"ONLY THE QUEEN MATTERS," PIERRE SAID.

Just then the servants began to clear away the remains of the banquet with a minimum of noise. The feasters ate silently as well. One would think that such a feast would be abuzz with conversation and laughter, but everything was oddly quiet, as if no one were allowed to speak above a whisper.

This was not a happy party.

Then the queen looked up and, seeing us, nodded her head.

At us.

At me.

Only the queen matters. I heard Pierre's voice in my head.

"Your Majesties, honored lords and ladies of France," Uncle declared, "we present to you the renowned skills of Troupe Brufort, as witnessed in the courts of Italy, Burgundy, and Spain."

I did not show on my face what was in my mind. I did what Uncle wanted.

I smiled.

He waved us forward and our first—and only—performance before the King and Queen of France began.

OTHER SPEAK BOOKS

QUEEN'S OWN FOOL

A NOVEL OF
MARY QUEEN of SCOTS

JANE YOLEN & ROBERT J. HARRIS

speak

An Imprint of Penguin Group (USA) Inc.

❧ *To David and Debby,*

who loved this book first

J. Y. and R. J. H.

Speak
Published by Penguin Group
Penguin Group (USA) Inc.,
345 Hudson Street, New York, New York 10014, U.S.A.
Penguin Books Ltd, 80 Strand, London WC2R ORL, England
Penguin Books Australia Ltd, 250 Camberwell Road, Camberwell, Victoria 3124, Australia
Penguin Books Canada Ltd, 10 Alcorn Avenue, Toronto, Ontario, Canada M4V 3B2
Penguin Books (N.Z.) Ltd, 182-190 Wairau Road, Auckland 10, New Zealand

First published in the United States of America by Philomel Books,
a division of Penguin Putnam Books for Young Readers, 2000
Published by Puffin Books, a division of Penguin Putnam Books for Young Readers, 2001
This edition published by Speak, an imprint of Penguin Group (USA) Inc., 2003

9   10

THE LIBRARY OF CONGRESS HAS CATALOGED THE PHILOMEL EDITION AS FOLLOWS:
Yolen, Jane.
Queen's own fool: a novel of Mary Queen of Scots / by Jane Yolen and Robert J. Harris
p. cm.
Summary: When twelve-year-old Nicola leaves Troupe Brufort and serves as the fool for Mary,
Queen of Scots, she experiences the political and religious upheavals in both France and Scotland.
1. Mary, Queen of Scots, 1542–1567—Juvenile fiction. 2. Scotland—History—Mary Stuart,
1542–1567—Juvenile Fiction. [1. Mary, Queen of Scots, 1542–1567—Fiction.
2. Scotland—History—Mary Stuart, 1542-1567—Fiction. 3. Fools and jesters—Fiction.]
4. Kings, queens, rulers, etc.—Fiction.] I. Harris, Robert J., 1955– II. Title.
PZ7.Y78Qu2000 [Fic]—dc21 99-055070
ISBN 0-399-23380-6

This edition ISBN 0-698-11918-5

Printed in the United States of America

www.janeyolen.com

CONTENTS

A NOTE FROM THE AUTHORS

Mary Queen of Scots is an historical figure. So is La Jardinière, one of her three female jesters.

We know much about the queen, though opinions about her vary widely. Her uncle, the opulent Cardinal of Lorraine, wrote that when she was still a child: "King (Henry II) has taken such a liking for her that he spends much of his time in chatting with her . . . and she knows so well how to entertain him with pleasant and suitable subjects of conversation as if she were a woman of four and twenty." But the wintry-souled preacher John Knox called her a "honeypot" and wanted to burn her as a sorceress.

At age ten Queen Mary was already writing to her mother about Scottish politics. At thirteen she composed and presented a speech in Latin to the French court. We know how she looked, what clothes she wore, what songs she admired, what friendships she had with her personal servants, and how—in the words of one critic—she was "Fond, foolish, pleasure-loving . . ." How could she not be? She had been brought up in the court of France, known as the most elegant, most joyous, and most lax in Europe. Of course she would share that court's virtues as well as its considerable vices.

We know only this much about Mary's French fool La Jardinière, all from the court records: that she was female, that she was given several expensive dresses, that she was given linen handkerchiefs, and that she was sent home to France with a large payment when the queen went off to England.

Where history ends, storytelling begins.

FRANCE ❧ 1559–1560

Did Destiny's hard hand before,

Of miseries such a store,

Of such a train of sorrows shed

Upon a happy woman's head?

from a poem by
MARY QUEEN OF FRANCE, 1560

1 ❧ RHEIMS

The rain poured down throughout the day, hard and grey as cathedral stone. One by one, we dragged to a halt. I stopped dancing first, then Annette, our skirts hanging in damp folds, tangling in our legs.

"It is like walking with dead fish," I said. "Slip-slap."

Annette giggled. But then she found everything amusing. Even in the rain.

Taking the tin whistle from his lips, Bertrand flicked it several times, trying to rid it of water. Nadine's tambourine went still, and she shifted little Jean to her other hip.

Now Pierre alone kept going, flinging the clubs into the air. One and two, three and four, five . . . I wondered if he were going to try seven at once, here on the drowned streets of Rheims where no one would see him fail.

"What are you *doing?*" Uncle Armand cried out, and began hitting the rest of us for stopping. "Troupe Brufort does not stop for mere rain!" His hand was like some small, fierce, whey-colored animal nipping and pinching where it could.

Pierre dropped one of his rain-slicked clubs. It landed with a loud splash in a puddle at his feet. He stooped to pick it up.

Uncle Armand turned and slammed Pierre on the head with the gold-topped cane. "Clumsy fool! Did I tell you to stop?"

Stepping to Pierre's side, I began, "But Uncle, there is no one on the street. Even the beggars have left the road to seek shelter. We have come to the holy city for nothing, and . . ."

Whap! This time the cane fell on *my* head, and I saw stars. Pierre had been smarter, going right back to his juggling. Would I never learn? One day Uncle would kill me with his cane.

"Mademoiselle La Bouche du Sud," Uncle said, meaning *Miss Mouth from the South,* "says we have come to Rheims for nothing. But *she* is the nothing, not we."

This time I bit my lip to keep from answering back. One day, I swore, I would break Uncle's cane over my knee.

Uncle was not finished speaking, though. His nose wrinkled as if he had smelled something foul. "We have come to Rheims for the young king's crowning. Fortunes will be made here. The new queen loves pageantry, songs, dances, mummery. All of which Troupe Brufort can supply."

"But Uncle . . ." I began, wanting to remind him that the city was draped in black for the old king's death—"A lance in his eye while jousting," a walleyed beggar girl had said. "The new king insists on a long mourning." So none of the grand folk racing to the coronation had heart or coins for street players.

"Dance!" Uncle commanded. "Now! Good will come of it."

"Wet will come of it," I mumbled. But not so he could hear.

Bertrand began to play a three-step on the pipe, and Nadine beat the tambourine against her sodden skirt once more. Annette and I shuffled our feet obediently in time and Pierre tossed up three clubs in a rotation he could do even in a pouring rain.

"*Bon!*" sang out Uncle, a rare compliment.

Just then a well-dressed merchant and his three dark-clad daughters hurried past us, holding cloaks over their heads. The girls squealed in their distress.

"Papa! My boots!" cried both the eldest and the youngest.

"The rain is ruining my skirts," the middle one added.

"Talk less," their papa responded. "Run faster."

Uncle insinuated himself into their way, smiling. He is like a serpent when he smiles—all lips, no teeth. "Pause for a moment, good sir. Witness the wondrous skills of Troupe Brufort, only recently returned from the courts of Padua, Venice, Rome."

Of course, Troupe Brufort had never been to any of those places. Only I, born in my papa's beloved Italy, had traveled beyond France. But Uncle always dropped great names like a horse with too much grass in its mouth letting fall the extra bits.

The merchant spun around Uncle and hastened his whining daughters homeward, the backs of the girls' tufted dresses looking like a dark rolling ocean.

"This is stupid, Papa," Pierre muttered, wiping his clubs one at a time on his shirt, a useless action, as his shirt was as wet as the clubs. "We will all come down with a fever, and for nothing."

Ignoring Pierre, Uncle strode over to Bertrand and snatched the pipe from his mouth. "Enough tiddly-piddly, boy! Do your tumbling. Nadine, strike up a beat."

Annette and I clapped in time to the tambourine, making soft smacking noises. *One and two and one-two.* On Nadine's hip, little Jean awoke and tried to catch the raindrops.

All at once, a clatter of hooves on the cobbles to our left, and a dark carriage approached, drawn by two dappled horses, their backs so wet, the hair looked black. On the carriage door was a coat of arms and a motto, but as I could not read, I did not know what it said. I glimpsed a red uniform under the driver's cloak, the only bit of color I had seen in the city so far. Then the driver drew the cloak more firmly around his shoulders and that brief flame was quenched.

Beside the driver was another man, shaking as with an ague.

Uncle nodded. "Ha!" he cried, as if the appearance of the carriage vindicated all the beatings.

The carriage pulled up close to us, so close that Bertrand hesitated in his tumbling for fear of frightening the horses. A gentleman with a thin mustache peeked out of the window.

"Do not stop!" hissed Uncle.

Bertrand leaped up again, doing first a double twist, then a series of no-handed cartwheels.

Annette and I added some shuffling steps to our hand claps, and Pierre lofted five clubs.

"Climb," I whispered to Annette.

"But my skirts . . ." she began.

"To the devil with your skirts," I said, locking my fingers together and holding my hands down low.

Annette was so shocked at my swearing, she climbed without further comment, scrambling to my shoulders and leaving muddy footprints on my bodice. I gripped her ankles. Luckily she was only six years old and very light.

"Smile," Uncle hissed.

We smiled.

The shaking man climbed down from his station on the carriage and stood at attention by the carriage door. He had a disgruntled air, as if he dearly wanted to be in a warm, dry spot.

The gentleman in the carriage just sat there, rubbing his mustache, while his servants got soaked, and all for the sake of our poor show. If he were to throw us a good-sized purse, Uncle might let us stop and find someplace dry. I smiled again, what Pierre calls my "winning smile" and Uncle calls "Nicola's grimace."

"Enough!" the gentleman announced abruptly. "You will do."

Gratefully I lowered Annette to the ground. Her little golden curls were now hanging in long, wet strands. Pierre tucked the clubs under his arms and Bertrand—at the long end of a tumbling run— came back unhurriedly.

"Do?" Uncle brightened.

The gentleman pursed his lips. "As I have seen no other troupe on this forsaken street, you will *have* to do. Jacques, show them the way to the *palais.*" Then he banged his cane against the carriage roof and called, "Get me home before I catch my death."

The servant Jacques jumped aside in time to avoid a splash of water from the carriage's wheels as it pulled away, though Bertrand had no such luck and was drenched to the knee.

As soon as his master was gone, Jacques let his shoulders droop. Glancing sourly at us, he rubbed his nose with the flat of his hand. "Follow me, and try to keep up. I do not want to dawdle in this weather."

"Whom have I the extreme honor and privilege to be address-ing, monsieur?" Uncle asked in the oily voice he used when speak-ing to rich people.

"It is no honor addressing me," Jacques answered, turning away and saying over his shoulder, "nor privilege neither. You had best save your fine manners for the new king."

For a moment Uncle froze, his lips silently forming the word "king."

The king. I thought. *With the pretty queen who loves pageants.*

Then Uncle stirred, bowed and waved at us, his face suddenly exultant, open like a dried flower bed after a good shower. "Come along. Do not just stand there. The *king* is waiting for us. And," he added, "remember—obey my every word if you wish to make a good impression. Nicola, you especially, do not open your mouth."

Pierre and I hurried to the wooden cart, each taking hold of a handle. The ancient cart creaked and protested, but for the first time ever it sounded like music to me.

Bertrand, Annette, and Nadine grabbed their sacks off the ground, slinging them into the cart, then followed behind us. For once there was no chatter. We were going to entertain in a palace. How could anyone complain—even of the rain?

Perhaps we had come to Rheims for something after all!

Marching ahead of the cart, a step behind Jacques, Uncle went proudly. His balding head was tilted at such an angle, he looked as though he were leading a parade rather than following a sullen servant along a rain-soaked backstreet.

Jacques looked as if he had a bean stuck up his nose. He never even glanced around to see if we followed. Clearly he wanted no one in Rheims to think he had anything to do with our ragtag troupe.

The rain began to ease at last, but the evening was drawing in. Rheims was still grey above, grey below, and grey in the middle, but there was a small, hopeful, golden glow in my belly. Each step I thought: *But one more step and one more and one more towards the warmth.*

I was so concentrated on getting to where we were going, I had no idea where we were, and so I was entirely startled when Nadine cried out, "Look, children, there is the king's palace."

Jacques sniffed at her. "No, madam, that is the palace of Charles, Cardinal of Lorraine and Archbishop of Rheims. The king and queen are but guests here. But it *is* our destination."

The cardinal's palace was certainly large, but not nearly as large as some we had seen in our travels. As for that stone wall—we were *connoisseurs* of walls: cathedral walls, palace walls, the walls of fortresses and castles. They were often the backdrops for our performances, though we had never actually been invited *inside* before.

Still—walls meant roofs. Roofs meant shelter. Suddenly I was filled with new energy. Grabbing my cart handle, I gave it a hard shove which skewed the cart so that it wobbled on the cobbles.

"Easy," hissed Pierre. "Do not overturn the cart. Not now."

"As if I could!" I countered.

"Amazon!" he said.

"Flea!"

"Fleabite!"

And then we looked at one another and laughed. We were as close as brother and sister. Closer, really, for although we were not the same age, we were of the same disposition. We had chosen one another as confidante and friend.

"Be quiet, all of you," Uncle said, "and Nicola especially." He raised his cane as a warning, for Jacques was talking to two guards at a small portal.

"Servant's gate," Pierre whispered to me.

"Peasant's bolt-hole," I replied.

The two guards stepped aside, lowering their spears, and Jacques waved us through.

After crossing a gravel-strewn courtyard, we parked the squeaking, protesting cart and took from it only those items we would need for our show.

Then we followed Jacques inside. The passages were narrow, whitewashed, but dimly lit. I had expected something grand, I suppose, but it was like a rabbit warren, with lots of doors along the halls. At last Jacques stopped in front of one door and pushed it open.

This was no luxurious apartment, but a plain room with a bare stone floor, bare walls, a single long table, and a couple of chairs.

"Not even rushes or hangings to take away the cold!" I complained, for in the fairy stories my mother had told me there were always such things in a palace. How I missed her stories. How I missed her and Papa, almost two years gone.

Jacques glared at me as if to say: *What do you know of such things?* And I blushed deeply—for shame, and for anger, too. To treat us so when we had done nothing to him.

Uncle made a quick movement with his hand in my direction, promising a beating. Then he turned and said to Jacques in his deepest voice, smooth as oil, "I thank you on behalf of our troupe for these excellent accommodations."

Jacques merely grunted in response.

"I am thankful, too," I said, trying to make amends. After all, there were three basins of water, several towels, and two small cakes of scented soap on the table. A warm fire crackled in the grate. What were rushes and wall hangings compared to those?

But Jacques' face got its bean-up-the-nose look again. "Try to make yourselves respectable," he ordered curtly. "*If* that is possible. Someone will come for you in a short while."

As soon as the door shut behind Jacques, Uncle wheeled on me. "Your mouth will get us all in trouble, mademoiselle," he said, with a finger flick at the side of my head. It stung, of course, but I did not care. We were out of the grey rain, the fire was beginning to dry our clothing, and perhaps there would be food as well.

Bertrand, Annette, and Pierre all made for the fire. As I went to join them, Uncle hauled us back, directing us to the basins.

"Clean yourselves first." He mimicked Jacques' voice exactly. "*If* that is possible. Only then dry your clothes."

"But Papa," Annette began, fingering her strings of wet curls.

"There will be no *buts*," Uncle told her.

So we did as we were instructed while Uncle Armand had the fire all to himself. I swear that if he could have, he would have soaked up all the warmth and left none for the rest of us.

After placing the sleeping Jean near the hearth, with a rag under his head, Nadine fussed over Annette and me, trying her best to wipe every spot of mud from our faces. Then she turned her attention to Annette's hair, spinning the curls around her finger and blowing on them.

I was left on my own, first drying my hair with a towel. If we were to perform before the king and queen, I would have to make myself presentable. Uncle often told me that I was the least talented member of Troupe Brufort, adopted and not born into it, but still I would not disgrace the others with my looks. However, when I tried to comb my plaits out with Nadine's hard brush, every tug hurt enough to make my eyes smart.

"Do not stop brushing," Uncle commanded. "Make something of that bird's nest of yours."

"It is harder work, Uncle," I said brightly, "tidying what is on top of my head than keeping straight what is inside it." I thought to make him laugh, but the look he gave me was so cold, I returned to the brush with a will.

My hair finally in order—though much was left in the brush—I went over to the fire to dry my still-damp skirts and sandals. The smell we made steaming out was musky and familiar. Many a time Troupe Brufort had taken refuge—like the Holy Family—in a farmer's stable, and glad of the shelter.

I closed my eyes and, despite my excitement about performing before the king, fell fast asleep in front of the fire standing up, like a horse.

The door opened creakily and I was startled from my sleep. An elderly woman with a heavily-lined face came in. She was dressed in a black silk mourning dress without a hint of ornamentation. Her eyes were the color of stone and her lips but two thin lines, one atop another, like folded linens. She glowered at us, as if adding up our virtues and finding us lacking a full measure. Then reluctantly, she stepped aside to admit a tall, delicately-boned young woman into the room.

This woman had amber-colored hair, enormous green-gold eyes under heavy lids, and a lovely long neck. Unlike her companion, she wore a dress of white and pale green. As she moved—spring to her companion's winter—the skirt swelled out with close-set pleats like a bell that parted to show a smooth green underskirt. Her velvet overbodice was embroidered with gold leaves and green florets. The ruff at her neck was tinged with green from which jeweled ropes of pearls and beads hung down. She was like the fairy princess in one of Maman's tales, and I drew in my breath in wonder.

The older woman made a downward gesture in our direction with the flat of her hand.

Only Uncle understood. He bowed deeply, motioning us to do likewise.

So I bowed, just like Uncle and the boys, and was embarrassed when Nadine and Annette each performed a graceful curtsy. I could feel the heat rise in my cheeks as I blushed again.

Uncle scowled at me. I think he would have beaten out his displeasure on my poor head, but the cane was lying too far away.

The tall girl did not seem disturbed by my bow. In fact, she

looked positively amused to see me act like a man. Perhaps she had
made a similar error in not wearing mourning? I felt a sudden compassion for her.

"What pretty young women and what handsome young men,"
she said brightly to Uncle. Then for the first time she looked around
the room. "But why is this room so plain? So . . . empty? I must
have rushes and hangings sent down at once to warm it up."

"Rushes and hangings—I asked for such," I blurted out.

All of Troupe Brufort glared at me.

But the tall girl smiled. "So should you all!"

I turned and grinned at the troupe, but no one smiled back.

The tall girl continued. "I am delighted that you have come to
us. Pray, do your very best to bring some joy into this dark day." She
shook her head and a wave of perfume wafted over us, like a wind
over a flower garden. "This *should* have been the happiest of times
for our new crowned king. But with his papa so newly and horribly
dead, he can take little pleasure in it."

"So the beggar girl said," I put in. Pierre grabbed my skirt and
pulled me back and I realized I had gone too far, so I gave a quick
curtsy.

But the tall girl nodded, as if she had heard from the very same
beggar. "Still, we must have *some* celebration today, a small token,
do you not agree?" She smiled again. "So tonight do not hold back,
Troupe . . ." She hesitated, looking for the name.

"Brufort, Your Highness," put in Uncle, his voice deeply oiled.

"Brufort," she said, dimpling at him.

Having finished her little speech, she turned gracefully and left
the room. Her silk skirts sounded like a rivulet rushing over stones,
but softer and more intimate and much more welcoming.

"Highness? Highness? Who *was* that?" I whispered to Nadine.

The elderly woman raised her eyebrows at me as though I had just spat upon the floor. "Stupid girl. That was the new queen, Mary. It is at her insistence this entertainment has been arranged." The scowl on her face was evidence that she did not herself approve.

"Queen Mary," I whispered with the kind of passion one reserves for a life's pledge.

3 ❧ GREAT HALL

We had barely gotten dry when two serving girls entered carrying baskets of sweet rushes and herbs which they scattered over the floor. Within minutes the sour odor was gone and in its place a fresh garden smell.

It was even better than the fairy tales had made it sound, and I clapped my hands together. "La! We are quite the upper crust now."

The servants giggled and left, but right behind them came three men with tapestries which they hastily hung on the bare walls.

When I tried to say something to them as well, they acknowledged my greeting with no more than a grunt, as though we were so far below them we deserved little more. Still, a kind word is never amiss. I was about to say so when another girl came in with a tray on which sat a carafe of mulled wine, a lovely baguette, and several cheeses.

"Shall we greet the food then?" I said. "Food, meet Troupe Brufort. Troupe—here then, the meal."

Annette's peal of laughter started us all off into giggles. We were soon a great deal jollier than we had been since coming to Rheims.

Uncle, standing with his back to the crackling fire, raised his hand. Surrounded by a halo of firelight, he looked like some old devil just up out of the pit, for his hair—what was left of it—stood up on two sides like little horns.

"Now, my children," he began, his voice like a great viol, low and singing, "this will be our finest hour. Troupe Brufort is to perform before the King and Queen of France."

The way he glared at us made my stomach hurt.

"Pierre, you must not just try, but must *do* the seven clubs."

"But Papa, I have only done the seven in practice, never while anyone was watching," Pierre reminded him. He rubbed his fingers through his hair.

"*I* have watched," I said. "And you did not drop them then."

Pierre smiled at me. "Amazon," he whispered.

"Flea," I countered.

Uncle barely glanced at me, but it was enough. I shut my mouth.

"And you, Bertrand—you must turn the cartwheels *en l'air*, no stops," Uncle said.

Bertrand nodded and Nadine knelt to massage his ankles.

"And my dancing girls . . ." Uncle smiled at Annette, not me, which I did not take amiss. I trusted his smile less than his cane. "The faces must *beam* at the royal couple." He touched his own face and his fingers shaped a grotesque smile across his lips. "Even if you misstep, the face must never show it. Now you—mademoiselle!" he said, turning at last to me. "You will keep your tongue to yourself. No little adages from Italy. No stories. Just silence. Do you understand? You are a member of Troupe Brufort by adoption, and I will not have you spoil our finest hour."

I nodded. What else could I do?

Nadine woke up Jean and made him eat something, adding much water to his wine. He is so delicious and charming, his giggles usually earn us an extra coin.

As for me, I stared out of one of the windows into the cold, grey day. I was warm. I was full of good food. But, to be truthful, I was very frightened. This was not stage fright. I had gotten over that more than a year before. But I knew what Uncle would not admit. We were only ordinary street players, used to rough audiences. Our meager dances and tricks would hardly be fine enough for the king and his court.

And if we failed to entertain them—as we surely would— Uncle's humiliation would be beaten into our backs come night- fall.

Once again it was Jacques who came for us. His face had not lost its sour expression. That bean was even more firmly up his nose.

We followed him through the long passages and the hurly of the servants' halls, past the bustling kitchens, and up a winding stone stairway, till we came into the Great Hall. I was the very last in line. When I arrived, I had to stand on tiptoe to see over Bertrand's shoulder what the others were already admiring.

What magnificence! Here were enormous tapestries of kings and queens, and armies of mounted knights and their foot soldiers hurled into a fray. Above us from the high rafters flew the banners of all the great families of France.

For a moment I could not take it all in. The height of place, the width. Why, a herd of horses could have trampled about in the hall and lost their way. Inside a palace seemed ever so much larger than any outside I had seen. It was almost too much and my mouth hung open.

Then Pierre nudged me. "Toad!" he whispered.

"Wart!" I countered.

"Look at the people," he said. "Not at the ceiling."

I looked.

There were at least fifty fine folk seated at long tables that ran around three sides of the room. Most were adults, but there were five children as well, sitting stiff in formal mourning wear.

On a dais at the high table sat the queen. Beside her was a young man in dark velvet, a pale, frail figure with a swollen face. He looked nothing like a king. Rather he was a plain—even ugly—boy with the reminders of pox on his cheeks. Frequently he raised a handkerchief to his right ear as if the ear pained him.

Next to him was an elegant older woman whom I took to be his mother—the old queen—for she was in the *deuil blanc,* the widow's dress, and covered with the transparent white veil that all new widows wear.

Next to the old queen sat a girl perhaps my age. And by the girl's side, an elderly grandmother who seemed, somehow, the most queenly of them all, with her straight back and raised chin.

On Queen Mary's other hand was the cardinal, opulent in crimson, and next to him a man so like the cardinal in looks, I took them to be brothers. But where the cardinal had a softer countenance, the brother's face was very stern. He sat upright as though on horseback surveying not a troupe of players but a troop of soldiers.

I could imagine none of these fine folk enjoying our show. I wondered what they would do if they hated us.

Curse us?

Beat us?

Throw us back out in the rain and the cold?

In front of the high table, at a small table of her own, lounged a dwarf no larger than Annette. She looked as if she were totally uninterested in either our troupe or the fine folk.

I had only seen a dwarf once before, a little manikin who had been in a tumbler's troupe. He had winked at me and made me laugh. But this dwarf was female, though dressed in dark velvet with a velvet hood and a cloak worn man-fashion, over the left shoulder. Her humped right shoulder rose up like a mountain on her little back, and the dress did nothing to disguise it. Still, she had the face of a fallen angel.

"Do not stare so," Pierre whispered.

"You *told* me to look."

"To look, not to gape." But he smiled.

"The dwarf . . ." I began.

"Play to the queen, not the dwarf," Pierre said. "Only the queen matters."

Just then the servants began to clear away the remains of the banquet with a minimum of noise. The feasters ate silently as well. One would think that such a feast would be abuzz with conversation and laughter, but everything was oddly quiet, as if no one were allowed to speak above a whisper.

This was not a happy party.

Then the queen looked up and, seeing us, nodded her head.

At us.

At me.

Only the queen matters. I heard Pierre's voice in my head.

Suddenly Jean—too young to be intimidated by the grand place, the fine company, the silent solemnity of the feast—pointed a finger at one of the high banners. He expounded in his piercing little boy voice. "Look, Maman! Red and green and blue!"

Nadine quickly grabbed his hand and shushed him while a titter ran through the audience.

At that very moment, a chamberlain prodded Uncle with his finger. In an instant Uncle returned to the perfect showman. Striding into the center of the room, he made a florid bow. Then he began a speech I had heard a hundred times before. Only now, in the presence of the court, his words took on a borrowed grandeur.

"Your Majesties, honored lords and ladies of France," he declared, "we present to you the renowned skills of Troupe Brufort, as witnessed in the courts of Italy, Burgundy, and Spain."

I did not show on my face what was in my mind. I did what Uncle wanted.

I smiled.

He waved us forward and our first—and only—performance before the King and Queen of France began.

4 &. PERFORMANCE

Bertrand made a series of tumbles the length of the room. He kept his toes pointed and we in the troupe cried out, "Hop-la!" and applauded.

Then Bertrand turned cartwheels and in-the-air somersaults, his legs like pinwheels, all the way up to the table where the king and the queen were seated.

The king was not paying attention to Bertrand, but leaning over to speak to his lovely young queen. She never took her eyes off Bertrand, but seemed also attentive to the king, for she laid a reassuring hand on his arm.

Taking a step forward—out of curiosity more than anything else—I saw that the young king's eyes were puffy, as if he had been weeping. And perhaps he had been. I certainly had wept enough for runnels to form down my cheeks when my parents had died. However, the king did not look as if his father's death had caused his puffiness. Rather he seemed like someone who had never known good health.

I was puzzled. How could anyone so sickly rule France? It was like expecting an infant to handle the reins of a warhorse. On the other hand, both the cardinal and his brother looked as if handling horse *and* infant would not trouble them at all.

But my woolgathering was soon stopped as Bertrand came to a halt in front of the high table, arms raised, always a signal for applause. He certainly deserved it. His tumbles had been perfect—numerous, elegant, and high.

At first there was an awful stillness, as if everyone were holding their breath at the same time. Then the queen began to clap enthusiastically, followed by the king. Soon the entire company was applauding loudly, except for the dowager queen, who kept her hands in her lap, her lips pursed in a disapproving frown.

Bertrand blushed and bowed, then blushed again.

Uncle motioned Pierre to step forward. Flinging the first two clubs into the air, Pierre started walking up and down the room as he juggled. He plucked a third club from his belt and soon had all three of them flying through his hands with dizzying speed.

When the fourth, then fifth, were spinning through the air, one of the women seated closest to me cried out, "Oh, la!"

For the space of about twenty heartbeats he kept the five moving. They arced a perfect rainbow overhead.

And then he slipped the sixth club from his belt and threw it into the rainbow.

It stayed in perfect rotation.

I whispered under my breath, "Dear Lord, let him add the seventh."

The room was silent with anticipation as Pierre pulled the last club from his belt and threw it up in the air.

I closed my eyes.

When I did not hear a club drop, I opened my eyes again.

Pierre had all seven clubs in the air and they moved around in perfect harmony. He made three more passes with them and then gathered them down one at a time, spun around on his toes, and bowed.

For a long moment the silence lengthened. Then, led by the young queen again, there was sudden, deafening applause.

Now the king looked as if he were starting to enjoy himself, talking animatedly to Queen Mary on one side, and then to his mother—the old, purse-lipped dowager—on the other.

As Pierre and Bertrand hurried back to join us, Uncle Armand laid aside his stick. He marched into the center of the room and puffed out his chest.

"Honored majesties," he announced grandly, "prepare to be dazzled by feats of magic which have baffled the sages of Venice, Alexandria, and Constantinople."

He produced a copper coin from his pocket, holding it between the two middle fingers of his right hand. He made a fist and when he opened his hand again the coin was gone.

"Ha!" Uncle said, smiling as widely as if he had made the moon itself disappear.

There were a few murmurs from the children, but no more than that. This company had seen such sleight of hand before.

Uncle repeated the trick, disappearing two coins, then three, verbally applauding himself each time. Then he passed some little balls from hand to hand, making them vanish as well. Finally he produced three colored handkerchiefs from his sleeve and stuffed them into his clenched fist. When he stretched out his palm, the handkerchiefs were gone.

"Ha-ha!" Uncle cried, holding up both hands as if awaiting the thunderous applause he was used to in the courtyards and street fairs where we usually performed.

But as he stood with uplifted hands, the dwarf woman got up ponderously. Turning her back to Uncle, she lifted her dress slightly, bent over, and let out a massively rude sound that was a cross between a horn and a donkey's bray.

The entire court broke into explosive laughter.

Uncle forced a broad grin onto his face, but his neck and chin flushed crimson. Backing away from the high table, he executed a rapid series of bows, his head bobbing like a duck feeding in water. When he neared us, he hissed, "Girls! Step lively!"

There was to be no more magic.

Annette and I came forward to begin our dance.

Let the queen at least like us, I prayed.

Bertrand began an upbeat tune on his pipe, while Nadine— striking the tambourine with vigor—sang a song from her village in Aquitaine. Her lovely voice with its grave trills filled the hall.

I saw the queen give the king a gentle nudge, encouraging him to watch. He did so, squinting at us as though his head now hurt. He dabbed at his ear again with his bit of cloth. *How odd,* I thought. *She treats him like I do Pierre or Bertrand, and not like a queen does the king who is her lord.*

Nadine finished singing, then began beating the tambourine faster and faster in time with Bertrand's piping. The rest of Troupe Brufort began to clap—encouraging the audience as well, though only the children joined in. Then Annette and I whirled each other round and round, till we were on the edge of dizziness.

I gave Annette our signal with a nod of my head.

We stopped at once, though the music and clapping continued, and I crouched to let Annette climb up onto my shoulders. I straightened at once, so that our audience would see no break between the dance and the acrobatic climax.

Gripping Annette firmly by the ankles, I turned slowly to encourage applause. It came only grudgingly, and I knew for certain that this gathering was not impressed by us.

Perhaps I was thinking too much about pleasing the audience. Perhaps I was worrying about Uncle's cane. But suddenly I slipped on the polished floor and lost my balance. Desperately I tried to stay upright, but could feel Annette toppling. Luckily I had the sense to let go so that she did not hit the floor face first, but managed to land on her feet and go into a quick forward roll.

I went right down after her into a similar roll, just as I had been taught to do.

Then everything went black.

It took me a moment to realize what had happened. I had rolled completely under one of the tables and was now hidden from view by the linen cloth. I could only dimly make out the legs of the gentlemen and the skirts of the ladies.

There was laughter and a man's voice calling out, "Disappearing girl? That's what I call *real* magic!" Another, a lady, cried, "Can you conjure her back, Brufort?"

I scrambled along blindly under the table thinking that if I could reach the far end quickly enough, I might salvage something from this disaster. But scampering on my hands and knees, I soon found myself at a corner where two tables met. I had been going in the wrong direction! I could not turn around in the narrow space without making my presence obvious.

I could hear footfalls and Annette calling to me. Shuddering, I thought that if Uncle hit me for imagined insults, how much more he would beat me for this!

A pair of black-clad legs suddenly stretched straight ahead of me. When I tried to maneuver around them, I came rolling out of cover right next to the dwarf's table. She glared at me with that dark angel face and stuck out her tongue.

All I could do was to try and make the best of things. Leaping up with my arms outstretched, I executed a few rapid dance steps, as we often did at the end of a particularly difficult routine.

When I stopped, I was face-to-face with the king and queen. The king was in the middle of a coughing fit, and had a kerchief pressed to his mouth, but he still managed to look amused. The queen was grinning broadly.

"What *were* you doing down there?" she said.

The queen had asked me a direct question. Despite Uncle's warning, I had to answer. So I thought quickly.

"In the course of my dance I grew very hungry, Your Majesty," I replied with a bow. "I thought there would be scraps of food under the table, but found none. So . . . the food must be very delicious or your nobles very, very greedy."

"And which do you think is true?"

Another direct question. What could I do? And then Pierre's voice spoke clearly in my mind: *Only the queen matters.* I would answer, though Uncle might well murder me later with his cane.

"I have not tasted the food, but I can see from the shape of your nobles that they never have enough."

The queen clapped her hands together. *"Quel drôle!"*

"I think she's referring to you, Uncle Charles," remarked the king with a laugh that turned immediately into another cough.

The queen leaned over and patted him on the back.

"I am sure it befits a nobleman of France to be . . . to be grand in every sense," I said.

Now there was laughter from all around the room. The dwarf stood again, mimed a big belly, then walked to where the cardinal sat and pointed at him. The cardinal—who was not really all that stout—grabbed up an apple and tossed it to me deftly.

"Have a care you do not grow too large yourself, girl," he joked.

"No fear, your lordship, for I am a peasant," I said. "We never grow big or we would outgrow the only clothes we own."

I bowed once more and backed away from them to scattered applause and laughter. As soon as I came within his reach, Uncle grabbed me by the skirt and dragged me out through the door.

Once we were out of sight of the courtiers, he shook me so hard that the apple fell to the floor with a bump. I watched it roll away with dismay, for I had really wanted to eat it.

"You stupid girl!" he snapped. "Do you think all these nobles came here to witness your clumsiness? Or listen to your peasant mouth? I should have told that priest where to take you the day he brought you to me." Uncle's voice was so cold it froze me to the very bones. "The streets are the best place for you, you stupid little witch."

Swallowing hard, I kept my eyes on the apple.

"But they *liked* her," Pierre protested. "They liked her jokes."

"Liked . . . her . . . jokes?" Uncle rounded on Pierre. "They enjoyed mocking her, that is all. The court is known for such mockery, which they call wit. *Mon Dieu!* I spent years building the reputation of this troupe and in a minute this loose-tongued urchin has ruined me."

He released my arm and cuffed me across the side of the head. The stars this time were the color of wine—both red and gold.

"I will *peasant* you!" he cried, raising his hand for a second blow. "I will show you real wit!"

Then Uncle struck me again, this time with one of his beefy fists. For the first time I began to weep. Not because of the pain but because of who I was not. Cruel as he was to his own children, he beat me all the harder because I was not one of them.

Uncle took another swipe at my head, but as he did so, Pierre pushed him from behind. I ducked under his swing and bolted through an open archway, running without thinking down a dim corridor. All the while, I was certain that Uncle would cast me out and I would have to spend the rest of my days begging in the streets.

5 ❦ THE GARDEN

he few servants I passed stepped aside to avoid being knocked over, and I continued to run until—more by chance than design—I found an outside door and burst into the open air.

I came to an immediate halt and tried to catch my breath. Knuckling the remaining tears from my eyes, I gazed around. To one side of the garden was a knot of kitchen herbs, the plants still green. To the other, a plot of autumn flowers nodded in a small breeze. A half-moon cast a puckish glow over all.

Had I, like Marie-in-the-Ashes in my mother's favorite bedtime story, found my way into faerie land?

Dry-eyed, I began to wander the little winding stone paths where drops of rain, like tears, glistened on petals and leaves.

"Do not weep," I whispered to myself. "The king and queen have spoken to you. The court has applauded your performance. And though you are about to be thrown out onto the streets by your wicked uncle, be content to have spent one evening here in faerie." I spun around and around making myself dizzy.

Just then I came upon a stone bench and sat down on it, gazing around in continuing wonder as if I had suddenly stepped out of my perilous world into a place of safety.

I do not know how long I sat there before I heard footsteps and that safe little world suddenly collapsed. It had to be Uncle coming to find me. I could already feel his cane on my head. This time he might actually kill me.

Then, to my great surprise, I realized that the person coming to-wards me was not Uncle at all, but a woman. Over the tip-tap of her footsteps, I could hear the *shush-shushing* of silk.

I sat still as a stone. Prepared for Uncle, I was not prepared for anyone else.

As the woman got closer, the half-moon cast her in a pale light so that she looked like a fairy queen. Instead of a crown of jewels, she wore a hood with a heart-shaped curve above the forehead, from which her auburn hair peeked out.

It was Queen Mary herself, alone and without escort.

I stood, making a quick and awkward curtsy.

She nodded and then giggled, as if remembering my earlier boy-ish bow.

"I thought I might find you here," she said. "When I was little and got into trouble, I always used to hide in the garden."

"I did not know queens could get into trouble," I said.

"Perhaps not queens of France, but a little girl surely can. And more often than you might believe. Are you in trouble, garden girl?"

I shrugged. "Uncle Armand is very cross."

"Well, he should not be. Yours was the only performance that brought a smile to my dear Francis. The king, that is." She gave an-other clap, and smiled. "And what shall I call you, pretty child?"

I blushed, being neither pretty nor—at well past ten—a child. "Nicola, Your Royal Highness. Nicola Ambruzzi."

"You are not a Brufort, then?"

"Only half," I said, then told her about my father, a poor shoe-maker from the plains of Lombardy in Italy. "My mother was French, Madam. Uncle Armand's little sister."

"So, do you speak both languages then?" asked the queen.

"*Si,*" I whispered shyly. It had been a while since I had said a word in my father's tongue. Uncle would not have it.

"How interesting," the queen said slowly. "I speak Latin and some Greek. And French of course. Also some Scots, as I lived in Scotland till I was six." Suddenly she said, *"Parli Italiano?"* asking if I spoke the tongue.

"*Si, parlo Italiano.*"

"Ah—I wanted to be certain that you were telling me the truth. I cannot abide being lied to, though all else I can forgive."

I blushed furiously. "I have many faults, Your Majesty—as Uncle will surely tell you. But lying is not one of them."

She smiled again. "Well said, Nicola. You are direct. I like that. Now tell me how you came to be a performer."

"Can you really want to know, Madam?"

She nodded, so I told her about the very last day I had seen my parents alive. How, returning from a market where Papa had sold many pairs of sandals and boots, we were crossing the Rhône, in bad weather. The boat had capsized.

"Oh, poor child!" Queen Mary cried.

I told her how the howling gale churned the river into a froth. How I blindly thrashed about in the water. As I spoke, I threw my arms about showing the motion of the waves. "I made it to shore and waited hours for Maman and Papa to find me. They never did."

The queen took out a square of linen from her long sleeve and wiped a tear from her eye. But she did not urge me to stop, so I went on.

"Eventually," I said, "some nuns came upon me. They took me to their convent and wrapped me in warm blankets. But I could not stop shivering." I was suddenly shaking as if wrapped in those blankets again. No one—not even Pierre—had ever had this much of the story out of me.

"Go on," the queen whispered.

"The kind sisters told me the Lord had saved me for some purpose, though they did not know what it might be. They asked if I had other family. I told them only my uncle, the famous entertainer Armand Brufort. So they gave me into the care of a priest who was on his way to Paris. When we reached the city, it was filled with mummers and troubadours, for the dauphin had just been married to the young Queen of Scotland, and . . ."

I stopped suddenly and raised my fingers to my mouth. "Oh, Madam—that queen was *you!*" I dropped a deep curtsy.

She laughed, tucked the linen in her sleeve, then put her hands on my shoulders, drawing me up. "So, Nicola, you were at my wedding!"

"Not exactly *at*, Your Majesty. Any more than a flea is *at* a dog's nuptials."

"Oh, dear girl, what a teller of tales. And a wit as well. Two souls in a single breast. But tell me, how did you and the priest find your uncle in all the crowds?"

"We asked every mummer and juggler and beggar we could find. There were *so* many of them! I lost count after a hundred."

The queen laughed at that. "But you *did* find him at last."

"Yes, Your Majesty. We were directed to a small square on the north bank of the Seine, and there someone pointed out Troupe Brufort. Pierre was performing, with five clubs."

"Ah, the handsome dark-eyed rascal. So he has come up in the world since. Seven clubs now. I am well impressed."

For a moment I was speechless. That any of us in Troupe Brufort could impress the queen.

"And your uncle opened his arms to you?"

"Oh no, Majesty. At first Uncle paid no attention to the priest. You see, clerics rarely have money to give to performers, and for this reason alone Uncle despises them."

"Clearly your uncle knows the wrong clerics," said the queen. "The ones I know are very rich indeed. But do go on, little teller."

I needed little urging. A story must come around to its proper end. This my mother had told me often when I was impatient with a tale. Her stories always finished with "Happily ever after," but my own story did not.

"The priest," I continued, "was forced to tug on Uncle's sleeve to get his attention." I tugged on my own sleeve to demonstrate. "And when Uncle finally noticed, he did not know me, having seen me last when I was four. He said he already had enough mouths to feed, and we should go away."

"So—it always comes down to money," said the queen.

"Oh, no, Your Highness. Not with everyone. Papa liked to say: *A good heart outlasts a big purse.*"

"Your papa must have been a very smart man."

"He was a cobbler, Your Highness," I said.

She sat down on the stone bench and spread her skirts about her like scallop shells. "At least you knew him," she said. "My own father died in a faraway place six days after I was born."

"I am sorry. Oh—may a peasant feel sorry for a queen?"

She shook her head. "It does not matter. I had a better father in the old King of France, God rest his soul." For a moment she was quiet, remembering. Then she smiled. "Tell me the rest, child. Your story touches me, here." She put a hand over her heart.

"Well, the priest reached deep into his own pocket and pressed some coins into Uncle's hand. Uncle Armand counted them and then said to me, 'Can you dance, girl?' So with a nod of encouragement from the priest, I tried a few steps of the tarantella my papa had taught me.

" 'I suppose you will do,' Uncle said grudgingly, 'though we will have to see if we can pretty you up a bit.' "

"You are pretty enough," the queen said to me. She put her head to one side as if considering.

I blushed again. Thankfully it was too dark for her to see.

"Hai letto l'Orlando Furioso?" the queen asked suddenly in Italian, then put it into English. "Have you read *The Mad Orlando?"*

"I cannot read at all, Majesty."

She seemed astonished. "You can speak two languages but read not even one? How appalling. Are all peasants like that?"

"All the ones I know," I said. "But I *can* count the coins we get in the hat."

The queen laughed, but not in a mean way. "I am sorry you cannot read, Nicola. There is so much beauty in the written word."

I waved a hand at the darkening garden. "With so much beauty all around, why waste your days staring at paper and ink?"

The queen paused for a moment as though giving this idea serious thought. "But what about writing letters to the people you care about?" she asked. "And to read the letters they send back? I who have not seen my mother since I was eight years old hear from her almost every day through letters."

"The folk I care about I *see* every day. As for the others . . ." I hesitated. "I do not think they deliver letters to heaven."

The queen sighed. "Talking to you is like playing a game of riddles, Nicola. Do you know any riddles?"

I confessed that I did not, hoping that would not disappoint her. I was not even sure what a riddle was.

"Let me try one on you then," the queen said. "My governess, Madam de Parois, taught me this. First I walk on four legs, then on two legs, and in the end I walk on three legs. What am I?"

Is a riddle some sort of test? I thought hard before answering, "You are a dog who dances badly before a king."

The queen looked baffled and her mouth pursed. For a moment she looked like the old widowed queen. Then she smiled and any resemblance disappeared. "Oh, no, that is not the answer."

"Then what is?"

She clapped her hands again. "The answer is *a man!*"

"A man?" I shook my head. "No. I do not think so."

"*You* do not think so? I, the queen, tell you it is so and *you,* a peasant, say you do not think so?" She turned her head slightly, looking at me out of the corner of one eye. "I will explain it to you as Madam de Parois explained it to me. It is simple: A man goes about on all fours as a baby. Then he grows up and walks on two legs. Finally, as an old man, he needs a stick—his third leg."

"That is cheating, Your Majesty!" I told her, surprised at my own boldness. "A stick is not a leg. And no amount of saying so can make it true. If I wear a hat and call it a crown, that does not make me a queen."

She did not seem to mind my boldness. If anything, she was intrigued and amused by what I had just said. "Then why did you think the answer was a dog?"

"You were walking on four legs just as all dogs do," I explained, "but then the king ordered you to dance on your two hind legs to entertain his court."

"But why do I have three legs in the end?"

"Because you found walking on two legs too difficult to do. You stumbled and knocked over the king's wine cup, so he had one of your legs cut off as a punishment."

The queen wrinkled her nose, as if smelling something bad. "That is a very gruesome answer, but it is also very clever. I think it is much better than the one Madam de Parois gave. Though I do not think kings are quite as cruel as you make them out to be."

"Perhaps not all kings," I admitted, "but it is what Uncle would do if he were king. Why—he beats us with his cane if we fall or make a mistake, or talk out of turn, and we are *family*. Imagine what he would do to a dog!"

"I do not think my Francis would ever beat anyone, let alone cut off a leg," the queen said reproachfully. "Perhaps you are wrong, and kings are kinder than showmen."

"I sincerely hope so, Your Majesty, for a whole country lies at the king's mercy, not just a few hungry children."

We both fell silent for a long moment, though I doubt our thoughts were the same.

Just then, as if he had an uncanny knack of knowing when people talked about him, Uncle appeared. His brow was still furrowed with rage. And because I was standing, he saw only me with the moon on my face, and not the queen sitting in shadow.

"So, it is not enough that you humiliate me in front of the king," Uncle Armand said, his voice loud and menacing. "You must also lead me a merry chase around the palace to make me look the fool." He made a low sound in his throat, almost like a growl. "You will pay for that, you little idiot, now and for days to come."

At that the queen stood, and she towered a full head over me. Her face was a royal fury. I do not think Uncle could have recoiled back any more fearfully if he had found a lion in his path.

He bowed and made abject apologies. "Please forgive my niece's insolence, Majesty. If I had known she was going to trespass, I . . ."

"Yes, I think you *are* the kind of man who would cut off a dog's leg for stumbling," she said. "So it is a good thing you are not a king."

At that Uncle's jaw hung slack, for of course he had no idea what she was talking about.

The queen's face suddenly got a sort of sly look. "I believe you were paid money to take Nicola into your charge," she said.

Uncle nodded dumbly.

"How much would you take, then, to give her up?"

"Give her *up?*" Uncle repeated, his normally deep viol voice rising almost to a squeak, like a badly-tuned pipe.

The queen reached into her sleeve and produced a purse, which she offered to him. Uncle took it hesitantly, then pulled it open. His eyes grew wide when he saw how much was inside.

"That is what we were intending to pay you tonight," she said. "I will double it if you will release Nicola into my service."

"Majesty," Uncle stammered, still fingering the coins in the purse. "You . . . you do me great honor."

"I do you no honor at all, Monsieur Brufort," the queen replied, "but I will not see you pull the petals from the prettiest flower in my garden. Does that suit you, Nicola? Will you stay with me, telling me stories and giving the king some joy? Perhaps this is what your nuns meant when they wrapped you in warm blankets—that the Lord saved you for *me.*"

I thought for a moment of the troupe, and especially of Pierre. I wondered briefly how Annette would perform without me. Who would keep time to Bertrand's piping? Or help push the cart? I wondered if any of them would even miss me.

I thought of them all for a moment.

But only a moment.

"Yes," I breathed. I was more than Marie-in-the-Ashes. I was the captive of the Queen of Elfland herself.

"Come then, Nicola," Queen Mary said, leading the way back to the palace. Then turning she called over her shoulder, "You will have the remainder of your money before you leave, Monsieur Brufort."

Uncle bowed to her, but it felt as if he were bowing to me, too. I straightened my shoulders and nodded majestically back at him, but he took no notice. Instead he was counting the coins.

And seeing him counting, I could not help but wonder exactly how much I was worth.

To Uncle.

To the young queen.

6 ❧ FAREWELLS

There was just enough time for me to go and collect my few belongings before Uncle took his family away. When I got to the forecourt where we had left the cart, they were all there but Uncle, who had gone back to receive his second payment from the queen's serving woman.

As I took my little sack out of the cart and set it on the ground, I told them about the queen and the garden.

"Magic!" Annette said, her eyes wide with awe. "Ah, Nicola—you *will* live happily ever after, just like Marie-in the-Ashes."

"A fairy tale," Nadine said with a sniff.

"But *this* tale is true," I said, suddenly realizing I needed to convince myself as well.

Nadine's mouth was pinched, and a little line I had never noticed before showed between her eyes. "The queen is toying with you, Nicola. Nobles are like that. Passionate about something one moment, forgetting it the next. Tomorrow you will be out on the streets, and this time without the family."

Only Pierre seemed genuinely hurt that I was going. He stared up at the stone wall of the palace as though he could see through it to the royal apartments beyond.

"Not even the queen can just buy someone like that," he protested. "You are not a slave."

"It is my *freedom* she has bought," I told him. "Freedom from hunger. And from constant travel. And from Uncle's cane. It is what I want, Pierre." I put a hand on his arm, pulling him from the others before adding: "You could stay here, too."

"I do not think the queen would pay much of a price for me."

"She said she thought you handsome and she was impressed with your skill. I could ask her. With what she has already paid, she could have us both—quite a bargain!"

He smiled but it did not go as far as his eyes. "Nicola," he said softly, "Father cannot afford to give away the entire family."

"Uncle did not *give* me away," I reminded him.

He grunted, and stared again at the wall.

"Pierre," I said quickly, "listen to me. It will not be long before you are old enough to start your *own* company."

"I am fourteen—that is old enough already," he said. "Father began Troupe Brufort when he was even younger than I am now."

"Well," I said, more brightly than I felt, "there will be other festivals, other royal occasions. I am sure the queen will send for you."

"I think not," said Pierre. "Queen Mary does not like Father."

"We could write to one another."

He looked at me as if I had just told him we could fly. "Do not be an idiot, Nicola. We do not know how to write."

"I am not an idiot."

"You are a flea brain."

"And you are a flea*bite.*"

He laughed, but it was not his ordinary bold laugh.

I put my hand on his. "The queen promised to teach me to write. How difficult can it be? A few scratches like a hen in sand." Turning his hand over, I made pretend marks on his palm.

Pierre laughed again, his old, bold laugh. "I suppose I could find a priest to teach me some such hen-scratchings."

Suddenly we threw our arms around one another. What had I been thinking? How could I leave the only family I knew?

"Still here, my fine lady?" Uncle's voice interrupted us, and we sprang apart. "Shouldn't you be upstairs with the lords and ladies, not down here consorting with the riffraff?"

I could not stop my tongue from returning a sharp answer. "Ah, Uncle—have you finished counting the queen's gold yet?"

Uncle sneered. "She drives a very poor bargain. I would happily have let you go for far less."

What he said hurt so much, I said what I was thinking. "She did well to be rid of *you* so cheaply, Uncle."

Determined to have the last word, Uncle said angrily, "If you treat the queen to such a wicked tongue, Nicola, you will be beheaded before the week is out. And good riddance."

Suddenly I had no answer. Giving Pierre a last goodbye glance, I seized my bundle and walked away.

When I got back into the palace, a serving woman in a deep russet gown and dark scarf took me in hand.

"Come!" she said, and nothing more.

Leading me up the stairs, she took me to a small but elegantly-appointed room where four young women, just a few years older than me, were sitting and chatting at their needlework. The language they spoke was neither French nor Italian but something filled with harsh sounds, between a cough and a growl.

The four were all in black velvet dresses with deep hanging sleeves, starched white lawn at collar and at wrist, and dark black veils descending from small dark caps.

The servant cleared her throat. All four turned to stare at us. Then the one whose striking good looks were all but overpowering waved a hand at the servant, who left at once.

For a moment there was a deep silence. The hand-waver cast her eye over me like a farmer examining a chicken at the market. There was something regal about her: the way she carried her head, the way she dismissed the servant.

"So *you* are the fool." Her accent was more pronounced than Queen Mary's.

All at once I realized that these four women must be—like the queen herself—from Scotland, for surely it was the language of the Scots they had been speaking together.

"A fool, madam? I do not think so," I spoke slowly but with great deliberation, my eyes lowered. "Though I am a peasant, and not nearly as clever as you, madam, I am clever enough not to insult a stranger at first meeting."

I glanced up. Her eyes were suddenly hard and shiny like pebbles on a beach. Instinctively my hand went to my mouth. Nadine had been right. I would surely be thrown out onto the streets.

"Oh, la! She does not mean that you are stupid, girl," said the prettiest of the four, her bright daisy looks easier to take than the other's deep rose beauty. "To be a *fool* is simply your title here. A fool is . . . a clown or a jester."

I knew clowns, of course. In their motley, they juggled and mimed on the streets at any market fair.

"Am I to wear a colored costume then? And a hat with bells?"

She laughed. "What a thought!"

"But . . ." I gestured down at my poor dress, with its neck kerchief and long apron. It had been good enough for a street dancer. Would it do for a court fool?

She laughed again. "Do not worry. We will dress you appropriately. Of course, now you must wear mourning as we do. The dowager insists. She does not give up her power willingly, that one. But . . ." She toyed with a curl of hair that had escaped from her cap,

then laughed again. "Mary is queen now. She will see us restored to
our former gaiety."

"You chatter too much," the regal one said.

"Well, I say only the truth."

"The queen prizes the truth," I said brightly, hoping to make
amends. "She told me so."

"See?" The pretty one made a face at the regal one, then turned
to me again. "There is money in the royal accounts for clothing for
all of the queen's people despite the old dowager's parsimony. Certainly the queen will have some costume made up for you." She
cocked her head to one side. "As for your duties—well, there are always fools at court. You will be above them all, of course, as you are
to be the queen's *own* fool. And won't that be a flea in La Folle's ear.
La!"

I had thought I was to be the queen's own friend, not her fool. I
tried not to let the disappointment show. "If that is what Queen
Mary wants."

"Oh, that she does," said the third of the young women, setting
down her embroidery frame. Her face was rounded. While she did
not have the fine looks of the other two, there was a vivacity to her
that shone out in bright spots of color on her cheeks. She stood up
and began viewing me from every angle.

"Even between the four of us, we are not *foolish* enough for the
French court," she said. "We are too Scottish. We say what we mean
without putting pretty twists upon it. The French court prizes the
quick answer that says one thing but means another. You—it
seems—can do both! And you have nothing to lose."

"Nothing but my head," I whispered.

All of a sudden she hooked her arm through mine so briskly I
half expected her to hoist me onto her shoulders.

"They say your name is Nicola."

"They say correctly," I replied. "Do I need to change it as I change my dress, now that I am a fool?"

This time they all laughed, even the one who had been silent so far, she with the set of amber prayer beads hanging at her waist. Rather plain and still compared to the other three, her large, kind eyes shone in her face like great dark jewels.

"La—Nicola," the pretty one said. "Perhaps *we* are the ones who should change our names, for we Scots are each called Mary."

"Each?"

"Each! I am Mary Beaton, and this is Mary Fleming, Mary Livingstone, and Mary Seton!" she said, pointing to one after another. Then she clapped her hands together as if she had just performed a great trick and was leading the applause.

"Five. If you count Queen Mary," added Mary Seton, the one with the prayer beads. "May she live long and rule well." Her right hand made a quick sign of the cross. She reminded me of the nuns who had taken care of me, and I liked her at once for that.

"I am indeed too foolish to distinguish all of you so quickly," I said. But I had already made up my mind to think of them as Regal Mary, Pretty Mary, Jolly Mary, and Pious Mary, their actions marking them out even if their clothing did not. However, I was not so foolish as to tell them this. "But you will all know me, lest they change my name to Mary as well."

"You may keep your name, little ninny," said Jolly Mary Livingstone, leading me away. "Four Maries is enough. But these awful clothes—pah! They will have to go." She tugged at the sleeve of my threadbare dress. "The dowager would have you put down like a dog for wearing such a thing."

"Nicola seems my size," Pious Mary observed. "I will give her my other mourning gown till the seamstress can come. But clean her up well or she will soil the good cloth." She picked up one end of a tapestry and disappeared through a door hidden behind it.

7 ❧ THE BATH

"ome," Jolly Mary said. "We are well prepared for you."

They led me into a small inner cham-
ber where there was a steaming wooden tub sitting on the stone
floor. I had never seen any pot big enough to heat this much water
before. I looked under it but there was no flame. How many times
must someone have emptied a kettle into it! And for what purpose?

Jolly Mary let go of my arm and said, "Now take off that hideous
apron and dress. The kerchief as well. And the cap. I am certain
you are going to look lovely when you are clean."

"Clean? But I am not dirty," I complained. "I washed my hands
and face before we performed and had a full bath not a month ago
in a stream near Nantes." I did not make a move to strip off my
things.

"Now!" Regal Mary's hand pressed into the small of my back,
pushing me forward again. "Into the tub."

"*Mon Dieu!*" I cried. "You are going to boil me like a piece of
mutton! Does Her Majesty know of this?"

"It is the queen's own order," Pretty Mary said.

"But the water is hot."

"Of course it is hot!" Jolly Mary laughed at me. "We could not
possibly bathe you in cold, could we?"

"Of course one bathes in cold water," I said. "Is not a stream
cold? And a pond?"

"Come," said Regal Mary, "or the water will indeed be cold." They grabbed me and began peeling off my apron and dress.

There was no point in trying to fight them. Besides, where would I have gone? I *wanted* to be here. Perhaps this was a test of courage, just as the riddle had been a test of wit. Both to determine if I were worthy of a place at court.

Suddenly I was quite naked, Pretty Mary having tossed my clothes as far from me as she could. I put one arm across my tiny breasts, shamed that anyone should see me bare, especially these Scottish strangers.

"How thin she is," Regal Mary commented, as if I were some piece of horseflesh at a fair.

"You would be thin, too, if you had had only a baguette to eat today," I replied, neglecting to mention the cheese or the wine.

Regal Mary harrumphed and turned her back on me.

"Now, Nicola, are you going to get in by yourself or do we have to throw you in?" Jolly Mary demanded, placing her hands on her hips and fixing me with a determined stare.

I had no doubt she was quite capable of tossing me into the tub on her own, so I took a reluctant step closer. When I dabbed one finger into the water, I found it was the temperature of soup that had been sitting in the bowl for some time.

Turning, Regal Mary saw my hand testing the water, and raised a haughty eyebrow. "Hot enough for you, little peasant?" she said. "We can always have more boiled water brought in."

There was no way I could delay further, so I lifted up one foot and dipped it in. The bath did not feel so bad! Slowly I climbed in, then lowered myself until the water came to my chin. The warmth seeped through my skin and down into my bones. *If this is torture,* I thought, *what a delicious way to die.*

Pretty Mary handed me a cloth and soap to wash with. I rubbed down my arms and legs and could see that already I was turning the color of a new babe. I laughed at the thought.

"You will need to wash your hair as well," said Jolly Mary. And without any more warning than that, she put a hand on the top of my head and shoved me completely under the water.

For an instant pure fear stabbed at my heart. My entire body remembered the great river Rhône that had swallowed my parents; it remembered the waves, the cries of horror, the black tide. I clutched the edge of the tub with both hands and pushed up as hard as I could.

Bursting out of the water, I gasped and spluttered, "Maman! Papa!" I screamed, again and again. "Help! Help!"

At first the three Maries laughed, but they soon stopped when they saw the great fear in my face. And the awful rage.

"You are trying to drown me," I cried. "Assassins! Help!"

At that very moment, Pious Mary came back in with an armful of clothes. My eyes were drawn immediately to the cross she wore, and as I stared at it, all at once I felt safe again.

She knelt beside me. "Poor child, are you all right?" she asked in her soft voice.

"We were just trying to wash her hair," Pretty Mary said.

"She thought we were trying to drown her," added Jolly Mary.

I did not want Pious Mary to think I was just being silly, and so hurriedly explained, my voice raw from screaming. "A year ago I saw my parents drown. I would have drowned myself, had the Lord not saved me."

Pious Mary glared at the others before turning back to me. "You are safe here, Nicola. No one would dare harm one of the queen's own house."

My panic faded and I sat back in the tub. Gradually I relaxed as the Maries scrubbed at my hair and chattered, sometimes in French, sometimes in their own strange-sounding Scots tongue.

I began to drift into sleep.

Jolly Mary's voice roused me. "You'd best get dried off and dressed now," she said, offering a hand to help me out of the tub.

The drying towels were so soft and sweet-smelling it was like rubbing rose petals over my skin. The velvet gown Pious Mary loaned me was very long and loose, but the silken hose were lovely. I had never had any but woolen before. However, they had no shoes that came near to fitting me.

"I have just the thing," I said, finding my sack next to the pile of my discarded clothes. I pulled out the last pair of boots Papa had ever made me. I had worn them but once before, when the nuns had taken me to a special mass for my parents. The boots had been too big for me then, and I had not tried them on since. But now they fit me nicely, snugged on over the new hose.

Regal Mary turned her nose up at the boots. "Peasant wear!"

But the others agreed they would do until proper shoes might be cobbled for me. However in my heart I doubted even the queen's shoemaker could make me anything half so fine.

Then the Maries brought me into a carpeted room where the walls were hung with rich tapestries. Two large canopied beds stood side by side. On a small table were several sets of inlaid combs and brushes.

"Sit here, Nicola," Pious Mary said, gesturing to a stool by the table. Then she tutted to herself as she stood over me, working out the snarls in my hair. "I will put it into a proper style in the morning."

At first I swore at each pull, crying out, *"Mon Dieu!"* And "Assassin!" And even "Mother Mary!" which, under the circumstances, with all the Maries around me, was almost laughable. But at each swear, Pious Mary gave me a sharp rap on the head with the brush. "Do not take the Lord's—or His Mother's—name in vain."

At last, the tangles being mostly *un*tangled, Pious Mary stood me in front of a mirror. I was startled, for I had never seen myself, except in a pond. I looked entirely different from *that* Nicola. My cheeks were now baby pink, not with blushes or with Nadine's paints, but with scrubbing. My hair, in two long plaits, shone an antique gold, instead of the dirty yellow I knew so well. And the dress made me look like a courtier. I ran my hand down the skirt.

"Am I . . . in the least pretty?" I asked, remembering what the queen had said.

"A fool does not need to be pretty," Regal Mary said with another sniff. "Mostly they have humps and bumps, crossed eyes and bad teeth."

"She is not that kind of fool, and well you know it!" Pious Mary picked up her embroidery frame again. "Those are God's own fools. It is a sin to laugh at them, poor helpless creatures."

Helpless creatures? I thought of the dark angel-faced dwarf letting go a fart in Uncle's face. She had not seemed helpless then.

"Oh, la! You make every occasion a lecture," Pretty Mary grumbled.

Jolly Mary whispered in my ear as she dabbed me with some perfumed oil that smelled like lavender. "You are *very* pretty. Especially cleaned up. They are just jealous, you know. Jealous that the queen has a need of more wit than theirs."

A wiser fool would have kept silent at that and simply held the compliment to herself. But I was not wise yet. "If *I* am to be the wit, then why are *you* all here? Are you all relatives of the queen?"

"No, not relatives," Jolly Mary replied, "though we all come from good Scottish families. We were sent here to France as children to become maids-in-waiting for the young queen." She spun around, her skirt belling out.

"Our mothers were promised we would be living at court," added Pretty Mary. "But the dowager queen sent us away to the convent at Poissy." Her mouth went all sour and she was suddenly not very pretty at all. "A long way away from the games and the fun of the court."

"They say little Mary cried for want of us," Jolly Mary added. "But still they did not bring us back."

"There are rather too many games in this court as it is," Pious Mary said. "It is a place of debaucheries. All Europe knows it. For the sake of our eternal souls it is good that we went to the convent." Her hands busily tied off a knot in her embroidery. "The Prior has been very attentive."

"*Too* attentive, if you ask me. Paying attention equally to our ABC's *and* our letters from home," said Regal Mary. There was a heavy bitterness in her voice. "Prior de Vieuxpont is a tyrant." She looked so angry that, for the first time, I was almost sorry for her.

"He is a holy man," replied Pious Mary.

I wondered how they could be speaking of the same person, but then I remembered that the way I saw Uncle was not at all the way Nadine saw him. Or his favorite, Annette, saw him. Or even Pierre.

"Why could you not stay with the queen," I asked, "having come so far to be with her?"

"Queen Catherine wanted her to be a *proper* French princess, as she was to marry the little prince," said Jolly Mary, pulling a face. "She was already a queen, you know, of Scotland. She had been so since an infant. But that was not good enough for Queen Catherine."

"And *we* were not French enough," Regal Mary said.

"Or witty enough," added Pretty Mary.

"You were children," I said. "How could they expect it?"

"How indeed," Jolly Mary said, hooking her arm through mine once again.

"It is no surprise they hid us away," Pious Mary replied, hardly looking up from her work. "The Scots lords brawled in King Henry's presence. They were drunk and they were rolling about on the floor pulling hair like peasants at a fair. What a disgrace!"

"Well, how can anyone lay the blame for that on us?" Pretty Mary's lower lip stuck out. "We were only children. And not even there, but shut away at the convent!"

"We are here now," Pious Mary pointed out. "And we must be ornaments in the young queen's crown. We must show them that not all Scots are drunken brawlers."

"Here today—and gone tomorrow." Regal Mary shook her head. "Once the coronation celebrations are over, it is back to the convent for us. And back to Prior de Vieuxpont."

I just did not understand. "Why not go back to Scotland, if you hate it so here in France?"

"We cannot just do as we will, little fool," Pretty Mary said. "We go or stay at the king's pleasure."

"But that almost makes you . . . slaves."

"Slaves!" Regal Mary drew herself up and glared at me. "We are of good families. Unlike . . . *some.*"

All my sympathy for her fled at once.

"We will get home anyway in a year or so," added Pretty Mary. "To be married off, most like."

"What about the queen? Will she go back to Scotland with you, as she is queen of that land?"

"Not if she has any sense!" Jolly Mary laughed. "It is much pleasanter for her here in France."

"And safer, too," Pious Mary said, crossing herself quickly, "for a Catholic queen."

8 ❧ MASS

That night, though I had been bathed in the four Maries' tub and was wearing one of their velvet dresses, I was sent to the servants' quarters. There I shared a cramped bunk with two other girls. Still it was the softest bed I had ever had. Far softer than the roadsides and hard pallets that had been my lot the past year.

The two girls with whom I shared the chamber kept their distance. I tried to speak to them, even asked them questions about the court. But they looked at me as though I were carrying the plague and turned their faces to the wall, falling asleep without a word.

I did not sleep well. Both of them snored.

In the morning I ate breakfast in the kitchen among the servants, many of whom were already hurrying about their duties. I filled myself to the bursting point in case I got no more food that day. But the others paused only briefly for a snatch of bread or a swallow of water. Their gossip was full of names I did not recognize, duties I did not understand. And all of them seemed wary of talking to me.

I could only guess that, as the queen's own fool, I was neither one of them nor one of their masters. Yet I had no idea what I was to do or where I was to go. Or how I could once again talk to the queen.

When I could not eat a morsel more, and it was clear I had no other reason to remain in the kitchen, a potboy pointed to the back stairs.

"You be wanted there," he said.

I climbed slowly, still marveling at the fairy tale my life had become. Who needed friends or duties, surrounded by such luxury?

On the second floor, I heard again the harsh jangle of the Scottish tongue and found my way to the room of the four Maries. They barely looked up from their embroideries to greet me, though Pious Mary eventually arose and came over.

"That hair!" she said, making a tsking sound with her tongue against the roof of her mouth, as Maman used to do when the cat got among the chickens.

She was but slightly gentler than she had been the evening before, pulling the brush through my hair stroke after stroke till it crackled like summer lightning. Then she parted my hair in the center, twisted and tucked it into a fluted cap. When she showed me the results in a hand mirror, I did not recognize the girl who stared back at me.

"That will do, then," Pious Mary said, taking the mirror away. "Any more is an invitation to the sin of pride." As she finished speaking, the cathedral bells rang out a cheery invitation.

"What am I to do?" I asked. "Where am I to go?"

"Why—to mass with us," Pious Mary said. "Where else?"

"With the whole court," Jolly Mary added.

"And the queen?" I asked.

"Foremost the queen," said Pretty Mary, standing. She had a small book in her hand.

"After the king, of course." Regal Mary's voice was stern. "Always after the king."

. . .

We went down to the cathedral where the young king had been crowned only the day before. But now, instead of watching cold and weary from a grey street while nobles hurried by, I was to be a part of the court's own worship service. I pinched the skin of my arm, thinking I was dreaming, but I did not wake.

The four Maries sat on special benches up in the front of the cathedral, only slightly behind the royal family. I was well in back, though not as far back as the kitchen staff. Squeezed in between a girl with crooked teeth named Eloise, who was a handmaid to the Maries, and a rather fat maid-in-waiting who had obviously never waited for a meal, we were on the same bench as the dwarf La Folle, who snored on and off through the entire mass.

Up in the pulpit, the cardinal in his brilliant crimson robes preached a long sermon about heretics. He called them traitors to both God and the king and said they should be burned at the stake. "The smell being an incense to the Lord," he roared.

Burned! I shivered with the thought of such a terrible punishment. But I could not follow his argument, for much of it was in Latin, which was like—but not like—the Italian I knew.

Suddenly a great fear took hold of me. The Maries had told me that the queen wanted someone amusing. But I was fool indeed if I thought I could be witty enough for this company. And if I failed, would I be judged a traitor to the queen if not to God? Would I be beheaded as Uncle had said? Or burned at the stake? I hardly heard a word more of the sermon, but sat trembling like an alder leaf, all those questions rattling around in my head.

Then, suddenly, mass was over, and we all stood while the royal party trooped down the aisle towards the door. They walked slowly, and were very grand and very, very frightening.

Because I now realized how my very life depended upon pleasing them, I turned to Eloise and asked, "Who are they all?"

She giggled, naming each as they went by. "The king and queen, of course," she said, nodding at the first two.

"Those I know. And the next man, with the white plume?" He had been sitting at the high table when we had performed. His handsome face was only slightly marred by a long scar.

"The Duke de Guise. He received that scar in battle," Eloise added. "He is the bravest man in France."

"Braver than the king?" I asked.

Her voice dropped to a scornful whisper. "The new king is a boy. He knows nothing of fighting. He is *not* his father." Then she put her hand partly over her mouth. "I did not tell you that."

"I am as silent as one in the grave," I said.

"Where we both will be if you repeat what I said."

I shivered. "I am only curious who they all are," I said. "I do not wish to spread gossip about them. But to please them, I need to know them."

She nodded. "The duke is Queen Mary's uncle," Eloise told me. "The cardinal, too."

I remembered thinking how much the duke and the cardinal had looked alike sitting together at dinner and nodded.

Eloise continued. "Since the old king died, the cardinal and the duke have been running the government. The old queen is not happy with either of them. But of course what can she say now?"

"They must be very important men," I hazarded.

"More important than the king, some people say." Eloise raised an eyebrow, then nodded at the next to walk by, the purse-mouthed dowager. "The old queen Catherine, the dead king's wife."

"She looks fierce."

"She *is* fierce." She leaned even closer, her voice dropping till it was scarcely a whisper. "After marrying the king, she was found to be barren."

"But . . . she has children. Sons *and* daughters."

Eloise put a finger to her nose and nodded. "She took every powder and potion she could get her doctors to make. Some even say she resorted to magic. She is a de Medici, you know."

A de Medici! One did not have to be Italian to know of them! Poisoners all. I would have to be careful around the old queen.

Eloise looked around, making sure no one could overhear her, then whispered, "The trouble with magic is that it cannot always be bidden. True, she has had children, but not a one of them in good health. The young king has had the pox and the flux and the ague. His ear is always leaking. He often finds it difficult to breathe." She stopped, then nodded again at the line of royals walking up the aisle. "Look, here come her other children, Prince Charles and the Princess Elisabeth."

As they passed by, I could see they shared their mother's features, but there was something very determined in her face they all lacked. She was a lioness, they lambs.

Back at the cardinal's palace I found myself rather lost amidst a new kind of bustle.

"What is going on?" I asked Eloise, who had become my only source of information.

"We will be leaving soon," Eloise told me. "You with the queen's court to the king's great house in Blois, and me with the four Maries back to the convent." She wrinkled her nose. "It is not so much fun there. Hard bread and hard stones to kneel on."

"Leaving? But how soon?"

"Why, tomorrow. Did no one tell you?" Eloise asked. "The king and queen are but guests here."

"No. No one told me," I said. I had known that the king and queen were guests, of course. It was the first thing that Jacques had told us. But I had not thought they would move on so quickly.

"Guests—even royal ones—are like fish who stink after the third week!" Eloise said. "There, that is my little joke. Do you think I might become a fool, too? Then I could stay at court instead of returning to the convent."

I was too stunned to answer.

She babbled on. "There is much packing to be done today. The wagons and carriages must be loaded first thing in the morning. You would be amazed how much those four brought with them, even from a convent. Gowns and laces and shoes and combs and jewels." And off she went.

Here I was, just learning the stairs and hallways of this great house. How would I ever find my way around another?

9 &~ WIT

ater that afternoon, when the light was beginning to fade, I received a summons to
go to the queen. I had convinced myself
she had forgotten me already. She hadn't sent for me since buying
my freedom, and I was only a peasant's child dressed in borrowed
velvet after all.

But when I was brought into her chamber, her face lit up. "Ah,
La Jardinière, my little lady of the garden," she greeted me. "I am
glad you have found your way."

She remembers, I thought. *She may be a queen, but she does not
forget the little folk who love her.*

A thick rug covered the floor and a warm fire burned in the
grate. Still, drafts seemed to find their way into the passages and
halls like mice squeezing through cracks in the stonework.

The four Maries were seated close to the fire, chatting as they
worked on their embroidery. Sitting near them, Princess Elisabeth
talked to her mother, the dowager. The king was on his knees playing with a pair of terrier puppies, holding out tidbits of food between his fingers and chuckling as the dogs jumped for the morsels.
His color was no better than when I had seen him in church, but he
was animated with the dogs.

By the fire, the dwarf lolled on cushions. Her humped shoulder
cast strange shadows on the far wall.

I made the best curtsy I could. It felt clumsy in the new dress and
my father's boots, but at least I remembered to do it.

"Have you been keeping yourself busy?"

"Not really," I admitted, as I straightened up.

"Not really, *Your Majesty*," the dowager said, looking up, her voice stern.

"Not really, *Your Majesty*," I said quickly. "I am not certain what my duties are. I do not know what things to pack or where to put them. And I have so little myself that . . ."

Queen Mary crooked her finger towards me and waited to speak again till I was by her side. She put her hand on mine and drew me to a cushion by her chair. Then she looked into my eyes and whispered fiercely, "You have only one duty, Nicola, and that is to be yourself. Be honest at all times, even when everyone else is telling me only what they think I should hear."

"That does not sound like any sort of work at all, Madam," I said. "Are you sure there is not more I can do for you?"

"You will be surprised at how difficult it is to do as I ask," she assured me with that same quiet intimacy. "But it is all I want."

I must have blinked uncomprehendingly at her because she went on.

"My governess taught me that when a Roman general celebrated his victory with a parade through the city, a slave was always beside him to repeat in his ear, 'Remember, thou art but a mortal.' Now you are no slave, Nicola. But you must speak such truth to me. You must remind me that as queen I rule over all the people. And that I am as human as they. *That* is your duty, child."

"To tell you that you are a mortal? Who would believe me?"

She smiled broadly at me. "More than would believe you if you said I was a dancing dog, I hope."

"Dog?" echoed the king, looking up. "Did you say something

about a dog?" His eyes were still puffy and close up I could see how badly his face was scarred with the pox.

The dwarf gave a series of short yips like a frantic pup, and Princess Elisabeth broke out into gales of laughter. The dowager only pursed her thin lips and looked annoyed.

Ignoring them, Queen Mary spoke directly to the king. "My dear, you remember Nicola, the girl I found in the garden."

"In the garden?" King Francis had turned back to feed his dogs. "Ah—yes! The one who fell under the table. The one who had some clever things to say."

The queen clapped her hands. "Tell him. Tell him, garden girl, your answer to the riddle, the three-legged dog."

Feeling like a performing dog myself, I did as she asked.

The king screwed up his face, puzzling over what I had said. "Can a dog really be taught that?" he asked the queen seriously. "We have never seen any of ours walk on two legs. Maybe we should teach them."

"No, do not do that!" I burst out without thinking, worried that he might also think to cut off the dogs' legs.

There was a sudden swift intake of breath from the four Maries.

The dwarf shook her head back and forth, back and forth. There was a broad impish grin on her face, as if she knew that now I was in for it.

The dowager's face was unreadable.

"I would not want any of the dogs to get into trouble. . . ." I said, lowering my eyes. "I mean, if they should fail, Your Majesty."

"Oh, do not worry about that," he said. "We would never mistreat any of our dogs." He patted one of the terriers on the head with great feeling. "It is all we can do to get some of our servants to walk upright." He laughed, throwing his head back and making a high braying sound. Everyone laughed with him, the dwarf loudest of all.

I tried to join in but made a poor job of it. I sincerely hoped that the king's next joke would be funnier so that laughing would not be such hard work.

A servant suddenly appeared at the door ushering in the queen's two uncles. The duke had a sheaf of papers under his arm. They bowed deeply to the king, then the duke beckoned him to a table set with writing implements on the far side of the room.

"If Your Majesty can spare us a moment," the duke said.

The king sighed. I could see he didn't really want to be bothered, but the queen gave him a gentle poke. So he stood and told the dogs to stay, but one of the terriers kept nipping at his heels.

"Yes, what is it now?" the king asked loudly as he crossed the room, making no effort to hide his impatience. Before either the duke or the cardinal could answer, he said in a sulky voice, "Mary, Mary, we want you here with us."

The queen got up and walked quickly across the room, waving me to come along.

I dared a quick look at the dowager, whose hands suddenly gripped the arms of the chair with such strength, her knuckles went white. This time her face was easy to read. Then as if forcing herself back into an iron control, her face went blank. I wondered whether she was furious with the king, Queen Mary, or me.

The duke did not look pleased, either. Indeed, he clenched his teeth and the scar on his cheek brightened. But he did not dare tell me to go away. I was there at the queen's bidding. Instead he ignored me, placing a single piece of parchment on the table. Tapping it with his finger, he said with some urgency, "This is the edict we discussed the other day, Your Majesty. Concerning the heresy laws."

The king looked puzzled, and squinted as if that might help him understand. So the cardinal explained, "Remember, you had decided that village houses used for illicit meetings should be razed."

"Had we? We do not really recall. But if you say so . . ." The king took the pen the duke offered, dipped it in the inkwell, then hastily scribbled something on the sheet of parchment. His writing looked a great deal like hen-scratches.

"I shall have the royal seal affixed and see that these measures are put into immediate effect," said the duke.

I found myself shaking, as if taken by a sudden ague. "Are people's houses going to be burned down?" I whispered to the queen, but my voice was louder than I had intended.

She nodded.

"Houses of people as mortal as you, Majesty?"

The duke's scar grew brighter still, and the cardinal's face was practically purple.

Queen Mary put her hand on her husband's. "Burning houses, my dear? Is that what we are about now?"

"Yes," the king said, ". . . but only ones that are misused. Is that right, Uncle?" he turned and looked at the cardinal, who nodded. "They can always have new ones built."

"Not unless they are very rich," I whispered again, quickly adding, "Your Majesty." I added a curtsy for good measure.

The queen patted my hand.

"These are matters of state," the cardinal announced, his great voice only moderated slightly. "Not the business of little girls. The head of a household does not consult his servants about where the furniture should be placed."

"Nicola is my fool, Uncle," the queen said, "and speaks only the truth. So, Nicola—what do you say to that?"

I dared a quick look at the queen. She was nodding at me, so I drew a deep breath and plunged ahead. "Even if he were not asked, a good servant would warn his master not to set fire to a chair. The flames might spread and burn the entire house down."

The queen laughed delightedly and, after a second, so did the king. "So be sure and set your fires carefully, Uncle," she said.

Neither the duke nor the cardinal looked amused.

"There are some other matters we should discuss in private," the duke said. "They are not for women's delicate ears." He nodded in the direction of the door. "*Important* matters."

"Matters," the king complained petulantly, "are *always* important. We were having a perfectly pleasant chat with the garden girl before you came in." He nodded at me and smiled sweetly, which totally transformed his thin, homely, pocked face. "About dogs. And . . . things."

The duke raised an eyebrow and then suddenly realized who I was. "Ah—the little tumbler under the table." He turned to the king, his voice dripping with condescension. "Your Majesty, the queen may call this child what she will, but such a peasant cannot possibly have anything of import to say to us."

The queen's lips drew down into two thin lines. "Nicola, be mindful of your duty."

I did not want to disappoint her. "I am certain everything the duke says is important," I began carefully. "When the duke sneezes, it is a very important sneeze and everyone should listen to it."

The king moved a hand to his mouth to cover a smirk.

"Have a care, girl, what you say next!" the duke warned me. The scar was an emblazonment on a pale field.

"Pardon me, my lord," I apologized. "Everything you say is very serious, so I am certain you always have a care before you say anything at all. But as I am just a poor fool, nothing I say matters in the least, so I might as well just say the very first thing that comes into my head."

"I do not think you can beat that argument, Uncle," said the queen, laughing.

"And what about me, girl?" the cardinal asked, his round face unreadable. "Do I think enough before speaking to satisfy you?"

"I could not rightly say, Your Sanctity," I admitted. "I did not understand a single bit of your sermon this morning."

"Ah, but I was merely preaching the Word of God," he said. He folded his hands over his belly, looking like a man who had just won at counters.

I was beginning to enjoy playing the fool and answered, "If God has only spoken *one* word—*the* Word—He must think very hard and for a very long time before He speaks, unlike a fool who thinks very little but talks without a pause."

"Perhaps it would be a good idea to preach a shorter sermon next time, Uncle," the queen teased. "Otherwise people might assume you have not been thinking hard enough."

The cardinal's face got as red as his robe but he did not respond.

"Enough of this nonsense," snapped the duke. "Such *wit* is for the dinner hour, not for the midday. And certainly not during a discussion of state matters." He beckoned the king, who—rolling his eyes dramatically—followed.

They paused in the doorway and the king looked back. He whistled for his dogs and they scampered after him.

For a moment, the cardinal scrutinized me closely. Although he was not as lean as his brother, there was a sharpness in his eye that led me to believe he was quite as capable of leading men into battle as the duke.

"Child, if you are to have the ear of the queen, you must be properly educated," he said. He started towards the door, then glanced back. "I will see to it." Then he was off in a swirl of rich crimson.

Educated? Me? I was only astonished that I had not been instantly beheaded for insolence. Even Uncle would have battered me senseless with his cane for such answers. But evidently as the queen's fool, I served at her pleasure. And her uncle, the cardinal, seemed to honor that.

For now.

The minute the men were gone, the four Maries—who had been silent the entire time—began to talk in a mixture of French and Scottish. I scarce understood one word in ten.

Looking secretly pleased at something, the dowager stood and held her hand out to Princess Elisabeth. "Come, daughter," she said. "We have much to do before tomorrow's progress."

The princess got up immediately, and she and the old queen walked out of the door without so much as a nod to the others.

"Your Majesty," Regal Mary began.

The queen waved her away with a flick of her hand. "Leave me. All of you. I am tired of chatter." Then she looked at the dwarf. "You, too, *ma Folle.*" When I started after them, Queen Mary said, "Not you, Nicola. Sit here by me." She gestured to one of the chairs near her.

I sat.

"So what do you think, Nicola?" the queen asked.

"I think, Majesty, that all uncles have some things in common, whether they are nobles, priests, or showmen."

"And what is that, my Jardinière?" asked the queen.

"They do not like girls who talk too much."

"But that is exactly why I want you here," she said, lifting one finger. "To talk and talk and talk as much as you please."

"Even if it is all nonsense?"

"*Especially* then." She leaned forward as if confiding in me. "If burning down houses is sense, then the more nonsense we have the better." She picked up her embroidery frame and looked at it critically, before plucking out one of the threads that made up the tail of a little monkey.

For a long moment we were silent, and then I sighed.

She shifted in her chair but did not look up from her work. "Yes?"

"Madam, is it true that we leave in the morning for the royal palace?"

"We leave for Blois, if that is what you mean."

Was there more than one royal palace then? "Is that the one where everything is made of gold and silver, even the knives and spoons? Like in the fairy stories my mother told me."

"I'm afraid there is nowhere as grand as that." The queen laughed. "Not even in France. But I am sure you will like the château at Blois when we get there."

10 ⁊ LESSONS

I did *not* like Blois, which was a great château in the valley of the river Loire. Or at least we were not there long enough for me to learn to like it. Soon after, we moved on to another château named Varteuil. Then to Château Châtelherault. And then to somewhere else.

I should have been happy. Did I not have all that I could possibly want and certainly more than I had ever dreamed of? Clothes as beautiful as a princess in a fairy tale. Food at my command. A soft bed. And the companionship of a queen.

Well—not quite all.

Perhaps it was foolish of me, but I had thought that once I became part of the court, my wandering days would be at an end. But it seems that the royal court is not a building. It is a great crowd of people who never stay in any place for more than a few months at a time. Where Troupe Brufort had followed a trail of fairs and festivals in search of coins, the royal court moved for its own reasons.

"It is too cold," the king would say, and off we would go to the south.

Then "It is too hot," he would complain, and off we traveled, like geese in summer, to the north.

Sometimes we stopped to host the Grand Council of France, where all the great men of the realm gathered. Then we would be gone again to some new place where there was good hunting to be had, or there was a special wine that did not travel well.

The king and his people were performers traveling from one place to the next, and the next, in the great play that was the court. Oh, we were warmer and better fed than Troupe Brufort. We did not worry about bedding or a roof over our heads. But we were just as often on the road.

"Travel," I said one time to the queen, "however it is done, is tiring. The brain simply longs for familiar things."

"Oh, my wonderful fool," she told me, "that is exactly why we take along those things which remind us of home. The cook has his pots. The king has his dogs. And I—well now that my dear royal sister Elisabeth has gone to her king in Spain, I have you! To remind me . . ."

"That thou art but a mortal?" I said.

She clapped her hands happily. "Exactly."

What a great train the traveling court made. As well as the king and queen and their family, there were other nobles who traveled with them and served as ministers and these, in turn, were served by dozens of clerks and scribes. There were priests, chamberlains, doctors, pages, porters, valets, stable hands, maids, barbers, laundresses, soup makers, musicians, seamstresses, guards—and fools. In fact there were more folk in the traveling court than in the village I had lived in with Maman and Papa.

One would think that with all of these folk I would have found at least one good friend amongst them. But I was neither a servant nor a noble, only somewhere in-between.

"Neither fish nor fowl," Maman used to say of such situations. Whenever I found myself moping, I remembered that. And forgot it again each time the queen called me in to play her fool.

It took me some time, all through winter and into spring, but at last I understood: I would never truly be Marie-in-the-Ashes, for at story's end she turns into a princess, and that did not happen in real life. However, I would never again be put out in the rain and cold like a traveling player. What I had lost in the exchange were good friends like Pierre.

At the time it seemed a reasonable trade.

Still, the queen constantly asked for me, and that was all that mattered.

She even surprised me by giving me gifts. Once it was three dresses.

"One for your lovely singing voice," she told me. "One for your laughter. And one for your wonderful peasant stories."

The first dress was of tufted velvet, the second, a grass-green silk with embroidered leaves vining across the bodice, and the third of a lighter green velvet over which embroidered flowers were sprinkled. I spent hours trying them on and staring at myself in the glass.

"You are my Jardinière, and so you must look like a garden," the queen said several days later, handing me a green velvet cap.

I had been so astonished at the dresses, I had hardly even thanked her. But when she gave me the cap, I blurted out, "You are the sun, Madam, and flowers always turn toward the sun."

She shook her head at me. "Now you sound like a courtier, Nicola, while I would have you say the truth."

"The truth, Your Majesty, is in the listening, not in the saying." It was something Papa had once said.

We traveled back to the castle at Blois for the beginning of Lent as winter was giving way to the first promise of spring. As all the châteaus and palaces, Blois was a maze of hallways, a puzzle of doors.

I was always lost and constantly asking directions from servants who seemed annoyed with me. The cook had long since taken to calling me "Madam Underfoot." The king's valet christened me "Little Wrong Turning." And the king's dog boy named me "Little Mademoiselle Gone Missing." I answered them back in kind.

It made them all laugh but it made me no friends.

As I settled into my own chamber, not far from the queen's apartments, I thought about how few friends I had. Only, in fact, the queen. And she had not recently called for me.

Hanging my dresses on hooks, I suddenly got a cold chill down my back, a strange foreboding. It felt exactly as if a dead fish had been laid against my spine. I shivered but could not think what such a chill might mean, except that I had lost the queen's favor.

I turned and looked out of the tiny window at the slight green haze on the far fields. If she deserted me, where would I go? How would I live?

Just then one of the chamberlains knocked on my door and ordered me to report to a study in the west wing of the palace.

"What for?" I asked.

He shrugged extravagantly, and then silently led the way.

It was lucky for me that he took me or I would have been lost for certain. Blois—like all the many châteaus we had stayed in—had its own logic, but I did not know it yet.

It was obvious from the dust that the study was but little used. There was a small desk, a pair of wooden chairs, and some shelves. Other than that, the room was bare. For a brief moment, I remembered the room into which our troupe had been ushered in the cardinal's palace—the one without wall hangings or rushes on the floor. This room had that same empty feeling.

I shuddered again, my back cold-fish clammy once more.

The chamberlain left me as silently as he had led, and I was all alone. I went over to the latticed window and looked down at servants scurrying across the courtyard below. How I envied them their busy-ness.

Just then a noise made me turn around. Entering the room was a thin-faced woman in a somber dark dress, the high collar closed tight with aglets. She carried a book and some paper which she set down on the dusty desk, then fixed me with a glare. Her black hair was parted in the middle and tied back so tightly under her hood, her eyes were pulled into slits.

"So you are Nicola the fool," she said without any niceties. "The one they call La Jardinière."

"Yes," I said with a nod of my head.

"I am Madam Jacqueline," she told me. "The cardinal has summoned me to be your governess."

Madam Jacqueline looked like my maman's old soured ewe, who had stopped having lambs and was bound for mutton. What lessons mutton could impart I did not know.

"It is very kind of the cardinal," I said, "but I have nothing to pay you with. And no room in my quarters for anyone but myself."

Madam Jacqueline frowned, as if uncertain whether I was teasing or as truly as ignorant as I appeared.

"You do not pay me, you stupid girl. I am no servant of yours," she bristled. "I am here to take charge of you."

"Take *charge* of me?" I repeated. "But I am quite capable of taking charge of myself. I am no infant. I can dress myself. And except for getting lost within a new palace, I am quite capable. . . ."

Madam Jacqueline let out an impatient sigh. Then she let loose a volley at me. "It is not enough to be properly dressed and washed. And we *all* get lost within a new palace on occasion. Though I understand that you have made such lack of direction a character trait. However, you are now part of the court, and it is well past time you were educated. Why I was not sent for before, I do not know. You must be taught whom to address and when. You must learn manners. Moreover, since you are the queen's fool, someone must be responsible for setting a limit to your folly."

"But if one puts limits on foolishness, it ceases to be foolishness at all," I said. "You might as well try to keep the wind in a box."

"The wind in a box!" she tutted, her face the color of the skimming off milk. "That is just the sort of nonsense we must stop."

"But it is my nonsense the queen loves," I said.

"I have no doubt she has sometimes found your rustic prattling amusing, an antidote to the more sophisticated wit of the court. And your tumbling and singing somewhat entertaining. But even she is tiring of it, which is why her uncle sent for me."

I must have looked shocked, for madam softened for a moment. But only a moment.

"Tell me, girl, have you any letters at all?"

"No, madam, I cannot read anything but the weather and people's faces." I pointed out the window. "I can see that it will rain before the day is out. And . . ." I paused for effect, "I can see in your face that you carry a great sadness."

Cold anger flared in her eyes. I knew at once—but too late, of course—that I should have kept my mouth closed.

"My only sadness is that I should be burdened with so ignorant a girl," she snapped. Her lips got as thin as her slitted eyes. "But I shall teach you, no matter how long it takes."

She looked around the room and her mouth got even thinner with distaste, though I wouldn't have thought it possible. "I will have one of the maids clean this place up tomorrow, but it will have to do for today." Then she returned her gaze to me, looking no more pleased with me than she was with the state of the study.

"Do you know your catechism?"

"My what?"

"The doctrines of the faith." She clasped her hands primly in front of her.

"I know we are made by God to love one another. My mother taught me that."

"You must learn more than that modest sentiment, because our faith needs to be defended against its enemies at all times."

"Defended?" I was surprised, and my head cocked to one side. "Like a castle?"

"*Exactly* like a castle." She nodded, pleased with my first lesson.

"But I do not understand. How can the faith of Christ possibly be besieged?" I was truly asea.

Madam Jacqueline smacked a hand down on the table and the sudden noise made me start. "Foolish child, it is under threat at this very moment from the Huguenots and their heresies."

"What are Huguenots?"

She hissed at me like an adder in the field, and I understood that we were off to a very bad start. "How little you know. How far we must go."

"Then, please madam, start by telling me how anyone can threaten faith," I said. I smiled in what I hoped was a winning way. I really *did* want to know. "That would be like . . . like threatening the sun or the moon. Surely not even Huguenots—whatever they are—could do such a thing."

But Madam Jacqueline was clearly not taken by my smile. "The Huguenots are heretics who have brought over their pernicious doctrines from Switzerland," she said, her voice, like her lips, thin and hard. "They deny the teachings of the church and the pope and that puts all of us in danger."

"I'm sure it is very foolish of them to go against the church," I agreed, "but how are they dangerous? Doesn't the church have soldiers to guard it? And the pope his own guard?"

"How little you understand," said Madam Jacqueline. "I can see that a long hard task lies ahead of me."

For all of madam's complaints, I could not help but feel that it was *I* for whom things were going to be hard.

11 ❧ MORE LESSONS

I soon learned that like Uncle, Madam Jacqueline had a cane. It was not grand like his, with a gold knob on the end, but only a rod of plain wood. While Uncle's stick was meant to impress the public, the only purpose of Madam Jacqueline's rod was to impress *me*. When I made mistakes in my work, she laid that rod hard over my shoulders. When I spoke to her in a way she did not care for, she brought it down across my knuckles.

I was determined to give her no reasons to whip me.

Still she found them.

"Huguenots are villainous, not just misunderstood," she said one day, and *whap,* down came the cane.

"The catechism is to be memorized word for word, not sentiment for sentiment," she said the next day. And *whap,* again down came the cane.

On the next day and the next, she disliked my manner. Or my mode of speech. Or how quickly I answered. Or how slow. Not a day went by that my shoulders and knuckles went unreddened.

But I learned things nonetheless.

My real education began with the alphabet, and for all that I did not care for madam, oh, I was pleased to be learning to read. I greatly missed the stories Maman used to tell, ones she had learned from her own mother. Once I was skilled with my letters, I was determined to find at least one book in the queen's library filled with those sort of tales. And once I knew how to write, I would send word to Pierre about all that had happened since we took leave of one another, for he was still my one true friend. I thought of him often.

So I embraced my lessons. I think madam was more surprised by this than pleased.

Sitting side by side at the table, she taught me each of the letters as they were written large on the page of a book and surrounded by pictures of things that began with that same letter.

"A," she said clearly, making faces as she pronounced each letter. "A for apple and arbor and acrobat."

I repeated them after her, making the same faces.

"B," she said, "for ball and baton and bear."

I said the B words.

"You have such a peasant's pronunciation."

"That is because I am a peasant," I answered.

The cane hit my knuckles. "I will make you sound like a lady," she said. "If it kills us both."

Some days I was afraid it might.

She made me repeat each letter over and over, concerned that my mouth should form the right shape as I spoke. I think she cared more how my mouth looked than what came out of it.

But in spite of her stick, I learned.

And in spite of her dislike of me, madam admitted, though grudgingly, that I was doing well. She forced the praise through her thin lips, like icing through a pastry bag: "It will not be long, Nicola, before you are reading with ease."

"Will I read more than the ABC's?" I asked. "Will I be able to read a book of stories?"

Her stick came down on my hand. "You will read the catechism," she promised. "For it is the truth. Stories are all lies."

I thought to myself: *Once I know how to read, you shall not keep me from reading what I will. No one shall.*

Learning to write, however, was altogether different. Try as I might, I could not please madam. She insisted on my holding the pen in a way that made it difficult for me to form my letters properly.

Time after time she took the pen and jammed it into my right hand, forcing it between my thumb and forefinger.

"Madam, if you would just let me hold the pen in my left hand, I could manage much more easily," I protested.

"The devil lurks in the left," she said, *whapping* the cane down so hard that my fingers went numb and I could not have held anything with the left then, even if she had given me leave.

I picked up the pen with my right hand and made the letters for *cat* and *dog*.

"What an ungainly scrawl," she complained. "Your letters must be elegantly formed, else there is no reason to make them."

I could not resist saying, "Surely, madam, *what* we write is more important than *how* we write it. Is not a hastily-scrawled truth better than a beautifully-penned lie?"

She rapped her cane so hard across my knuckles for that, the pen fell to the floor. Then she snatched the parchment away.

"There is no sense in going any further with this," she said. "It is a waste of paper."

"But I had hoped to write a letter to my cousin one day," I said, making my eyes round with innocence.

Madam Jacqueline raised a skeptical eyebrow. "Really? And do you suppose he will be able to read it?"

I smiled at her. "He has promised to learn from a priest."

She clasped her hands primly before her, the rod still clutched between thin fingers. "Even if your writing improves and he learns to read, paper is far too expensive to be wasted on whatever fiddle-faddle you scribble. No, we shall move on to other things."

And we did.

There were matters of court etiquette to be mastered: how to enter a room, when to curtsy, when to speak, when to be silent.

Next I was taught how to address a prince or princess ("Your Royal Highness"), an ambassador ("Your Excellency"), the duke ("Your Grace"), and the cardinal ("Your Eminence").

"Always with the eyes down. Do not stare into a noble's face," madam instructed.

"Papa always said not to stare at a wild animal," I said. "Or it would bite. Perhaps nobles are the same."

Whap! The cane sliced through the air.

"Madam," I objected, "if I behave just like everyone else at court, I will cease to be a fool and will be cast out into the street."

Madam continued the lesson in a tone of voice that was even thinner and frostier than before.

During those spring weeks at Blois, I grew quite lonely for the queen. Although I was often summoned to entertain after banquets—singing songs from my childhood and telling Maman's tales—I rarely had the chance to speak with the queen alone.

I felt that what Madam Jacqueline had said was true: that Queen Mary was tiring of me. She was losing interest because that which is familiar always loses its glitter. But there was something else— under madam's instruction, I was becoming less and less myself, my peasant wit blunted by my newfound learning.

Even when I was not with Madam Jacqueline, I found myself shying away from any speech or behavior that she might disapprove of. It was as if I cringed not from the rod but from the shadow of the rod.

Only once that spring did Queen Mary have me read to her, from a book of verses, which was quite a change from the dry books of letters that Madam Jacqueline had me practice on.

The day was blustery and a persistent cold had kept the queen in from the hunt. She had a large white linen square which she pressed to her nose.

"Nicola, dear, you see me unlike my usual self."

"You are never less than your self, Majesty," I said, smiling greatly. I was sure she could see the joy written large on my face that I was once more in her company. But she acted as if we had never been apart.

She handed me the book. "Read. I would see how well your lessons are going."

I read, stumbling through the unfamiliar words.

"Brava!" she said after I had struggled through several pages. "Everything sounds so much better when spoken by you."

"But all my mistakes . . ." I began.

She laughed. "Pious and pies *do* sound alike."

"And priests and presses?"

"I made the same mistakes when first learning to read," she said. "To sound-out words is a hazard, is it not?"

"To mistake a priest for a press, perhaps," I said. "But if one pressed a priest into a pie—what a greasy meal that would be."

She roared with laughter then. "That's the Nicola I adore. Read on!"

• • •

When I finally became adept enough at my reading—no longer confusing priests and presses—Madam Jacqueline resumed the business of my catechism.

"This is what all good girls must learn," she said, presenting me with a list of definitions of God, His Son, the Holy Spirit, and other matters of our Catholic faith.

"A long list, madam," I said, my nose wrinkling as if it were not only lengthy but smelled.

"God's length is not measured by man," she said sniffily. "But you must learn all the definitions. Lest you be taken for a Huguenot." And shaking her index finger at me as if I were one of their dreaded race, she added, "The Huguenots' entire purpose is to destroy the church and deliver mankind into the hands of the devil."

"Oh, madam," I replied, "can they do it?"

"They will," was her thin-lipped reply, "if we are not vigilant."

Of course, I had never met a Huguenot. But now I imagined they were like the pictures I had seen of demons and imps, with hairy buttocks and arms dangling by their sides. I wanted to know more. Did they have horns? Did they have tails? Did they eat people? Or did they—as madam said—just infect people with *pernicious* ideas? *Pernicious* was a favorite word of hers. But I did not ask, in case it invited another great thwack with her stick.

"Are they close by, these Huguenots?" I asked. The walls of Blois were thick. But all walls have chinks in them. Perhaps the impish Huguenot could scale walls or slip through spaces.

"The Huguenots are a very long way away," she answered.

"Then why must we worry?"

"Because pernicious ideas can travel faster than a man."

This was puzzling. I shook my head. Surely it takes a man to carry an idea. So I asked, "Will not the cardinal and the duke set them aright?"

"With God's help, they will indeed."

That led me to hope that the cardinal and the duke would discuss the Huguenots with the king when I was within hearing. But the several times I was invited to be with the queen in the king's presence, no such discussions took place.

To tell the truth, in all the times I had been in a room with the king, he rarely seemed to listen to the things the duke and cardinal or anyone else reported to him. It did not seem to matter if the subject was the armies, taxes, or edicts. He would just blink his puffy eyes, nodding and grunting at the person who brought him news until they left him alone. Then he would go back quite happily to his dogs, his gaming, and hunting. For someone who was so unwell, he certainly loved to ride. Perhaps it was that on horseback he could let the horse do for him all the things his sickly, swollen body could not.

It occurred to me that I might ask the queen about the demon Huguenots. But at Blois, more than any other place, she kept by her husband's side, riding with him when he was well, faithfully attending his sickroom when he was ill. Except for the one time we had read together, it had been weeks since she last sent for me except to entertain in a crowd.

I had no one to pour out my worries to. Madam Jacqueline would surely not care that the queen saw little of me. And the cooks, the maids, the clerks and scribes, chamberlains, doctors, pages, porters, valets, stable hands, barbers, laundresses, roasters, priests, soup makers, musicians, seamstresses, guards—they were none of them my friends and all had duties of their own. Perhaps if the

Maries had been there, but, no, they were not. They were still at the convent.

So with nothing else to keep me busy, I spent more and more time with my lessons and this eased my longing for the queen's company. And my reading skills, at least, grew.

Madam Jacqueline finally felt I was ready to memorize the Creed of the Apostles in Latin. Unfortunately, I kept getting the words wrong when I recited it, lapsing into French or Italian no matter how hard I studied.

Each mistake meant another great whack with the cane.

"Does not God understand us whatever language we use?" I asked. We were sitting across the table from one another, I in my green dress and she in her accustomed black. My hand was on the table, palm up. Madam required it, the easier to give me a blow.

"Wicked child, you dishonor God Himself by making so light of His holy word," she cried and the cane—like a stroke of lightning—crashed down.

My right hand went so numb from the blow I could not pick it up from the table except by using my left. I pulled it to my chest and willed myself not to cry.

And at that very moment, the queen walked into the room.

She glared at my governess as though she had caught madam in an act of treason. "What exactly is going on here?"

Madam Jacqueline bowed her head. "Your Majesty, I am endeavoring to teach this dull girl the rudiments of her faith."

"With beatings?"

"If it is required. Willfulness is not a virtue in God's eyes. It stands too close to pride. She is an *extremely* willful girl."

I could not read the queen's expression, except that she seemed disgusted. The feeling began to return to my fingers, hot pricks like needles held in the fire.

"I do not think God sees cruelty as a virtue," Queen Mary said. "Else He would have made it a commandment."

If I had said any such thing, I would have been beaten twice. I dared to grin at madam.

"Come, Nicola," the queen said. "We will talk to the cardinal about this."

Madam Jacqueline did not move, but I glimpsed the tension in her old ewe's face as I followed the queen out the door.

"I think Madam Jacqueline is trying to please God," I said, hurrying down the stone corridor and trying to keep up with her. The queen was a head taller than I, with long legs to match.

"She has not pleased *me*," said the queen, stopping and turning so suddenly that I almost ran into her. Her skirts murmured around her. "None of *my* governesses ever treated me in such a fashion."

"But you are a queen, Majesty," I reminded her. "And I expect you were a clever child who was not such a trial to teach."

"My dear Nicola, you have learned to read in record time. Even the king has taken notice. We left you alone to get on with it—and get on you certainly have!" She smiled.

Made bold by her revelation, I dared to ask: "Majesty, why did you come to the study now? You have not been before. I thought that you did not . . . did not . . ."

"I have just been given a new book from Italy which I want you to read out to me," she replied. "I was eager to give it to you. It is a book of tales. But it can wait."

A book of tales! I would wait as long as I must!

12   THE CHESS GAME

We entered one of the salons where the king and the duke were hunched over a table playing chess, the king's dogs asleep and snoring loudly at his feet. The cardinal looked on, bending down occasionally to recommend a move to the king.

A few courtiers were seated in small, gossipy groups near the fire where the dwarf, La Folle, paraded up and down in a suit of armor made to fit her small, humped body. Brandishing a tiny sword in the air, she squawked loudly and made mock attacks on various of the men, all of whom roared at her antics. Even the duke laughed.

Just as we got to the king's game table, La Folle charged at us as though we were an invading army. The queen waved her away impatiently and went over to the chess game, where she spoke to the cardinal in hurried whispers that I could just make out.

"I must talk with you, Uncle, about Nicola's governess."

The cardinal raised an eyebrow. "Is the fool dissatisfied?"

"*I* am the one who is dissatisfied, Uncle. I just saw Madam Jacqueline beating Nicola with a wooden cane."

"Did you not want her educated?"

In a controlled voice, she answered: "Yes, I want her educated, but I do not mean to have her *beaten.*"

"Madame Jacqueline comes with the very highest of recommendations," the cardinal assured her calmly.

"I am not questioning her loyalty, Uncle, only her methods."

"You will find, dear niece, that difficult children are taught all over France with the guidance of the rod." He folded his plump hands over his ample stomach.

"I do not care what happens elsewhere. I will *not* have that woman treat my Jardinière in such a way."

"I am sure Madam Jacqueline will make whatever modifications to her regimen you demand," the cardinal conceded. "If you insist, I will speak to her at once."

"Do so." It was a royal command.

The cardinal bowed stiffly and left the room.

Throughout this conversation the king and the duke had continued their game, the duke with great concentration and the king sullenly, the linen cloth now to his ear, now to his nose.

I had seen chess played before at court, but never with such magnificent pieces. They looked just like little people—soldiers and nobles marching bravely across a wooden field of battle. The black pieces were made of ebony, the white from bone.

"The king seems to have fewer pieces than the duke," I whispered to the queen when she returned to my side. "Is he losing?"

She nodded, replying in a hushed voice: "Uncle insists that the king play. He says monarchs need to learn strategy. He says that chess is good preparation for life. The king hates it."

Hearing us, the king looked up, his face even thinner than last I had seen it, the pockmarks more pronounced. "Ah, little garden girl, perhaps you can help save the day and advise me. My wife's uncle seems to have me cornered." He winked.

"Oh, no, Your Majesty, I do not know the game at all," I said.

"Then in the further interests of your education, you should learn," he said, beckoning me forward. "No matter how hard I try, I cannot defeat the duke. Perhaps a fool could do better."

Reluctantly I moved to where the cardinal had been standing moments earlier. "I do not think so, Majesty. It looks very difficult."

"Nonsense, girl, the moves are simplicity itself. It is just the outcome that is so damnably hard." He tapped one of the pieces with his forefinger, a white figure in a crown. "Now in this square is me, the king. Here by my side is the queen. Over there is a castle, this is my knight, and all those small ones are called pawns."

"And this piece?" I asked, pointing to the figure of a jester.

"It's called *Le Fou*, the fool. There are two of them, and at the beginning of the game one of them stands in the square beside the king, the other beside the queen." He looked up and smiled at me. "As you do with my dear Mary."

Instead of looking down at my shoes as madam had taught me, I smiled back.

"In some countries," the duke put in, "that position is occupied by a bishop." His voice was hard as ice. "I for one find that far more appropriate."

Aha! I thought. *Now I begin to understand the game.* I chose my next words very carefully.

"I am one fool who knows better than to put myself in the bishop's square, Your Grace." I started to move away but the king grabbed my hand, holding me to the spot.

"Since you have already taken the cardinal's place here beside us now," he said, "perhaps we should also let you take his pulpit for the mass." He laughed at his own jest.

I knew I was well out of my depths here. If I said one thing, I angered the duke, another I angered the king. Either way, I chanced drowning. The only hope I had was to be amusing and so anger no one. *Think, Nicola, think!*

Then at last I had it. "I do not believe my governess would agree, Your Majesty. She would tell you that I know even less about religion than chess."

"Indeed," Queen Mary said, coming to my rescue just in time, "Nicola confuses priests and presses, pious and pies. Do you not remember, Francis?"

He laughed. "Oh, yes—that was quite a joke. Priests. Pies. And grease. We liked that a lot! Well, we cannot help you with religion, garden girl. That is Uncle Charles's domain. But we can with chess. The pieces move like this." The king demonstrated the movements of each in turn.

Clearing his throat loudly, the duke said, "Girl, you will notice that the chess king can hardly move at all on the board."

I nodded.

"That is why he needs these others to protect him—a strong castle, a brave knight."

"And a fool," I added, from the safety of the queen's protection.

"Yes, even a fool," the duke conceded at last. "Though the fool must always remember its place." He smiled a grim smile.

This time I looked down before asking, "Why is that, Your Grace?"

"Well, since the fool moves along the diagonal, it may only move onto squares the same color as the one it began on. Half the board is barred to it. Any fool should beware moving onto squares where she is not allowed."

Again I thought carefully before answering. "Then I suppose a fool must choose that first square very carefully."

"Brava, Nicola!" the queen whispered.

When I let out my breath, it was the first I realized I had been holding it.

The duke lifted a finger and stroked his scar, then said as carefully back to me: "The fool has no say as to which square it is placed on."

"Nor do any of the others, Uncle," the queen reminded him. "In that way, at least, they are all equal."

"In that and in that alone," the duke replied.

"Then . . . how do you win?" I asked.

"You win the game, child, by using your queen to capture the king," said the duke with a slow smile. He moved his queen into position, looking very pleased with himself.

The king scowled and leaned his cheek against his fist. "You have taken over the cardinal's position, fool. What do you recommend?"

"I think . . . I think that as you are the king, you should make all of your pawns into knights," I said.

"There's an idea!" The king roared his approval, his homely face lighting up with his delight.

"It is not allowed under the rules," said the duke evenly. "Even a king is bound by the rules."

"Well, he should *not* be," the king protested. "We prefer the way our fool thinks." He snatched up a piece and moved it carelessly across the board.

"You have placed your king in great danger," the duke chided. "That move will give me checkmate." He picked up one of his castles very precisely between two beringed fingers. But before he could place it, a crazed war cry shook the room.

La Folle came galloping across the room, making a mock charge at the duke and crying, *"Au secours!* To the rescue!"

Instinctively, the duke raised an arm even as the dwarf tried to pull up short. However, she had left it too late, and her slippers skidded on an uncarpeted part of the floor. Barging feet-first into the table, she overturned the board and scattered the pieces.

The queen and I jumped back to avoid the cascade and La Folle collapsed on her bottom, her sword clattering to the floor.

"We have been saved by the Queen of the Amazons," giggled the king, thoroughly enjoying the duke's discomfiture.

Gritting his teeth, the duke angrily leaped to his feet, tossing aside the ebony castle that was still gripped between his fingers.

"Clumsy buffoon," he hissed at La Folle, so enraged that I believe he would have lashed out at her had he a weapon to hand.

Luckily for the dwarf, however, the duke's attention was distracted when the door flew open and an officer dressed in rough riding clothes burst into the room. The man had not even taken the time to wipe the mud from his boots before coming into the royal presence.

"I bring word of La Renaudie!" he gasped and knelt down.

The duke hurried across the room and held a hushed but urgent conversation with the messenger before dismissing him.

"Fetch my sword and pistol," the duke ordered one of his servants.

"What has happened?" I whispered hurriedly to the queen, but she seemed not to hear me. "What is La Renaudie?"

"Come, Your Majesties," the duke said, turning to the king and queen, "we must leave Blois at once."

"At once? But we had planned to go hawking in the morning," the king objected, his voice rising to a squeak.

The queen put a hand on his arm. "Listen to Uncle, my dear."

"*Must* it be at once?" the king asked again.

The duke looked at the king with narrowing eyes. "At once, Your Majesty. If we make a wrong move now there will be no one to save us by knocking over the board unless it be God Himself."

13 ☙ THE GARDEN AT AMBOISE

I had not known the court to move with such haste. One would have thought the palace at Blois was about to collapse around us. Servants and soldiers darted about like stags driven by dogs. I could not guess the reason for all this hasty activity, and no one I asked—from stable boy to waiting maid—could tell me.

Without even riding costumes or proper cloaks, the members of the court were bustled into carriages guarded by mounted troops, something that had never happened before.

"Are we in danger?" I asked a cook I knew.

He shrugged. "We—or they?" he asked, pointing to the nobles.

When I asked the same question of a soldier hurrying by, he waved me away with irritation.

I finally saw the king on a fidgety brown mare. He wore a sword whose red hilt matched his coat and looked the very dandy, though there were two red spots of fever on his cheeks.

"Sire," I cried out, thinking to ask him. But the duke rode between us.

"It would be better, Your Majesty," the duke called out, "if you stayed in the carriage with the queen."

"I am the king!" King Francis said stubbornly. "It is my duty to lead our cavalry, even in a retreat." He spoke with such unusual authority that de Guise had no option but to let him go, though I could see from the duke's face what he thought of the idea.

"Your Grace . . ." I cried out. "Please . . ." But I found I was speaking to his back.

"Nicola!" The queen spotted me and called from the carriage window. "Come here." Before I could get to her, the coachman had started the horses with a crack of his whip, and they were gone, galloping down the road at such speed, I was choked by the dust.

Was I to be left? In a danger I had no name for?

"Here, girl," a man said from behind me. "Into my wagon." He put his beefy hands on my waist and lifted me up before I could say a word.

I grimaced when I saw that Madam Jacqueline was aboard the same open wagon, along with two of the kitchen maids. Madam had made certain that she sat as far from them as possible—which was not actually very far. It was not a very large wagon.

The man with the big hands climbed up onto the front, picked up the reins, and slapped them against the rumps of the two great geldings. "Walk on!" he cried, and the horses began pulling us through the gate.

We were bounced along as the cart drove across the cobbles and onto the dirt road with a change of tune, from a *racheta-racheta* to a softer sound.

And still no one had told me why we were away.

Madam Jacqueline said nothing, but brought out a book of devotions, silently turning the pages. The two kitchen maids, though, chattered to one another, full of gossip which held my attention for some way down the road. But I guessed from what they were saying that they knew no reason we were hurrying from Blois.

I glanced back at the château, where heaps of baggage still sat in the courtyard. We had never been so separated from our belongings before, and it only served to emphasize how quickly the court was moving.

For what purpose? I wondered. The image of stags being driven by hunters with their dogs would not leave my mind.

"Why are we leaving?" I asked the driver.

"La Renaudie," he said.

"Where are we going?"

"Amboise." He parceled out his words like a miser his gold.

We were first in the line of wagons that followed the royal carriages along the north bank of the Loire. The river wound green and lazy through the countryside, like an adder in the sun, but our wagoner pushed the horses to their limit.

As the day went by, my stomach announced the hours as surely as a church bell. Luckily the kitchen maids had wrapped some food in a kerchief before leaving Blois—big hunks of cheese and two small baguettes. Shyly they shared this with me, and with the wagoner, who pulled out a bottle of wine which he likewise passed around. It was not very good wine, being bitter and raw, but I had had much worse with Troupe Brufort. At least it was wet. Madam Jacqueline made a point of being absorbed in her book and did not share our small meal.

"You should not speak with them, Nicola," she whispered to me. "They are beneath you."

"They are beside me, madam," I said, pointing.

She sniffed and turned back to her book, but evidently the maids thought as she, for they did not include me in their conversation.

It was only when the sun was sinking that we came in sight of our destination. The cart rumbled over a bridge to the southern side of the river, crossed a small island, and entered the town.

"Amboise," the wagoner said, grinning and showing a mouth full of teeth like old gravestones. "We go up there." He pointed to a castle perched high on a corner of a nearly vertical rock. "The locals call it a château, but it is well fortified."

As we wound through the town, I was surprised at the empty streets. But then I began to notice faces appearing furtively at windows. I wondered what the people of Amboise made of this sudden visit by the king and queen. Were they used to such invasions? Or was this as new to them as it was to me?

The road looped upward from the town, approaching the castle from the west. Now the road was filled with people—all foot soldiers—checking us out as we drove up.

The wagoner called out, "A fine burden I have here."

"Save some for us!" a couple of men shouted back, gesturing at the maids and me.

The maids giggled and I smiled, but Madam Jacqueline sniffed loudly, burying her nose further into her book.

We rode on, now through a wide, terraced garden and orchard in the midst of which was a chapel of grey stone. Above the doorway a curious carved scene on the lintel showed a huntsman kneeling before a magnificent stag with a crucifix set between its antlers.

"Who is that?" I asked, pointing.

"Saint Hubert," Madam Jacqueline said. Her tone implied we should have recognized him. "A nobleman whose love of hunting caused him to neglect his religious duties." Her sniff informed us all what she thought of such behavior. "One day he came upon a stag with a crucifix between its antlers. After that Hubert abandoned his self-indulgent ways and took up the religious life."

"That is quite a story, madam," said the wagoner, winking at me. "A stag with a crucifix. I never seen any such in all my years."

"It is true, every word of it," she replied haughtily. "Eventually he became a bishop." She turned back to her book.

Every word true? I did not believe that for a moment, any more than I still believed every word of Maman's tales. But that the story was true in some deeper sense, I was certain.

Above us, more soldiers came trooping out of the castle. There must have been two or three hundred of them descending towards the town. They were oddly quiet as they passed us. Whenever I had seen soldiers before, there had been pounding drums or braying trumpets.

We rattled on through the arched gateway into the château courtyard. I had not even time to leap from the wagon before servants rushed to unload what few supplies were on it.

All around us more soldiers moved about briskly. Cannons were shifted as if they were mere toys. The newly-arrived wagons were drawn up in rows of twos and threes, like some sort of barrier, while the horses got led away to the stables.

Suddenly I glimpsed the duke striding past, issuing sharp orders as he went.

"You there!" he called to one man, showering him with curses. Another he sent back the way he had come. A third waited patiently by the duke's elbow for orders which never seemed to be given.

The king was watching all the furor from his horse, but he did not say a word. It was as though he was suddenly stunned by what was happening, recognizing that here was a game far beyond his meager grasp of strategy. His face was the color of the tops of waves.

"What is this all about?" I asked, turning to the wagoner, but he was gone. As were the maids and Madam Jacqueline.

• • •

Madam Jacqueline had found quarters for herself, and for me as well. Although she was annoyed with me, I was still in her charge. When I caught up with her, she had already organized her room, setting her book of devotions in the very center of the desk.

Of course we did not have our belongings yet, other than what we stood up in—she in her familiar dark dress and me in my second-best black velvet gown. So settling in took no time at all.

We sat down to a quick supper with other low-ranking members of the court: the king's valet, several coachmen, the chambermaids. La Folle was at one end of the table and I at the other. The valet laughed and said, "We now have a parliament of fools."

Neither La Folle nor I was amused.

The talk then turned to our headlong rush from Blois.

At last! I thought and tried to listen to every conversation at once.

"Astonishing," Madam Jacqueline pronounced to the valet.

"But necessary," Henri, the valet, said. "These are times of unrest, and the Huguenots were rioting near Blois."

Madam Jacqueline drew in a deep, frightened breath. "Those filthy imps of Satan."

"But, madam, you told me they were very far away." I said it with much aggrievement, but she simply stared at the wall, toying with the topmost aglet on her collar, too agitated to respond.

A coachmen across the table from me shook his head grimly. "Not so far away, my girl. Not so far away at all. La Renaudie himself has set his evil eye on this town. He and all his fellow Huguenots."

Henri interrupted. "Not to worry, little one. Amboise is much more defensible than Blois. That is why we are here."

• • •

The room Madam Jacqueline had picked out for me was little more than a closet, but I was glad of the chance to be alone in it. I wanted to make sense of all that had happened.

I could not ignore our headlong flight from Blois. The duke certainly thought there was something to worry about. Otherwise why flee so quickly? Why gather so many soldiers and set out the cannon? Why erect barriers of wagons? Why wall the court up behind great stone walls?

And yet one part of me was fascinated by the Huguenots. Madam's stories about those imps of Satan made me curious. Perhaps at last I would actually see their hairy hides and impish faces. Perhaps even hear their pernicious doctrines.

Of course I did not want to get too close. Still, I wanted to see them from behind the defensible walls of Amboise.

I was not *that* much of a fool.

Between these two warring armies of sense and nonsense, I fell asleep at last on the small, hard bed. I dreamed all night of a garden. Not Eden exactly, for there was no serpent in it, no Adam, no Eve.

In the dream, I sat high in an apple tree which was some magical kind on which both blossom and fruit grew at the same time. The tree overlooked a wild garden where wildflowers grew in weedy profusion. Below me a great stag came on silent hooves to eat the windfalls, a crucifix glowing between his antlers. When he looked up at me with his soft brown eyes, I saw my own face reflected as if in a mirror, darkly.

Suddenly out of the woods came a hunter, seven small dogs at his heels. He looked just like the king, puffy-eyed and a pasty complexion. But he had the king's mother's fierce anger pinching his pockmarked face. Raising his bow, he killed the stag with a single arrow, then slit its throat. The blood fountained down for the dogs. Then the hunter broke off the crucifix, slung it over his shoulder, whistled to his dogs, and off they went.

I climbed down from the tree and held the stag's bloody head in my lap, weeping for the king and for the stag and—I guess—for me as well.

I woke, shivering, and thought about that dream garden. And about the other garden, in the cardinal's palace in Rheims, where I had first really talked with the queen.

Dreams are supposed to mean something. At least that is what Maman always told me. But what could my dream possibly mean?

Then I thought about the carved stag I had seen above the chapel door as we arrived at Amboise. *Perhaps,* I mused, *I am supposed to find the answer in the garden here.*

The more I thought about that, the more certain I was. The dream wanted me to go to that terraced garden by the chapel outside the château gates. So I stood up, smoothed down the skirts of my dress, and buttoned the top aglet at my collar which I had loosened for sleep.

Then I crept out of my room and down the unfamiliar corridor, alert for signs that anyone else was awake.

Pausing at each window, I peered out through the gloom to get my bearings. At last I saw trees and flower beds below me, though they were little more than dark shapes in the early dawn.

There was a small door nearby, and when I pushed through it, I found the stairs that ran down into the walled garden.

A thin ribbon of pale crimson was visible between the eastern hills, and slowly the garden began to come into focus, filled with early spring flowers. I remembered my mother's small plot where onions, turnips, and beans had grown in intimate connection, one with the others.

Flowers were a luxury only a king could afford.

Or God.

This garden, with its tidy borders and careful plantings, was certainly not the unkempt garden of my dream.

Standing on tiptoes, I looked over one of the stone walls. Below, the terraces descended to a weedier place. There I saw Saint Hubert's chapel in its grey solitude, shrouded by an early morning mist.

That, I knew, *is where I am meant to go.*

Carefully, I stepped into one of the beds of flowers to get to the wall. I checked over my shoulder and saw no one around. Fitting my right slipper into a chink, and my fingers into others, I started to climb. For a moment—only a moment—I gave a care to my dress. Then I scrambled up to the top and over.

It was a long drop to the terrace below, and it had been a while since I had done any acrobatics. But my training stood me in good stead. Without planning, I landed with knees bent, did a forward roll through a small bush, and stood up again only slightly out of breath.

Brushing my dress off as best I could, I made my way around to the entrance and stared up at the carvings on the lintel.

There Saint Hubert, his hands clasped in prayer, gazed at the crucifix between the stag's great antlers. It was a meeting the saint had not expected but it had changed his life forever. I knew nothing else about him, but I knew we had that much in common, for hadn't I been changed by a meeting in a garden as well?

Is that all the dream wants me to know? It had certainly not been worth the ruin of my dress.

It was then that I heard a cry of alarm from somewhere below. I squinted down at the orchard that stretched between me and the town.

Suddenly I felt terribly alone and foolish. I was unarmed and exposed. Shaking, I pulled back into the shadow of the chapel. Where was everyone? What had become of all the king's soldiers? Could I get back to the castle before being seen?

Then there came the crack of pistols and the blast of muskets followed by an uproar of voices—screams and shouts and cheers, all intermixed. I heard orders being bellowed and the beating of hooves, as though a battle were taking place.

What a fool I am indeed, I thought, looking back at the high wall I had just leaped from. Climbing down was certainly easier than getting back up. I might have to go by the road.

The road!

The road was where the horses and riders and soldiers would be. I could not go there.

I turned back to stare at the trees below. Were those shadowy movements coming towards me?

And then there came the odd flash and puff of smoke.

Was I to die, then, for a dream?

I do not know how much time passed by as I stood in the shadow of the chapel, unable to make a decision. I moved as if through water, as if in a waking dream.

Just as I had that thought, I was startled by the sound of running feet. I pulled back behind a corner of the building when an enormous bearded man, with neither hat nor helm, came rushing through the orchard. He held a bloodied sword in one hand.

Halting by the chapel, he gasped for breath. Blood trickled from a wound in his thigh, staining his cream-colored breeches. His hair looked clammy with sweat in spite of the early morning chill, and his jerkin was smeared with mud and grass, as if he had been crawling across the ground.

I thought: *Clearly he is not one of the king's soldiers.*

And then I thought: *Is he a Huguenot?*

Eyes darting about, he came forward again, and I shrank back, hoping my black dress would make me invisible in the shadows. But the grass was slick with dew and I slipped, falling against the wall.

A bit of the wall crumbled and the pebbles struck the ground with a sound that was no louder than a whisper, but loud enough.

The stranger rounded on me, his sword raised to strike. When he saw who I was, he laughed.

"Jesu—just a girl," he breathed, lowering his sword. Then he added in a hoarse whisper, "Come to me, child. What are you doing here? This is no place for children."

I took a stuttering step forward. "I . . . wanted to walk in the garden. I had a . . . a dream."

He threw a quick glance over his shoulder before speaking again, his voice still low. "From your clothes, you are from the château."

I nodded, too frightened to speak again.

Then the man said something surprising. "Can you take me to the king?" His voice was almost imploring, "I *must* get to the king, before we are all taken or killed."

I backed away from him and he followed until I was pressed right against the chapel wall.

"King Francis *must* understand," the man continued, his voice rushed and heated. "We are not His Majesty's enemies. I swear to you, child, we are his loyal subjects, as loyal as any in his court. All we want is an end to the persecution the de Guises have inflicted upon us."

"Are you . . . a . . . a . . ." I stammered at last, "a Huguenot?"

He nodded and opened his arms. "Yes, child, but I am not your enemy."

"But what of your *pernicious* doctrines?" I asked, drawing back. Then added, "Are you not imps of Satan with hairy hides and tails?"

He shook his head irritably, his gaze darting about for signs of pursuit. "Girl, you repeat nursery stories. We are as human as you." His right arm moved as if to grab me, and then he must have thought better of it, for he placed his hand—filthy and bloody—to his breast. "The king, child, where is he? I swear all I want to do is plead our cause. Quickly. I have but little time."

"That much is certain," interrupted a voice from behind him.

It was the Duke de Guise, dressed in a steel breastplate and helmet, a very large and bloody sword in his hand. He was mounted on a huge black warhorse and he reminded me of nothing so much as the black knight from the chess game.

A dozen foot soldiers, their armor much muddied, charged up behind him and quickly surrounded the Huguenot.

For a moment, I thought the big man was going to fight. But then, as if assessing the odds, he tossed aside his sword and allowed the soldiers to seize him. There was something wonderfully heroic in the gesture.

One soldier began to bind him roughly with a length of rope. The Huguenot winced at each twist of the rope but did not make a sound.

"Your rebellion is as slippery as a serpent, La Renaudie," said the duke, "but I know how to stop such a creature. Cut off its head!" His voice was venomous and in the morning light the scar on his cheek shone blood red. If anyone looked like the serpent in this garden, it was he.

"Someone revealed our plans," La Renaudie said through gritted teeth. "Or we would have trapped you at Blois instead of having to quick march here to Amboise. If we could have spoken to the king there . . ."

I took a deep breath. So that was why we had moved so quickly! I pulled back into the shadow of the chapel.

"Is it such a surprise that traitors should find themselves betrayed?" The duke smiled. His horse began to paw the ground impatiently.

"I *demand* the chance to speak to the king," said La Renaudie, his head unbowed. "As a nobleman I have that right."

A nobleman? Madam had never said any such thing.

"You are in no position to demand anything," the duke replied.

"By your own admission you were trying to trap the king. That is not the way a nobleman acts. But you *shall* have an audience with the king."

At that I breathed out again, relieved.

"His Majesty will watch you swinging from the gallows. And he will applaud your final dance," the duke finished.

"Oh, no, Your Grace," I said aloud and without thinking. "That is too cruel. . . ."

"What about the girl, my lord?" asked one of the soldiers. Taking me roughly by the arm, he hauled me out of the shadows and dragged me over to the duke. "I found where she came over the wall." He held something in his hand which he gave to the duke. "Is she a traitor? Is she one of the rebel band?"

I suddenly could not speak out, even in my own defense.

Despite the rope around his throat, pulled so tight that he was beginning to choke, La Renaudie bleated out, "Leave her, de Guise. She's . . ." He gasped for breath. "None of mine."

The duke took what the soldier gave him and held it between his fingers as he had held the chess piece. It glistened in the light of the sun and I saw it was one of the silver aglets from my dress. For a moment the duke looked at me with interest.

"Over the wall? My, you have put your tumbling skills to good use, little dancing girl. And *are* you a Huguenot?" he asked. "Or a good Catholic loyal to the king?" He smiled his serpent smile.

My tongue suddenly loosed and I answered him by reciting the catechism, first in French and then in passable Latin, for once never stumbling.

He threw his head back and laughed uproariously at my performance. Then he said dismissively, "She is only the queen's fool. Get her inside. See that she keeps out of the way." He tossed me the aglet and I caught it in one hand with as much grace as Pierre caught his clubs, though my palm was slick with sweat.

By the time I was taken back into the castle the sounds of conflict from the town had roused everyone. Soldiers and servants scurried from place to place, and Madam Jacqueline was there to scowl at me as I was pushed into my room by the duke's man.

"Where have you been? Look at your dress! Your collar is torn, an aglet gone." She did not pause for any answer.

I held out the missing aglet.

She shook her head and did not take it, saying, "You are an untrainable peasant, Nicola. What *can* the queen be thinking?"

Then she kept me at my studies till dinnertime in a small library at the rear of the castle, as far from the town as we could get.

"We must act as if this is an ordinary day," she said in a deadened voice. There was a tic in the corner of her right eye which betrayed her nervousness. "The soldiers will do what they do best, and so must we. So must we."

Her cane had disappeared, and without it she was less intimidating. But she was also distracted throughout the lessons, often halting in midsentence whenever the sound of hoofbeats or musket shots echoed below the castle walls.

I was distracted, too, remembering the dream, the courtly Huguenot, the duke. And remembering that the answer that had saved me was the rote taught me by Madam Jacqueline.

Finally madam slammed shut her book of grammar and stared at me. "Now do you see the importance of your catechism, the importance of keeping the faith strong against any attack?"

Little did she know!

"They are such devils, the Huguenots," madam said. "They hate us all. We could have been murdered in our beds."

"I met one of the Huguenots outside," I told her. "La Renaudie. He is not an imp of Satan but a man. In fact a nobleman. He said he was loyal to the king."

Madam's mouth opened and closed. She looked like a great perch out of water. "Of course . . . he said that. They are all liars. Satan is the king of liars. No true nobleman would threaten the king."

"He did not seem a liar, madam. At least I have no proof of it." On the contrary, I had had proof of his honesty. La Renaudie had saved me by telling the duke I was not one of his.

"We have proof enough," she countered, offering none.

"He seemed most sincere, madam, with a rope around his neck to guarantee . . ."

"It is more than a peasant like you could possibly understand," Madam Jacqueline broke in testily.

I began to shake with anger and I should have held my tongue, but I did not. "I have sense enough not to make enemies out of those who would be my friends, madam."

Madam Jacqueline sniffed. "But not enough, it seems, to learn from those who would teach you." She turned and walked out of the room, her skirts making a sound like muffled drums.

And there I was again, left alone. But this time I knew I must see the queen. I must tell *her* about the duke and La Renaudie.

And then I thought: No, *I must tell her more, I must relay the Huguenot's request to speak with the king.*

So asking directions from several servants—for I did not know the way—I finally found one who could show me.

Soldiers stood guard at key points throughout the castle, and especially as I neared the queen's apartments. Those guards I could not avoid, I managed to charm. Luckily my velvet dress with its silver aglets and discreet white lawn at neck and wrists—while slightly the worse for my garden adventure—still proclaimed me as one of the court.

As I trod carefully down one dimly-lit gallery, I heard the sound of weeping ahead of me. A lone woman sat on a chair, all hunched over, her shoulders heaving with the force of her sobs.

To my astonishment, as I drew closer I realized that it was the queen. She was crying into cupped hands, unaware of anything except her own misery.

Gently I laid a single finger on her arm, something I would have never dared had she not been so overwhelmed. One does not *touch* a queen!

She looked up, startled, through red-rimmed eyes. Tears ran freely down her cheeks and her fingers trembled. She did not seem to recognize me.

Then all at once she knew me.

"Oh, Nicola," she said between sobs, "I could not bear to watch anymore, even though my uncles insisted. What must the sight be doing to my poor Francis? He is not well. Not well at all."

She waved me away, down the gallery, and lowered her head again, covering her tearstained face with pale, slender hands.

If she had been an ordinary person, I would have put my arms around her for comfort. But she was the queen and besides, she had just dismissed me.

What could I do to help? What could I say? Suddenly I was at a loss for words, so I did as she asked, and kept walking down the gallery, only too aware that she still wept behind me.

Ahead a large doorway gaped into a room. When I peered in, I saw that there was another doorway opening onto a balcony. A number of grandly dressed figures were crowded there, looking into the courtyard below. It took me a moment to sort them out: the king, the dowager Queen Catherine, and the king's two younger brothers. They were flanked by the duke and the cardinal. On either side were a pair of armed guards standing rigidly at attention.

Not a one of them saw me, for their eyes were firmly fixed on what was before them.

I crept past four tables on which the remains of a light supper lay. When I reached the balcony, I had to stand on tiptoe to see.

At first the scene came to me only in small snatches: a peek under an elbow, over a shoulder. Then I gasped in spite of myself.

Surely, I thought, *this is some sort of tableau of silent players. A charade. A game. Nothing so awful could really be happening.*

But in another instant I realized that it was all too real.

From balconies and high railings all around the courtyard hung at least two hundred bodies, perhaps more. I could not have borne counting them. The faces were hideously discolored. Eyes bulged. Mouths hung open, slack and lifeless; limbs were limp.

Oh God, oh God, oh God! I thought in a rush. *An orchard of horror in a garden of death.*

I was not naive. I knew of war. Our poets sing of battles and the hundreds slain. I had heard how the duke had killed many of our country's enemies, which was surely an honorable thing to do.

But these hanged men were not some foreign foe. They were Frenchmen loyal to the king and to France.

La Renaudie had said he wanted only to speak to the king. He had come with a company at his back to beg for help. Yet here their poor tortured bodies were, being displayed as though their deaths were but some sort of dumb show.

I did not understand, I did not *want* to understand.

But I knew I had to witness it all, for this was the sight that had made my poor queen weep. So I continued to stare.

Then I saw in the very center of the courtyard a crude gallows where a man swung back and forth, the rope creaking loudly. I recognized the dead man at once by the beard, and by the cream-colored breeches with the slash in one leg. As the duke had promised, La Renaudie had been hanged in front of the king.

At the gallows foot stood a bloody wooden block over which hunched a grim, hooded figure. He held a long-handled axe in his right hand. There was already a wide streak of crimson along the edge of the blade.

Now a struggling prisoner, a young man no older than my dear Pierre, was dragged forward by a pair of soldiers. Forcing him onto his knees, they pressed on his shoulders so that his neck was laid square on the block.

The headsman lifted his axe.

I stuffed a hand into my mouth to stifle the scream that rose up—like bad wine. Then, spinning around, I dashed away as fast as I could across the room, through the door, down the corridor, to collapse at Queen Mary's feet.

"The axeman," I sobbed. "The blood . . ."

She put her hand on my head. "Oh, Nicola, what fools we all are. What grief we bring down upon our own heads by this cruelty." Her voice choked with pain. "How will we ever pay for what has been done this day?"

15 ❧ DEATH OF A KING

We did not stay long at Amboise. The grounds of the palace were contaminated, the rivers as well. Those conspirators who had not been hung or beheaded had been tied hand and foot and thrown into the Loire. Some said it was the spirits of the dead that drove us away, others that it was the smell.

I was glad to leave, for I had constant nightmares.

It seems I was not alone.

The king's valet told me that the king cried out in his sleep: *"Au secours!"* over and over. Nothing seemed to help.

As for the queen, she was pale and feverish for days. It was one of the few occasions that King Francis had concern for her health instead of his own. He forsook his games to sit by her side. We chatted often while she slept, about dogs, about hawks, about the life of a player on the road.

"You must miss the safety of your troupe, Nicola," the king said, compassion in his puffy eyes. "No hangings. No bloody axe."

I nodded in agreement, but really Troupe Brufort and Uncle's cane had never seemed all that safe to me.

Once the queen was well enough to travel, the court left Amboise. There was great relief at all levels of the court that we were quit of that cursed place, going first to Fontainebleau, next to St.-Germain-en-Laye, and then on to other châteaus.

While we traveled, the soldiers scoured the countryside, arresting those Huguenots who had escaped from Amboise and those who had been in league with them. News of executions always seemed to await us at each new place, spoiling our welcome. The de Guises put down their Protestant enemies ruthlessly, with as little compassion as a farmer gives mad dogs.

If the misfortunes that followed the killings were meant as punishment from heaven, why did they fall so heavily upon my poor queen? She had played no part in the Huguenot deaths. Indeed she had openly wept for them.

Yet it was she who suffered the most thereafter.

News came but a few months later of the death of her mother, Mary de Guise, who had ruled Scotland in her daughter's name for so many years. The queen had been eight when her mother last came to France, but they had remained close through their letters. Now there would be no more letters from that cold land.

The queen spent weeks grieving, and there was little I did that consoled her, though I tried. I made up little verses and read them aloud, my handwriting as wobbly as my meter.

"Like that dog on its hind legs," I told her.

"No more dogs, Nicola," she said. "I have no heart to laugh. Just read."

I read:

> "Madam looks up towards heaven's gate,
> That opens briefly, then shuts tight;
> There both queens and peasant mothers wait,
> The dawn that comes after each dark night."

"Thank you for the sentiment, dear Jardinière," she said, her eyes puffy and red. She did not comment on the meter.

After that I tried dancing, jests, tale spinning, singing, even tumbling. Nothing worked. She could scarcely manage a smile.

We did not know that the worst was still to come.

The court wintered that year at Orleans, and the king returned one Sunday from hunting, complaining of an intense pain in his ear. He sat through dinner with a linen square to his discharging ear, while the queen fed him by hand as if he were a child.

"Sing, Nicola," the queen commanded. "The king always likes your jolly songs."

"No songs," he whispered. Then he got up unsteadily and went off to his own apartments, still moaning about his ear.

The next day he fell into a swoon. Doctors flocked around him like gulls at a fishing boat, but they were powerless to steer him to safe waters.

So as not to worry the court, the duke announced that the winter fogs over the Loire had given the king a cold. Therefore, no one worried—except the queen and the dowager, who hovered in the sickroom as helpless as the medical men. No fools allowed, of course. No one felt like laughing.

For the next two weeks the king grew steadily worse.

The queen's hairdresser came to my room one morning, her own hair all startled wisps. "You must come to Her Majesty at once," she said. "She is distraught. I can do nothing right."

I hurried after her, and when I entered the room, the queen was sitting before her mirror, dark circles under her eyes.

"Oh, Nicola, what shall I do?" She did not look at me but at my reflection in her mirror. "How can I possibly live without my sweet brother?" She meant the king. "No one is dearer to me."

"He will live many years more, Your Majesty," I said. "God would not be so cruel," proving I was a better fool than a seer.

She sent the hairdresser away and turned to gaze at me with such sadness, I thought my own heart would break.

"Come with me, Nicola," she said, standing and taking my hand. Then she led me to the king's sick chamber. His mother was there already, keeping the doctors at bay.

The chamber smelled of sickness, that heavy, musky, dank smell of wet beds and poultices.

"I thought Nicola might entertain Francis," Queen Mary whispered to her mother-in-law. "He enjoys her wit."

"Anything to take his mind from the suffering," Queen Catherine replied. She gestured me to stand at the side of the great bed.

The king's face was puffier than ever, his cheeks mottled with scaly patches. A bandage had been placed over his left ear, but there were traces of inflammation around its edges, like the crust of a tart.

"Your Majesty," I said in a voice in which cheer and dread battled, "I have a riddle for you, one that has to do with dogs."

His eyes fluttered open and I took that as a good sign. So I began: "Two legs sat upon three legs, with one leg in his lap. In comes four legs, and runs away with one leg. . . ." I did my best to amuse him with that country riddle and others, as well as foolish songs and stories, but my heart was no more in it than was his.

Once or twice he lifted his heavy eyelids, but I am not certain he even saw me. Dearly as I wanted to bring a smile to his face—if only to please the queen—I felt as disheartened as on the day Uncle had forced us to perform on the empty, rain-swept streets of Rheims.

After many minutes the queen said, "It is enough, Nicola."

She knew, as I did, that my efforts had been in vain.

I was relieved to be dismissed. The pervasive odor was making me feel ill as well, and I hurried to a side chamber where I waited in case the queen wished to call upon my services again. To my shame, I hoped she would not. I could not bear to be in that room again.

I had brought with me a small book of Italian poems the queen had lent me some months before. The poems were full of shepherds and shepherdesses falling in love amidst willows and crystal springs. I wondered that their life was not harder, seeing that here in the king's own palace, life seemed very hard indeed.

Curling up on a cushion, I read by the failing evening light, and fell into a doze, dreaming of sheep.

I was woken—I do not know how much later—by the sound of the door closing. Still soothed by the dream, I merely opened my eyes.

The queen came in and flung herself onto the chaise weeping in long, wrenching sobs. I kept silent. Indeed, what comfort could I give when her best friend lay so ill?

At last her crying subsided, the rainstorm dwindling to a harmless drizzle. She looked up, dabbed her eyes with a bit of embroidered linen, and only then noticed me.

"Nicola," she said, composing herself, "I had no idea anyone was here. . . ." Her voice tailed off. "You heard me weep?"

"I hope you are not angry, Your Majesty."

"Angry? How could you think that? When a loved one dies, how doubly dear are those who remain to us."

"The king . . . the king has *died?*"

She nodded, tears waterfalling from her eyes. "At least . . ." she stopped, then tried again. "At least we can be assured that his pain is at an end. But France will never know how great a ruler he might have been. Poor Francis. Fate is cruel, though God is not."

It had never occurred to me that the silly and games-loving King Francis might ever become a great ruler. But then Saint Paul on the road to Tarsus had changed. Perhaps Francis could have as well.

"He always treated me very kindly," I told her truthfully.

"You made him laugh," Queen Mary said, trying bravely to smile at me and failing. "I shall always love you for that." Then she lapsed into silence, knotting her fingers together.

Just then the door opened and the dowager came in, her face grim but settled. There were no tearstains down *her* cheeks, no red eyes. It was as if she had already put aside her grief.

Behind her followed the duke and the cardinal. The cardinal discreetly closed the door.

Queen Mary rose and the two widows embraced briefly. It was the dowager who pulled away first, brushing a hand down her skirt.

"We must bear up under this tragedy," she declared firmly. "Neither the king nor France would expect any less of us."

Seeing me, the cardinal raised an eyebrow. "Surely we can dispense with the fool's presence."

"On the contrary," Queen Mary said. "I wish her to stay. She was as much a favorite of Francis's as mine." She held out her hand to me. With an uplifted chin to show my defiance of the others, I took it.

"It is of no consequence," said the dowager. "Death will make fools of us all in the end."

"*My* concern is with the living," said the duke. "We are hedged about with enemies ready to leap at the first sign of weakness. We must address the question of who rules France."

"You may set your mind at ease upon that score," the dowager announced solemnly. "I rule now."

I held back a gasp. What could she mean?

The duke and his brother exchanged dark glances, then the cardinal spoke. "Surely, Your Highness, there should be some discussion of what is best for the country and . . ."

The dowager cut him off with an impatient gesture. "My son Charles is next in line for the throne. As he is only eleven—not old enough to rule on his own—I am assuming the office of regent. I shall rule until he comes of age."

"Are you entirely sure you are ready for the responsibility?" the cardinal asked in a voice that oozed concern. "To rule France is far different from sitting at the king's side and offering a few words of counsel, however wise."

"Do not condescend to me, Charles," the dowager snapped, her voice as hard as her face. "The only other person with a legitimate claim to the regency is the King of Navarre." There was something almost triumphant in her manner.

"Navarre? But he is a friend of the Huguenots." The cardinal fingered the jeweled cross that hung around his neck. "His own brother, Louis de Conde, is awaiting execution for planning the attack at Amboise."

"Exactly," said the dowager. "Under such circumstances, would you uphold Navarre's claim against mine?"

"No, of course not," the duke put in quickly. "In fact, Madam, that is the very reason why you will need our protection. Navarre will surely contest your claim. We should raise an army at once to forestall any move on his part."

"That will not be necessary," said the dowager. She smiled thinly. "I expect Navarre to give his full support to me."

"And why, Madam, should he give you his support?" The cardinal could not disguise his astonishment.

"I intend to purchase it . . . by freeing his brother."

"Freeing de Conde? But the man is a traitor!" blustered the duke.

"He is a Huguenot, but as much a nobleman of France as you are. I think we have had enough of death these past months."

Queen Mary gave my hand a squeeze and gave me a small smile, as if relieved at the dowager's words. Remembering the awful deaths at Amboise, I was relieved as well.

Meanwhile the duke and his brother continued to exchange uneasy glances.

"Madam," said the duke with a small bow, "we stand ready to offer you our guidance and assistance."

"That is very generous of you," the dowager replied. It did not sound to me as if that was what she meant at all. "However I will be appointing my own ministers."

The cardinal could not have looked more startled if someone had slapped him across the face in the middle of mass. The duke's face was unreadable.

I glanced again at Queen Mary. She was biting her lower lip.

The dowager turned to her daughter-in-law, her voice like ice. "Mary, in order to ensure the smooth transfer of power, you must return the royal jewels to the treasury at once."

This time I could not control myself. I gasped out loud.

"Of course," Queen Mary replied, dropping my hand and smoothing down her skirts. Though her voice was equally cool, I could tell she was shocked by the abruptness of the request. Her palm had gone suddenly wet.

"From now on," the dowager continued, "you are free of the burdens of royal office. At the end of our period of mourning, you may retire to your estates in Touraine or Poitou."

"Away from court . . . ?" I began, my passion running ahead of caution. However, a hooded look from the dowager was enough to stop my mouth, like a cork in a bottle.

Queen Mary only nodded but did not otherwise move.

"Now, gentlemen, I leave you with your niece. I am sure you have many personal matters to discuss. As regent, *I* must begin arrangements for the royal funeral." Her head was high, neck rigid, the veins running like sharp ridges from under her chin. Then she turned in a swirl of dark silk and went out the door.

We all bowed as she left, even my queen.

That sorceress!" the cardinal fumed. "That witch! She has been planning this move since Francis became ill, I am certain of it. What a heartless mother. What a . . ."

"Brilliant conniver?" put in the duke.

His brother nodded. "I would not be surprised if she has already been in contact with Navarre."

They spoke as if neither the queen nor I was in the room.

The duke snorted. "Of course she has. How else could she be so confident of his support?"

"The object of the game," I said suddenly under my breath, "is to capture the king."

The duke turned and barked at me, "What was that, fool?"

I glanced at the queen. Her face gave me no clue. In fact she was staring into space, grieving—I guessed—for both the loss of her husband and the loss of her throne.

"I asked a question, girl," said the duke, his voice like a newly-honed knife.

I shrugged. If he wanted an answer, I would give it to him. But I spoke my answer quietly. "In chess, Your Grace—at least as I have observed—there comes a time when even the cleverest of players will be beaten and swept—queen and all—from the board."

The duke scowled, but he did not deny the truth of it. Instead he turned to the queen, who had sunk down onto the chaise longue and was staring dejectedly at the floor.

"We have much to discuss, Mary," the duke said.

She looked up, glancing from the duke to his brother and back again, her eyes still red from weeping. "Yes?"

"We must decide on a new husband for you at once," said the cardinal, fingering his cross. "Only through marriage can you regain your influence."

He did not add: *and we ours.* But I heard it.

The cardinal continued. "Now, marriage to Don Carlos, the heir to the throne of Spain, would create a most Catholic alliance. When he succeeds to the throne, you would be the most powerful queen in Europe. Even greater than France's queen."

"My beloved husband, my best friend, is just minutes dead and you speak of marriage to me?" Her green-gold eyes suddenly blazed.

I rushed to her rescue with as little thought to my own safety as when the dwarf La Folle had skidded across the floor for her king.

"Madam," I said, addressing her in the voice I used when entertaining, light and frivolous. "Don Carlos is a small boy. And an ill-behaved one."

"What would *you* know of such things?" the duke demanded.

"Even fools have ears," I said. Standing up for the queen made me bold.

"And they should be boxed!" the duke retorted.

"Is it true, Uncle?" Queen Mary asked, her voice quiet, but firm. A queen's voice. "About Don Carlos?"

The duke turned his back on her.

"Surely these minor faults," the cardinal said pleasantly as he maneuvered himself between me and the queen, "these *very* minor faults, count for less than the nobility of his blood."

Queen Mary's voice drawled out slowly. "And how will Queen

Catherine feel about that? We can make no such a move now without consulting her. As regent she . . ."

"*She* will oppose it." The duke turned around again and looked directly at the queen. "*If* we give her the chance. She wishes Don Carlos to marry one of her own daughters."

The de Guise brothers were a wall between the queen and me and I could do nothing to break through. I could not even see her.

"Then I do not see how we can proceed with such an alliance," the queen said. I noticed she did not use the word *marriage*.

"There are other alternatives." The duke counted on his fingers. "The kings of Sweden and Denmark are both in need of a bride. And there is Archduke Charles of Austria."

"Then there is the Duke of Ferrera, recently widowed and a fine gentleman," added the cardinal.

I could not stand their two against one any longer. I said—as if to myself—"And very old. An oak surrounded by acorns."

The cardinal turned to scold me. "The duke's lands are very well placed. He wields considerable influence in many of the courts of Europe."

But now I could see the queen. Moving towards her, I forced them all to watch me. It was a trick of Uncle's. *Catch the eye of the audience,* he used to say, *and they are halfway to being yours.*

"If the queen must marry again, why not find her a Prince Charming?" I said, as if talking to myself. "Even if his kingdom is very small. Though Mary is no longer France's queen, she is still Queen of Scotland. Surely she deserves a happy ever after in this once upon a time."

"These romantic fancies are all very well for fairy tales," seethed the cardinal. "But in the real world, the queen's duty to family and nation determines whom she must marry." His voice was a controlled fury. He looked directly at me as he spoke, but his message was clearly for his niece.

The queen suddenly stood. There were two spots of color on her cheeks. "You are wrong in this, Uncle, and my fool is right. I need no marriage to make me great. I am still a queen."

"Of Scotland," the cardinal said, speaking the name as if it were a burr under the tongue. "Scotland is very small and very far away. It has little influence upon the affairs of France, which is the greatest country in the civilized world." He spoke angrily, as if chastising a child. "And while the title sits well upon you, Highness, I think you would find it less comfortable to actually rule that troublesome country."

"I do not remember it being so . . . so troublesome."

He threw his hands up, clearly tired of her arguments.

"Childhood memories gild even the poorest surroundings." He started to pace and matched his sentences to his steps. "The Scots castles are grey and bare. Their palaces lack the most basic amenities. The land itself is mountainous and infertile. The weather freezing in winter, scarcely warmer in summer. The people are hostile, ill disposed to strangers, and mean." He stopped and glared at her. "To call Scotland 'bad' is to libel the word."

"But, my lord," I said in my fool's voice, "is it not better to eat bread in your own small house, than to dine on venison in prison?"

"Brava, Nicola!" said the queen, clapping her hands and smiling.

"The Scots," the cardinal said in a rush to the queen—and ignoring me completely—"are an ungovernable race. Their barren land has fallen into the hands of the Protestants, who have renounced the rule of the pope and made the saying of mass a crime."

The queen shook her head. "Tell me, Uncle, how can they make illegal that which God has ordained?"

"They have done so," the cardinal said, "under penalty of death. Would you hazard your life for the dubious honor of ruling such a place?" His face was now as red as his robe.

At last coming to his brother's aid, the duke said, "To go there without an army to impose your will on the people would be sheer madness." He hesitated, then added, "You can no longer count on support from France, not while the dowager holds the throne."

"An army? Why would I need an army? I want to be the Scots' beloved queen, not their conqueror," said the queen.

Brava, Your Majesty, I thought. Aloud I said, "Madam, His Grace, the duke—being a soldier—of course believes every problem can be solved by sending in an army."

"I need no army to settle *your* insolence, peasant!" the duke roared, raising his hand to strike.

"No!" screamed the queen, rushing towards him and standing between us. "You will not touch her. She is *my* fool, sent to me by God. I have given her complete leave to speak the truth."

The duke was so taken aback to hear her address him in such a manner, he lowered his hand, but slowly.

"Is it not enough that I have lost my husband today? Will you now harm the sweetest flower in my garden?" the queen said.

"A nettle more like," said the cardinal in a low voice.

"If so, Uncle, then it is one that stings in my defense. Please leave me with Nicola. I will speak to you both again later."

There was no room for argument, so the two men left the room, backs stiff, like dogs beaten in a fight trying to retain some bit of dignity in retreat.

Walking over to the window, the queen gazed wistfully out at the night sky. "Nicola, my Jardinière, what am I to do? Should I retire to a château in the country and pass the time dancing and hunting until everyone has forgotten me?"

"You are a queen, Madam, not yet twenty years old. You are both beautiful and wise. You cannot be hidden away any more than you can hide a bonfire in a cupboard."

Still looking at the sky, she asked, "Then should I marry again, as my uncles advise?"

"They would have you marry only in order to restore their own power," I said. "And the dowager would not have you marry at all."

She nodded. "That sounds very sensible, as sensible as something my uncles would say. But I want you to speak like a fool."

She was putting so much trust in my counsel, I took a long moment before answering. "A fool," I said at last, "would set aside all counsel and go where her heart leads."

"And what if she does not know where her heart is leading?" she asked, turning away from the window and gazing full at me.

I shook my head. "I am only a girl, Your Majesty. Fool is the name you have given me. What wit I have is used in jest. You want me to give you *real* advice, but I can only tell you a story."

"Tell it then," she said, holding out her hand to me and leading me to the chaise.

We sat down together, not like queen and servant, but like friend and friend.

I took a deep breath, and began. "A man set sail in a boat, but he could not decide where to go. So, he let the tide take him, for that was the easiest course. To his horror, the tide began carrying him towards jagged rocks that would clearly dash the boat to pieces."

"Was he shipwrecked?" the queen asked.

I shook my head, as if I knew the ending already, but in fact I was making up the story as I went along.

"He raised his sail, and the wind blew him away from the rocks and out to sea. Now he let the wind take the boat where *it* would, but it blew him into treacherous waters full of sea serpents whose long necks rose out of the waves, whose teeth snapped hungrily."

"How did he escape?" The queen leaned towards me intently.

"He took out his oars and started rowing. And just in time, too. One of the serpents caught an oar between its jaws and was about to bite it in two. The man grabbed back the oar and rowed and rowed until he was safely out of reach."

"Good," the queen said. "Go on."

"Now he knew that he could surrender to neither tide nor wind without being destroyed. He could not do what was easy. The only wise course was the most difficult one. He had to keep rowing, though his arms were sore and his muscles ached. But at least now he followed a course of his own choosing."

The queen gave my story some thought. At last she said, "Nicola, your little parable points the way clearly. My heart tells me to go to Scotland, to be a queen in more than name. But I am afraid."

I nodded. "That is because being a queen without a king is hard work, like rowing the boat."

"Hmmmm," Queen Mary reflected, "Elizabeth rules England without a king at her side. And the dowager is now regent of France and *her* husband is dead." Her face grew determined. "Why should I not rule Scotland alone? It is smaller than either England or France and so surely easier to govern, whatever my uncles say. Even *I* can row a little boat."

She placed her hands on my shoulders and gazed at me. "But

what of you, Jardinière? How can I take you to such a northerly land where the wind and frost might wilt your tender petals?"

I had not considered my own fate in this. Yes, I had thought I might go back to Italy some day. But Scotland? I knew nothing of that cold place.

Still, the queen had asked a direct question. As always, I had to answer. But my mind boiled like a kettle with questions: If I decided to stay behind, what kind of a life could I make for myself? Would the duke and his brother punish me, without the queen to stop them? Could I ever find Pierre again? Pierre was sixteen now, would he leave the troupe so that we could go off to make our own future? All these questions collapsed around a final one.

"Am I not bound to follow you, my queen?"

"Bound, no." She released her hold on me and sat back. "I freed you once from the cold grip of a tyrant. How could I force you now to go where you do not want to go?"

I remembered then what the Maries had said, of how a Catholic queen was safer here than in Scotland. The duke and the cardinal had said much the same.

Yet I—no more than a peasant in a fool's costume—had told the queen to go there. And she—poor Madam—had accepted my advice.

Then I recalled La Folle racing to King Francis's side when the duke was about to checkmate him. If a dwarf could save a king, surely a fool might do likewise for a queen.

"Take me with you," I said. "The fool belongs at her queen's side."

17 ❧ ACROSS THE WATER

I thought we were bound for Scotland, but it was six months more before we left France. A queen's time is not like that of a traveling player's. It took weeks to pack everything and weeks to outfit the two great galleys and the two escort ships.

One of the galleys was fitted out in red, the other in white to match the queen's mourning colors. Aboard the queen's galley were to be the four Maries, now finished with their education in the convent, and their crooked-toothed maid, Eloise. Also the young poet Châtelard, who was meant to entertain us with his verses. He was handsome in a pasty sort of way, with parti-color eyes, one blue and one green. The old chronicler Brantôme, with his sour mouth, was to come along, too.

We also had physicians, perfumers, a Latin tutor, page boys, milliners, embroiderers, laundresses—all those folk who worked hard to give the queen her ease. And of course musicians. The queen could not do without them.

And me!

To my relief Madam Jacqueline was not to go, for the queen decided I needed her no more. And the dwarf stayed in France, too. She was Queen Catherine's fool now.

I had a favor I wanted to ask of the queen. I waited for days, trying to think of the best way to approach her. At last one evening we were in her chamber and she was in a happy mood, having beaten me once again at chess.

Carefully I drew a folded letter from my pocket. "Please, Madam," I said. "I have written to my cousin. The boy who threw the seven clubs in the air."

"Ah, the handsome Pierre. You have not spoken of him for some time," she said, putting the chessmen back in their oaken box.

"I have told him that we are going to live in Scotland. In the city of Edinburgh. I asked that he send me word there." I held out the letter. "But I do not know how to get this to him."

Smiling, she took the parchment from me and without unfolding it, said, "Surely if a priest could find your uncle for you once, a messenger of mine can find Troupe Brufort again."

The queen had commanded the Maries to teach me the Scottish tongue. So, even though I was not a friend to them, I was often at their sides.

"Scots is a barbaric language," I complained to Jolly Mary one evening as we sat by the fire roasting chestnuts. "How it jangles."

She laughed. "It is not as pretty as French," she said. "But once we are in Scotland, you will see how it exactly fits that rugged land."

"Surely the queen in England does not sound like she is clearing her throat with every syllable, or they would not call her Great Elizabeth, only Great Elizabelch."

Pious Mary, sitting on a nearby chair, smiled. "Elizabeth in England speaks English, which is like—and yet not like—the Scots tongue. Just as the language spoken by people in Normandy differs from that spoken in Picardy."

"At least," I said, *"they* all speak French."

"La, Nicola, you will keep the cold Scottish court warm with that tongue of yours!" Pretty Mary said.

The dawn of our departure from Calais was so dull and misty that when we boarded the ship, the dock and all of our beloved France was hidden from view.

The gulls cried mournfully as they flew through the mist, and a small rain began to fall.

"The country weeps for its loss, Highness," I said.

The queen did not seem to hear me. I thought that her eyes and heart were already set upon Scotland. But mine were turned backwards, to France, and I began to weep.

Pious Mary came over and put her arms about my shoulders as if to draw my sadness to herself. She smelled of lavender water. "Do you weep for the country or the queen, Nicola?"

I shook my head. "I am only afraid of going so far away and leaving behind everything I know. My family . . ."

"We are your family now, Nicola."

"That does not make me any less afraid."

"There *is* much to be afraid of," Pious Mary agreed, letting me out of her lavender embrace. "Elizabeth of England has refused to grant us safe passage."

"Will she send ships against us?" I asked.

"No one knows," Pious Mary said. "My father has written to me a warning. But we must not borrow trouble, as the prior used to say. Only be ready for it. Commend yourself to God and all will be well."

At last our rowers began to move our galley out of the harbor and onto the cold expanse of the North Sea.

I looked about for the queen and spied her at the stern, that part of the boat still closest to France.

In her white widow's veil she looked like the ghost of a queen and not the queen herself. She held her little terrier to her breast and was staring off to land.

I went to offer what comfort I could but stopped when I heard her whisper, "Farewell, my beloved France. Farewell. Farewell. I shall never see you more."

If she had turned around, I am certain I would have seen tears running down her cheeks. But she did not move or speak again till we were far out to sea. Then she called for her bed to be brought up on deck and remained there the rest of the voyage.

How could I have been so wrong? She was not looking ahead to the journey. There was nothing familiar for her in Scotland. It was a foreign country to her, no matter that she was its queen.

Three days out, a fleet of ships was sighted to the southwest, close enough that we could see their banners flapping from the masts.

"Are they pirates?" I cried to one sailor. I put a fist to my chest and added, "I will fight. I can, you know."

"No, not pirates, miss," he told me, laughing. "They are English, which is worse." Then he spit over the railing with a sound like "Ptah!"

"How can you tell?" I stared over the railing at the ships.

"By their flags, miss," he replied.

"Will they attack us?" the queen asked.

The sailor shrugged. "I do not know, Majesty."

Standing at the railing, where she had spent much of the trip, Regal Mary said stiffly, "I think they are as uncertain as we."

"Uncertain? What do you mean?" The queen spoke into the wind and her questions were blown back to us.

Her face the color of soured milk, Regal Mary said, "They do not know if Elizabeth will knight them or behead them should they bring the Queen of Scots captive to London." Then she bent over the railing once more.

The queen shook her head. "No—I do not believe this. Elizabeth is my sweet sister. She has written me these very words. We need not fear her ships."

By evening the English ships had dropped out of sight, and though we never saw them again, I did not stop checking the horizon hour after hour, just in case.

In all it took five long days to reach the mouth of the river Forth, and our journey ended very much as it had begun in a thick, grey, blanketing fog. We could scarcely see the shore.

I had thought the French court a fairy-tale realm.

Not so Scotland. The hard, rugged coast appeared and disappeared in a grey mist.

"Madam," I said to the queen, "perhaps giants or savage monsters dwell here."

She smiled. "Some call the Scots that. But I was born to love them. Just as they were born to love me." She leaned over the railing and opened her arms wide. Little tentacles of mist curled and uncurled around them.

Suddenly, like stars appearing from behind a cloud, bonfires ignited along the shore to greet us. It was as though the hard granite face of a stone giant had just smiled at us, revealing him to be a friend and not the ogre I had feared.

Queen Mary ran to the front of the ship. She stood on her tiptoes and cried out, "My people—I have come home!"

SCOTLAND ❧ 1560–1567

To ease my sorely troubled mind,

I keep to no one spot confin'd

But think it good to shift my place,

In hopes my sadness to efface;

For now is worst, now best again,

The most sequestrate solitary scene.

from a poem by
MARY QUEEN OF SCOTS, 1560

e docked at the port of Leith, and the queen was the first to cross the gangway.

If there were ever a last moment when she could have abandoned her Scottish venture, this was it. If she had turned then, calling to her sailors to man the oars, I think not one of us would have felt regret at going back to France.

But she simply squared her shoulders beneath the flowing white widow's veil, and strode forward to meet the tall and grizzled Scots nobles who had gathered to welcome her.

I followed right behind.

"Greetings, Your Majesty," a tall, square-chested man called out in Scots as he moved towards us. Dressed in a shirt decorated in blackwork embroidery and a black velvet doublet, he did not look comfortable in his finery. Not like the French nobles I knew.

"Thank you for my warm welcome, Lord James," the queen replied. "My most trusted kinsman."

Lord James had a heavy, unhandsome face. There was a crude honesty to his features, I suppose. At the same time something seemed withdrawn in his eyes, as though part of him was purposely hidden. The queen called him trusted. But *I* did not trust him. Not so easily. Not yet.

I set my lips together. Lord James would get no smile of me.

Lord James gestured to the small man at his side. "You remember William Maitland, your mother's secretary of state."

The queen inclined her head towards Maitland.

Maitland was much shorter than Lord James, with a long nose, well-trimmed beard, and a receding hairline shaped like a large heart. He wore a velvet coat with a broad lace collar and was very refined in his movements. Much to my relief, he spoke French. His witty flourishes, however, seemed labored, and he went on and on.

"Why is it that people who have the least to say are those who take the longest to say anything?" I complained in a whisper to Jolly Mary, who had come up behind the queen.

"You must be patient," she whispered back. "This Maitland is a diplomat and so is prone to flowery speech."

I made a face. "I think diplomats are like chameleons," I whispered back. "They change color wherever they stand."

The gist of Maitland's welcome was that fair winds had brought us from France more swiftly than expected. The royal palace of Holyrood was not yet ready. We were to be fed there at Leith while preparations at the palace were completed.

Not ready for the queen! In France all royal houses were kept in a constant state of readiness.

Not a good beginning, I thought.

It took until late that afternoon before we proceeded on to Holyrood Palace. The queen seemed to take everything in stride, but I became increasingly angry. As did the chronicler Brantôme.

In rapid French, Brantôme cursed the Scots, the cold, the sea fog—which everyone here called a *haar*—and the Scottish tongue.

"They are brutes," he said.

"Beasts," I countered.

"Fleas on beasts," he said.

"Fleabites!" For a moment I felt as I had with my cousin Pierre, and smiled at Brantôme companionably. But he turned away, still muttering to himself.

The city elders then presented a grey palfrey to the queen. I was appalled all over again. In France she had been used to the finest, swift-running, spirited steeds, with shiny coats. This small, bowed horse seemed an insult.

I was not the only one to think so.

"Your Majesty, you cannot possibly accept such a horse," said Brantôme. "To sit on it would be like placing a lily on a dunghill."

"Hush," the queen said. "He is a lovely boy. Aren't you?" She whispered into the horse's ear while feeding it a handful of grain. Then she looked back at Brantôme. "The dunghill encourages much growth, my old friend. Do not despise it."

I was glad then that I had said nothing. It is awful to be rebuked in public by the queen.

Brantôme continued to grumble as the queen was helped into the saddle, but the palfrey seemed to take on a certain pride with the queen on its back, like that humble donkey carrying Our Lord through the streets of Jerusalem.

And indeed, with the wind teasing out a stray curl from her cowl, the queen was as beautiful as I had ever seen her, set on that humble little horse.

Perhaps, I thought, *I have been too quick to condemn.* If the queen on her little palfrey could find the good, so could I.

With Maitland and Lord James flanking her, the queen set off along the road to Edinburgh. The four Maries and the noblemen rode directly behind on small mountain ponies.

I was near the rear of the procession, perched atop a wagon-load of royal baggage, swaying perilously as we made our way along the muddy, rutted road. From so high up, I could see mobs of people—families with young children, gangs of young men, giggling clusters of girls, settled groups of elderly women and men—all gathered on the road waving at Queen Mary and calling her name.

Though it was August, the onlookers were dressed in heavy, coarse woolens of two and three colors in checkerwork, rough country wear. Many had broad blue caps with sprigs of holly and hawthorn, myrtle or yew. Their long embroidered mantles were pulled tight against the cold. I shivered in my lighter, more fashionable dress and envied them their heavier wear.

The closer we drew to Edinburgh, the denser and more boisterous grew the crowds. I could see them jostling one another to get closer to the queen on her palfrey and I could hear wild applause and enthusiastic cheers as the royal party neared the city gates.

"The queen!" people shouted. "Long live Mary!"

"She be a rare beauty!" called out a redheaded man, and his words were quickly picked up and echoed through the crowd.

The people were still cheering when my wagon reached them, and they cheered me, too. I smiled and waved, calling back to them in my broken Scots. "Happy to be here. It was a lang, lang journey."

A ruddy young man thrust a handful of flowers up at me. I took the bedraggled bunch, waving them at the sea of rough but friendly faces. The hoorays in the crowd grew louder. I could only suppose that not knowing who I was, they assumed I was someone of importance because I was riding in the cart.

Either that or fools were held in high esteem in Scotland.

We crossed an iron drawbridge to the palace of Holyrood. Its towers and turrets reminded me of a French château, and for a moment homesickness washed over me. Then I scolded myself roundly: *I will not disgrace Her Majesty. I will take this as a good sign, a welcome.*

I looked then for things to like. There was a row of thirty-five windows in the castle's long facade. I counted them! And a series of gardens beyond the walls.

But when we came to the stone gate and I looked at the lintel, I began to tremble, for there was a carving of a stag with a cross set between its antlers, the same as at the little church in Amboise.

"That is the holy rood, the cross of Christ," Lord James explained loudly, pointing to the carving. "King David the First saw such a deer at this very spot and so had the palace built here."

"Is that true, Jamie?" the queen asked.

"Every word, Majesty," said Lord James, bringing his fist in a salute over his heart, but he smiled as if to put a lie to it.

I wondered then if the Scots lords all lied with smiling faces. Even if no one else was on the lookout for them, I would make it my duty to find them out and protect my queen.

Holyrood Palace lay a good way outside the city walls, under the protection of a long, looming, rocky hill. Every window in the palace seemed guarded by iron gratings.

"And what are these for," I asked in French when I caught up with the Maries. "Proof against thieves and brigands?"

"Perhaps against wolves and bears," Pretty Mary replied in Scottish, gesturing up at the great rocky expanse behind Holyrood. "It is said such beasts live up there on Arthur's Seat."

I gasped and she laughed at my frightened face.

"La, Nicola, be happy for the protection of the iron bars. Do not borrow dangers once danger is past. Did you see how the Scots all love the queen?"

I remembered Lord James and his hooded eyes. And the small

ponies. And the palace not ready in time. I thought again about the iron bars. "They did *seem* to."

"They are friendly enough today," Pious Mary warned, whispering in French, "for now they have an excuse for celebration. But when the light fades, the queen's enemies will sneak out under cover of darkness, mark my words."

Once inside the palace, I was escorted by an unsmiling maid to my little room. How would I ever make it feel like a home? The hangings on my bed here were simple woolen plaid, not the embroidered damask of France. There was no private water closet, only a closestool hung with coarse sacking in the common room I shared with Eloise and the other ladies' maids.

Shivering and exhausted, I climbed into bed, a hot water bottle at my feet, and tried to sleep.

I awoke in the middle of the night with a fearful start, thinking that Pious Mary's prophecy had come true all too soon. Outside the palace walls came a bloodcurdling wail and an awful chant of dissonant voices as if the spirits of the dead had risen from their graves to drive us back to France.

"Mother of God," I whispered, flinging aside the covers. I jumped up, took the crucifix from over my bed, and, holding it before me, threw open the window.

What a sight greeted me!

Below, hundreds of Scots—men and women alike—capered and sang and played loudly upon their ill-tuned instruments. Some sawed away vigorously at fiddles and rebecs. Others bore strange pipes such as I had never seen before, that had not one but four tubes for fingering and blowing sticking out from a kind of bladder.

The resulting noise was an earsplitting wail more suited to the battlefield than a serenade.

Not ghosts, then, but a happy crowd, made happier—I am certain—by much drink. The songs drifted from reverent psalms to bawdy ballads and back again. In between were cheers—for the queen, for Lord James, for the four Maries, and even, when someone spotted me at the window, for me!

Three rooms from where I watched, the queen stood on a balcony, wrapped in a violet robe, gazing down at the revelers with a smile, like a mother looking proudly upon her boisterous children.

One huge woman raised a tankard and shouted, "Mary, lass—I drink yer health. Yer father was a generous man."

In France such familiarity might have cost the woman her head.

The queen clapped her hands and called out in perfect Scots, "Haste ye back, my people. Come again tomorrow."

My one thought was: *What an invitation! What if they take her up on it?*

But luckily they soon left for their own beds.

I crawled into my uncomfortable cot, and fell gratefully into a dream.

But the next night and three nights after as well, the people of Edinburgh took the queen at her word, robbing us all of our much needed rest, until even they finally had had enough.

Surely, I thought each night as I tried to sleep with my head under the covers, *surely no queen was ever so beloved by her people.*

Or so loudly.

19 ❧ MASS AND MOB

But, as I soon found out, not everyone so loved the queen.

That very first Sunday in Holyrood, as we went to mass, this was revealed to all of us.

The queen walked slowly at the head of our small congregation towards the chapel royal, stepping daintily through the mud. She did not speak but read her breviary as she went.

The four Maries came dutifully behind her, Regal Mary with her skirts hiked well above her ankles so as not to drag her hem through the mire.

I strode along next to the black-robed acolyte, Michel, who clutched the fat white altar candles to his chest. He had a shaven head, protruding front teeth, and the look of a frightened rabbit.

Directly in back of us came several of the queen's French servants, who had been given permission to attend Catholic worship with us. They were carrying a gold altar cloth.

Suddenly the queen stopped and Regal Mary, eyes on her own hem and the mud, almost crashed into her back.

I was too far back to know at first what was happening, though I heard angry muttering, so I slipped from my usual place and ran towards the front.

It was then that I saw our way was blocked by a knot of men.

"Blasphemer!" cried one, his face red with anger, or drink. He raised his fist and waved it in the air like a weapon.

"No more idolaters!" cried another, who actually spat at us. Though, as he was too far away for any precision, the spit fell on his own boots.

"Hang the priest!" shouted a third, a thin-lipped man with narrowed eyes. Leaving the safety of his fellows, he dashed forward and tried to seize the candles from Michel's hands.

"I am . . . I am no priest!" cried Michel. For a moment, he held on to the candles before dropping them in terror.

At that, half a dozen of the men ran at us, grabbing the cloth and ornaments from the serving girls, who screamed and let go without a struggle.

"Stop!" I cried out in French. "Stop it, you monsters!"

But laughing at me, and mangling my French back at me, the men trod the cloth into the mud until it was brown and ruined.

"Run!" Michel cried in a high rabbity voice. "There is sanctuary in the church. Run! Run!"

And suddenly we were all running headlong towards the chapel, which meant running *through* the mob. So intent were the men on their little acts of destruction, they let us go, though the spitter caught up a serving girl and kissed her, despite her screams.

All of us ran. Me, too. And when I turned to find the queen, I saw that she had maintained the same stately pace she had had before, head held high, breviary now closed and clutched to her breast. She walked right past the laughing men. None of them dared lay a hand on her.

When she reached the church door, she turned to face them. There were two bright spots of color on her cheeks. I knew that look.

The queen was not afraid. She was furious.

Suddenly Lord James, who had been waiting inside the church, came out and stood by the queen's side. He puffed out his broad chest like a frog on a lily pad, and looked both comical and fierce. With him were two soldiers, like angels of the Lord, swords drawn.

Lord James glared at the mob with those great hooded eyes. "What loathsome wolves have we Scots become?" he thundered. "Chasing down women and boys as if they were rabbits on the hill."

At his words, a number of the men glanced away, or down at their feet. No one answered his challenge.

"I have given my word," said Lord James, "and with it the word of Scotland, that the queen may worship as she will in the safety of her own house. And no men as small as ye—shall make a liar of me."

The men stood silent but restless before him.

Then Lord James put his head to one side. "I know ye, Patrick Lindsay. And ye. And ye." He pointed to one after another, naming them all. "Go home, lads, and sober up. Or go to the kirk and ask the Lord and his preacher John Knox to forgive ye, for I canna."

One by one, the members of the little mob sneaked away, looking thoroughly chastened, though Patrick Lindsay threw down the fattest of the altar candles like a gauntlet at Lord James's feet.

We went in then, though Lord James and his two men remained as guards outside the door. But I could not keep my mind on prayer, for the chapel thrummed with tension. The bald-headed priest was shaking so much with remembered terror, he could scarcely manage to elevate the Host.

I glanced at the queen out of the corner of my eye. As she prayed, her clear, pale face had the calm of an early martyr waiting for the lions.

The very next morning the queen issued a proclamation confirming Protestantism as Scotland's official religion. She knew such a measure was necessary, as she said to us that night at supper in her chamber. "For my kingdom's stability and also because I hope it will confirm my people's affection for me."

"Most already love you, Your Majesty," said Pretty Mary. "How can they not?"

Behind us a young Scottish musician played upon a lute. He had a sweet touch on the strings though his voice was a bit harsh.

Jolly Mary added, "They love the music and poetry, the dancing and gaiety you have brought. To lighten their dour lives."

"God is watching over you," said Pious Mary. "And when He is ready, He will help you bring the old religion back to the land."

The queen smiled. "Play us another air," she said to the Scottish boy.

He began again, his fingers flying over the strings.

They were all so happily unknowing that I had not the heart to tell them otherwise. I did not say what I had overheard in the kitchen that very morning when I had gone down to fetch up the tea.

What cook said was that it was the preacher John Knox who had whipped up his followers to stop us from going to mass. That Knox—that "old black crow" as the cook called him—said we were leading the Scots to make a counterfeit France here!

What good would it do to tell the queen and the Maries? I asked myself as I watched them.

So I failed in my one duty to the queen.

In the end, I did not have to warn the queen about Knox's follies. They became all too evident to everyone at court.

First, from his high pulpit, practically within the shadow of the castle, he began preaching ferociously against our Catholic faith. Then he took up against what he called the queen's "frivolity," as though it were a sin to believe other than he did, and a double sin to do so cheerfully.

Knox called the queen "Honeypot" and "Sorceress," and he did not mean them as compliments.

Soon Knox's name was on everyone's lips. The four Maries talked of nothing else at the table, at their embroideries, at cards.

And the queen? She was baffled by the man. She said so as she played chess.

"I have sent him warnings and appeals. He ignores them all. Who is this man who dares to speak against me in this fashion?" As she spoke, she moved her pieces willy-nilly, as if unable to concentrate on the game. "What have I done that he seeks to separate my people from me?"

"In France he would have been beheaded for such treason," Pious Mary pronounced blithely, her busy fingers at work on yet another embroidery. She did not notice that her words made the queen shiver.

"Pitch him into the sea," Regal Mary said. "Let the fish eat his black heart." She moved her bishop carefully. It was not often she beat the queen.

"Madam, if you tempt him back to the one true faith, then all the rest will follow," the poet Châtelard suggested, "as dogs follow their master."

"Oh, yes, Majesty," cried Pretty Mary. "Send him to a monastery. That will cool his blood!"

On and on they jested, making light of the dark. The only one who did not jest was the one who had the right to make jokes.

The queen's fool.

Me.

Day after day I added nothing to the jests, for I felt I had already failed my queen by having said nothing at first. And day after day Knox, that old black crow, added fuel to the fire. But still the queen did not speak out publicly.

"I have promised my people—all my people—freedom to believe as their consciences dictate," she said, her chin high.

Who could not have loved such a monarch!

And then John Knox finally went too far, demanding that Queen Mary become a Protestant herself or be driven from the throne. I did not bring the news to her. Lord James himself, puffed out with the story, told her as she sat surrounded by her Maries.

I was on a cushion by her chair, one of the dogs in my lap.

"That," Regal Mary said plainly, "is treason, Your Majesty. Simply treason. It cannot be ignored."

Lord James agreed. "Even I, a Protestant, know he has gone too far. You must speak to him, Madam. You must tell him as his sovereign that such talk will not be tolerated."

The little terrier bit down on my finger with its sharp teeth. A love bite. But still I cried out.

"And you, my fool," the queen said, "who have been silent all these days on the matter of this Knox? What say you?"

I replied in Italian: "Our village priest had a crow once that spoke. Until it said what it shouldn't during mass. Then he wrung its neck."

"What did she say?" asked Lord James, who did not understand the language.

"That I need to speak to the black crow in person, Jamie. Make it so," the queen said.

So Knox was summoned to the palace for an interview with the queen.

How I longed to be at her feet while she filleted him. I said so in French as we sat by the fire.

"No, Nicola," she said. "He would take *your* presence as an insult and therefore would not listen to a word I say. This is a man who prizes himself highly. I will hang him on his own monstrous vanity." She spoke in Scots and I answered her in the same tongue, for my use of it was improving daily.

"How I want to see that, Your Majesty." I turned from the hearth. "Please."

"You cannot, Nicola," she told me. Her mouth got that stern expression that was a warning to me that she was about to say something extremely important and that I must listen with care. "The man already froths at the mouth where women are concerned. He even tried to raise rebellion against my mother."

"But Majesty, I will be as quiet as a sleeping babe. . . ."

She shook her head and held out her hands to the fire. "No, *my fool.*" She said the two words in French, which softened her refusal.

"Then may I conceal myself behind a tapestry in the council chamber?" I asked. "He will never know I am listening."

"Not even hidden will I have you there, my sweet fool."

"I could be as silent as the grave." I made the sign of the cross over my heart.

"I would rather you be lively," she answered. "Now run along."

• • •

Treated as a child, I vowed I would act like one. But what could I do? I was loath to go against my queen's wishes.

And then I had it: I would hide but not *inside* the interview room—for she would see me there—but behind a hanging *outside* the chamber.

I was too old at twelve to believe Knox would have flames leaping from his eyes or brimstone gusting from his jaws. I had learned that lesson at Amboise. Still I wondered what kind of man he could be who was both an old crow—and a firebrand.

So when he was due for the interview, I carefully concealed myself behind a hanging, and arranged the heavy tapestry to conceal the bump that was me. The wool in the tapestry made my silk dress cling unbecomingly to my legs, which was annoying. But I made myself stand still and waited for John Knox to arrive.

I knew when he entered the hallway. The great doors let out an agonizing squeak as the guards opened them. Then a second squeal as the doors were shut after him. I heard his heavy footsteps going directly across the stone floor.

The footsteps were all but past my hiding place when I peeked out. He was so intent on the door to the throne room, he never noticed me.

What a disappointment! At the very least I had expected a man as dashing as La Renaudie, with a winning smile and a piratical manner. But Knox looked more like a wandering prophet. His hair was grey and worn long, with a beard tumbling down his chest to his waist. He wore a homely black bonnet and a long black robe, as if he were in permanent mourning for the world.

When he entered the audience chamber, I had a moment's glimpse of the queen sitting under a gold canopy, the great multicolored window at her back. Her mother's diamond and ruby cross hung from a chain around her neck.

She was a swan to his crow. But she also looked, somehow, v
nerable.

And mortal.

Then the door closed behind him with a crash and I could see
more.

So I sneaked from my hiding place to listen like a child at
keyhole. Alas, I could make out little they said.

Knox's voice, more powerful than even the cardinal's, rose a
fell like a raging gale. I could distinguish one or two of the act
words—"idolatry" and "Nebuchadnezzar" were said with mu
rolling of r's—but I got no real sense of what he was saying.

I pressed my ear even harder against the keyhole.

There were long silences which I took to be when the queen v
answering Knox. I could just imagine her gentle, reasoned arg
ments, possibly leavened by the occasional bit of poetry.

Quiet versus thunder, light against dark, their conversation w
on for some time. I strained to make sense of what little I could he
when suddenly footsteps approached the door from within
chamber.

I leaped away from the keyhole and almost fell over backwar
There was just barely time for me to run back to the tapestry. I ma
little effort to conceal the sound of my shoes on the stone floor.

Wriggling back behind the heavy arras, I held my breath, w
ing the heavy hanging to stop moving.

Just then I heard Queen Mary emerge from the throne room,
light tap-tap-tap of her shoes accompanied by the heavy march
steps of a number of heavy-footed men. They swept down the p
sage towards the banqueting hall. As she passed, I peeped out a
saw on her face traces of freshly dried tears.

I did not doubt that the queen had met the stern preacher w

a spirit as resolute as his own. He had not cowed her. But he *had* made her cry. I wriggled out of my hiding place and started after her. She needed me—*me*—and not that gaggle of men following close behind her.

At that very moment, John Knox emerged from the chamber, and I turned to stare at him. His robes flapped behind him like the wings of a giant crow. His face was locked in a scowl so dark that it could almost have extinguished the torches blazing on the walls.

"And what are ye gawping at, lass?"

I stepped back involuntarily, as if thrown off balance by a driving wind. Blurting out the first silly thought in my head, I said, "I was wondering, sir . . . how many times you have to run a comb through that beard when you first get up."

"Often enough to make a decent appearance and little enough to avoid the sin of vanity, too." He answered me seriously, as if he could not possibly conceive of a jest.

I opened and closed my mouth several times, chewing on his answer.

"I see from yer gaudy attire, mistress, that ye apply no such restraint to yer own conduct." He had turned my feeble joke into some sort of lesson.

"I . . . I dress to please the queen," I said, recovering some measure of poise. I pulled feebly at the silk which tried to wrap around my legs. "I am her fool."

"A fool ye are indeed, to please the queen and not to please God." He leaned towards me, glaring with two coals for eyes.

I smiled and said lightly, "Do you mean that only what's plain pleases God? Did He not make the lily and the rose, the rainbow and the . . ." I struggled for another word.

"The de'il can show a fair face as an inducement to sin."

"Well, then I am sure that you are no devil, sir," I retorted tart｜
folding my arms in front of me. "For your face is hardly fair."

He frowned, not prepared to acknowledge such a barb from
mere girl—fool or otherwise. "This place is already full enough
de'ils, lass. They bring with them their wicked music and want
dancing."

"Does God not like dancing, either?" I asked, holding up ｜
skirts and taking a few steps forward. "I thought it said in the Bil｜
that David danced before the ark, and surely he was loved by Goc

"In its proper place, where it is done to honor the Lord, I can a｜
prove of dancing. But not the frivolous cavorting that aims mere
to intoxicate the senses."

"I should have thought . . ." I said quietly, matching his serio｜
tone, "that there are so many more serious sins that merit Goc
anger, He can have none to waste on so light a thing as dancing.｜
smiled.

But Knox thundered even more loudly, as if his voice could n｜
be moderate, either. The sound bounced from stone wall to sto｜
wall, and not even the heavy tapestries seemed to dampen it. "G｜
willna overlook any occasion of sin through weariness or inatte｜
tion, as a mortal judge might do." His r's rattled alarmingly.

"I am certain the angels dance," I said, taking a few light step｜
"and that they do so for the sheer joy of it. I think if you saw the｜
you would change your mind."

My little dance seemed to make him even grimmer. His li｜
thinned down till they were no more than a slash across his face.

"Change my mind?" His voice rose to new heights. "Inco｜
stancy is the mark of the feminine nature. Women are weak, fra｜
and foolish creatures whose rule can only bring ruination. As ye a｜
showing me even as ye show yer legs."

I stopped dancing and glared at him. "If God were as set against womankind as you say," I shot back, "I hardly think He would tolerate France, England, and Scotland to be ruled by queens as they are this day."

"He will set matters right in His own gud time," Knox threatened darkly. Then he seemed to catch himself up and cocked his head to one side, looking entirely like a dark bird. "Och, lass, I have no quarrel with a child. And I tell ye, yer accent is execrable. Are ye French?" He peered at me and looked, for a moment, almost human.

The change of subject caught me off guard. I curtsied but kept my head up. "No, Italian. But I came with the queen from France."

"And what of yer parents? What manner of folk are they to let ye fall into such a nest of vipers?"

"A cobbler and his wife, sir, and they are long dead and in heaven. So take care how you speak of them. I follow the queen now."

"Then I can hardly wonder at yer ignorance, lass," Knox said, shaking his head. "I shall try to be gentler. It is not yer fault ye are a captive of the Church of Rome and that sorceress, and so are being dragged down to perdition. Raised in the wicked ways of the French court, ye have been denied the true word of God."

"I believe I have heard rather a lot about the *word* of God," I said, remembering a similar conversation with the cardinal months earlier. "I am beginning to think it must be a very long word and very difficult to pronounce."

Knox made a disgusted noise at the back of his throat and waved my reply away like a bad smell.

"Lass, ye have fallen into damnable ways. Let me take ye from this cage of folly and find a decent godly Scottish family who will take care of ye and see to the gud of yer immortal soul."

His absolute certainty only made me madder. No wonder the queen had cried. But he would not catch me so.

"If this palace is a cage," I replied, "I would rather dance here a prisoner than let misery be the price of my freedom."

"Poor lass," he said suddenly in a softer voice. "How little ye understand of the world." He reached out a tentative hand, as though to pat my head. Then, as if thinking better of it—or fearing contagion—he withdrew his hand, stuffed it into the bosom of his robe and stalked away.

"It took only a single serpent to destroy paradise," he warned over his shoulder before going through the door. "One vain woman might yet put an end to this entire kingdom."

21 ❧ ANGELS AND IMPS

f John Knox had been the only devil in our garden, Scotland could have become a paradise for us. The land had its own hard beauty and the people were honest and ready to love the queen. But to borrow a phrase from the old crow himself, the devils were many and came in pleasing guises. The angels sometimes looked like imps. In truth, though I thought I was on the lookout for them, I did not know them one from the other when they came.

I was strolling in the formal garden behind the Holyrood abbey one morning soon after my encounter with Knox. Often I walked there alone. They were not extensive gardens, not like the queen's palaces in France, but still a maze for one who did not know them.

In Scotland as in France I had no true friends. *Who would fool with a fool?* I told myself, making the choice sound my own. But in truth I was lonely. On this day the queen and the Maries were still abed. So I did not even have them as companions.

As I turned a corner of a hedge, I heard the sound of coarse laughter and voices raised in mockery.

"Why, lads, look! Here is a toad in peacock's feathers!"

"Pluck it, Duncan, and see if it squeals."

I rounded the corner cautiously, having no wish to become involved in a brawl between any of the Scots lordlings. Their crude humor could turn to quick cruelty, especially if they had been drinking.

Up ahead were two young, brawny Scotsmen, six-footers clad
rough plaid with claymores—those two-handed swords—at the
sides. They had penned in a third man, a small, hunched figure
dressed in a salmon-colored doublet with matching sleeves slashed
and pinked in a diagonal pattern. Beneath a jeweled bonnet and
mop of glossy black curls, the little man's face was distorted,
though seen through a poorly-fashioned mirror.

"I think it be a witch's bairn," one of the Scots said, "fathered
a boggle."

"What do ye say to Duncan's guess, goblin?" challenged the
other. "Hae ye a father who will own up to the deed?"

They laughed raucously at their own poor humor.

"Je suis ici avec le Duc de Savoy," the little man told them defi-
antly. I am here with the Duke of Savoy.

"It hisses like a snake, Malcolm." Duncan gave the hunched
figure a shove that almost knocked him over.

Clearly neither of them understood French, so they did not
know that the man was here with the Duke de Savoy.

"I skinned an adder once," said Malcolm, grabbing his victim by
the pickadil collar. "And I can skin this little snake, too."

The Duke de Savoy's man pulled away and the delicate collar
ripped, prompting further guffaws from the burly Scots.

Cursing under his breath, the foreigner turned his mangled face
away from his tormentors and saw me, but did not call out.

"I know a lassie that this finery would suit," said Duncan. "Peel
that peacocking off, wee mannie, and I'll make her a present of it. Or
I will peel ye mysel'." As he spoke, he pulled out a dirk, chuckling
when the little man flinched away from the blade.

I could no longer stand still and watch. Picking my skirts up, I
stepped out boldly and strode towards the men with as much dig-

nity as I could muster, trying to sound like Regal Mary. I lifted my chin, straightened my back till it felt like a rod was there instead of bone, and spoke loudly as I walked.

"Your Magnanimity, I am so glad I have found you. The queen humbly begs the honor of your presence."

"The queen humbly begs?" said Duncan, disbelievingly. He squinted at the little man. *"Him?"*

I pretended surprise. "Do you not recognize the Archduke Galliard of Barcarolle-sur-Mer, Prince of Saraband and Chief Regent of all Tarantella?" I rolled my *r*'s and added flourishes that would have made even Uncle Armand proud. "The prince has come to offer an alliance by which Scotland may stand or fall."

"This is a great prince, this wee bogie?" gasped Malcolm.

"Can you not tell he is a prince by the richness of his clothes?" I demanded. "Who but a prince dares dress so . . . flamboyantly?"

Both of the Scotsmen stood back and stared.

"And who might ye be?" Duncan asked suspiciously.

They did not know! Then—I would tell them! Drawing myself up proudly and putting on my haughtiest voice, I announced: "I am Lady Laetitia Hilaria de Moquerie, daughter of the Count of Brufort, first cousin to the Grand Margrave of Ambruzzi, chief lady-in-waiting to Her Majesty the Queen. You do not recognize me?"

While the young Scots tried their best to absorb this torrent of imaginary titles, I pushed my way past them.

"Come, Your Preponderance," I said in Scots, "your army has just landed, and the queen wishes to review the troops." Then I added quickly in an urgent whisper, *"Venez avec moi, monsieur,"* beckoning to him to follow me.

"What army is that, then?" growled Duncan.

"Five thousand Dragonard mercenaries," I explained gravely.

"The most bloodthirsty warriors in Christendom, each one hav
sworn an oath to die rather than see his prince dishonored."

Nervously fingering the hilts of their claymores, the Scots
changed unsettled glances. Malcolm finally said what was worry
them both. "But he was out here alone, without escort."

I nodded. "I know, I know. And the queen worries about th
But it is the custom of His Grandiloquence to test the characte
those nations he graces with one of his visits." I looked around a
afraid to be overheard, then added in a low voice, "I believe he o
went to war against the Palatinate of Haute Majestie because
heard a minstrel there singing out of key. What a slaughter there v
that day!"

"I've not heard of any such massacre," said Duncan slowly.

"That is because there were no survivors to tell the tale."

"But how then do we know . . ." Duncan said.

"It is a puzzle, is it not?" I nodded. "But never fear, this is j
a friendly visit," I assured them. "So far."

They were looking more puzzled than satisfied, but I turn
and made a deep curtsy to the little man. In a low voice, I said
French, "I have told them you are a prince, monsieur, and that I
the queen's lady-in-waiting. Please act accordingly."

He gave a curt nod, smiled slyly, put his hand out, and bid
rise.

We left together, though I walked—as was befitting his su
posed rank—a few paces behind.

"We were just having a wee joke with him," Malcolm call
after us. "Tell him we meant no harm."

Once we were inside, he turned to me and in elegant, cour
French proclaimed, "My dear young lady, my most profuse than
David Riccio at your service forever."

"I am not a lady, David Riccio, only the queen's fool."

"A prettier fool and a prettier bit of foolery I could never hope to find," he said. "How old are you, child?"

"Twelve. Well, almost thirteen," I said.

"Thirteen! My heavenly child!" His accent betrayed him.

"Italian?" I asked.

"*Si.*"

I said back in the same tongue, "I, too. Nicola Ambruzzi. Well, part Italian anyway. My mother was French."

"Italy's loss, Scotland's gain," he said, bowing low, or as low as he could manage with his crooked back. "It was foolish of me to go out alone, but who could have expected such rough treatment within the grounds of the royal palace."

"You are not hurt, are you?"

Fingering his torn collar with one hand, he waved away my concern with the other. "I am hardened to such cruelty. Since a small boy I have been the object of beatings and humiliations."

"I, too, have known beatings," I replied. And then, for some unknown reason, suddenly out of me poured the story of Troupe Brufort and how I came to be in the queen's court.

"Ah, Nicola, here you are—so lovely a form and a fool. But my family thought that *because* of my deformity I should spend *my* life as a buffoon." His eyebrows knotted in a frown which did not improve his looks.

"Your own family called you . . . *deformed?*" I whispered the word, not wanting to offend him. "Did that anger you?"

"They told me no more than does my glass. How can I get angry at my mirror?"

"Then your mirror is false," I said, not entirely telling the truth. "A man is counted by what is in his mind."

He bowed to me again, a mocking gesture under the circum-

stances. "Noble sentiments, dear Nicola. My parents were more
alistic. They told me that my appearance would amuse wealthy ¡
trons, that I could live the cosseted life of a court clown. But ɪ
mind is as agile as my body is clumsy. I choose a harder way. Oft
that means that I am mocked by those who despise me on sight.

I thought immediately of La Folle's ridiculous capering and w
suddenly embarrassed at how often I had laughed at her. I tried
imagine David Riccio submitting himself to such an audience.

"What did you choose?" I whispered the question.

"To learn letters and music and be a book for my master, no
buffoon for his amusement."

"You were right to choose as you did, David," I said.

He smiled at that. "Please, if we are to be friends, you must c
me Davie."

Friends! Could it be? I drew in a breath. *My mouth must ha
known what my mind hadn't, for I had already told him my life's h
tory.* "Davie—what kind of work do you do for the duke?"

"As yet I am merely an assistant to his secretary of state. Bu
will not be an assistant forever. And since I can sing and play t
lute as well, the duke has brought me along to Scotland."

A sudden inspiration struck me. "The queen's valets are pla
ning to sing tonight in a little entertainment, but they have be
looking for a fourth member for their company. If you can sing
French, perhaps you could join them?"

"Sing for the beautiful queen of the Scots?" He grinned, and
was an imp's countenance. *"Eh bien,* I would be honored."

"Bring your lute," I said. "She loves music and poetry, and t
lute best of all instruments in the world."

22 ❧ A FRIEND AT LAST

So I took Davie to meet the valets, who were delighted to have a fourth, even though his twisted face and humped back took some getting used to in one who was not a fool.

I left him to rehearse, and that night he performed before the queen. Once he had completed the set of songs with the three valets, he brought out his lute and begged the queen's indulgence.

She clapped her hands. "I hope you have good tone."

"And good tunes, Majesty," he said in reply.

The queen was delighted by his quick wit and was the one person there who seemed oblivious to his appearance.

As Davie sang, he seemed to cast off his misshapen body and rise upon wings of music, like a butterfly emerging from a cocoon.

We were all entranced, the queen above all.

She leaned close to me. "Who is this charming fellow, Nicola? He reminds me of one of the puppies we had back in France, the weakest of the litter. Francis thought it not worth keeping, but I nursed it till it grew strong and loved me entirely." She put her hand down and that same little dog, now full grown, licked her fingers.

"David Riccio, Your Majesty. He is in the keep of the Duke de Savoy. I met him walking in the garden." I thought it best to say no more than that, lest I spoil the evening.

"We must persuade him to stay for a while," the queen said.

I nodded eagerly, pleased for Davie that he had found favor
the queen's eyes. And even more pleased for me.

In fact, I was only able to snatch an hour or so at a time in Davi
company over the next few weeks, for he still had duties to perfor
for his own master. But in those moments we discovered that
shared a love of Monsieur Ronsard's poetry and knew the sar
songs from Italy. I entertained him with my maman's stories, esp
cially the fables in which foxes and lions and mice play their par
He told me all the news from Italy and France. I had not enjoy
such moments of friendship since Pierre had gone.

Yet a cloud over every meeting was the knowledge that day
day the time was coming closer when he would be sailing back
France with the duke.

Two days before that departure I was sitting in the queen's pa
lor with Pious Mary, who was—once more and with little success
trying to teach me embroidery.

"Why is it," I complained as I laboriously unpicked my late
disaster—a leaf whose bough looked mightily like a caterpilla
"Why is it that I can dance and garden and tumble and my han
give me no problem. But set an embroidery hoop in them and ea
finger becomes a thumb. Ow!" I dropped the hoop into my lap ar
sucked on the thumb I had just pricked.

She laughed, then leaned towards me, picked up the hoo
looked at it critically, and set it back in my lap. "It will come. A
things come with patience. And time."

I sighed deeply. "I can no more stop time than catch smoke ir
basket."

Just then the queen entered with two attendants at her hee
Pious Mary and I stood and the hated embroidery hoop tumbled
the floor. I did not bother to stoop and retrieve it.

"Good day, Mary. Good day, Nicola. Why is your face so long, child?" the queen asked.

"It is nothing, Your Majesty," I said. "A mere pinprick." I showed her my thumb.

"That face is not for a small hurt, I wager," she said, "but a large one. Come, you must tell me." She sat and we did the same.

"I cannot bother you, Madam, when you have so many more important things to worry about." I looked down at my hands.

"And if I cannot worry about my people, what kind of a queen would I be?" She took my hand in hers. "All these little finger-sticks do not add up to a fool's distress. If my fool is unhappy, then so am I."

"Oh, Madam," I blurted out, "it is Signor Riccio. I will miss him."

Pious Mary put her embroidery up before her face as if she was smiling at my misery.

The queen leaned back in her chair and signalled to one of the servants for a glass of wine to be brought to her. "We will all miss his lovely voice, Nicola."

"And his lute," said Pious Mary from behind the hoop, her voice almost strangled by laughter.

I nodded, unable to say a miserable syllable more.

Then, as if bringing out a trump card from the deck, the queen said, "Which is why I spoke today with the duke of my desire to re-tain Signor Riccio in my service."

"Oh, Madam!" I cried, and then was suddenly tongue-tied.

Pious Mary dropped her hoop into her lap and clapped. "Oh, Madam, it is *so* hard to hold secrets!"

The queen laughed. "But you were letter-perfect, my dear Mary. She never guessed. Did you, Nicola?"

I shook my head but was silent, overcome by happiness.

"What kind of fool has nothing to say back?" asked the queen. Still I could not speak.

"It has all been agreed," the queen went on. "Davie will remain here as my master of music, and he seems delighted at the appointment. His belongings are even now being moved into an apartment in the east wing. I expect you will find him there."

I jumped to my feet and was halfway to the door before I remembered myself. I whirled around and bobbed excitedly before the queen. "With your permission, Majesty?"

"Of course," the queen said, waving a hand to speed me on my way. "Go quickly to your friend before you burst!"

I sped down the corridor and galleries and only when I reached the east wing did I realize that I did not know which apartment Davie was in. Suddenly I felt like little "Miss Wrong Turning" all over again.

A servant on some errand of his own came around a corner and I seized him by the sleeve.

"Please. Signor Riccio, the queen's music master, do you know where his apartments are?" I asked.

"You mean Signor Monkeyface?" he asked. "Little man, big hump?"

My stone expression must have told him all.

"Right at the end of the corridor there, two doors down."

I left him without a word of thanks, so angry that he should call Davie names and not know the good in him. I stomped away down the corridor, made the turn, and found the right place.

The door was slightly ajar and I could hear Davie's voice within. Suddenly I worried he might be with the duke, making his farewells. I knew better than to burst in on a nobleman.

Widening the doorway a crack, I peered in. At first all I could see was Davie's lute propped in a corner, and a trunk next to it, on which was piled sheets of music. A wardrobe flung open revealed all his finery.

I stepped further into the room and there was Davie hunched over a table, entirely alone. He was so absorbed in whatever he was doing, he did not hear me come in.

"The queen here . . ." he was saying. "The knight next. I will move the swords there . . ." He chuckled.

I tiptoed closer and saw he was playing a card game, placing some cards in piles, and others faceup in orderly lines. The cards were of the Italian style, with suits of swords, batons, cups and coins, and four dress cards: king, queen, knight, page.

"And to complete the court . . ." Davie muttered.

"You need a music master and a fool!" I said.

Startled, he spun around and lifted an arm to protect himself, a move of such instinct, I almost burst into tears.

"Have you no caution, Nicola?" he demanded, then walked past me to the door of the chamber and shut it.

I was stunned. "But you were only playing a game. What is the harm in that?"

He turned. "Suppose someone should find you alone here with me? A pretty young girl with Signor Monkeyface."

My jaw dropped. "You know . . ."

He smiled sourly. "What I am called? I make it my business to know. But what does it matter what I am called?"

I put my hands on my hips. "Then what does it matter if some-one sees us together."

He shook his head. "Little Nicola, I have been to many of the courts across Europe and they are all hotbeds of malicious gossip. I say this for your sake, not for mine."

"There is nothing between us to give rise to gossip."

He took my hands, his face serious. "Do not be a child. Gos
needs no substance to nourish it. It feeds upon itself."

I squeezed his hands. "This court is not like those others, fo
is ruled over by a queen like no other."

At last his face softened into a smile. "Perhaps you are rig
Nicola Ambruzzi. I have spent so much of my life flinching fro
blows, I shield myself out of habit. Come, let me teach you a ne
game I have just had from a traveler. It is a game for one player."

"What fun is that, when you have a friend to play with?"

"It teaches one the art of patience," he told me, spinning r
around so that I looked at the table where the cards were laid.

"Oh, patience!" I said. "I have had enough of that for one day

Laughing, he plucked the ace of batons from its lowly positic
then fingered it thoughtfully for a long moment.

"Davie," I said, "card games are for fun, not for such gri
study."

"Like chess, cards can teach us strategy." His voice was serio
but he put the card back on the table.

Sighing, I said, "Strategy is for kings and queens, Davie, not f
us. Surely we must learn to be happy over turns of chance."

"For chance it was that brought us together, Nicola?" he aske
I nodded.

"Or was it *fato*," he said in Italian. "Fate?"

I had not heard that word since leaving Italy. I shuddered. "C
fate," I said.

avie quickly became a favorite of the queen's, singing and playing for her evening dinners and entertaining her with gossip from the European courts.

Soon Scottish nobles began to vie for a place at the queen's table because of the gaiety there and because the queen was unwed. At nineteen and a widow, she was now the most eligible royal in Europe, except for her cousin Elizabeth. The question of who Queen Mary's next husband would be led to an enormous guessing game that went on for month after month. Toasts were offered on the subject at almost every dinner the queen gave. I overheard people in the streets talking of it.

Even in the quiet of our own chambers, who the queen would marry—and when—was the topic most discussed.

"Don Carlos of Spain," said Regal Mary, laying out cards for a game of solitaire.

"Why not the young King of France?" asked Jolly Mary, looking over her shoulder. "Or even her cousin Henry de Guise? Then we could all go home."

"You *are* home," Pious Mary reminded her.

"Whom do you favor, Nicola?" Pretty Mary asked me.

"Why must the queen marry at all?"

Pretty Mary giggled. "For the succession, of course, silly fool. If she does not have a child, she will be like Mary Tudor, whose kingdom went to her sister, Elizabeth, who looks not to wed at all." She stared in the mirror, examining her face for blemishes.

"I favor Sir John Gordon," Jolly Mary said.

"That cockscomb?" Having gotten stuck in her game, Regal Mary reshuffled the cards and laid them out again. "He is nothing."

"Well, at least he is Catholic," Jolly Mary said. "His father has lands and money. Besides, *I* think he is quite handsome."

"Very handsome," Pretty Mary said to her reflection.

Handsome, Sir John certainly was. Even I had to admit that. He had hair the same auburn as the queen and an open, guileless face. His eyes were a merry blue and he smiled rather a lot.

"Rather *too* much," I remarked to the queen. "Like a fox, after the hen." That made her laugh.

"The man is a dandy and a fool," she said.

When I made a face, she added quickly, "And not a wise fool like you, Nicola."

But Sir John must have thought that his handsome face would commend him to the queen as a fine husband. When it did not, and she turned him down, Sir John decided to try a different approach. He tried to abduct her as she toured her northern Highland provinces, thus forcing her to marry.

I had not gone on that trip, being abed with a flux called "The New Acquaintance." Davie brought me a box of comfits.

"Sweets for my sweet friend," he said. He also handed me a book of Italian verses I had admired in his room. But he did not stay long for fear of catching what I had. And he kept his handkerchief over his face all the while he visited.

When the queen returned from the Highlands progress, she came directly to my sickbed to recount her adventures.

"Now it is my turn to tell you a tale," is how she began.

"Are you not worried you might get this flux, Majesty?"

She smiled and sat down beside me. "The doctor says you are well on the mend and no longer able to pass on the contagion."

"Then tell on, Majesty. Though if you are any good, I may have to make you my fool!"

How she laughed. Then she suddenly grew serious. "Sir John's men dogged us during the journey. The silly creature had not listened to my rejection." She smoothed down the front of her dark riding skirt. "I believe the man is in love with himself."

"Not a good husband, then, for he should love his wife."

She smiled at me. "A good point, my little fool. Another reason against Sir John's suit. Well, we bypassed him, setting him a trap, and all with the help of my loyal Highlanders." She took off her hood and laid it on my bed, then took the pins from her hair.

"Are they as fierce as I have heard, those Highlanders?" I sat up weakly and she fluffed the pillows behind my back.

"Fiercer. They wear nothing but skins and plaids, and sleep out on the heather. Neither wind nor storm drives them in. I wore plaids to please them and they rewarded my small gesture with a loyalty I could not have bought." The queen looked serious, remembering.

"What happened then?"

"It turned from a silly escapade into a full-scale rebellion," the queen said, "for Sir John's friends and his father whipped some of the towns into a frenzy against me. *That,* of course, I could not countenance."

"But you won, Your Majesty?"

"With God's help, how could I have failed?"

"What will happen to Sir John now?" I asked.

Her smile faded. "That is yet to be decided. But I am afraid, Nicola. Of more hangings. Of more beheadings. Of more death."

She stood and went over to my window, staring out as if she could see something awful there.

And suddenly remembering the bodies twisting from the balconies at Amboise, and the bloody block beneath the gallows, I was frightened, too.

The queen was right to be afraid, for Lord James and Maitland and the other ministers informed her forcefully the very next week that she must personally witness Sir John's execution.

I was up from my sickness by then, and was in her chamber as her hair was being combed when they came to tell her this.

"If you do not attend, Madam," Maitland said, his voice urgent and low, "rumors will surely spread that you encouraged his mad plan to abduct you."

She turned from her mirror to stare at him, her hair around her shoulders, looking like some beautiful ghost from a story, just rising from the grave. "But why would I do such a thing when it would have been so easy just to say yes to his suit?"

"You have lived so long in France, Majesty," Maitland replied smoothly, making a deep bow. "The Scottish people believe that the French love the romantic gesture. And with this execution, you could say the choice to marry Sir John was not yours, so that the other nobles could not be put out that they were not selected to be your king."

"Yours is a devious mind, Lord Maitland," the queen said, turning back to her mirror.

"A diplomat must know which way the wind blows, Madam, and trim his sails accordingly." He gave a little head bob.

"You *must* watch the beheading, Mary," Lord James put in. "You have no choice."

I gasped at the use of her name that way, but she was so appalled at what he said, she never noticed.

So the queen had to witness Sir John's execution. She begged me to be at her side.

What could I say? She was my queen and needed me.

I went.

Sir John cried out to a hushed crowd, "Your presence, great queen, brings solace to me in my final moments, for I die of love." Then he put his head on the block in one elegant movement.

The queen put her hands to her breast. The look she gave him was not one of disdain. Not even pity. It almost seemed to be a look of love.

The executioner was clumsy and it took three strokes to finish what he had begun. Sir John's merry blue eyes remained wide open, as if he stared at the queen even after his head had rolled to a stop.

I closed my eyes and fought back the tears.

Unlike at Amboise, the queen could not run to a dark corner and weep. But, immediately after the execution, she left for her chambers, pulling me by the hand.

"Only Nicola stays with me," she commanded her maids. "Only Nicola."

So I was the one who held the bowl in which she was sick, and the one who bathed her forehead with scented water. I sang to her in French till she slept. And, when she woke, I held the bowl again till all she heaved up was green bile.

There was no one to hold a bowl for me, though. I had to keep my sickness within.

And then silly Châtelard, not content with making poems to the queen's beauty—as any court poet does—became so smitten with her, he dashed into her chamber and hid under her bed. Luckily he was found by the grooms of the chamber and sent away from court.

He then made things worse by following the queen to the holy city of St. Andrews.

While we sat in the queen's chamber—Queen Mary, Jolly Mary, Pious Mary, and me—he burst in declaring his great love for her, putting his hands on her shoulders and calling her "beloved" right in front of us. He even tried to embrace her and, in doing so, shook her so hard, her glorious hair tumbled down around her shoulders. Pins scattered everywhere—in my lap, on the floor.

Taking her embroidery hoop, Pious Mary hit him on the head, which only seemed to inflame his ardor. Jolly Mary ran screaming from the room for help. The queen's terrier bit him on the ankle and I grabbed hold of him from behind, crying, "Leave go, you stupid loon. Leave go."

But he would not—or could not.

Just then Jolly Mary returned with Lord James in tow, and spying him over Châtelard's shoulder, the queen cried out, "Run him through, Jamie, run him through."

Weeping hysterically, she kept trying to pull away from Châtelard's encircling arms. All the while Châtelard—I can only believe he was totally mad—called her his "desire" and his "mistress" and his "lady wife."

Lord James grabbed hold of Châtelard and tore him from the queen. Ripping a bellpull from the wall, I handed it to Lord James, who quickly bound the poet's hands behind his back. Châtelard was still calling on the queen to witness his great love, when at last he was dragged from the room.

He was executed a month later, going to his death—so it was

reported—with the words "Adieu, the most beautiful and the most cruel princess in the world."

This time we were not forced to attend.

It was Châtelard's final words that made me understand at last the power majesty and grace holds over men. And I understood at last that if the queen did not choose a husband for herself, it might not be long before another ambitious lord or crazed commoner scaled the castle walls and tried to seize her. I no longer asked why she needed to marry, but entered the guessing game with the others.

Once more the name of Don Carlos was proposed. But fresh news from Spain came by ship that he had taken a fall while chasing one of his serving maids. The resulting blow on the head had left him subject to fits of homicidal mania.

"Hardly a suitable suitor," I said in Scots at a royal dinner. It was a phrase which was picked up and spoken around the court and even—so Eloise said—on the streets of the city, where it was put into a scurrilous song called "The Seven Loves of Queen Mary," the first two lines of which went:

> *Sir John came a courting upon his high horse,*
> *A suitable suitor, a saleable suitor . . .*

On the very next ship came word that war had broken out in France between the Huguenots and the Catholics.

Queen Mary, hearing the news at dinner, was stunned. "What can this mean?" she asked for days after hearing.

I knew she had to be thinking once more of Amboise.

Then another boat landed with a report that her uncle, the Duke de Guise, had been killed, shot down by an assassin who had known him by the white plume in his hat.

I was in her chamber, losing once again to her at chess, when the message came. She turned so pale that her face looked like milk, then put her hand to her forehead and swooned, for though she had often quarreled with him, he was part of her family.

Regal Mary and I had to carry her to her bed. We loosened her collar and took the heavy pearl drops from her ears. Jolly Mary sent Eloise for a glass of red wine.

But this turmoil so afflicted her, she was struck down by a nervous fever.

Once again the Maries and I sat by her bedside, and just as she was getting better, she heard that another uncle, Grand Prior Francis, had died.

"My family," she cried in French. "My poor family." She put her hands to her head as if trying to keep her head from exploding. "Oh my dear companions, the happiest people are not those who continue longest in the world."

Not one of us could console her, I least of all, though I knew what it was like to be without family.

I prayed for an end to her troubles, my brave beautiful queen. I prayed for a return of her health. Above all I prayed for a handsome prince to appear at her door, one with the charm and grace and youth her Scots lairds so badly lacked, and with the wits Don Carlos had lost.

And one spring day—but three years later—he came.

I had asked the queen for a bit of garden. "My mother used to say that the seasons mean nothing without a bit of dirt beneath the nails," I told her. What I didn't say was that I could no longer remember what my maman looked like. I thought that if I could make a garden, it would recall her to me.

The queen had smiled and granted me a corner of the south garden at Holyrood, without my needing to ask further. I do not think the gardeners were pleased.

Such a change from the endless card games and dicing, backgammon and chess, and I was glad of that!

Once the February snows were past, I set out paving stones, and planted the borders with bulbs. As I lifted a clump of earth to my face and breathed in the dark, damp smell, I remembered my maman with such clarity, I burst into tears.

Just then the queen was taking a turn in the gardens with her little dog and the four Maries. She stopped to admire my corner and, ignoring my tears without comment, said, "When spring comes roaring in, so will your flowers, Nicola."

On this particular spring morning I was planting some more bulbs, but kept changing my mind about where to put them. Near the castle wall? Away from it? Within the herbal knot I was planning?

At last I found a spot sheltered from the wind but still open to the sun. Perfect!

As I was patting the earth down, I heard the clatter of hooves. Turning, I saw a party of riders in close-waisted doublets and short Spanish capes approaching the gate.

For some reason I watched, though they meant little to me.

One of them displayed some documents to the sentries and they were let in. Dismounting, the three dandies left their horses in the care of their servant and walked in my direction. They gazed about in grudging admiration, and one—a stout bearded man—snorted through his nose like a horse.

"It will not make a bad home, Lord Henry," he commented in English to the tallest of the three. It was not a language I knew well, but close enough to the Scots we spoke that I could understand most of it. "What say you, Giles?"

"Not bad—if it is kept clean." Giles, a thin stork of a man, spoke in a high-pitched voice. His feathered bonnet and yellow leggings completed the bird look. "Do the Scots do that, do you think, Lord Henry? Keep clean?"

What right do these English have to talk that way about the Scots? I thought, then laughed silently at my defense of a people I had often complained of myself.

Lord Henry treated the stout man to a light punch on the chest. "You assume too much, Toby." It was a reprimand, but said with a grin. "I have not yet commenced my courting of Queen Mary and already you have my feet under the kitchen table."

Coming to court the queen? I decided to take a better look.

Lord Henry was dressed like a great noble. His crimson doublet had long vertical slits through which showed bright gold; his crimson hose was of silk; an otter-skin cloak hung jauntily from one shoulder. I thought him a bit lady-faced, for he was beardless, with the soft skin of a child, and he wore his gold hair shoulder-length. He was very tall. And certainly very handsome.

The three of them suddenly noticed me staring at them and sauntered closer, nudging each other and winking.

"Look, a mudlark. Does it talk, do you think?" piped Giles.

"Mayhap it can be persuaded to fly in our direction and then we will find out what is under all that dirt," said Toby.

Only then did I realize how filthy I must be from all my digging. But such talk needed an answer. "Unless you are raiders, sirs, come to pillage my garden," I said, "I see no reason for flight."

"It *does* talk!" Giles exclaimed in mock surprise. "And in English."

"With quite a bite for a bird," Toby added.

"Your tongue has a queer touch to it, mudlark," remarked the young lord.

"I am from France," I explained.

"And are you a little piece of French soil that follows the queen around to remind her of her former realm?" Lord Henry asked. He softened the question with a smile of surprising charm.

"When she had a husband to keep her warm?" Toby added.

I glowered. "It is dirt honestly come by, which is better than stolen finery, sir."

"*Stolen?* What do you mean, minx!" Lord Henry was suddenly outraged and moved towards me. "Do you call us thieves?"

"I mean only that your companions take their splendor from you, my lord," I responded, with an expression of complete innocence. "As everything on earth receives its light from the sun."

In truth, he did look very magnificent. I had seen tapestries and paintings depicting the gods of ancient Greece. He resembled them closely, with his gold hair and his jewel-like eyes.

"So you have a sweet tongue after all." He laughed, flattered as easily as he had been provoked. "Girl, find the queen. Tell her Henry Lord Darnley, great-grandson of Henry the Seventh, humbly seeks the honor of entering her presence." He sounded any-thing but humble.

"Her presence is not here, sir, for you or for anybody else to enter. All that is left is her absence, if that is any honor to you."

"What are you talking about, you noisy little sprat?" Darnley was quickly upset again. "Where might she be found?"

"She can be found for certain in Fife," I replied, pointing to the north with my trowel. "At Wemyss Hall. Gone hunting."

"That puts a crimp in your own hunt, I should say, Lord Henry," fat Toby brayed, as though it were all a great joke.

Silencing him with a cold look, Darnley turned back to me. "Girl. Bother—what is your name?"

"I am Nicola, the queen's own fool," I answered, stepping out of the flower bed and making a curtsy.

"The queen's fool, eh? Are you a particular favorite of hers?"

"She likes to hear me jest and sing, or watch me dance, sir."

"A dancer, eh?" said Giles. "Perhaps you will show us a pretty leg." He made a rude gesture which I pretended not to understand.

"If you are a favorite of the queen," Darnley said, ignoring his companion, "perhaps I can become one also. Will you say a kind word to your mistress for me?"

He reached into his pouch and pulled out a silver coin which he tossed high above my head. I jumped and snatched it from the air, making Lord Darnley and his friends laugh heartily.

"You see what a generous fellow I can be, pretty fool?" said Darnley. "I wager that will buy you more than a few flowers."

"Indeed it will, sir," I answered lightly. "I shall be head gar-dener before the day is out." I wondered, though, why a stranger should reward me so richly for nothing yet accomplished.

"Remember, you and I are special friends now, and you must

speak of me so to your mistress, the queen." Lord Henry smiled.

"Ho! Look what comes!" cried Toby, motioning at a small hunched figure making his way towards us followed by a lanky companion.

Giles murmured into Toby's ear and the pair of them sniggered.

I reddened, for they were mocking Davie, the one person at court who was my true friend. And the queen's friend, too, for she had raised him up to be her own secretary. In the queen's absence, Davie was in charge of seeing that the palace was run properly. He was a bear for rules, was Davie. Not everyone in the palace was pleased. At times not even me.

Slowly Davie approached Lord Darnley and, bowing low, said, "Sir, I have just been told of your arrival. Welcome indeed. This chamberlain will show you and your companions to suitable quarters. The queen is expected back in a day or two."

"*Indeed,* fellow." Darnley raised an elegant eyebrow, for as ever Davie was dressed like a popinjay, in a bottle-green doublet decorated with gold braid. "And who might you be?"

"David Riccio, your lordship, secretary to the queen."

"Stand straight in the presence of his lordship," Giles demanded, as if he had not noticed Davie's crooked back.

Davie smiled, but it did not reach all the way to his eyes. "I could stand no straighter, not if all the kings and princes of the world were enthroned before me."

"I like a man who is always bowing to me," Toby snorted. "I believe I like it very much."

I thought to answer for Davie. A fool can say much that a secretary cannot. But Darnley spoke first.

"I shall take a downstairs chamber. I am so fatigued from my journey, I do not wish to be further vexed by a set of stairs."

"I shall see that it is as you desire," Davie responded.

"And perhaps later you will tell me where in this fair city a gentleman might pleasurably pass the lonely hours of the night."

I think my mouth dropped open; the chamberlain's certainly did. Giles sniggered again.

Even Davie seemed caught off guard by this request, but he only smiled amiably. "I will give it some thought and make my best recommendations to you, my lord." Then, with a sweep of his hand, he indicated that the chamberlain would lead them to the palace.

As he went, Lord Darnley cast a final glance over his shoulder at me. "Little mudlark, you may come and dance for me in private, once you are cleaned up."

"Was that an order?" I blushed and whispered to Davie in Italian as the men left with the chamberlain.

"Do not worry, Nicola. I will see he finds ample distraction. He will not remember asking you to his chamber."

"Do you think he has really come to woo the queen?" I asked.

"So, I believe, he intends."

"And in her own house he asks for a place to . . . to . . ." I could not say the words.

Davie looked somber and nodded.

"But he *is* very handsome, is he not, Davie?"

"Handsome?" Davie almost spat out the word. "Yes, I suppose he is handsome. But he is a carrion crow in peacock feathers, Nicola. The queen will not be fooled. . . . And neither should you." Then he added, "Now, once you have bathed, come take supper with *me*. I have a new card game. Once you learn it, you can teach it to the queen."

I nodded and waved to him as he turned and made his slow careful way back to the palace.

It was two days before the queen returned, by which time Lord Darnley was already notorious in the alehouses and gambling dens of Edinburgh for carousing and drinking till daylight. I had the reports from the cook and the potboy, and from Davie as well. A carrion crow indeed!

But for the queen's benefit, Darnley assumed once again the appearance of a perfect prince when she returned, even reciting a poem for her which he claimed to have composed on the spot, though I had heard him practicing it out in the garden.

> *The turtle-dove for her mate*
> *More dolour may not endure*
> *Than I do for her sake . . .*

The queen was quite taken with him.

"Is he not a very godling?" she said at the banquet and ball given in his honor where—dressed in white with gold ornaments at his neck and breast—he performed competently on the lute.

"Apollo or Pan?" I asked.

Although most everyone laughed, even Lord Darnley, the queen's eyes narrowed. I took this as a warning. And as I never wanted to displease my queen, I did not pursue the jest.

25 ❧ A HUSBAND FOR THE QUEEN

For many days after, I do not believe I ever saw the queen without Lord Darnley at her side, walking together, reading poetry, or dancing with a special lightness of step. She put away her mourning clothes and was now dressed in cramoisie or blue or carnation or sometimes even yellow. And she went fully bedecked with a rich *parure*—the belt with the long end, brooches, broad chains from shoulder to shoulder, clasps, rings, ear bobs, and pearls. She had not seemed so happy in a long time, certainly not since King Francis had been alive.

I believe I was a little jealous, and said so to Davie. "The queen rarely sits with just the Maries and me now."

"She *will* have to marry someday, you know," he said, then added with a twinkle, "and you are not a suitable suitor!"

I understood what he was saying. That even were I Queen Mary's sweet sister—as England's Elizabeth styled herself in letters—I could never come between Queen Mary and whoever was her king.

So I *tried* to like Lord Darnley. Really I did. But he exercised no charm over me. Nor over the rest of the court. When the queen was not present, he cuffed servants for the slightest fault, upbraided courtiers for their shortcomings, made mock of the Scottish nobles as "untutored brigands." I even saw him kick the gardener's dog, and a sweeter old gentleman one could not find in the canine world.

Once Lord James tried to raise the subject of Darnley's behavior with the queen in her bedchamber, where only the four Maries and I sat with her. It was an early morning, so Lord Darnley had not yet risen.

The queen gave Lord James a frosty reception.

"Lord Darnley has learned his manners in a very different court from this," the queen said. "If my Scots nobles are offended with his etiquette, he has every reason to take issue with them."

"*Take issue?*" Lord James's voice rose alarmingly. "You call striking Lethington on the head for laughing an *issue?* Or spitting ale in Maitland's face because he dislikes the man's politics an *issue?* Darnley is a spoiled child, vain and silly, Majesty."

Her look sent Lord James from the room.

What surprised me more than Darnley's behavior, though, was that Davie had begun making a show of befriending him.

"How can you do such a thing?" I asked when we were taking a walk in the garden. "You whom he has called a 'black hump' and a 'pasty, undercooked piece of . . .' "

"He makes the queen happy and he galls the dour-hearted lairds," Davie answered smoothly. "He is as much an outsider as I am, yet I do not dare provoke the Scots as he does. I take as much pleasure in their upset as I would in insulting them myself." A wind blew a bit of a feather from his hat across his forehead.

"You told me he was a peacock, Davie."

"Even a peacock can sing," he said, "though you nor I may not like its tune."

"Oh, Davie," I said, putting my hand softly on his humped back, "I sometimes think we two are twins separated at birth."

"Well, then, you have got the face and I the brains," he jested. "Which is why you are loved and I am not."

But we both knew that the only person who truly loved either one of us was the queen. It was part of her nature, I believe, to love best those whom she pitied. A saint's nature, some might say.

Oh my poor queen, who could have guessed that very nature would in the end be your undoing.

"Nicola, you must come at once," said the queen, some weeks after my accounting with Davie. With an unusual abruptness she swept into the room where I sat with the Maries.

I looked up from my needlework. Pious Mary had been teaching me to embroider decorative letters which she then used to embellish her own religious mottoes.

Setting aside my work was no sacrifice at all, as I had little talent for it, my *S*'s looking like sick snakes and my *R*'s as badly humped as poor Davie. I stood up briskly. "Where to, Majesty?"

"To Lord Darnley's sick chamber, Nicola," she replied. "He is on the mend at last and has expressed a desire for some entertainment. I suggested that you might sing for him, and dance, and he agreed readily."

Nodding obediently, I followed her out the door.

I wondered that she should be so excited over Lord Darnley's recovery. It had only a been a case of the measles, after all, not the pox. Others had gotten through the same disease with much better grace. Yet here the queen was acting as his messenger. It was not seemly, but how could I task her for it? She was the queen, after all. She had the right from God to choose how she would.

As we rushed along the corridor, she said, "Nicola, while I have always exhorted you to be honest with me, I must ask you not to say anything which might vex Lord Darnley now."

"I would not knowingly do that, Your Majesty," I said, hurrying to keep pace with her.

"Oh, I know you would never *intentionally* cause hurt," she said.

"But you do have a wounding wit, my little Jardinière. Set an extra guard on your tongue. Lord Darnley has only begun his recovery. I would not have anything pose fresh hazard to his health."

"I shall be the very soul of . . ."

"Discretion," she finished for me.

When we entered the room, Lord Darnley was propped up on his pillows, eyes closed. The appliquéd satin hangings were askew, and his embroidered coverlet had fallen to the floor. There were still patches of red on his cheeks from the measles, and for a moment he reminded me of the poor, dying King Francis.

But only for a moment.

Hearing our footsteps, he opened his eyes lazily. A smile flitted across his face, giving him the satisfied look of a cat who has been feasting solely on cream. Then, sighing, he put his hands over his eyes as if the light suddenly hurt him.

The queen hastened to his side. "I have brought La Jardinière to brighten your room till you can walk in the palace gardens again."

"*You* are all the garden I need, lady," Darnley responded in a pathetic voice that was as badly formed as my embroideries.

The queen did not seem to notice his counterfeit—the crow beneath the feathers, the wolf under the sheep's skin. Wetting a linen cloth in a bowl of water, she began to stroke his brow.

"Pray, begin, Nicola," she said.

So I sang a rude Scottish song that I had learned from one of the maids. Darnley laughed out loud, as I knew he would. I followed the song with a quick jig, another gift of the maid's. Then I told them a story, which ended with a wild scream and a pounce. The queen giggled and put her hand to her breast.

At the end of my performance, Lord Darnley clapped weakly and then squeezed the queen's hand.

"You are so attentive, so considerate of me, Madam," he said. "If an angel came down from heaven to sit at my bedside, it would display less compassion than you, my dearest, dearest Majesty."

"Hush, dear laddie," cooed the queen. "Do not tire yourself."

Until that moment I had convinced myself that the queen was merely amused by Darnley, happy to have a dancing partner taller than she. But this conversation went well beyond friendship. My head suddenly ached.

You are simply jealous, I told myself.

But I had not been jealous of King Francis.

And then I recognized the emotion I was feeling: I was afraid.

How can she love this monster?

But she had loved the weak and sickly Francis. She loved Davie despite his warped back and misshapen face. She had loved me first because I had been beaten by Uncle. It was what made her such a noble queen: loving the neediest of her people.

She must love Lord Darnley from pity.

"Let me mix a tonic for you," the queen offered, sliding her hand gently out of his grasp. "To put the color back in your cheeks."

Darnley nodded and blew a kiss to her as she left.

However, as soon as she was gone into the next room, he beckoned me closer. Thinking he wanted to thank me for my performance, perhaps even reward me with a coin, I drew near.

But as I got within reach, he suddenly seized my arm.

"Come here, pretty fool," he whispered huskily. "You are growing into such a lovely young woman. A kiss will mend me quicker than any physic."

He pulled me down so that my face touched his. From the smell on his breath I guessed that wine was the only physic he had taken that day. His lips touched mine, then parted, and his tongue thrust into my mouth.

My cheeks ablaze, I wrenched away, overbalanced, and tumbled to the floor with a thud.

At the sound, the queen hurried back into the room, afraid—I guess—that her patient had fallen out of bed.

"Nicola, whatever are you doing on the floor?" she asked.

"She was demonstrating a new dance step to me," Darnley drawled. "One from Spain. She lacks skill . . . in some things."

"A difficult step indeed," the queen said, helping me to my feet. "And one best not attempted without practice."

I straightened my dress and stared at Lord Darnley. His face was the picture of innocence.

Should I tell the queen what has just happened?

But who was I—a commoner—to lay a complaint against a noble? And which of us was the queen more likely to believe?

"Yes, Your Majesty," I said. My voice was rough like a goblet ill mended. "I will practice before I attempt it again."

"Yes, you had better, if you would please me," said Darnley. His mocking tone was quite lost on the queen.

How could the queen not have guessed what had happened? My face must have been bright red; I could feel the heat of it. My voice was tremulous, my hands shaking.

She *had* to know.

But clearly she did not.

Escorting me to the door, the queen said, "Fetch the four Maries to the drawing room. I will be along presently."

I was relieved to be out of the chamber, and hurried away to do her bidding.

Pious Mary was still in the drawing room, picking out my unfortunate *R*. I found Jolly Mary and Pretty Mary Beaton in the library playing cards. But it took some time to find Regal Mary—until I glanced out a window and saw her strolling in the garden with Sir William Maitland. He was joking with her as if all the affairs of state were forgotten.

For a moment I watched them, surprised at my growing sense of unease. Certainly I had seen the like before in the French court. I was fifteen, after all, the age at which most young women were already married and mothers.

But the memory of Darnley's tongue in my mouth made me shudder. I pushed the awful thought aside and ran down the stairs to the garden, interrupting the two at their play. I was even more surprised that they did not seem at all flustered. In fact they both seemed to preen themselves at my discovery.

"The queen," I said, my voice carefully distant, "wishes to see all the four Maries in the drawing room at once."

Regal Mary smiled and Maitland bent down to kiss her hand. She plucked it away before his lips could quite touch her fingers, and swept indoors laughing while I scurried after her.

"Do you know why the queen wants to see us?" Regal Mary asked, a blush remaining on her cheek.

I shook my head. Even had I known, it would not have been my place to say so. But my temple had begun throbbing again.

"Perhaps it is to do with the young cockerel," Jolly Mary suggested, using one of the many mocking terms they all called Darnley.

"You don't suppose—" Pretty Mary began.

"Hush! Not a word!" cautioned Regal Mary, raising a finger to her lips. "Let us not even think on such a thing."

We had not long to wait before Queen Mary arrived, with a radiance of face that should have been a pleasure to behold. Yet that radiance troubled me.

We stood, as if standing could help us all bear the news.

"I have the most marvelous thing to tell you," she said, "and I wish to share it first with you, the dear friends of my childhood."

"Does it concern Lord Darnley?" Regal Mary asked, looking as though she were firmly braced for the answer.

"Yes it does," the queen replied, her face glowing. "I should have known you would guess, dear friends. It must be obvious I am in love. And he declares his heart mine. Is that not wonderful?"

She looked at each of us in turn, seeking our approval.

There was a long silence, which Regal Mary finally plucked up the courage to fill. "He is very comely," she said.

"Very," Pious Mary agreed.

"And tall," said Jolly Mary. "A goodly height for dancing."

There was a further pause, then Pretty Mary added quickly, "He carries himself nobly. Like a gentleman."

"Yes," Jolly Mary agreed. "His carriage is beyond reproach."

"And he is of the royal blood," concluded Regal Mary, as though that finally settled the matter. Her fingers twisted together till they grew white.

"And you, Nicola?" the queen asked, turning to me. "What does my dear fool, who ever speaks the truth to me, have to say?"

What could I say? That Lord Henry was a bully and a sot? That he was unfaithful to her? That he was not fit for her anteroom, much less her bedchamber? Did she *really* want to know the truth?

"A godling, Your Majesty," I answered, giving her a curtsy. She would think I meant Apollo, but I knew he was really Pan. But the half-lie hurt my head and I closed my eyes against the pain.

The queen did not notice. She clapped her hands together,

blushing furiously. "Oh, I am so happy that you love him as I do, for I do love him so. And it will please you to know that Lord Darnley and I are to be married as soon as suitable arrangements can be made."

There was a fresh silence, even more profound than the first. This time it was Pious Mary who broke it.

"Suitable arrangements should take time," she pointed out. "That is . . . if they are to be entirely *suitable*."

"It will take no time at all," the queen declared airily, waving her right hand. "I will command it." Into the silence that followed that declaration, she added, "I already have the most beautiful dress in mind. Of white silk, with an embroidery of golden flowers and insects on the bodice, sleeves, and skirts."

"Oh, it will be a grand day!" Pretty Mary exclaimed, as though she could already see the queen in her wedding gown. "Masques and . . ."

"Music and dancing!" cried Jolly Mary.

In their sudden excitement they seemed to have forgotten the identity of the groom.

So it was left to me to speak out, the only one foolish enough to try. The fool charged with always telling the truth.

"One should be careful when taking such a step as this," I said. "A mortal marrying a godling. For you *are* mortal, oh queen."

Queen Mary laughed. "Such caution, Jardinière. But I need no such warnings now." She put her hand on her breast. "I shall simply follow my heart as you once advised me to do. Lord Darnley and I shall be wed as soon as possible, even if the world calls it folly."

"Your Majesty," I tried again, my voice trembling as I spoke, "it is *my* duty to play the fool . . . not yours."

"Am I a fool at last?" She laughed gaily, taking my hands and spinning us around. "If I am, then it is love that has made me so."

I pulled us to an abrupt stop. "Then I shall dance at your wedding," I said, "one fool with another."

The queen left to spread the word of her wedding plans. Standing uncomfortably in the midst of the Maries, I wondered which of us would be the first to say what was on the minds of all.

"If she must marry a toad, there should at least be some advantage to be gained by the union." Regal Mary sighed.

"There are many weeks yet before the ceremony," Pious Mary reminded us. "There will be time for her to come to her senses."

"Dear Lord, I hope so," I said, and broke the circle apart.

26 ❧ DISASTER

Later that day I ran into Davie in a corridor with a sheaf of papers under his arm. I seized him by the sleeve.

"Davie, have you heard? The queen and Lord Darnley are to be wed."

He nodded, glancing over his shoulder at the empty corridor, then answered in guarded tones. "Yes, I know. I was there when she broke the news to Maitland and Lord James." There was mischief in his voice. "None of Lord James's bluster or Maitland's honeyed speech could dissuade her."

I shook my head. "It is a disaster, Davie. There is no other word for it. Did they tell her what they thought of him?"

Davie's homely mouth contorted into a grin. "Aye, and with little enough prompting. She called them jealous and uncaring."

I thought quickly. The queen could ill afford such a falling-out with her two chief ministers, particularly over such a creature as Darnley. Touching Davie's sleeve again, I asked, "Was there no peace offering?"

He shrugged his hunched shoulders. "After a bit, they left off their bombast and tried to reason with her. Maitland maintained that to marry a man who is kin to the English royal family would only provoke Elizabeth, who could then reasonably claim her cousin was trying to steal the English throne."

"Is that true?"

"True enough," he said quietly. "Like most politics."

"Well, everyone says English Elizabeth already envies our queen her beauty. I wager that when she hears, she will not be able to bear that Queen Mary will enjoy the pleasures of marriage while she does not."

Davie laughed at me. "Then you are as naive about these things as your mistress and you will lose your wager."

I glared at him, which only made him laugh longer, so I turned the subject. "What I cannot really understand is why Queen Mary loves Darnley. I can only believe it is out of pity."

"You yourself called him handsome."

I shuddered and Davie's eyes narrowed, as if he guessed what had happened between me and Darnley in his sickroom. But I did not say anything about it aloud. Instead, I asked, "What did Lord James say?"

"He declared that for the queen to marry a Catholic would offend the Protestants. They would fear she planned to persecute them, as the French have the Huguenots. He said they might well rise up in arms."

I sank down on a small couch, and put my head in my hands. "Oh, Davie, that sounds more a threat than an argument."

He plunked himself down next to me. "That is exactly how the queen took it." His voice was low. "But neither reason nor threats sway her, Nicola, so firmly set is the course of her love."

"What a *disaster*," I said.

"Not such a disaster actually."

I turned to stare at him, astonished. "Surely you do not think him a *fit* husband, much less the *best* husband for our queen."

"Have you not understood yet, my innocent one?" He smiled sadly. "There is no *best* husband for her. There is not even a *good* one. Whoever she chooses will be the cause of disputes and intrigue. She may as well marry this girlie-faced braggart and be done with it."

"But he will not be faithful to her." I wiped the back of my hand across my mouth with remembered distaste.

After a pause Davie said slowly, "As long as Darnley pleases the queen, what does that matter? The marriage question will be settled at last, and perhaps there will even be an heir."

"Darnley does not *matter?*"

"He is too idle to interfere in the business of governing," Davie explained. "He desires a crown, but not the tedious burden of ruling, which will be left to those who know what they are about."

"Like Lord James?" I asked. "Like Maitland?"

He smiled broadly and waved the sheaf of papers in front of my face. "No, Nicola—like . . . *me.*"

The pounding of boots on the floor made us both turn. Down the corridor came the queen's spurned ministers marching towards us. Lord James was a raging bull, with Maitland a fidgeting goat by his side.

"Well, Signor Riccio, are ye satisfied with yer handiwork?" roared Lord James before even coming to a halt. "Ye hae done all ye can to set that English whelp on the throne of Scotland."

Davie stood to face them. "I am satisfied that I have committed no offense against the queen, my lords. Can you say likewise?"

Maitland was more conciliatory, his hands spread out before him. "Our sole concern is for the queen's welfare."

"And that of the realm of Scotland," Lord James added.

Maitland nodded. "Who benefits if the court is divided into two hostile camps?"

"If it benefits those the queen favors," Davie retorted, "and ruins those she despises, then it is a division I can tolerate gladly."

"Ye are as much to blame for this farce as Darnley," Lord James said. "Ye have been his supporter from the beginning, taking his side when all others opposed him."

"I know what it is like to be opposed by all," Davie said.

Lord James sneered. "This ill-advised marriage will bring chaos upon our nation and well ye know it!"

"Perhaps you would rather the queen married one of your Protestant friends," Davie said. "If you had spoken up in time, she might have married Mr. Knox while he was yet a widower."

I must have gasped out loud at his remark, for all three suddenly turned towards me.

"*You* are the fool, David Riccio," I said. "Not I."

"He is worse than a fool." Lord James turned to Davie. "Ye are a mischievous goblin! I should box your ears for yer insolence."

"If it is insolent to speak the truth, sir," Davie said, "then I am the King of Insolence and my kingdom knows no bounds."

"I will set bounds to it!" Lord James said, lifting a brawny hand and swatting Davie across the face.

Reeling back, the papers scattering everywhere, Davie pressed against the wall, arms over his head to protect against further blows.

Lord James drew his sword, a sound that sliced the air.

Though I thought Davie a fool—or worse—I could not see him killed. Stepping in front of Lord James, I raised my hands.

"It does you no honor, sir, to strike down an unarmed man." I was so frightened, I could feel my heart all but leap from my breast.

"His vile tongue is weapon enough, little tart!" cried Lord James, trying to push me aside. "He has used it overmuch already."

"Have a care!" Maitland called out. "You will not knock sense into the queen by beheading her secretary and her fool."

Lord James's face was flushed, but slowly he saw the sense of Maitland's argument and sheathed his sword. Then he turned, saying over his shoulder, "I will not stay a moment longer. Let the queen take that pretty doll to her bed. I will have none of it!"

Then he stormed off with Maitland following close behind.

When their footsteps had faded, Davie looked up, his face pale. Smiling nervously, he straightened his tunic.

I collected his scattered papers and handed them to him, but my hands were trembling and the papers clattered together.

"Oh, Davie," I whispered, "I would be your dearest friend, but I think you are your own chiefest enemy."

There was no apology, no thanks. All he said, in a voice thick with venom, was, "I will see Lord James driven clean out of Scotland, Nicola. You mark my words."

There was to be no reconsidering. Lovesick and adamant, the queen married Darnley in the chapel royal at Holyrood just after dawn on the last Sunday in July, having first named him "King of this our Kingdom." She was twenty-three years old and he scarce twenty.

I could barely say his name without a clench in my gut. But for the queen's sake, I hid my feelings and went to the wedding in a new dress of green silk with a high lace collar and velvet shoes.

Queen Mary was escorted to the chapel royal by Darnley's father, the Earl of Lennox, a heavyset man who looked nothing like his slim, elegant son.

To signify that she was a widow, the queen wore a black robe with a wide hood, the very robe she had worn at her husband's funeral. But it was clear that Darnley had spared no expense in his own garb. He was dressed sumptuously, with a doublet of gold and hung about with jewels.

With the summer sun just lighting the chapel's windows, he placed three rings on the queen's finger. The middle one bore a diamond as large as a quail's egg. I wondered that Darnley's mouth was able to speak the word "faithful" in the wedding vows without a sneer.

When the ceremony was done, the newlyweds proceeded to their individual chambers.

In the queen's room, the Four Maries unpinned the queen's black mourning robe.

"Careful," the queen cautioned when Pretty Mary—in an excess of excitement—was too quick. "I am not some virgin so eager for the marriage bed I would tear off my clothing! Remember, while I am Queen of Scotland, I am also the dowager Queen of France. By taking off my mourning clothes, I come afresh to this new marriage." But then she giggled, which put a lie to all her protests.

"Let me help," I said, but I was warned off with a look from Pious Mary. I had no place in this ceremony. So I stood back and simply watched.

When they had peeled the robe off, what was revealed beneath was the glistening wedding gown the queen had promised us, with its intricate embroidery of golden flowers and insects on bodice, sleeves, and skirts. She looked every inch the Queen of Faerie I had believed her to be in the garden at Rheims.

I applauded, my hands ringing out in praise. For *her*. But not for him.

A royal wedding is not like a commoner's. The celebrations continued for days. I was well tired of the drinking and dancing and masques long before they were over. I was overfull of both wet and dry confections. If I had to eat another caramelled or candied fruit or another bite of Nuns' Beads, or any other sweet, I might die of a surfeit of sugar. My voice was rough with all the singing and story-telling and the lack of sleep.

Each night, the queen and king—his title hateful in my mouth—threw handfuls of coins from the balcony to the crowds of well-wishers who had poured down from the city. The queen had her arm around the king's waist. But his hands were busy only with the coins.

A number of the Scots lords got wildly drunk at the feasts, and there were more than a few fistfights among the queen's devoted

Highlanders. From the second day forward many of the dancing men sported blackened eyes.

On that second day, the royal heralds proclaimed that Lord Darnley—now King Henry of Scotland—would henceforth sign all documents along with the queen. This declaration was met at first with utter silence by the assembled Scots lords.

Only the Earl of Lennox, the English father of the king, was heard to cry out, "God save His Grace!"

I was not the only one to notice that Lord James was missing from the celebrations. As good as his word, he had refused to return to Edinburgh for the wedding. Instead he had fortified himself in the midst of his vast estates, declaring that the queen planned to bring back the hated Catholicism to Scotland. And further, he called for the Protestant lords to join him in denouncing the queen.

"That long-legged pup and his father plan to assassinate me," Lord James was reported to have said of the king and Lennox. Davie told me this in a delighted whisper out in the garden. I had forgiven him his bad behavior of before. One does that for a friend. Forgiven—but not forgotten. And he had forgiven me what he called my silly innocence.

"Lennox," he added, rubbing his hands together, "has just warned the queen that Lord James intends to kidnap the king and ship him back to England."

"Is it true?" I asked. "Oh, if *only* it were true."

Davie threw his head back and laughed uproariously.

"I am serious, Davie," I said.

"So is the queen," Davie said, grinning at me. "She is putting Lord James to the horn!"

"You mean—she will outlaw him?" My hands went to my mouth.

"Aye." Davie's expression was one of impish delight. *"And* she's taken away all his lands!"

I was shocked that the queen would condemn one who had stood so closely to her in times past, and I remembered how Lord James had faced down the mob at the chapel door for her. But I was even more shocked at what I read so clearly in Davie's face—that he had encouraged the queen so that he might have his own revenge.

Revenge, Papa had always said, is a tainted meal. *Strange meats,* I thought, *for a wedding feast.*

Davie had even more revenge than that. Goaded by Lord James's stubborn opposition, the queen and her new king had no choice but to lead an army against him.

I watched them ride out from the gates of Edinburgh at the head of their troops. The king was dressed in a glossy suit of gilt armor. I thought he seemed like a knight from a fanciful romance.

But the queen—she looked every inch the soldier—wore a plain soldier's armor and had sword and pistol at her side. There was an expression of such determination on her face, I did not believe that anyone could stand against her.

Indeed this proved the case. Word came back to us through a messenger to Davie that Lord James had found little support for any uprising and had been forced to flee into exile in England with the few Scots nobles who remained on his side.

As he told me all this, Davie did a sprightly jig, right there in the corridor.

"Hush, Davie," I cautioned, but he did not stop his dance.

Queen Mary returned to Edinburgh in triumph. Even John Knox was forced to acknowledge her courage.

For a brief, glorious moment, it looked as if all was well.

I said so to Davie as we viewed from a balcony the return of the troops. "Maybe it will be 'happy ever after' after all."

"History compressed into one of your fairy stories?" Davie asked.

"Well, why not?"

"Because history, my dear Nicola, is never so tidy," he replied. "And because history does not stop for an ending, happy or otherwise."

28 ❧ SPILLING GOOD WINE

How often is the passing of one storm only a prelude to another. With Lord James gone, who had served her so well, the queen needed to appoint a new lieutenant general to command the royal armies.

Did she name someone safe and reliable? Someone with only her safety at heart?

No.

She awarded the post to the Earl of Bothwell.

Bothwell!

I wish I had never heard his name.

Where the new king was handsome, weak, willful, Bothwell was the opposite. Short and stocky, with the heavy good looks of a scrapper, he said things bluntly, but left out much in the saying. A fox and a wolf together. I believe the queen saw in him a man who could command her armies with energy and cunning.

Oh, but what a price she was to pay for his services.

The king had hoped his own father would be appointed to the position. When Bothwell, a Scot, was named, it became the first of many grievances he nursed against the queen. He still smiled and danced and paid her pretty compliments, of course, but as yet she did not suspect the poison that was growing in his heart.

Should I have told her? How often since I have asked myself

that. The truth was, I thought she had turned to Bothwell *because* she knew the king's venomous soul.

But I was now rarely at her side, and there was no good time to say what I thought. She was too busy—with her husband, with Bothwell, with the business of governing.

Who will speak truth to the queen now? I wondered.

No one took more satisfaction in Lord James's exile than Davie. He and Darnley toasted one another over the great laird's downfall, gloating excessively in the king's chambers.

But alone with me, out in the garden—Davie called it the only safe place for conversation—he spoke differently of his master.

"What a lackwit," he said. "What a wastrel."

"How can you serve a master you despise?" I asked, bending over to work the soil.

"And do you so admire yours?" he said, smiling.

I stood, hands on hips. "You know I do. She is the kindest, the sweetest, the . . ."

"Kind and sweet she may be," Davie said with that same teasing smile. "She knows poetry and music and is good to her dog. But that is not what makes a great monarch, Nicola. The queen is led too often by her heart. To reign well, one must lead with the head."

"And *you* know how to reign?" I threw down my digger. "You who bend knee to a king you consider a wastrel? You are spilling good wine on bad soil, Davie."

He laughed. "This garden has gone to your head, little fool."

I walked away and did not look back.

For weeks after that conversation we did not speak, ignoring one another in the corridors every time we passed.

But as Davie himself would have been the first to admit, calling a log in the water a fish does not give it gills. Darnley never rose to the task of being a true king. Rather he pulled the office down around him. And seeing the wreckage Darnley made of everything he touched, Davie finally fell out with him, just as everyone else had.

Everyone, that is, but the queen.

As winter drew on, Queen Mary was subject to another bout of ill health, a flux contracted on one of her rides. She asked for me specifically to nurse her.

Me!

How could I refuse? I even slept on a small cot by her bed in case she should cry out in the night.

The king was never by her side during her illness. Sometimes he was gaming and drinking with his low friends, Toby and Giles, finding every alehouse in Edinburgh. Or he went off on hawking and hunting trips with the few Scots lords who could still abide his company.

Often in her fever the queen would call out for him. And I—to my shame—always lied to keep her quiet.

"He has been to see you while you slept, Madam. He sat for an hour by your side," I told her not once but many times.

"That he should care so," she would whisper, and slip back into her fevered sleep.

He had not been there, of course. He never came. But I could not tell her so.

When the queen had recovered enough, we went to her palace at Linlithgow, with its beautiful view of the nearby loch. Even illness could not alter her long French habit of changing houses on a whim.

"I always feel better there, near the water," she told me before we left. "With you and the Maries to entertain me, I will be entirely well soon."

She was carried to Linlithgow by litter, rather than riding there, and this led to a fresh flurry of rumors about her health.

"She is just tired," I would say when asked. "She is recovering."

And she *was* tired from the days of fever. But it was more than that. She sighed often when she thought I did not notice, her face as pinched and white as when King Francis had died. She was tired and Darnley did not come to visit. Nor did he send letters.

What the queen had, I was certain—though no doctor told me—was a depression of the heart. All my little evasions had not fooled her. Deep down she now knew Darnley for a knave.

It was a dreary December day in Linlithgow when I came upon Davie sitting on a bench by the great fireplace in the parlor. His back was to me and he was intent on a book which I took to be a volume of poetry such as he and I used to enjoy together.

Weeks earlier I would have avoided him, hating him for his championing of Darnley. But since his break with the king, and especially here in Linlithgow, we had come to a sort of peace, occasionally even chatting companionably, though with none of the closeness we had had before. Of course he was now high in the government and had little time for card games with the queen's fool.

I *missed* him, if one can miss a person one sees every day. So I peeked over his shoulder, to be near him again. I saw then that he was not reading poetry at all but rather a treatise on the laws and statutes of Scotland.

"That looks very dull," I said. "Have you given up on the poems of Monsieur Ronsard?"

He looked up guiltily, then smiled his monkey smile. "I have found that the law has a poetry of its own, Nicola." He laid the book aside. "There's a rhythm to smooth governance, a meter like a poem."

I sighed. "I thought such matters were Maitland's domain."

"Ah, Nicola, Maitland earned the queen's disfavor when he opposed her match with Darnley. He will not easily win it back."

"But he is *still* her secretary of state," I pointed out.

"Retaining a title is not the same as being in power," he said, a strange note of ridicule in his voice. The flickering flames from the hearth cast odd shadows, so that his face was now dark, now light.

"But Maitland is here at court all the time," I said.

"Courting Mary Fleming, rather," Davie snapped.

I could not stand the contempt I heard in his voice. For Maitland, for Regal Mary, maybe even for the queen. "Davie, what has happened to you? Who have you become?"

"What have I become?" He grinned and puffed out his little chest. "I have become more powerful than the king."

I must have gaped. *"More . . . ?"*

"The king is a child who plays instead of learning statecraft."

I shrugged.

"Did you know that his latest piece of petulance is to sulk because he has been refused the crown matrimonial?"

I looked at him blankly. "What is that?"

He patted the bench. "Come sit, little fool, and I will explain."

I sat.

"Darnley is king only by virtue of being married to the queen. If she were to die, then he would lose his throne."

"Oh," I said, "as the queen did in France."

"Aye," Davie agreed. "But the crown matrimonial would make him king in his own right, so that he would continue to reign whatever happens to Queen Mary."

"Darnley reigning unchecked over Scotland!" I was appalled.

"Oh, I agree such is unthinkable. But there are those who, failing to find advancement with the queen, have tied their futures to Darnley. They fill his head with notions of his own greatness."

"As you did once, David," I reminded him, shaking a finger under his nose.

He had the grace to look embarrassed, and his monkey face suffused with color. "Do not task me, Nicola. I did it for the queen."

"Davie, let us have truth between us as we used to. You did it for yourself."

He nodded. "I hide nothing from you, my dearest friend."

"Good," I said, smoothing my skirt.

"I did it for the queen." He grinned.

"Oh, you! You are impossible," I said.

"If I did not have the queen's ear, there are many who would even now be urging her to take second place to her husband," he said sternly.

"Surely the queen would never agree to such a thing."

"Not so long as wiser heads prevail," Davie responded, slapping first his head, then his chest. "I have here, under my tunic and over my heart, the solution to Scotland's woes."

"Who is the storyteller now?" I said.

He looked a bit peeved with me, his face wrinkling in displeasure. "No, it is true."

I stood. "David Riccio, you would not know truth these days any more than . . ."

"Nicola, listen. I will prove it." There was a battle being waged on his face, between wanting to boast and wanting me to believe him.

I sat again, the fire warm on my face. "Prove it then."

"The king's pleasures are what, Nicola?"

I shrugged and counted on my fingers. "Drinking, gaming, hawking, drinking, hunting, dicing, cards, drinking, wenching..."

He nodded approvingly at my count. "In fact everything but the *business* of the land. He hates being called away from his pleasures even to set his signature to royal proclamations."

"So..."

"So—a solution was proposed," David replied smugly.

"By whom?" I asked, suspicious.

"By me!" He reached inside his tunic and pulled out a metal disk on a length of chain. "Now do you see?"

I leaned closer, but could not make out what it was. "What am I supposed to see, Davie? It does not *look* important."

"Ah, but it is a mistake to be fooled by appearances, Nicola. The beautiful Darnley is little more than a shadow of a king, while I—his ugly and despised servant—possess a stamp with the king's signature."

Now I could see the signature picked out in raised metal.

Davie laughed. "With this stamp I can imprint his name upon any document I wish."

"And he has agreed to this?"

"Agreed? My dear friend, he was *delighted!*" Davie dangled the metal amulet before me.

I reached out a finger to touch it. It was cold and hard and unfeeling. The very coldness of the thing chilled me through and through. So I stood and went over to the hearth, hoping that the fire would give me back some measure of warmth.

I turned and saw Davie still eyeing his prize as a drunkard eyes his wine.

"Oh Davie," I cried, "these games are too dangerous for the

likes of you and me. You may love the workings of power, the poetry of the law, but you have no army at your back, no powerful family to save you should anything go awry. We are like mice scampering about the feet of angry lions. If we squeak too loudly, they will eat us."

Davie was unmoved. "And what of the fable you once told me of the bound lion that owes its life to the mouse that chewed through its bonds?" He stuffed the disk back in his tunic.

Just then the door banged open and in walked the king in mud-spattered hunting gear. Close behind him came Lord Ruthven, a hawk-faced man with the unblinking eyes of a snake.

Davie and I leaped to our feet. One does not sit when the king is standing, but I had to repress a shudder.

Davie showed no such alarm. "Here comes the little lion now," he whispered to me, "and one of his keepers."

Neither of the men acknowledged us. The king strode across the room, calling out loudly for food and drink as he pulled off his leather gloves. Then, warming his hands before the fire, he turned his handsome, arrogant face upon Davie and me.

"There stands as unlikely a pair of cards as I ever drew from the deck—the knave and the jester," he said. "What trick should we make with such cards as these, Ruthven?"

He looked to Lord Ruthven to laugh at his jest, but was met with a calculating stare. Ruthven remained at the far end of the room, as though the warmth of the fire was an enemy to his icy nature. Finding no ready audience in Ruthven, the king ambled towards me.

"You have not yet delivered that kiss you promised, pretty fool," he drawled.

"I made no such promise, sir!" I stepped backwards.

"Oh, no?" He raised an eyebrow over one elegant eye.

I repressed yet another shudder and said in my light fool's voice: "I recall, Majesty, that you stole a kiss, like a brigand."

"I heard you distinctly," he purred, grabbing me by the shoulder. "You pleaded with me to commit further robbery. You are not calling your king a liar, are you? That would be treason."

From the corner of my eye I saw Ruthven moving towards us while Davie stood frozen, eyes flickering back and forth between the king and his companion. My foolery could not save this situation. I would have to speak the foul truth and hope to shock the king.

"Sire, a traitor is a man who would betray his queen wife," I said, wriggling to free myself and failing. "If the queen knew of this outrage to her fool . . ."

"The queen does not wish to know. I should hardly be surprised to learn that she disputes my very existence!" His hand snapped out and caught my face in a vicelike grip.

I tried to protest, but my mouth was squeezed too tight.

"Yes, pout those rosy lips," the king said. "I fancy I will dine sweetly on those cherries, and more besides."

All at once, Davie seized the king by the arm and tried to pull him away. "Think of your position, my lord," he warned.

The king narrowed his eyes. "Touch me again at your peril, you misshapen frog. I'll have your ugly head on my wall."

Ruthven came from behind and shoved Davie away, almost knocking him into the fire.

"Is this your field then, Davie?" the king asked, wrapping an arm around my waist. "Is no one allowed to plow it but you?"

Davie made another feeble attempt to reach me, but Ruthven blocked his way. "You interfere in things that are not your concern, Riccio."

All the while, the king pressed me against him, keeping one hand across my mouth so that I could not cry out.

Just then the door opened and the queen walked in with Bothwell and the Earl of Huntly right behind. She had a rolled up parchment in her hand.

At the sight of his wife, the king spun me around and released me. Then he stepped away, his hands wide apart, like a boy who has been caught stealing biscuits from the kitchen.

Halting abruptly, the queen placed one hand over her breast. "What is happening here?" she asked in a tight voice, looking from the king to me to Davie and back. Ruthven she ignored altogether.

"I was having a joke with the fool, as I am sure you jest with your own intimates," the king answered airily. "Have you never played such a game with bonny Signor Monkeyface?"

The queen's eyes were coldly furious. It was the look I had seen when she had ridden off after Lord James. "What you call play, sir, decent men call scandal." She advanced on him, the hand with the parchment upraised as she would to a misbehaving dog. "Bad enough you shame me outside the walls of my palace. Oh, yes, I knew of it, but have said nothing, thinking that you were still young and would change. But to do so here in my own parlor—I would that you choke on your shame!"

The king fell back before her. "I see I am as unwelcome here as ever." It was a weak attempt at defiance. "Come, Ruthven, we will find our amusement elsewhere." He turned and walked past her and out of the door.

Ruthven cast a quick glance around the room, assessing the mood of the queen and her men, then followed the king.

Once they were gone, the queen sank down on the seat by the

fire and dropped the parchment she was carrying. When Davie tried to speak to her, she waved him back.

"All of you leave me," she said, "but Jardinière."

Davie bowed, picked up the piece of parchment, then left with Bothwell and Huntly.

I knelt in front of the queen. "Your Majesty," I began, my palms both sweating. "I swear that I did nothing to invite . . . nothing to encourage . . ." *Please Lord,* I prayed, *let her believe the truth of it.*

"He needs no encouragement, Nicola," she said. "I have been aware longer than I care to admit what sort of man my husband is. And I have always known *your* heart, my loyal fool."

For a moment we were both silent, and I could measure the time by the hard beating of my heart. Then the queen said suddenly, "Did you know, dear Jardinière, that I was born in this very castle?"

I shook my head.

"I had hoped that being here would work some healing magic between the king and me. We need that now more than ever."

She met my questioning gaze and rubbed a hand gently over her belly. "I am carrying his child, the child who will one day rule Scotland. And—if Elizabeth does not marry and bear—this child will rule England as well." There were tears in her eyes.

Ignoring all propriety, I placed a sympathetic hand on her knee, searching for something—some song or story to comfort her. Then I looked up again and realized that there was no need.

She was smiling, and the tears she was shedding were tears of joy.

29 ❦ MURDER

Though he moved back to Holyrood, Darnley was in no way improved by the prospect of becoming a father. If anything, he got worse. His drunken parties became notorious. Tavern wenches were sneaked in and out of his bedchamber by day and by night. It was disgusting behavior and we all tried to keep word of it from the queen.

"Darnley and the queen are rarely together now," I told Davie as we walked into the queen's chambers. We had met by chance in the hall and Davie held the door for me.

He smiled broadly at me, which lent but little beauty to his face. Still, I smiled back. And suddenly it was as if our differences had never happened.

I said over my shoulder, "I sleep in a cot by her side, should she need to rise in the night. She will have no one else."

Did I boast? Perhaps. But it was sweet to be the queen's dearest fool again. And sweet to have my best friend back.

I was wearing the new silver-piped dress the queen had had made for me, and my hair was caught up in a silver net. I knew that I looked well enough in it, and wondered if Davie noticed. But he spoke of other things.

Compliments, I thought with sudden understanding, *were what Davie reserved for the queen, not her fool.* It did not hurt me as it once might have.

Davie said plainly, "Darnley knows that once the queen has an heir, she has even less need of him."

So I replied as directly. "And if it is not a boy?"

He smiled again. "It will be."

"As if you could know."

He smiled again, this time his face full of mischief. "You notice how Darnley is referred to less and less as the king and more and more as the queen's husband. Have you noticed?"

"I wasn't aware of that." In fact I tried to be *un*aware of Darnley, since the very thought of him made my stomach hurt.

We crossed the antechamber towards the stairs to the queen's bedroom.

"No?" Davie said. "Well, it pains him like a nail hammered through his foot."

I stopped and turned. "Fortunes do change, Davie," I warned him quietly, "just like the seasons. For a while the queen did not ask for me, now she does. You and I were friends, then we fell out, now we are friends again. Of all people you know how changeable folk are. Be careful of the enemies you make."

This time Davie laughed, but there was a bitter note in it. "My enemies should be careful of *me!*" he said, striking himself on the chest. He seemed to be becoming dangerously swollen with pride again.

"Oh, Davie—perhaps I should tell you Maman's story about the good girl who spoke in rubies and pearls but whose prideful sister had only toads and vipers fall from her lips."

Taking me by the hand, he stared into my face. "Perhaps you should, Nicola. But not now. Now we dine with the queen, and I will bring her the latest gossip from France. Pearls from my lips." He dropped my hand and went before me up the stairs, going slowly on his shortened leg.

I thought of how Davie's intimacy with the queen aroused not only Darnley's envy but that of many Scots lairds. They felt the same of me, of course, only as I was a girl and the queen's own fool, they could excuse it. But they did not excuse Davie. So I tried once more to warn him.

"I have heard that you exercise control over who is admitted to the queen's presence," I said. "And that you make the nobles pay you for an audience with the queen. Davie—is this wise?"

He stopped abruptly, turned slightly, and glared at me over his hunched shoulder. "Surely *you* understand what I am doing, Nicola. In the queen's present condition, she should be disturbed as little as possible. And if I demand some recompense for arranging an audience . . . well, that only serves to discourage those whose business is unnecessary." Then he smiled his monkey smile, as if to say: *Aren't I the clever boy?*

I drew in a breath to keep from answering back, then stopped right where I was, thinking what a dangerous game Davie was playing.

But Davie continued on without me and was already on the final step. I had to lift my skirts high above my ankles to catch up.

"Davie," I said softly in Italian in case anyone should overhear, "you know there have been threats made against you. Everyone says so. Take care! Take . . . care!" My voice almost broke in two.

He spun around and looked at me disdainfully. "Talk, talk, nothing but talk, Nicola," he said, also in Italian. "The Scots will boast, but rarely perform their brag." Then he turned on his heel and walked towards the room where the queen was already entertaining her guests.

"Majesty," he called, arms upraised, "the news from La Belle France has arrived. And *such* news! Wait until you hear . . . ."

I sighed. My poor Davie. His pride had hardened so much,

nothing could dent it. The queen's favor only served to make him more daring.

Queen Mary was seated in the small supper room that extended from the far left corner of her bedroom enjoying a late night meal with five or six of her courtiers. The Countess of Argyll was at the table while the others—all men—stood at various points around the room.

As I approached, my eye went to the stairway on the right which led down to the king's chambers. Would he come to dine tonight? That door had not been opened of late and it did not stand ajar now. *Fine!* As far as I was concerned, each day away from the king was a holiday.

The queen greeted Davie and me merrily. "Come in, come in, sweet friends. Though where you shall sit I do not know. As I have brought an extra guest," she joked, folding her hands across her bulging belly, "there is hardly room for us all."

A ripple of good-natured laughter went around the little room. It was cramped indeed, but made cozy by the glowing fire and the golden light of a dozen candles. The queen enjoyed this kind of intimacy with her friends, all the more since she had grown so distant from her husband. A place was made for Davie at the table, and I settled myself on the floor by the fireplace.

"So far away, Jardinière?" the queen asked. "Why not sit there by the countess?"

"Forgive me, Your Majesty, but I am so cold, I prefer the embers from the coal to the members of the court," I announced. The fire crackled at that moment, as if putting an exclamation point to my sentence.

Everyone laughed and the queen added, "Would that I could sit by the fire with you. But once down, how would I get up again?"

Davie put his hand out to her. "As to that, Majesty, you would have my hand, which always follows my heart."

The queen applauded his words, as did the others. I did not, thinking how he saved his compliments for when it would do him the most good.

Laid out on the table were bowls of Soupe de la Reine, Veal Floury, cold mutton pies, raisins, dates, almonds, and honeyed wine, from which we were invited to help ourselves. Davie began at once, but I was not hungry. I was still annoyed with him. My anger filled me so much, I wanted nothing to eat.

For a moment the room was full of light chatter led by the Countess of Argyll, then the queen broke in. "What of the news from France that you promised, Davie?"

"For dinner or dessert?" he asked.

They all laughed and shouted, "Now! Now!"

So Davie began a series of wicked anecdotes from France, many of them pointedly against the dowager Queen Catherine, all the while stocking his plate. Davie always did love good food.

I sat by the fire stony-faced for most of his recitation, but the fire had gotten too hot for comfort, and I rose, moving to the table.

"You must sing for us later, David," Queen Mary said. "You have not done so in a long while." As she spoke, she held out her hand for me, and I put my warm hand in hers.

"My throat is quite raw from discussing the business of the Parliament," said Davie. "I can barely outcroak a frog."

"Then you must play the lute and Nicola here can sing," the queen insisted. "Some of the jolly Italian songs perhaps?"

Davie shrugged. "I have so little time to practice I will make a worse din than the bagpipes." But he said it in a way that everyone knew he was jesting.

Just then I heard a noise from the bedchamber and leaning for-

ward, saw Darnley appearing from the private stairway looking very
pale and drawn. *Too many late nights,* I thought. *And too many low
wenches!* There was a hush in the room and I recoiled instinctively,
glad now that I had not eaten, for it would have come right up into
my throat.

The queen was probably the most surprised of us all, but she
kept her composure. "Make room for the king," she said.

Darnley squeezed in and took a place at the table, reaching immediately for the wine jug.

The moment he had appeared, the conversation died. Now the
queen made an effort to resume it, asking him two or three trivial
questions which he answered with only a few grudging words.

I wondered why he had even bothered to come up, since he was
obviously taking no pleasure in the company. He carefully avoided
looking at Davie, who now addressed him directly.

"How fares your kinsman, Lord Ruthven?" Davie asked, pop-
ping a grape into his mouth. "I hear he is abed with the fever."

Darnley shifted uncomfortably. "I believe he is now much recovered," he muttered, taking a deep draught of wine.

As though conjured up by the mention of his name, Lord
Ruthven suddenly appeared at the door of the king's private stairs.
If he was recovered, he did not look it. His face was white as ash, his
eyes rimmed with crimson, as if he were deathly ill still or—worse
yet—possessed. Strangest of all, he wore a metal breastplate, with a
sword and pistol strapped to his side. I thought he looked ready for
war and not the queen's dinner room.

An awful hush fell over the conversation. The Countess of Argyll put a hand to her breast. Even the courtiers were still.

Of us all, only the queen was not cowed by Ruthven's appearance.

"Lord Ruthven," she said curtly, "I sent you no invitation to supper."

Ruthven's flinty voice cut through the room like a jagged knife. "Let it please Your Majesty that yon man David Riccio come out of your chamber, where he has been overlong."

"Davie is here at my request," she answered sternly. "Have you lost your wits, man, that you speak to me like this?"

"That man has offended against your honor," Ruthven said.

The queen turned to her husband. "Is this your doing?"

Looking down, the wineglass still in his hand, Darnley muttered, "I know nothing of this."

The queen then turned back to Ruthven. Her hands gripped the table with such power, the knuckles went white. "Leave here now," she told him in a steely voice, "or I will brand you a traitor."

"I will not go while he yet remains," said Ruthven, pointing an accusing finger at Davie. "While good Protestant lairds who have served you languish in exile, this misbegotten, devilish creature has made a place for himself at the heart of your court."

All the warmth of the hearth left me in an instant, and I went stone cold. My temples pulsed: *danger, danger.* But I could not move.

As Ruthven spoke, armed men emerged from the private stair, gathering at his back. No one had yet drawn a sword, but the threat alone was devastating. There were gasps from the standing courtiers and the countess put a second hand to her breast.

"I warn you, sir," the queen said. "And will not again."

Davie suddenly jumped up from his chair, pressing against the window, as far as possible from the armed men.

"Sir," Ruthven said to Darnley, "take your wife to you."

Now Queen Mary stood, her hands held protectively over her

belly, and I reached to help her. But Darnley was quicker than I, seizing the queen in his arms and pulling her to his side.

Ruthven charged into the center of the room, heading for the window where Davie cowered. Everyone fell back before him except the queen's equerry, Arthur Erskine, who summoned the nerve to try to hold Ruthven back.

"Lay not hands on me, for I will not be handled!" Ruthven roared, drawing his pistol and brandishing it in Erskine's face.

Erskine staggered away, as if driven back more by a curse than by the threat of a bullet.

"Davie!" I cried out. "Take care!"

But he stood as if paralyzed, a mouse mesmerized by the roaring lion.

The other intruders now piled into the room, shouting curses. In the confusion, the table overturned, spilling food and wine in all directions. Candles toppled to the floor—save one that Lady Argyll managed to snatch up—and the room was plunged into near darkness. In the struggle, I was knocked to the floor and almost rolled into the fire.

I heard the queen cry out.

Then a squeal.

Davie!

Getting to my feet, I tried to make my way to him, thinking to shelter him behind me. Surely these men would not strike a girl. But at that very moment, Ruthven turned and came towards me. In the light of the single candle, his face was demonlike, his teeth bared in a vicious snarl. He pushed past me and marched back into the bedchamber. Behind him came his men, dragging Davie. Two of them had hold of his arms; a third wound his fingers in Davie's black curls.

"Davie!" I called.

"*Justizia! Justizia!*" He cried out in Italian. And then in French, "*Sauvez ma vie, Madam! Sauvez ma vie!*" Finally, "Save my life, Madam! Save my life!" Each cry was more pitiful than the last.

But no one could save him, for two of Ruthven's men held us at bay with drawn swords and pistols while the rest dragged him away.

Arms outstretched, the queen sobbed loudly as Davie disappeared into the room beyond.

That was the moment I saw my chance. Diving to the floor like a tumbler, I scrambled between the legs of the guards, upending one. When I ran into the antechamber, I saw Davie being forced into an alcove.

He spotted me and in his terror cried out my name. "Nicola!"

Ruthven turned, saw me as well, and lashed out with the back of his hand. He struck me so hard, I was sent spinning to the stone floor and lay dazed, a tumult of voices echoing in my head.

I do not know how long I was down. When I woke, as if from a nightmare, I was alone in the chamber. On the spot where I had seen them drag poor Davie, the floor was stained with blood.

Pushing myself up, I ran to the stairs. More patches of blood stained every step. I started down so swiftly, it is a wonder that I did not take a tumble and crack my foolish skull.

"Davie!" I cried. The only answer was an echo of my own voice.

I reached the landing where baggage was piled before being carried up to the royal apartments. There lying backwards over the lid of a trunk lay Davie's poor, twisted, bloodstained body. A bald-headed porter was bent over him, stripping off his rings.

"You filthy scavenger! What are you doing?"

The porter looked up unabashed, fingering a jeweled earring. "He was an ungrateful knave and deserved his fate," he said, an awful epitaph for my only friend.

Fato! Suddenly I remembered Davie speaking the word so long ago when we looked at the cards in his room. *Fate.* For friendship's sake I would dare it.

Running at the porter, I pushed him with both hands. He glowered and tried to return to his ghoulish task. So I swung with all the anger I had left, and raked my nails across his cheek. He fell back from my attack, touching the scratches, finding blood on his fingers.

"I will have your eyes next if you do not leave him in peace," I shouted. "And the queen will have your head!"

The porter edged towards the door. "The queen will be lucky to keep her own head before this night is out." He spat as he spoke, the flecks spattering between us. Then he darted off.

I turned and touched Davie's dear face with trembling fingers. Tears poured down my cheeks, hard as an Edinburgh rain. He had been stabbed more times than I could count.

"Oh, sweet friend," I whispered. "To be so hated. . . ." Then I leaned over and embraced him as best I could.

Wandering into the corridor, I heard orders and cries of alarm shouted behind me as the queen's guards were forced to surrender their weapons.

I stumbled along as though lost in a strange realm. *Would I be next to die?* I wondered. *Would the Maries? Would the queen?* I put my hand over my heart, remembering the bodies hanging from the balconies and railings of Amboise.

Perhaps I *should* have remained with Troupe Brufort. I could have married my cousin Pierre and raised a crop of baby acrobats. What was a rap on the head compared to a knife in the breast?

Then through a window I saw a band of townspeople assembling in the courtyard, all of them waving pitchforks, cleavers, and knives. They were calling out for the queen.

For the queen. Calling her "Our Mary" and "Our Sovereign."

I realized in a rush that the uproar from the palace had brought them racing to protect her. They needed to be told what had happened.

I tried one door. Then another. And another. But at each a sentry blocked my way and would not let me past.

"I am the queen's fool," I told the guards. "I am on the queen's business."

But they looked at my disordered hair, the blood on my dress, and would not let me through.

That was when I heard Darnley addressing the crowd from a window of the royal chambers.

"Have no fear, good people," he called, his hateful, reedy tenor voice floating above the courtyard. "I am safe. So is the queen. Return to your homes and sleep well." Then he went inside.

There were some grumbles amongst the crowd, low mutterings. And then someone shouted, "Come oot again, Darnley, ye silly man. Tell us aboot the fuss."

Someone else cried out, "Show us the wee queen."

"Is the wee bairn safe?" a woman added.

But gradually, when there was no more information, the crowd dispersed. I wept afresh to see them go, to see their honest Scottish instincts baffled by Darnley's deceit.

I knew that the queen would have addressed them herself if she could. She must be in her chambers, held prisoner.

Or worse!

That last thought was almost too terrible to contemplate, and it lent wings of panic to my feet. I darted back to the west wing, where two armed guards now blocked her doorway.

"Step aside!" I told them sharply. "I have to see the queen."

I must have been a dreadful sight, stained as I was with Davie's blood, my eyes ablaze with anger and fear. One of the guards made to stop me but the other held him back.

"It is only the fool," he said. "Let her pass."

I climbed the stairs desperate to find the queen safe, yet afraid, too. Was she alive? Was she injured? Was the babe in her womb still well? These fears tumbled about in my head like small boats in a rain-swollen river. I could not see the safety of the shore. The stairs seemed longer than I remembered; it took ages to get to the top.

But when I burst into her bedchamber, there she was: alone, sitting on the bed, weeping. But alive.

Alive!

"Madam," I whispered.

She looked up and stood, less quickly than she might have done because of her condition.

"Nicola!" she cried and opened her arms to me.

I ran over and we embraced, and this time I was not at all worried about touching her.

"Thank God *you* are safe, Nicola! What news do you have of Davie? The guards will tell me nothing. Nor will the king send word."

Should I have lied? Should I have given her a night of calm sleep?

I could not. She was the queen. I forced the words out, as if saying them for the first time made everything true.

"He is dead, Majesty." I touched one of the bloodstains on my dress. "Murdered."

The queen sank back onto the bed and for a moment I thought she was going to weep again. But she did not.

"No more tears," she declared in a calm voice. "I will think instead upon revenge. And so should you, dear Jardinière, for Davie was your friend as well. So should you."

Revenge?" I breathed the word. I felt it like a sharp spike under my breastbone. "For Davie!"

"And for me," the queen said, her cheeks the color of a new rose. "These conspirators intend to murder more than Davie."

I took a step back, my worst fears spoken aloud. "They would not dare murder *you*, Madam?"

"Once Darnley has the crown matrimonial, I will be no more use to them. Only dear Davie stood in their way. And now he is gone."

"Oh, *mon Dieu!*" I fell to my knees, put my head in my hands, and wept, my dreams of heroism drowned in a storm of tears.

Leaning forward, the queen smoothed my hair. "There, there, child. I believe we are safe for this night at least. Else they would have killed us already."

Suddenly I sat back. "Majesty, the townsfolk came racing here to Holyrood with pitchforks and cleavers. To save you." My nose began to drip and I passed a hand under it. "They will not let that viper Ruthven touch you."

"My dear Scots," the queen whispered. "If I could only promote all those honest pawns into knights. But they will not be able to stand against armed guards with only pitchforks and cleavers. If the serpent really wants to bite me . . ."

I sobbed again.

The queen pulled a square of linen from her sleeve. "Here,

Nicola. No need to ruin that poor dress further. Dry yourself and sit by me. We must come up with some sort of plan. But—oh dear—I have never been any good at this sort of thing."

She spoke lightly, as if to comfort me, and I must admit that it worked. Though my chest still felt tight, the storm of tears had passed. I sat by her on the bed and handed back the linen square.

With that calmness came a sudden canny thought, as if a measure of Davie's cunning had seeped into me with his blood.

"Majesty," I said hurriedly, "was it Lord Darnley who gave Ruthven and his men access to the private stairway?"

For a moment she looked away, biting her lip. "Yes."

Now I saw—as Davie had done from the beginning—that it was the king who was key to the entire chessboard.

"Then . . ." I said slowly, "who holds the king, wins the game."

She turned back to me. "The *game,* Nicola?"

I smiled sadly. "Your uncle, the duke, taught me more than he taught the King of France, I think, when he showed me how to play chess. We must take this king of yours."

She gazed at me intently. "Brava, Nicola!" she whispered.

"Where is Darnley now?" I asked.

"In his own apartments, the door locked between us. As it will stay. Forever!"

I stood, went over to the window, and looked down. We were a long way from the courtyard—three full stories. I trembled, but did not let the queen see that, for she was counting on me with Davie gone.

By great good fortune at that very moment Darnley poked his head out and breathed deep of the night air. I had seen him do this before when drunk, trying to quell the heaving of his stomach.

I tiptoed back to the bed. "Majesty . . ."

"Do not suggest an escape through the window, Nicola," she whispered hoarsely. "Even had we a rope to lower to the ground, I am in no condition with a child in my belly for such an adventure."

"Could you persuade the king to open his secret way for you?" I pointed to the locked door.

"It would scald my tongue to speak a single kind word to him."

"But suppose . . ." I said, raising my hand when she opened her mouth to object again. "Just suppose he came to you as a supplicant, begging your forgiveness and obedient to your will?"

The queen stared at me as though I had suggested we both sprout wings. "Nicola, I have not the spirit for jesting right now."

"I speak as a fool, yes, but not in jest. Lord Darnley is weak of mind and easily swayed, is he not?" I knew the answer already.

"Like a dandelion seed puffed this way and that by the wind. Especially an ill wind." She laughed bitterly.

I put a finger to my lips to quiet her. "Then . . . perhaps, Madam, my foolishness might sway him as easily. Have you some token I might take to him?" *Please,* I thought, *make it so.*

She looked at me quizzically, then went to a small bedside chest and took out a large brooch studded with sapphires. "He has always admired this," she whispered. "As he has my kingdom, he may as well have this bauble, too."

I took the brooch from her carefully, never having handled anything so magnificent. Then I fastened it under the folds of my skirt, where it could not be seen. *But,* I thought, *where I can reach it easily.*

"How will you get to the king's apartments?" Queen Mary asked. Her voice never raised above a whisper. "The door to our private stair is locked from his side and the entrance to his chambers will be well guarded."

"Perhaps *you* cannot climb down," I said quietly, "but I have

only myself to carry. His window is open and it is no great distance."
No further, I thought grimly, *than the depth of a grave.*

"We have no rope." She looked around the room. "Except the bellpull?"

"Not strong enough," I said. "Nor long enough."

"The bedsheets?"

I nodded. "You are better at these games than you think, Majesty. The bedsheets will do." *I hope.*

"I forbid it, child."

"Your Majesty," I whispered, "I am almost seventeen, a child no longer. There is another child we need worry about now." With an intimacy that bordered on insolence, I placed my hand flat on her stomach.

She looked at me gravely, then covered my hand with her own.

I set to work at once, stripping a pair of sheets from her bed and knotting them tightly together. Then, with her help, I maneuvered the table out of the supper room and we picked it up and carried it to the window—not daring to drag it because of the sound. There we tied the end of the sheets to a thick table leg.

Looking out the window again, I saw a sentry strolling below. As soon as he disappeared around a corner, I threw the end of my makeshift rope over the ledge.

Kicking off my shoes, I hiked up my skirts, then slung a leg over the sill. I took hold of the sheet with both hands and spoke to the queen as casually as I could.

"Once I am down, Madam, and into the king's chamber," I whispered quickly, "you must pull the rope back into the room before anyone below catches sight of it." *And do not be slow!*

"I will, Nicola. You can count on me. But what if the king becomes . . ."

The word *lustful* hung in the silence between us.

I shook my head. "Say a prayer to Our Lady for me, and that will be my best protection." *Or a kick where it will harm him most!*

I wished I were half so brave as I sounded. Half so brave as in my own thoughts. My heart was beating in my breast like a carpenter hammering nails.

Lowering myself by the makeshift rope, I began down, moving right hand below left. All the while, I planted my feet as firmly as I could against the grey stone.

Inch by slow inch I descended. It seemed impossible that I would complete my journey before a guard came by again and spied me. Glancing up, I saw the queen. She nodded her encouragement.

"Go on," she mouthed at me. "Hurry." And something else. I think it was, "Godspeed."

I felt the sheets give as the table shifted slightly and feared the knots were about to come loose and send me plunging helplessly down the full three stories.

For a moment I could not move. But the queen's prayers must have worked, for the line held. I looked up and she nodded again.

I started down once more and, having reached the end of the sheets, felt around with the tips of my toes till I touched the open window. Then my toes found the bottom of the casement itself and I positioned myself on the stone sill.

There was no sound from within. Silently I thanked God that the king had not spotted me. Nor had any guard. I let go of the sheet, stretched out my arms, and pressed my palms hard against the jambs of the window. It was all I could do to hold in a whoop of triumph.

Seeing me secure, the queen began reeling in the sheets while I surveyed the room before me. Darnley was seated with his back to me, so absorbed in his contemplation of the fire in the hearth, he had not heard a thing. There was a small table beside his chair on which sat a bottle and a half-filled glass of wine.

Carefully I sat down on the window's sill, then edged down to the floor. I crept up to his chair, making no sound in my stockinged feet. *How to best attract his attention without starting an alarm?*

Before I could come to a decision, Darnley let out a long sigh, then stood up, and turned around.

His eyes grew wide with astonishment and his hand leaped for his dagger. Then realizing who I was, he demanded, "Where in damnation did you come from?"

"Through the window like a bird," I replied lightly.

He glanced at the window, then back at me scowling. "Well, little bird, I will toss you out again. We will see how well you fly."

"Your Majesty," I said with a deep curtsy, "if you wish me to fly away, I certainly will. Only let me finish the small errand I was engaged to do."

He eyed me suspiciously. "What errand?"

"The queen beseeched me—so humbly I could scarcely bear it—to make my way here and bring back word that you are unharmed."

"Unharmed?" he repeated, staring at me. "What harm should come to me now that I rule undisputed in Scotland?"

He spoke boldly but his pale brow was slick with sweat and his right hand trembled involuntarily. He reached for his wine cup. It was clear he had had little stomach for the night's horrors. He probably had not counted on all the blood.

The blood! My dress was still stained with it. Darnley was trembling because of it!

He set the glass down again without tasting it.

"What harm could *you* come to?" I touched the bloody spots

on my dress for emphasis. "That is exactly what I asked the queen. But I could not abate her anxiety. She gave me this as a token of her continued love." I turned my back, reached under my skirt, undid the brooch, then turned and offered it to him with a flourish: "Voila!"

Darnley reached for the brooch tentatively, as though it were a viper coiled to strike. Then he held it up, as if admiring the play of the light on the blue stones.

"Does she seek to buy her life with this bauble?"

"I am sure the queen is quite safe, Your Majesty," I told him with another respectful bow.

"Why should you think that, girl?" Darnley snapped. "There has been more than one murder here already tonight."

"More than David Riccio?" For the moment I was stunned and it showed on my face.

Darnley seemed almost pleased at that, and he grinned at me. "One of the royal chaplains, the Dominican, Adam Black." He said it casually, then looked back down at the jeweled brooch.

"They murdered a priest!" This was as shocking to me as Davie's murder, though I was scarcely acquainted with the man.

"Ruthven's men had daggers drawn for Bothwell and Huntly, but those two escaped, leaving the hunters hungry for a kill. When the fox eludes him, a hunter will as gladly kill a badger." He smirked. "A badger, you know, is black-and-white, like a priest. A pretty conceit I think."

Play the pretty fool, I reminded myself, and answered: "Better than any I could invent, Highness. But . . ." and I bowed again, "do you think that they might yet do injury to the queen?"

"If so, she has brought it upon herself."

The man was impossible. But I was not there for pleasure. I was there to turn him to my will. *Flatter him,* I reminded myself. *Flatter till it is done.*

"You are *so* right, Majesty. She is my own queen but I see now how weak she is, how fragile her hold is on the throne. She was foolish not to have submitted to your will from the first." I hoped I had not overdone it.

"That she was. She has not the spirit to rule as a monarch should, but is easily led astray by ugly, guileful foreigners."

I wanted to snap back that for all his handsome face he was not worth half of what Davie had been. But I had the queen to think of, and my plan.

"As you say, Majesty, the queen is easily led. Especially now that she is with child. Women change when a child grows in the womb, you know. Perhaps that change will be enough to save her. Though it will depend upon your friends. They must be intelligent men. I am sure you would not consort with dullards." I looked into his face with what I hoped was complete innocence. The kind Davie had so often accused me of.

"They have more than a sufficient measure of wit." Darnley was relaxed now, and picked up his glass of wine to take a sip.

"Oh, then they might . . . but no." I put my hand to my mouth as if uncertain.

"What are you talking about, fool?" He stuffed the precious brooch into his pocket with his other hand.

"I *am* a fool," I said, simpering at him. "I mean since they are intelligent men, rather than fools, they would never act contrary to their senses of honor, not even should they gain by it."

"Speak plain, girl. Is this some tiresome riddle?" He drank another sip of the wine.

"I mean that their loyalty to you surely outweighs any advantage they might gain from *your* demise." *There. I put out the bait boldly. Now if the fish will only take it.*

"*My* demise?" He laughed shallowly. "My *demise*? Nothing will happen to me. Why, within a matter of days the crown matrimonial will be mine, then I will reign supreme."

"And justly so, I swear, though not all might agree."

"Might they not?"

I moved closer, as if confiding a secret. But not so close that he might lay his hands on me. *Take the bait,* I kept thinking. "Ruthless men, Majesty, might think otherwise. They might see some . . . great benefit in retaining the queen in power."

"How so?" Intrigued, Darnley stepped into the circle of my confidence. I wanted to back away but I did not dare. I had to let him close enough to make him believe.

So I lowered my voice even further. *A well-spoke whisper,* Uncle Armand always said, *makes the audience lean in.* And Papa said often, *The nearer the neck, the nearer the knife.*

"Well, in a mere three months, sire, the queen will give birth. Once the baby is born, if the queen were to suffer an accident or to retire to some isolated tower, Scotland would have an infant king."

"No infant can rule unaided, fool."

Who is the fool now, I thought. *You have taken the bait!* "Then what would be done?" I actually batted my eyelashes at him.

"A regent would be appointed. Do you know nothing?"

"I know very little of such grand matters, I am sure," I said. Though of course I knew what a regent was. The dowager Catherine de Medici still ruled France as regent for her son. "So will this regent . . . and is that a gentleman again, sire? Re-gent? A small foolish joke. I apologize. La!—Great doings make my poor head spin! Will this regent be a commoner or a churchman?"

"He would have to be a noble. Or a council of regents."

"Ah," I said, opening my eyes wide. "Now I understand!" *Though of course I had understood all along.* "So a group of nobles could rule Scotland in the baby's name."

"Aye, that might suit them, if there were not already a king upon the throne. Me!" He smiled witheringly.

I stared at him, feigning a dawning realization. "Of course, Your Majesty. If they have any such regency plan in mind, it will come to naught if you are already declared king."

"Exactly."

Bait taken, I now set the hook! "Surely there is no question of their loyalties. But wait, sire. I have just remembered. They have already broken their oaths to the queen. Would they dare do any such thing to the not-quite-yet king?"

Darnley stepped back from me as if from a poxied wench. He drained the rest of his wine in a single gulp.

I continued. "Only a fool would suppose them to be more concerned with their own gain than with the good of the nation." I kept my voice the innocent's. "But then, I *am* a fool."

The wine had brought an uncomplimentary flush to his face. "I have guards to protect me."

"Guards? Oh, yes. Right." I put a hand to my temples. "Such things escape the mind of a fool."

Darnley was trying to affect an air of unconcern, but he was now hanging on to my every word. *Reel him in,* I thought. *Be careful, though. Don't overdo the drama.* But Darnley seemed unaware of my overacting, so I went on.

"But sir," I said, looking around as if afraid to be overheard, "how good are these guards? True, they may save you from a knife in the back or a lance in the side. Yet there are subtler methods, the kinds sorcerers are wont to use, like poisons that cannot be traced. Still . . ." and I paused as if musing, "what Scottish noble would possibly sink to such base practices? This is not Italy after all."

Darnley was tugging at his jerkin and his eyes had become glazed, as if he were in the grip of a fearsome vision.

"Have you heard . . . talk of Lord Ruthven?" he asked.

"That he indulges overly in ale and wine, do you mean?"

"No, fool, have you heard that he practices magic!" His flushed face was now an odd shade of green.

"Magic? That is surely nothing but empty gossip. He studied abroad. Alchemy, I think. And yet . . ." I looked around again. This time he looked around with me. "They do say that where there is smoke a fire must be burning."

"Ruthven *has* been called a warlock," Darnley muttered to himself, clenching and unclenching his fists.

I hugged myself and shivered. "I wish you would not speak of such things, Your Majesty. Tales of witches and their poisons are frightening to a simple fool like me."

All at once he leaned forward intently. His breath stank of wine and fear. "Listen, girl, there may be danger here you do not comprehend, danger to both the queen and to me."

"To you?" I exclaimed aghast. "Surely not, Your Majesty!"

"If I say there is danger, then there is! Do not contradict me!"

I hung my head. "I am a fool, sir, indeed."

"Tell the queen that she and I must look to each other, as our own best friends. Only in that way can we find safety."

"I doubt the queen would believe such a story from my lips, Majesty. She will think it the ravings of a . . . mere fool. Can you not explain these matters to her yourself, in the language of the court?"

"Yes, of course," Darnley agreed. "That is exactly what I will do.

But you must be out of here, before anyone knows you have come."

I spread my hands helplessly. "As you surmised, Your Majesty, I cannot fly, for all that my head is full of feathers."

He pulled a key from his jerkin and started for the rear stairway. "These steps will take you to a passage that leads to the servants' quarters. Go soft now and be sure that neither Ruthven nor any of the others get wind of this visit."

He unlocked the door and signalled me to be gone. I paused for a final curtsy, prompting him to turn me around and give me a shove in the small of my back. Then he slammed the door shut after me. I heard the key turn in the lock. Praying that this desperate move would be blessed with success, I started down the steps.

King to queen.

Check.

31 ❧ ESCAPE

I had trouble falling to sleep that night. And when I did, I dreamed of the bloody stag again, its noble head in my lap. Awaking in the pearly light of morning, I checked in the mirror to see if I were still soaked with blood, but my night shift was unstained.

Sighing with relief, I thought suddenly: *The queen—she is the one who needs my help now.* So I dressed at once, in a plain, dark dress with but a touch of lace at the collar.

"Forgive me, Davie," I whispered. "I have no mourning clothes but these."

I had not been able to get back to the queen's chamber after leaving Darnley. Two new guards had been at the door and would not let me in. By now the queen must be desperate to know.

Unless . . . unless Darnley had already gotten to her himself.

There was an unnatural hush as I walked down familiar halls. Doors and gates normally ajar were now closed and guarded. The passageways through which clerks and scholars had gossiped only yesterday were now patrolled by armed men. Even those few courtiers I met became tight-lipped when they saw me, refusing to divulge by so much as a glance where their loyalties lay.

And I did not ask.

I did not dare ask for fear of giving the game away.

When I got to the west wing where the queen had her apartments, I found it the most heavily secured of all.

The devil owns this place, I thought.

But still I was determined to report back to the queen.

How?

And then I had it! Even if her regular attendants had been forced to leave, someone still had to fetch her meals. *I* would be that someone!

I found the nearest stair and fled down to the kitchens, where cook was barking orders. I watched from the doorway as his big hands slapped the heads of his assistants for spilling the milk or using too much salt. It was such a homey, familiar tumult that, for the first time that day, I felt almost safe.

Lazing on a stool in the corner near the hearth, a red-faced soldier sampled any food that was carried close to him. He looked at ease, but I noticed he never stopped eyeing the hurrying servants. *He* was in command of the kitchen now, not cook.

Cook had finished preparing a tray of cold mutton, kippered salmon, cheese, bread, and wine on the silver tray used for the queen's meals. "Hamish!" he called. "Perhaps she will eat this. Puir lady hasna supped all day."

A gangly boy, not more than thirteen, answered the summons, loping across the kitchen to stand before cook. He rubbed the side of his pointy nose with one bony finger.

"Ye take that up to the queen and mind ye come directly back," cook ordered gruffly, casting a quick glance over at the soldier. "Dinna wander any place yer not supposed. And dinna speak to a soul or I will gie ye sech a clout, yer head will spin round three times widdershins on yer scrawny neck."

I backed away from the doorway and found a spot further along the passage where I could intercept Hamish. Soon I heard his footsteps on the stone floor.

"Where are you off to then, Hamish?" I asked, stepping directly into his path.

He jerked to a halt, almost dropping the tray. Though he knew me as one of the queen's intimates, he had been warned not to speak to a soul, so he bobbed around, trying to find a way past.

"Well, Hamish?" I asked.

His need to obey cook warred with his wish to please me.

"To the queen," he said at last. "I mun hurry."

I let my mouth drop in surprise. "Hurry? I would have thought you would be dragging your feet, Hamish."

He stared at me, a puzzled frown creasing his thin, freckled features. Hamish was not particularly bright. "Be this some of yer jesting, Fool Nicola?"

"Peril is never a jest, Hamish," I said. "You are either a greater fool than I or a braver man than any I have ever encountered."

"Why say ye so?"

I stared back. "Are you unaware of the danger? Surely you know what happened to Sir John Gordon and the poet Châtelard?"

"Beheaded?"

I nodded ponderously. "They would be alive today if they had not fallen under the queen's spell. Coming into her presence led directly to their execution. First the bewitching, then the beheading."

Hamish looked like he wanted to scratch his sandy thatch of hair but was afraid of dropping the tray.

"And now David Riccio has fallen victim to the same fate," I said. "The king is jealous of any man who comes near his wife."

"*Any* man?"

"Even that old priest Adam Black. Simply because the queen met him in the confessional, he was put to the knife."

I could see that Hamish was paling. "I be only a humble . . ."

"Low rank offers no protection," I said with a grim shake of my head. "In fact, it makes the imagined insult all the greater."

His hands shook so hard, the cutlery rattled on the tray.

"Look, Hamish, *I* am in no danger, being a woman. I will take the tray for you. Master Cook need never know."

"Would ye do that, Fool Nicola? Would ye really?" He was so ponderously grateful, I almost felt guilty for tricking him.

I took the tray from his unresisting hands and made off with it as though it were the greatest prize in Christendom. When I reached the royal apartments, I held it under the noses of the guards, saying haughtily, "The queen's repast. To be delivered posthaste."

They laughed at my fine words, looked under each bit of food for the Good Lord knows what, then let me by.

Inside the antechamber there was a surprise awaiting me. Lord James was there talking with the queen. His heavy, bony face looked gloomier than ever, and she was making a great show of gratitude and friendship towards him.

I set down the tray and kept my distance, head bowed.

"Whatever wrongs you think have been done you," Lord James said gravely, "these men were acting for the good of their country. You must be prepared to practice forgiveness."

Forgiveness! Davie's body with its hundred wounds seemed to rise up before me.

"Forgiveness? Ever since I came to Scotland," the queen snapped, "I have been given opportunities to practice that particular virtue!"

I looked up at her words, and she nodded at me, as if my presence was all that kept her calm. Suddenly I understood the problem, even without Davie to explain it to me. A confrontation with Lord

James now would do the queen no good. She needed to keep him on her side if she were to go free.

"We will talk about the return of your lands at another time," she said to Lord James. "When I have the *freedom* to do it!" She stressed the word *freedom* so he could not miss her meaning.

"Madam," I said, offering the tray.

She clutched her belly and groaned. "You must leave me, Jamie. I suffer labor pains and would have only my maids attend me."

Lord James got a peculiar expression on his face, almost one of fear. He made a perfunctory bow and departed.

"Men!" the queen said when he was gone. "Heroes in the bedroom till it comes to the birthing of babes! My midwife tells me she always puts the husband out else he faints at the first blood." She seemed entirely well now. Her pains had been all pretense.

I put the tray on a little table by a chair, and turned. "How does Lord James come to be here, Madam? I thought him in exile in the south."

She sat down heavily on the chair but did not even look at the food. "He has just returned. He knew I would have need of him now."

"But if he is here, he must have known what was going to happen," I said. "Perhaps he was even part of the conspiracy."

"You are much less the fool than the court thinks you, Nicola," the queen said. "Is his timing not exquisite? If Parliament had met today—as I had originally intended—all his lands would have been confiscated. But nothing can be proved against him without Davie. And so I now need Lord James as an ally." She sighed and put the back of her hand to her forehead. "How I dislike deceit, Nicola, and how much of it there is in kingship. But I must rise to the challenge."

Going into her bedroom, I poured rose water into a flowered bowl. Then, dipping several of linen cloths in the water, I wrung them out, and brought them to her.

She patted one cloth on her forehead and another on the back of her neck. "I cannot fight them all, Nicola. For my child's sake, I must befriend those I can and take my revenge on the rest."

"And what has become of Davie?" I asked tentatively.

"Buried in a makeshift grave like a pauper," the queen whispered bitterly. "But that will be corrected! As can much else." She smiled suddenly, like the sun after a Scottish shower. "Nicola, I do not know what you said to the king last night, but he came early this morning, declaring his love, begging my forgiveness."

"There is much to be forgiven," I whispered back sourly. But inwardly I smiled, and thought: *The fish has been truly caught.*

"The king is like a selfish child," said the queen, still in that same quiet voice. "But he is only as dangerous as the company he keeps. Now, Nicola, listen carefully to what we have planned."

I moved by her side.

"Tonight we will make our way down the back stair to which my husband has the only key. From there we will go to the quarters of my French servants, who stand ready to help."

"May all the angels guard you on your way, Majesty."

"I have a further favor to ask of you, my Jardinière," the queen said, taking my hands and speaking in a hurried whisper. "You must contact Dougal at the stables. See that there are horses waiting for us beyond the abbey graveyard just after the midpart of the night. The postern gate is always kept fastened, but in such disrepair, we will be able to squeeze through. Even me!"

"I will, Majesty. But what then?"

"Lady Huntly . . ." she glanced around again. "Lady Huntly

has already smuggled out a letter for me instructing those nobles still loyal to gather their troops at Castle Dunbar." Her eyes were bright and she seemed to have an inner glow as she spoke.

"Do you know how many will be loyal, Madam?"

"With God's help we will find out tonight." She leaned back in the chair smiling. "Now I believe I will eat. Plotting is such hungry work."

I marveled that six months pregnant, surrounded by vicious men who had threatened her life, she showed no sign of fear nor would she entertain any suggestion of defeat. Gone was the grave woman of the night before. Here was the true Mary of Scotland.

If courage were a crown, I thought, *there could be no greater queen in all the world.*

That evening, past the quarter of twelve, I waited on the far side of the graveyard with Dougal and the queen's escort—Sir Anthony William Standen, Arthur Erskine, and Lord Traquair. The horses' hooves had been muffled with cloth, and the men held their hands on the steeds' noses to keep them from making any extra noise.

Fidgeting with the lace collar of my dress, I fretted uncontrollably. A dozen things might yet go wrong this night:

Darnley might change his mind again.

A turncoat servant might speak out for a purse of gold.

Lord James might come upon us on the road.

Lord Ruthven might spy us out with magic.

The queen might miscarry.

As the moon made its passage across the sky, I saw that the men around me were no less agitated than I. It was now half-past the hour and the queen not here yet. Even the horses were beginning to stamp their muffled hooves and snort restlessly.

"Hssst!" It was Dougal. He pointed a shadowy arm.

Ahead, two dark figures detached themselves from the darker bulk of the palace and made their way towards us, darting between the gravestones and pushing through the postern gate.

Beside me I heard the click of a pistol being cocked and the metal sigh of a sword drawn from its scabbard.

"Wait!" I said. "The moon will tell us whether friend or . . ."

But the moon was hidden behind a wisp of cloud and the figures were all but on us when the bulkier of the two figures cried out in sight of me.

"My dear friends," came the queen's hoarse whisper, "your loyalty to a lonely fugitive is more eloquent than any devotion offered a queen upon her throne."

Darnley said nothing but made straight for a horse. Seizing its bridle, he hissed impatiently. "Come, we must be gone."

We helped the queen onto Erskine's horse, and she put her arms around his waist, riding pillion behind him.

"You, too, Nicola," cried the queen. "I will not go without you."

Till that very moment, I had not suspected I was to accompany her in her flight. Indeed I had not looked beyond this moment.

"To me, girl," Lord Traquair called, leaning down and pulling me up behind him.

I held as tight as I could to his ample waist, for I was suddenly shaking with the cold, and feared I might fall.

Then, eager to be away, we all galloped down the road past the dark hump that was Arthur's Seat, the moon now full above us.

We rode like the dickens, but it was the king who drove us most fiercely, his voice straining with terror.

"Come on! Come on!" he yelled once we were away from Holyrood. "By God's blood they will murder me if they catch us!"

"The queen is with child, my lord," I called over Lord Traquair's shoulder to Darnley. I was furious else I would never have spoken so. "No one pursues. Would you have her lose the babe?"

He glared at me and turned in his saddle to shout at the queen. "If this one dies," he cried, "we can have others."

We rode for five hours, stopping only once to change horses. It was an hour past dawn, the early spring light pearly on the hillsides, when we came in sight of Castle Dunbar.

"Madam, look!" I cried, pointing with one hand, the other still secure around Lord Traquair's waist.

There were hundreds of men camped round the castle—thousands even—like a great hive of buzzing insects. A cheer went up when the queen was recognized.

Bothwell rode out to meet us, proudly gesturing at the army he had gathered, the beekeeper showing off to the queen bee.

"Huntly, Atholl, and Fleming are already here," he said, his voice booming out in the soft spring air.

Bothwell seemed so loud, I actually winced. And then I realized it was the first time any of us had spoken loudly in days. Not since Davie had been killed. Our voices—like our bodies—were now free.

"Brava, Majesty!" I cried out. Raising my hands above my head, I began applauding, which almost led to me falling from Lord Traquair's horse.

The queen laughed. Then she took off her bonnet and shook loose her hair. Though she had just come through twenty miles on horseback, pregnant and frightened, she looked as fresh as if she had just risen from her bed.

Bothwell laughed with her. "Madam, more have sent word that they will arrive before the day is out," he boomed.

There was no missing the way he ignored the king, and the queen did not correct him for it. I saw Darnley bristle, but secretly I was glad. How irrelevant he had become now that the queen was free and among her own supporters. That he should know it fully gave me the greatest pleasure. I turned in the saddle and stared at Darnley, my lips forming the words: *Who is the fool now?*

The queen was so overcome by the sight of her many followers massed before the castle, she had to swallow twice before she could speak. But at last she said, "It is as grand a company as ever I saw."

"In a day or two we will be ready to march on Edinburgh," Bothwell told her. "And the devil take any who stand against us!"

As it turned out, no one did.

Only a week after her escape, the queen rode back in triumph into Edinburgh at the head of an army of eight thousand men. Her "dear Scots" crowded the streets to cheer her on. Lord James came in person to welcome her home and—at least publicly—rejoined her cause.

As for Ruthven and his murderous crew, they were long gone. With no queen for a prisoner and no king for a figurehead, they had nothing to play with. Abandoning the palace, they had fled for their lives, and were already halfway to England, hoping to find sanctuary there for their treacherous souls.

Checkmate.

SCOTLAND ⁊ 1567–1568

A longing haunts my spirit day and night,

Bitter and sweet, torments my aching heart.

Between doubt and fear, it holds its wayward part,

And while it lingers, rest and peace take flight.

—poem by
MARY QUEEN OF SCOTS, 1568

Davie's body was removed from the common grave and given a proper burial at the chapel royal. I was there, of course, sitting behind the weeping Maries.

But I had no more tears to shed. I had already grieved in his blood, and had spent the rest of my sorrow in the terror of the days that followed.

However, I remained behind after the funeral mass, standing by Davie's grave site. There was much I still needed to say.

I had made a small bouquet of flowers from my own little garden—a mallow which meant "ambition," a wallflower which signified "fidelity in misfortune," and a bunch of snow-white anemones for "withered hopes." I had bound the flowers round with a cypress bough for mourning. Davie would understand.

I also took one of the golden roses from the altar because the priest had said that the rose stood for the mortal body and the gold color for the immortality of the soul. It was the last thing I would be able to do for Davie, and I wished to do it well.

Finally satisfied with the positioning of the garland, I knelt in prayer, hoping that whatever wrongs Davie had done would be forgiven him. I thought that if I could love him with all his faults —his ambition, his pride, his bitterness—how much more Almighty God must love one who had suffered so much.

"You see, Davie," I whispered, "your faults are now graces. Sing well before the throne of heaven. God will love every song."

I pricked my finger on purpose on a rose thorn and left a drop of my blood on the grave. If there was any magic, blood for blood, Davie would have it of me.

Standing, I crossed myself, and turned towards the abbey.

And there, walking towards me, was the last person in all the world I could have thought to see.

"Dear Lord!" I cried out, crossing myself again. What had that single drop of blood wrought?

It was an apparition—Davie as he would have looked had not nature's cruel hand afflicted him at birth. There were the same black curls, the same sparkling green eyes, the same eyebrows like crow's wings.

Davie indeed.

Yet how could it be?

I began to tremble violently, and I think I opened my mouth to scream, though no sound came out.

The apparition came closer and I stood, unable to run.

"They tell me you are Nicola Ambruzzi," said the apparition, greeting me with a bow. Even the voice was the same, with its Italian lilt.

"Y-yes," I stammered. "Da . . ." Davie's name died on my lips.

"You think I am my poor brother," the revenant finished for me. "All the family wears this face." He touched a hand to his cheek. "I am not David. I am Joseph Riccio, come from Paris to take Davie's place."

I continued to stare at him, looking—I suppose—very much the witless fool many took me to be.

"His brother," I repeated, stupidly.

Joseph Riccio nodded and smiled, not unkindly. "Poor dear Davie," he lamented. "He had so many gifts. Yet he felt his life blighted by a curse: crooked back, shortened leg, misshapen face."

"Yet he achieved so much, you know, despite those," I said, my voice halfway between a whisper and a cry.

"He did," Joseph Riccio agreed.

"He did," I repeated stupidly.

Again Joseph smiled. "And however high he rose, he never forgot his family. Year after year, he has sent us money, presents, letters; letters that were filled with your name."

"*My* name?" I echoed in surprise. I had not known Davie had any family, let alone that he had told them about me.

"He told us many times of your kindness—and your beauty."

"Beauty, no. He could not have said that." I blushed and looked down.

"He did. And now I see for myself that he wrote in truth." Joseph offered me his hand. "You have an angel's face as well as an angel's heart. I hope that we, too, Nicola, can be good friends."

I clasped his outstretched hand in mine and could not help but feel that my prayers and my blood had brought me a great gift.

For this, I thought, *is how Davie must look in heaven, his twisted back and leg set straight by the gentle hands of angels and the boundless love of God.*

"We will," I assured Joseph, knowing that it was true. "We will be true friends indeed."

33 ❧ A WEE LAD

ere months after Joseph's arrival, Queen Mary was brought to childbed. For the purposes of safety, we carried her by litter from Holyrood to Edinburgh Castle, a mile away. Lord Bothwell had insisted. Edinburgh Castle, he said, was that much easier to defend, as it perched like a great eagle on top of a granite aerie.

The queen did not object. I think she hated the idea of giving birth in the rooms where David had been so brutally slain.

We brought her up to her new apartments, in the southeast corner of the old palace. Her bed was hung with blue taffeta and velvet. In the next room stood a cradle with almost ten ells of Holland cloth wrapped around it waiting for the child.

"I can be happy here, I think," she said as she gazed through the window at the town way below. From so far away it looked like a gentle and quiet place, not the bustling city I knew.

On the nineteenth of June, before eleven in the morning, after a long and difficult labor, the queen gave birth to a healthy boy, whom she named James after her father. He was born with a thin, fine caul stretched over his face, like a spiderweb.

I shuddered to see it.

Mistress Asteane, the midwife, wiped the baby off, reserved the caul, and put him in his mother's arms.

"Did I nae tell ye it would be a boy?" she said to the queen as one of her old women helpers sopped up the blood. "And a braw laddie he is, too."

The queen's face was drawn and white from the long labor. She coughed slightly as she took the child. But then she smiled down at him and looked like a Madonna painted for a church wall: content and unworried about the future.

Braw young Jamie was. He certainly had iron lungs and did not stop wailing for the first three hours after he was born. But that caul worried me. My mother had always said of cauls that they brought the sight to some, and bad luck to others.

Some of the bad luck was surely Darnley's, for the birth of his son moved him further down the line for both the Scottish and the English thrones.

But—I wondered, listening to the baby's unceasing wails— *where else might such bad luck fall?*

Pretty Mary ran to bring the news to Sir James Melville, who rode to London to give word of the birth to the English queen. He sped so fast, he covered the near four hundred miles in five days, a feat few could match. When he returned, he told us that Elizabeth had fallen into a chair weeping. "The Queen of Scots is lighter of a fair son, while I am but of barren stock," she had said.

"If she remains barren," Regal Mary said as we sat attending to our sewing, "you know who will be king of England."

"Who?" I asked.

"Oh, la, Nicola—only a fool does not know," said Pretty Mary.

"The young baby, of course. Our Jamie," Jolly Mary said.

Regal Mary added, "He stands closest to the English throne

from both his mother's and his father's sides. Imagine—our Jamie king of England *and* Scotland, too."

I thought of our Jamie, red-faced and bawling in his carved oak cradle with its sides of inlaid wood. I thought of that caul.

Sometimes, I thought, *it is best not to think of the future.*

"To our Jamie!" I said, picking up my glass of wine.

And we drank to the wee babe.

Darnley finally left his parties to come and view the child, but he took his time doing it. There was a persistent rumor about in the town—so Joseph reported—that the child was not Darnley's. His reluctance to see wee Jamie at once lent a measure of truth to such slanders. I could have cheerfully throttled him for lending credence to such lies.

When he arrived at last, he was directed into the queen's bedchamber, for she was not yet recovered from her long labor. She was also weakened by an insistent cough that had kept her awake for nights, as well as Jamie crying for his feedings, for she had insisted the baby stay in her own room instead of the nurse's. To my certain knowledge, the queen had had little sleep for days.

She told us that the door to her bedchamber must stand ajar. "So that I can call for help if needed," she said before another fit of coughing took her.

The four Maries and I sat in the outer chamber, our embroideries to hand, though we hardly worked a stitch. Jolly Mary kept using her embroidery hoop as a fan.

I was closest to the bedchamber door, Pious Mary closest to the hearth, though it being the end of June there was no fire going. But that was the side on which the fire tools stood.

"What are they saying?" Pretty Mary whispered.

"Hush!" Regal Mary told her.

For the most part the queen and Darnley kept their voices low. We could hear little, though it was not for lack of trying! But all at once their conversation heated up and their voices were raised.

Darnley protested loudly. "I never . . ." he said.

Just as loudly, the queen replied, "The slander has been laid at *your* door, my lord, that the child is Riccio's and not your own."

Pretty Mary's hand went to her mouth.

I stood and started towards them, my fists clenched.

"Sit!" hissed Regal Mary.

Queen Mary's voice got even louder. "God has given me a son begotten by none but you. He is so much your own son, I fear it will be the worse for him hereafter."

"What does she mean?" I whispered.

All four of them rounded on me, fingers to their lips. "Hissssst!"

"Sweet Madam," the king's voice whined, "is this your promise that you made to forgive and forget all?"

"I have forgiven all, but can never forget."

"Madam, these things are all past."

"Then let them go."

Darnley fled the room, whey-faced and shaking. If he noticed us in the outer chamber, he did not so much as nod.

As soon as he had gone, we crowded in to see what the queen might need.

She lay ashen against her pillow. "Pull the curtains, Nicola."

I did it at once. When I turned back to look at her, she had her eyes closed.

"I would sleep till tomorrow or beyond," the queen said.

The Maries hurried out of the room, but I stayed and knelt beside her bed.

"What would you have me do to him, Madam," I whispered to her. "Whatever you ask, I would do and gladly."

But she was already asleep.

As summer gave way to a golden autumn, our Jamie grew into a fat and happy child. He could now almost sit on his own and he loved playing games of peekaboo. He had his own company of violers who fiddled him to sleep.

I adored the wee child. We all did. He had the sweetest disposition—*her* child, not his. But I worried where others did not.

"He shall be spoiled rotten," I told Joseph as he sat with me outside the child's chamber. "Like a fruit too much handled."

"How is that different from any royal child?" Joseph asked.

"If I have a child," I said, "there shall be no spoiling."

Joseph laughed. "You shall be the worst of them all."

Being a father did nothing to change Darnley's ways. In fact he had continued to risk disgrace and scandal at every turn. The strain of his behavior eventually wore down the queen until—in the course of a visit to Jedburgh—she fell dreadfully ill.

The four Maries and I were sent for, and we arrived tightly packed in a single carriage, like threads in a sewing basket.

"How is she?" Regal Mary asked the question for all of us as we were shown up the stairs to the queen's chamber.

The chamberlain who led us said, "She came home from a ride to the Hermitage to see Lord Bothwell and collapsed."

"And you let her ride so far?" Regal Mary asked. "Why, that is over fifty miles the round-trip, man, and she not yet well."

The chamberlain, a storklike figure, shrugged. "She is the queen, my lady. Would you have had me tell her no?"

"I would have!" I said. "Who is the worst fool?"

Pious Mary laid a hand on mine. "Hush, Nicola."

We had reached a landing, but none of us were willing to stop for a breath. We simply followed the long-legged chamberlain as he continued his awful tale. "She was taken to bed swooning and vomiting. For nine days she has lain in her bed unseeing, unable to speak no matter what Dr. Arnault has tried. A priest is standing by to hear her last confession."

"And you only just now sent for us?" I cried.

"God forgive you," Pious Mary said under her breath. "I shall not."

"And the king? Has he come?" asked Regal Mary.

"No, my lady, though we have sent for him." He pointed to a doorway, and we crowded into the small room.

A servant was by a window, starting to open it.

"It is too cold for that," Pretty Mary cried, dashing over to him.

The servant stepped back. "The stench is bad, my lady, and the queen is beyond caring."

"No!" I shouted. "It cannot be true." I turned towards the bed but could scarcely believe that the woman lying there was the queen. Her face was grey, her mouth shut so tightly that I could not distinguish her lips.

"Be quick," Dr. Arnault said, wiping his hands on a towel, "if you would say your farewells."

One by one the Maries knelt by the bed and, weeping, whispered into the queen's ear. She did not so much as move a finger to say she could hear.

"Madam," I said when it was my turn at last, "think of your baby. Think of wee Jamie."

She answered with a groan so awful, I turned to beg the doctor to release her.

But the doctor dropped the towel, crying, "Miracle! A miracle! Out, out, all of you. She still has some life. I must do my work."

The others fled, even the priest and the maids who had been helping the doctor, but I did not.

"Tell me what to do," I said. "And be it ever so bloody, I will do it."

"If you faint, Mademoiselle," he said, "I shall have you removed to the midden heap."

Dr. Arnault had me help bind the queen's limbs tightly with bandages. I did the arms and he her legs from the toes upward.

Then he said, "You must hold her mouth open for me. Do not shrink from what I ask. It will be difficult."

I nodded and sat behind the queen, holding her to my breast.

"Trust me, Majesty," I whispered. "What I do may seem foolish now, but we will laugh about it after." Then I reached around and opened her mouth with ungentle fingers, as one would the resisting jaws of a horse or a cow.

Dr. Arnault poured wine into her gaping mouth, and much slopped over on her nightdress and the bed linen, and me. But still I held her, saying fiercely, "Swim, my queen, swim back to the shore."

She suddenly shuddered in my arms, then threw herself forward and began to vomit up quantities of blood.

"Good, Madam, good," the doctor said.

Good? It did not smell good. It smelled like something long in the grave.

"You will see," the doctor said, as he wiped his hands once again on the same towel. "Now. *Now* she will recover."

"She will," I said, suddenly bursting into tears. "But will my favorite dress?" I looked down at my sodden skirts, once the bright green of spring and now an awful purple.

We both began to laugh loudly, hysterically, and our laughter called back the others.

Upon seeing the queen sitting in a pool of her own vomit, Pious Mary immediately took the filthy sheets away for washing, and the queen's nightgown as well. The other three rolled up their sleeves and began to set the little room to rights.

I wrapped the queen in two blankets. Then the doctor and I

moved her into a different room, where we set her on a mattress next to the fire. I would let no one else near her, and Dr. Arnault agreed. I unwrapped the queen's bandages tenderly and bathed her all over with a soft cloth and warm water till she was as pink and clean as a newborn child.

Only then did I get out of my awful dress and into a clean shift.

Once the queen was entirely well again, and back in Edinburgh, the little prince was baptized. Queen Elizabeth sent a gold font with a little note saying that if the font were too small for the prince, Mary must keep it for her next.

News came that Lord Ruthven had died in England, in a town called Newcastle, having escaped the queen's justice and entered under God's. Those who had fled with him petitioned for forgiveness. Lord James even came personally to plead their cause, saying, "Madam, they must be forgiven if the country is to be united."

"Forgive them? How can I forgive them?" the queen said to me later as she dandled the little prince on her knee. "You saw Davie's wounds. Can you forgive and forget?"

In fact, as she turned from Darnley and anyone else she suspected of having had a hand in Davie's death, she relied increasingly on Bothwell. He alone of the lairds had remained steadfastly loyal.

I tried to like the man. But I found it impossible.

For one thing, I could not stand his looks.

But Davie had been uglier by any measurement, and he had been my great good friend.

So I tried to understand what it was about Bothwell that bothered me.

He was a good few inches shorter than the queen, with a round and swarthy face, and short, bristly hair. He had little piggy eyes.

Piggy eyes? That was it!

Bothwell reminded me of the wild boar that can so cruelly disembowel an unwary hunter with a few, quick, powerful, cruel thrusts of its tusks.

There were many who admired his courage and his leadership; many more who were cowed by his ruthless energy. But no matter whom I asked, there were few who actually cared for him. Not even—the gossips said—his pale young wife, who had been forced to the marriage and then divorced by him.

I said as much to Joseph one time when we were alone in the queen's chamber.

Joseph did not look up from the lute he was tuning, but said in a quiet voice, "Wild boars have their place in nature, Nicola."

"But not, I think, in a queen's bedroom. I think Bothwell would be there if not for the king." I was repeating something I had heard.

"Best not say such a thing aloud," Joseph reminded me. "Not even in jest. Not even to me."

"It is said everywhere already," I pointed out, pacing back and forth before the fire. "And if I cannot say what I think, then how can I do what I must? I am the queen's fool."

"Playing the fool and being a fool are two very different things, Nicola," he said, and looked up. "Promise me you will take care."

"I will take care," I said.

"You must promise." He held out his hand.

I did not hesitate for a moment, but put my hand in his.

In January Darnley fell desperately ill in a common pub in Glasgow, after a night of carousing.

"Do you think it wrong to hope that God will relieve the queen of this unhappy match?" I asked Joseph when the news came. We were walking through the grey winter gardens of Holyrood.

"So you are not yet reconciled to the king?" he teased.

I made a face. *"Reconciled?* He is going behind the queen's back in everything. Why, Mary Beaton says that he has been writing to the pope, asking to be given precedence over the queen as the only true champion of the Catholic faith."

"Rumors have a life of their own," Joseph said. "Do not give them *your* breath as well."

He was so like Davie then, I stuck out my tongue, and he laughed at me. "Sweet Nicola, if God really wanted Darnley to decorate the courts of heaven, He would have taken him by now."

"Heaven? That one? He will not even get as far as the gates."

Laughing, Joseph took my hand and I trembled with the delight of it. Daringly I twined my fingers in his.

Joseph did not look at me, but he did not disengage his hand, either. He continued the conversation as if we were not touching. "Darnley has only a slight case of the pox and lies in Glasgow already on the mend. Perhaps we should be thankful. If the queen were free of this one, she might make an even worse marriage."

"Surely *that* is not possible," I said, raising my eyebrows.

"Surely *anything* is possible." Joseph looked serious. "There are many lords who would be only too happy to be king. Including your beloved Bothwell. What a stir that would be among those sharp-taloned hawks."

"A chicken fight more likely," I said, and we both laughed.

The wind sharpened, so we turned back towards the palace, still hand in hand.

Joseph said, "It probably galls them that the queen has softened towards the king now that she has visited his sickbed."

The queen at Darnley's sickbed. I suddenly shuddered, not only from the wind, and pulled my hand from Joseph's to set my cape tighter around me. "I thought she was off hunting in Fife. Or playing golf there. Surely she cannot possibly be deceived by him again."

Joseph shrugged. "She is not just a queen, but a woman as well. A woman is guided by her heart as much as her head."

I stopped and turned to look at him straight on. "Joseph! How can you say such a thing? She is *queen* first."

He shrugged again. "In this country, people change their minds as often as they change their clothing. One day they are high-ranking councilors, next in exile, then back in court again. The king has been involved in scandal, treason, and . . ." He hesitated and got a faraway look in his eye. "And murder."

I longed to embrace him, to help him over the hump of horror. But before I could act on my thought, he had come back again from whatever far country he was visiting.

"The queen is having Darnley moved back to Edinburgh, where she can nurse him personally," he said.

My mind was suddenly filled with images of the queen tending first the ailing Francis, then Darnley.

"Oh, no, Joseph," I whispered hoarsely. "Dangerous times are come again."

"You are the court fool," Joseph said with a laugh. "Not the court soothsayer." Suddenly he leaned forward, as if to kiss me on the lips.

The awful taste of Darnley's tongue in my mouth thrust itself brutally into my memory. Much as I wanted Joseph's kiss, I ducked away and ran off, suddenly afraid of my own wishes.

35 ❧ KIRK O'FIELD

Much to my dismay, Darnley arrived back in Edinburgh on the first day of February, carried by horse litter. At his own request he was lodged in a substantial house on a square known as Kirk o'Field. It was a house often used for convalescents, for it had good air. Joseph told me there was a particularly broad and pleasant garden there.

"You might even enjoy it," he teased.

I looked out of the window at my own little garden below. "Not as long as Darnley lies within," I said bitterly.

Typically, Darnley complained about every aspect of his quarters until a small army of servants began ferrying comforts up the hilly streets from Holyrood: carpets, cushions, chairs, tables, tapestries, and his favorite bed—an ostentatious thing hung with violet-brown velvet and trimmed with cloth of gold.

The queen stayed on at Holyrood with the little prince, who was safe there from any infection, but she visited Darnley every day, even staying the night twice in a downstairs room on a small bed of yellow and green damask.

I was glad not to be asked along.

The eighth day of Darnley's convalescence was a Sunday. One of the queen's favorite valets, the Frenchman Bastian de Pages, had been married that day, and there was so much jollity, it was possible to forget all about the ailing king. At least we should have done so had not the queen made a point of remembering him.

"Since my lord is not well enough to join us, we must take the festivities to him," she announced.

There was an immediate silence and more than one sour face. Mine included.

What if she should fall in love with Darnley again? I thought. *The sickbed had proved a powerful love token for her before.*

"Come, come," said the queen, "we can make happy faces there as here. And think how it will please the king."

And if we do not, I added silently, *it will give him something else to sulk about.*

The queen and her attendants mounted horses and set off down the winding lane while I followed with the entertainers and musicians. People stopped to clap as we wound our way through the streets of Edinburgh in our gaudy party clothes. More than once we dawdled to play a tune, and I was roundly cheered when I sang a rouser about the great hero Wallace. In fact, the good humor of the people on the streets almost made me forget our mission.

By the time we got to Kirk o'Field, the house was full. Company filled every room, dicing and drinking.

Darnley lay on the bed, his head on a white satin pillow. His face was covered by a taffeta mask to hide the disfiguring pox. I was secretly pleased to note he had lost much of his golden hair.

Close by the bed was a small table, and next to it a high-backed chair covered with the same violet-brown velvet as the bed. Some few feet away stood a bath covered now by an oaken door. Frequent bathing was a vital part of his cure. This left but little space for revelers.

When we arrived, Joseph was immediately summoned by the queen to play upon his lute. Seeing him, Darnley turned sharply away, groaning and clutching his belly.

A bad conscience leads to a bad stomach, I thought, something Papa used to say.

Angel that he was, Joseph merely shrugged off Darnley's rudeness. Still it took little to sense the king's fear even through the taffeta mask.

"Play on, Joseph," the queen instructed, and Joseph played. His touch was never as lilting as his brother's, but it had a raw power of its own.

Lord Bothwell arrived soon after we did, a dark figure keeping company with his wineglass more than with the other revelers. As the evening drew in, he strode over to the king's bed, where the queen was sitting.

"Madam," he reminded her, "you promised Bastian to be at the castle for the masquerade. You are not one to forfeit your promises."

The king snorted at that, and the taffeta mask rippled.

As if Darnley's response was some sort of signal, the queen stood. "We will go," she said.

When she stood, so did everyone else in the room except the king, and soon the whole company began to file out.

The queen stopped to give Darnley a ring to comfort him for her absence, and passed a few more words with him. I waited for her in the doorway, reluctant to leave without her.

Once again I was in position to overhear things I shouldn't. But as dear Maman had once said, *Once in the ear, twice in the heart.* I do not think she meant it for eavesdropping.

"Is it true Morton has returned to Scotland?" Darnley asked.

For a moment the queen was unable to meet his gaze. Morton

had been one of those known to have colluded in Davie's murder, fleeing to England with Ruthven. It was said that he bore a grudge against Darnley for betraying the conspiracy.

"He had a hand in *yon foul fact,* you know," the king added. He never spoke of the "murder" directly. It astonished me that he talked as if he'd had no part in it himself.

Such astonishment may have been in the queen's mind, too, for she took a long time to respond. At last she said, "Morton's pardon was necessary. Lord James insisted the old wounds be healed."

"*Insisted?* But you are the queen, Madam," Darnley said. "And I am the king. And they are . . ."

"It is done."

He put a hand out to her.

"I must go," she said.

"Why, Mary? Why must you leave?" His voice rose to an unbecoming whine. "For a mere servant's wedding. When your wedded lord lies here so sick—and lonely. Once you cared for me like an angel."

"I go because I promised a *loyal* servant I would," she said.

And I thought: *Take that in your cheating mouth, you knave, and swallow it!* And then I smiled.

Darnley propped himself up on one elbow, which caused the taffeta mask to slip. The discolorations on his face looked less like pox and more like the poxie, or love disease. "You must beware, Mary. Our noble friends intend to make mischief between us."

You hardly need any help with that, I reflected silently.

"Do not upset yourself so," said the queen, pushing him gently back against the pillow. "In the morning, you will move to Holyrood and all will be well." She blew him a kiss and went out the door, passing me in a cascade of silk.

I followed behind her, saying, "Any man may step in a bear tra[p] once, Madam, but only a madman does so twice."

She did not look back at me. "Whatever he has done," she sai[d] "I married him willingly, so I am as much to blame. Besides, th[e] church allows for no divorce."

"You have asked me to remind you, Majesty, that you are n[ot] god to make a bad man good. You are but a . . ."

"I need no reminding," she said, cutting me off.

What good is it, I thought, *to be told you have the queen's e[ar] when she does not listen?*

We walked down the stairs and on through the rest of th[e] house in the kind of silence that happens between enemies, n[ot] friends.

But once we emerged into the square, she suddenly threw o[ff] that mood and began to chatter about the masquerade.

I chattered back happily, glad to be away from that house th[at] was so thoroughly infected with *Darnley*.

It was quite dark now, but pages were standing by with torche[s] Bothwell's manservant, Paris, helped the queen into the saddle. A[s] he stepped back, I saw by the torchlight that his clothes were b[e] grimed with dirt and black powder. It was odd that he should be s[o] dirty and still be allowed to touch the queen.

"Your master has not made a miner of you, has he?" I joked.

Paris flinched but the queen laughed at my jest.

"He *is* a mucky cur," Bothwell commented laconically. "I sha[ll] toss him in the river later to see if that will make him clean."

At the palace the partying went on until late. I sang an[d] danced—most of the time with Joseph. His arms about my wais[t] his hand on mine in public, brought a flush to my face. I came in for much teasing from the Maries and from the queen, too.

But by the time the newlyweds retired to their chamber—amidst much ribald joking—the queen looked exhausted.

"May I help you to your room, Madam," I said.

Noting my flushed and happy face, she shook her head. "The Maries will help me. Take to your own room, child. I will not need you tonight."

Joseph and I walked for about an hour more, through the palace corridors, mostly talking about our childhoods. But at last my eyelids were fluttering closed even as we spoke.

"I will see you on the morrow," he said, taking me to my room.

He opened the door and I turned to say good night. But before I could open my mouth, he leaned over and put a kiss on my forehead, so light that it might have been the touch of a moth's wing.

I looked up at him for a moment, then without speaking, I ran into the room and flung myself on my bed. I heard the quiet *snick* of the door as he closed it, the sharp *tip-tap* of his footsteps as he moved away down the hall.

In spite of being tired, I was suddenly in no mood to sleep. The very air seemed charged. I could still feel Joseph's kiss on my forehead, burning like a brand.

Air, I thought. *I need air.* I went over to my window and opened the shutters, but it was not enough.

So I left my room and went down the stairs and outside, feeling giddy and wild. Standing by the doorway, I could hear isolated voices laughing and singing snatches of earthy songs. The party had not ended entirely. I put my hand to my forehead and once again could feel Joseph's kiss there.

But suddenly I shivered. It had turned cold, as Scottish nights often do, and I was not dressed for the weather.

I thought that if *I* could not sleep, perhaps the queen could not sleep, either, though for different reasons. After all, the confrontation with her husband had not been pleasant. And if she was still awake, I could apologize for all my sour back talk.

So I went back inside, up the stairs, and down the long corridors towards her rooms.

When I got there, however, I heard voices from inside, the loudest of which I could not fail to recognize.

"Speak plain, woman!" It was Lord Bothwell. "Will you be done with him or no?"

What is he doing in her rooms so late? I wondered.

"Why do you press me so?" the queen pleaded, like a child to a scolding schoolmaster. "What can I do but make the best of this burdensome situation and pray to God to deliver me, for you know I can never divorce him."

Bothwell made a disgusted noise, as though spitting out a piece of bad meat. "God is deaf to those who will not shift for themselves."

Suddenly his footsteps approached the door and I darted down the stairs, squeezing into an alcove to hide. When his steps died away, I came out from hiding and went back up.

As I prepared to knock, I heard weeping from within. Would I upset the queen further by intruding? Clearly she needed me now. But just as clearly I did not dare go in.

So I sank down by the door, struggling to stay alert. The cold stone floor sent a chill through me that at first kept me lively. But it had been a long day and, in spite of my best efforts, I was soon a-drowse, remembering Joseph's kiss as if in a dream.

The sudden opening of the door at my back jolted me awake. When I looked up, the queen was standing over me, as startled to see me there as I was to see her.

Jumping to my feet, I tried to present a seemly face to her.

"Nicola," she said, "what *are* you doing here?"

I had no answer. The truth was I had no idea why I was there.

"I thought . . . I thought you might need me, Madam," I answered lamely. "But I did not want to disturb you if you slept."

The queen regarded me curiously. "How could you know?" she said, as much to herself as to me.

"Know what, Madam?" I asked.

The smile she gave me was wan, as if she were trying to put a brave face on a troubled heart. "Come in, Nicola. I have a task for you. Surely *this* is the reason God preserved you from the river when your mother and father died. *This* is the moment—more than the comfort at Amboise, more than scaling down from my window, more than the flight in the night from Holyrood—for which you were sent to me. You are here tonight to save the life of one appointed by God, a life which no man has the right to take."

36 ❦ DEATH IN THE NIGHT

I followed her into the bedchamber, nervous and eager in equal measure. She opened a drawer in her bedside table, handing me a small diamond-studded crucifix that she had carried from France.

"I know the hour is late, but please take this to Kirk o'Field and give it to the king," she said. "Let it protect him through the night until he comes safe to Holyrood in the morning."

Protect him? I thought. *I would rather slay him for all he had done to my sweet queen.* I did not say this, of course, but instead asked, "Should I carry so valuable a thing through the city late at night, Madam? What of robbers? What of footpads? I will be a girl alone."

"My grandmother gave me this when I was very sick," the queen explained. "I have always been certain it summoned angels from heaven to protect me. It will protect you as well, Nicola."

On the way there, perhaps, I thought. *But once given, how will it protect me in Darnley's presence? Or on the way home?*

"The crucifix is very beautiful indeed, Madam," I said. "But surely the king is in no danger now."

It was as if she had not heard me. "I did not know who else to entrust this mission to. And then God sent me you."

"Are you sure you want *me* to be the messenger?"

"Who in all the court should the king trust better, Nicola? Without you, we would both have been dead a year past."

"I will do all I can for your safety, Madam. You know that." I placed the cross around my neck and started to leave.

"It has grown cold outside, Nicola." She fetched one of her fur-lined cloaks from the wardrobe and wrapped it round my shoulders.

It was much too long of course, but I felt quite the royal lady until I caught sight of myself in the mirror. *This will surely bring out the footpads,* I thought. Still, I could not fail the queen, who asked so little of me, so I bowed low to her. She patted my head and then kissed me on the brow, in the very same place where Joseph's kiss lay.

Hurrying through the night city, I held the cloak tightly about me. Once I lost my way in the dark. Closes and lanes and wynds seemed to rise up and plunge away again, twisting around each other like overgrown vines. But a partial moon finally enabled me to mark out a few familiar places—like Cowgate—and so I went safely on.

At last I saw the Kirk o'Field square, and headed straight for it. Before I could set foot in the open, I caught sight of two men huddled in the shadows by the king's dwelling. The moment they spied me, they vanished into the shadows like accomplished thieves.

How queer, I thought. *Why did they not come forward to rob me, a mere girl without the protection of an armed man?*

I paused to see if they would reappear, but when they did not, I drew in a deep breath and started quickly across the square.

Just then the door of the king's house opened and Lord Bothwell stepped out into the street, a pistol stuffed into his belt and a long dagger at his side.

I made a sound then, between a scream and a sigh of relief.

He turned, saw me, and his boar's eyes narrowed. He did not look pleased.

I thought to run off into the shadows then, but my arms were suddenly gripped from behind and I was dragged off, kicking at my abductors, into a dark alley.

This time I did scream, or at least I tried to, but a hand clapped down over my mouth. Twisting my head around, I saw that it was Bothwell's servant, Paris, who held me so tight. Another man stood by, his face hidden by a hood.

Suddenly Bothwell himself loomed over me. "Girl, what stupid fancy has brought you out here this night of all nights?"

Paris lifted his hand from my mouth so that I could answer. My voice squeaked with fear. "I am on an errand for the queen."

"As am I," he responded. "And I will tolerate no interference."

"I plan no interference, my lord," I managed to say. "Just give me leave to deliver my message and I will be gone."

"Is it done?" asked the man in the hood.

Bothwell nodded. "The fuses are lit. In a few minutes it will be over." He turned back to Paris. "You know what needs doing. So do it—and quickly."

"No," interrupted the hooded man, "She is just a girl. And on the queen's errand."

"Is she any less dangerous for that?"

They glared at each other, with Paris caught uncertainly in the middle. For a moment, his grip slackened. I took the chance and tore myself from his grasp, leaving the fur-lined cape in his hands.

I ran wildly, without thought, fear nipping like a wolf at my heels. When I reached the edge of the square, I was suddenly confronted by three more men. I drew in a ragged breath and looked around for some avenue of escape.

"Take her!" Bothwell called after them.

I swerved away and dashed back towards the king's house as fast as my legs could carry me.

Bothwell cursed and I heard several pairs of feet pounding behind me. Not daring to look back, I ran for the door, flung it open, hurled myself inside, and slammed the door behind. In the fading firelight from the hearth, I saw a small chair. Grabbing it, I jammed it under the door's handle.

Then hands on knees and breathing in great gasps, I tried to think. *Why are they chasing me? What had they said?*

Fuses!

Oh, dear Lord!

I had jumped out of the skillet, into the fireplace.

"Your Majesty!" I cried out. "Your Majesty!"

A servant's sleepy groan answered me, so I ran up the stairs to Darnley's room and burst in noisily. He leaped out of bed, almost tumbling into the open bath. His servant Taylor, who slept at his bedfoot, was awakened as well.

"What?" Darnley cried. "What is going on?"

"Murderers, Your Majesty," I gasped. "Assassins. At least half a dozen of them outside. They have set fuses."

"Fuses?" He repeated. "Do you mean gunpowder?"

"Gunpowder, yes!" *Why is the man so slow?* "The fuses are already lit." *I could kill him myself.* "We must leave this place at once, but not by the front door."

"But why?"

God's wounds, would he not stop talking and move.

"There are men outside the door and armed."

"Armed?" he echoed again. "Then how am I to escape?"

I—not we—he gives no thought to Taylor or me.

Taylor's eyes searched the room that was made shadowy by the flickering of the dying fire.

"Over there, sir," he said. With remarkable presence of mind he snatched up a piece of rope, tied it to a window rail, then dropped it over the side.

His nightgown flapping about his legs, Darnley climbed over the rail and began to slide down the rope. Grabbing a cloak for his master and a dagger to defend him with, Taylor started after him.

I had no option but to follow and hope we could all get clear before the place exploded.

When I was but halfway down the rope, I twisted around and saw Darnley running across the garden with Taylor at his heels. Before they got to the far gate, a half-dozen men jumped from hiding on all sides and grabbed them.

"Mercy!" the king cried.

But they were without any mercy, and one of the men whipped a cord round the king's throat. Taylor lashed out with his dagger but was quickly wrestled to the ground, and strangled as brutally as his master.

Dangling from the rope, the cold wind buffeting me from side to side, I was too frozen with horror to move. Had my wishing killed the king? But I had not wished Taylor dead, and there he lay in the garden by his master's side.

And what of the other servants in the house? Surely I had to go back and warn them as well.

Do I have time?

My cold hands gripped the rope and I tried to shift upward.

Suddenly the knot came loose under my weight, and I was dropped the last few feet to the ground. I landed in a heap on the brittle grass and for a moment lay there, stunned.

Any bones broken?

Then, not waiting for an answer, I scrambled, frightened, to my feet. I was terrified. Had my fall been heard? If so, I had to get away at once. Only . . .

Which way?

I feared the rope around my neck more than any blast of gunpowder. It seemed more real. So I raced away from the garden, that place of quick death, and around the side of the house, where I ran headlong into a man who was every bit as solid as a wall.

"You are serving your mistress ill this night," Bothwell said, drawing his long knife. "She demanded this favor of me, with her heart if not her lips, and I cannot let you betray us."

I stared at the knife and suddenly remembered Davie's poor body and all its bloody wounds. I tried to move but could not. All I could do was scream.

But my cry was drowned out by a massive detonation as the house exploded with a noise like the end of the earth. The force of the blast knocked us both off our feet. Clouds of dust and shards of splintered stone flew everywhere. Desperately I rolled away, then stood and ran blindly through the smoke and the dust and the shattered brickwork, coughing and vomiting as I ran.

37 ⮑ REFUGE

Bothwell bellowed a command and, when I risked a backward glance, I saw three men chasing after me. I knew they meant to silence me, and I pelted down the street, crying loudly.

"Help! Help me!" I called, my voice echoing in the stone canyons of the streets as I ran. A few of the houses came blearily awake with lighted candles.

I did not dare stop running. To ask for refuge would give my pursuers all the time they needed. So I ran on, into the maze of twisting streets that snaked over the steep hills.

At last a pain stabbed though my side and I collapsed against a wall, sucking in a burning breath. A part of my mind was yelling at me to keep moving, but my body refused to listen. I was dizzy with running, my ears still ringing from the blast.

"Which way did she go?" I heard a voice call behind me.

"There, over there!" answered another.

I lurched back into motion again, feeling as if my insides were about to burst.

As I rushed along the deserted roads, the footfalls of my pursuers got closer. Or was it the pounding of my blood in my ears? I dared not stop to figure it out.

Then I saw a dark shadow coming towards me, a single candle like a star in its hand.

Towards me, not behind!

I tried to call for help, but only a rasping breath came from my lips as I pitched forward at the shadow's feet, my knees scraping on the cobbles.

A large hand took me by the arm and helped me up. The candlelight passed over my eyes, blinding me.

"I know that face, do I not?" said a dour but familiar voice. "I have seen ye many times passing in the queen's retinue, singing verses not fit for a lass's ears never mind her lips."

I looked up into the frowning features of John Knox.

"I remember now," he said. "Yer the queen's own fool."

He released my arm as Bothwell's men came charging up to us. They skidded to a sudden halt before him.

"What manner of men are ye that pursue a wee girl through the streets at this hour?" Knox's voice rang out as though he were addressing a church full of people and not three armed men.

The men looked at one other in confusion. Obviously they recognized him and were doubtful about how to proceed.

One who wore a black bonnet stepped forward, making an unconvincing show of dignity. "She is an escaped thief, sir," he said, pointing at me. "We must take her to the sheriff."

"Is it true, girl? Are ye a thief as well as a fool?" Knox asked.

I took a gulp of breath and shook my head. "I snatched my life from their knives and their gunpowder, sir." I thought better of mentioning the king's death till I could find out what it would mean for the queen. Whatever he was, Knox was no friend of hers.

"She lies," black bonnet said.

"Then what is she accused of stealing?" Knox's voice was loud. It seemed he had only the one way of speaking.

"We know not the details, only that she must be taken," the man said, stretching an arm to grab me, but Knox drew himself up and interposed his tall crow's body between us.

"This toon is awakened by a loud crack and when I come out to learn what is afoot, I find it the hand of man and not God that has done this terrible thing. Then ye loons come running fully armed in pursuit of a lass!" Knox did not moderate his voice, and all about us, house lights flickered on. "A lass!" He let the words speak volumes. "Beware, for the just God knows what we do and why we do it." He raised his hand and pointed up towards the heavens.

The men glanced up nervously, as if God's all-seeing eye might even then be scrutinizing their guilt.

"Our orders, sir," black bonnet began, but his voice died away before Knox's hard countenance.

"I will take her into my ain custody," Knox said. "If she be guilty of a crime, I will bring her to justice. Ye hae my word on it."

They gave way before him as though confronted by a force of nature, cowed simply by the power of his voice. If God Himself had spoken, I doubt they would have retreated more quickly.

Once they were gone, Knox returned his attention to me.

"Have ye escaped at last from that den of vice and iniquity?"

"From the king's house, you mean?"

"Nae, girl, from the court of our idolatrous queen," he boomed. "Is that why those cutthroats are chasing ye? To haul ye back?"

I stared at him, but my breathlessness gave me sufficient excuse not to answer. He took me by the arm again, but not at all roughly, and led me into Trunk Lane near the High Street.

"This be my manse," he said, taking out a key and unlocking the door of a large house. He motioned me inside.

In the front room before a blazing fire, a girl scarcely older than me was pacing the floor with a baby over her shoulder. The baby's eyes were fluttering but it was still fighting to stay awake.

"How is she?" Knox asked, closing the door after him. His voice was suddenly sweet and low with concern.

The girl put a finger to her lips. "Hssst, John, she is almost dropped off. Dinna ye be waking her. And who is this ye have brought home now? Another waif? Though not poor, by her dress."

"This lass was being pursued through the streets by ruffians," Knox explained. "Whether she be guilty of aught, I dinna know. But one thing I do know: There be all manner of mischief afoot tonight."

"What mean ye, John? And what was that noise?"

"Gunpowder," I answered without thinking. "An explosion."

Knox fixed his gaze upon me. "And what do ye know of it?"

"Only what I heard said on the street," I said quickly.

Knox frowned. He knew as well as I that the only ones on the street this late at night were evildoers and . . .

And me! I shivered, having been caught so easily in a lie. I resolved to hold my tongue, for the queen's sake, if not for my own.

Knox's frown deepened. "Lass, ye will stay here with my wife, Margaret, while I discover what haunts the streets."

His wife? Surely not! Knox was fifty years or more and his wife more like my own age. I had supposed her the maid or the baby's wet nurse or a daughter come home with her own infant. But I schooled my face. I would not embarrass the man who had saved me.

"Thank you," I said, my gratitude genuine.

When the door shut behind him, I turned back to Margaret. The baby was now sound asleep on her mother's shoulder, a bubble of milk on her pretty mouth.

"Come," Margaret said, "I'll find ye a bed for the night."

As I followed her to the back of the house, through the long dark hallway, I thought that she looked and sounded as if she came from an upper-class family. Strange, then, that she should be wed to the old preacher.

But perhaps no stranger, came the answering thought, *than my own Queen Mary should have married such weak kings.*

In the morning one of Knox's sons brought me a plain white bowl of water to wash in, then took me back to the kitchen to join the family for breakfast in a crowded, low-ceilinged room made graceful by daylight.

I bowed my head with the rest of them as Knox said a lengthy grace. Then we set to our salted porridge and oatcakes.

No one spoke, not even to mention the explosion.

How can they just sit in silence? I wondered. *Even pigs at the trough say more.*

I was desperate to learn what Knox had discovered. So by way of opening a conversation, I said, "The sun seems to be shining this morning after so foul a night."

Margaret and the boys lowered their eyes.

"We dinna converse at the table," Knox informed me. "Our thoughts should be filled with gratitude to God for all His gifts. Besides, idle talk interferes with the digestion."

I finished my breakfast in silence.

When the interminable meal was done, Knox summoned me to the dark-paneled front room, where he gestured for me to sit down opposite him on a straight-backed chair.

"This be what I learned last night," he said.

At last, I thought, leaning towards him.

"The king's house was blown up, and he and a servant were found dead in the garden with no mark of fire or bullet or knife upon them." While he spoke, he kept his flinty eyes on my face. "The queen's cloak was discovered nearby."

I did my best not to reveal what was running through my mind.

"Do you know who was responsible?" I asked.

"Do *ye?*" He raised one bushy grey eyebrow.

My head pounded. Part of me wanted to confess all. But the other part of me held back, thinking. I knew that Knox had been the queen's enemy for years. I was certain that all he wanted from me was information he could use against her. But if I accused Bothwell, I might also bring danger to the queen.

"I know nothing," I said.

"Liars be the de'ils disciples," Knox warned me. "Ye have lied to me once already, lass. We both know it. So say it plain—why were those armed men chasing ye last night?"

I could feel my cheeks flush. *Take care, Nicola,* I warned myself. *Speak plain, but with the wisdom of the fool.* "I bumped into them in the street," I said. "They asked me for things I am ashamed to describe. So I fled and they chased after, accusing me of theft." I looked directly into Knox's eyes as I spoke, hoping to make him believe me.

Knox made a tsk sound with his tongue and clasped his hands over the beard that was like a cover on his chest. "Yer story sounds closer to the truth than theirs, but by how much I canna say." He closed his eyes for a minute, deep in thought. When he opened them again he glared at me. "So ye know nothing of this murder of the king?"

"Nor any murder at all," I maintained. "Not the king's or David Riccio's or anyone else's." I was so nervous in the old crow's presence, that for all my warnings to myself, my tongue began to run away with me.

"Aye, yon scoundrel Riccio. He richly deserved his fate."

I could hardly contain my outrage. "How can you say that, sir. He was the queen's secretary and a faithful servant." *And my dearest friend,* I added, but only to myself.

Knox appeared surprised by my outburst. "He was a spy and a plotter."

"A spy? Davie?"

"Are ye truly such an innocent, lass? Will ye fight God's own truth? Yer Davie was an agent sent by the pope to destroy the reformed religion and set idolatry up in its place once more." Righteous fury flamed from his eyes and I had to look away.

Fato, I thought. A wild fate had deposited me in the home of the queen's greatest enemy. I could only save her now by remaining mute, like the girl who sewed nettles into shirts in the fairy tale. I set my lips together, prepared to say nothing more.

Just then there was a knock at the front door. One of the boys answered it and came to the study.

"Father," he said, "Master Donald is here along with Master Gordon. They must talk to ye on a matter of some urgency."

Knox rose. "Tell them I will be with them presently." Then he turned to me. "I think we will have much more to say of this later." He shut the door on me but neglected to lock it.

I waited until his footsteps had receded, then made my way quietly to the back of the house and down a dark corridor and past the sunlit kitchen where Margaret was busy kneading bread and talking in baby talk to her little girl.

I knew there had to be another way out of the house. Knox's house was no place for a Catholic on a day when there was conspiracy and murder in the air. I might make an easy scapegoat, and then there would be no one to bear witness to my innocence except the queen.

Finally I found the door, a black oak barrier with a single latch. I lifted the latch and escaped into a small walled garden. But I knew how to climb walls, and a scraped knee notwithstanding, I was soon over it and into a twisting lane, and free.

38 ❧ SAFETY

Instead of going directly to the palace, I found myself drawn back to Kirk o'Field. I kept to the side streets and wynds, till I came to the square. From one of the lanes, I stared at the place where the king's house had stood and shivered, though the morning sun was warm.

There was nothing left of the king's house but a heap of rubble and a scattering of bricks. What furniture or hangings might have survived were gone already, picked clean by human scavengers. But the bitter stink of gunpowder still clung to the air.

If I had been but a minute longer dangling on the rope, I would have been rubble as well. A minute sooner in the garden, and I would have been strangled alongside the king.

Such a crowd was gathered—hawkers selling pies and pastries, peddlers offering their wares. It was like a holy day fair. A line of soldiers held the townspeople back from the garden while some officials strode about as if they knew what they were doing.

On the edge of the crowd I spotted a familiar head of curly hair and I edged over to him, taking care not to be seen by the guards.

When he saw me, Joseph's face lit up with incredible relief. Taking me by the arm, he led me quickly away, back to that same small alley. His arms went around me.

"Nicola, little fool, we all feared the worst," he said, his voice trembling. "The queen sent me to look for you. My heart . . ." He hesitated, looked deeply into my eyes. "My heart was in pieces, like the house." His arms were trembling, too.

"I saw what happened," I told him. "Last night. I saw it all."

He moved us further into the shadows made by the overhanging wood balconies. "Speak softly, darling Nicola. I doubt we have come to the end of this business."

"Lord Bothwell was here," I whispered. "He lit the fuses himself! I warned the king to flee, but they caught him in the garden. And his man, Taylor."

"You saw that?"

I nodded.

"Where have you been since? All night we worried."

"Would you believe in the house of John Knox? He saved me from Bothwell's assassins."

Someone ran past the alley, towards the crowd, and we shrank back even further into the shadows.

Joseph shook his head. "Fortune chooses strange helpmates."

"I do not think we can look to the old crow for any further help, Joseph. He would have me curse the queen and leave her."

"Poor lady," whispered Joseph sadly. "In the middle of the night, when the news came about the explosion, the four Maries were convinced that the queen, too, was to have been blown up. They routed me from my bed and told me, and as it seemed likely, we warned the queen. She has taken the child and fled to the safety of Edinburgh Castle."

I shook my head and pulled away from him. "I do not know what to think, Joseph. She sent me to Darnley with a token to keep him safe. But safe from what? Safe from whom? Did she suspect? Did she know? Oh, Joseph, my poor head is roiling with bad thoughts." I put both hands to my temples.

Joseph looked at me oddly. "It was only by the grace of God the queen did not sleep at Kirk o'Field last night. The grace of God and a servant's wedding. You know that."

I bit my lip so hard, I drew blood. "Joseph—I am certain it was Darnley alone they intended to kill, though they blew up the whole house . . ." I sighed deeply. "A cannon to kill a flea."

"No evidence," said Joseph. "And no witnesses."

"None but me."

We stood apart from one another, our backs against the same crumbling stone wall, both thinking furiously.

"Servants in another part of the house were killed in the explosion, Nicola," Joseph said at last. "The cook and several potboys."

I crossed myself at the thought of those innocents. "I must go to the queen, Joseph. I must tell her what happened. I must find out what *she* knows."

"No," Joseph said, turning towards me. He put his hand on my arm. "I forbid it."

"How can you forbid . . ." I stopped when I saw the concern in his eyes.

"Bothwell's men are everywhere. He says it is to protect the queen, but now I think he is waiting to seize you if you return, for you are a witness."

I was near to tears. "But surely no harm will come to me once I am under the queen's protection."

"So my brother thought, Nicola."

I started to tremble violently and Joseph put his arms around me. We stood together, breast to breast, without speaking. Without feeling the need to speak.

Suddenly there were shouts from the crowd.

"Look!" cried one man, then another. "Look what they have!"

A woman screamed, a high horrible keening that went on and on.

Joseph stepped out of the alley to find out what had caused the excitement. It seemed forever before he returned.

"Two more bodies, Nicola. Dug out of the ruin. They have been laid out on boards and are being carried into a nearby house. You do not want to see. They look like . . . like meat too long on a spit."

I shuddered again, then wiped the tears from my face.

"We must get you away from here immediately. It is not safe," Joseph said.

Just then two men walked by the alley and one said in a clear voice as they passed, "Who would do such a thing to that braw laddie, the bonnie king?"

"Who do ye think?" his companion answered. "Her that took him to her bed has seen him to his grave. They found her cloak."

Nearby a minstrel tuned his instrument and hazarded the first few lines of a ballad he called "The Tragedy o' the Bonnie King."

I stiffened with astonishment. "Fickle hearts and feckless souls," I whispered to Joseph when they were well past. "One would hardly believe how much Darnley was loathed while alive."

"Death can turn things topsy-turvy," Joseph replied.

"Joseph, if I cannot go to the queen, you must. Tell her what I saw."

"Speak out against Bothwell? When he is the queen's closest advisor and I but a secretary and a foreigner to boot." He shook his head. "No, Nicola, no! It would be suicide. And for nothing."

I put my hand on his. "But you would be telling the truth."

"I would be repeating the tale of the court fool, whose only function is to make others laugh." Joseph made a face. "What is more, that fool is a girl, a foreigner, and a Catholic."

"Joseph, you cannot be so . . . fainthearted." For a moment, I despised him for being so cautious with so much at stake.

"I am *not* being fainthearted, Nicola. I am being sane in an insane realm. There are already murmurs that this assassination is the work of the queen's French and Italian attendants."

"But that makes no sense at all!" I cried, flinging myself back against the wall.

"If a vengeful mob comes to drag me to the block, I will be sure to tell them so," he whispered fiercely.

I let my shoulders slump. "Then what can we do?"

"If Bothwell can be separated from the queen and his hold on the court broken, then it may be safe for you to return."

"And when will that be?" I suddenly thought: *Davie would have made such a thing happen, not just waited for justice to take its own course.* Then I remembered that Davie had died for such meddling.

Joseph's comforting hand rested on my shoulder. "Many already suspect Bothwell. Let the matter come to open court, and then you can step forward." He turned me round to face him. "In the meantime we must get you to safety."

I straightened my shoulders. "What would you have me do?"

He thought a moment. "Meet me near the market cross at noon tomorrow. In the meantime stay out of sight."

"Give the queen this," I said, slipping the crucifix over my head. "Say I was unable to deliver it, but at least it kept *me* safe."

Joseph put it back over my head and kissed me on the brow. "Let it keep you safe still," he said.

I found a deserted spot by the north wall of the city, below the brooding castle crag. Very few folk passed. Those who did gave me but a passing glance.

I waited and I tried not to think, but there was nothing to do *but* think.

I thought about the queen and her wish that Darnley have her crucifix on that night of all nights.

I thought about Bothwell, who had said the queen wanted Darnley dead though she'd not said so aloud.

I thought about Joseph's arms around me, and the full silence between us.

Then the sun was overhead, so I knew it was noon. I picked my way slowly, carefully, through the small hidden wynds to the market cross.

To my disappointment, it was not Joseph who awaited me there but Pious Mary. She had a cape and hood pulled up over her head and one under her arm for me.

"Put this on quickly and follow me," she said with quiet intensity. "No talking till we are there. We go straight into the face of danger."

She led me through back alleyways and—though I was dying to question her—I did not speak. Partly I was quiet out of fear. Partly I was trying to keep up, for she set us a fast pace.

At last, on a small street that ran up to the Royal Mile, in front of a rather substantial stone house, she turned to me. "Here is where you will be safe, Nicola. Master and Mistress Carwood have agreed to take you in," she said in a low voice.

For the first time since we had begun our mazed travels, I felt a bit of relief.

We went around to the back door, like beggars or tradesmen, and Pious Mary said in a low voice, "You know their eldest daughter."

"Do you mean Margaret Carwood? The queen's bedchamber woman?" I asked in the same low tone.

Mary rapped on the door. "The same. Their younger daughter died of a fever last year and it is her room that will be yours."

I put a hand on her arm. "Why are they doing this for me?"

"They are doing it for the queen."

The door was opened by a round-faced woman who looked little like the elegant Margaret. But she had Margaret's same clipped pattern of speech. "Come in, come in quickly, my dears."

She led us to an upstairs chamber in which a bed with serge cover and curtains, a bedside table, a large blanket chest, and a wardrobe were all of the furnishings. A picture of Our Lady hung over the bed and I was almost in tears when I saw it. I crossed myself.

Mistress Carwood watched me carefully, her head cocked to one side like a plump little sparrow. "You are just our dear child's size," she said at last. And taking out a simple dark blue woolen dress from the wardrobe and handing it to me, said: "Pray wear this instead of . . ."

She did not have to tell me how awful my own dress looked.

"Are you certain, Mistress Carwood?"

"It will honor my dear daughter's memory, Nicola," she said.

Pious Mary must have instructed the Carwoods to be discreet, for they never asked specifically why I was in hiding, though I remained for the rest of February into the middle of April. It was enough for them that I was a friend of the queen's.

Joseph visited when he could, but was always wary of being followed by Bothwell's spies. Each time he came—once early in the morning, but the other times long past ten o'clock at night—he brought news, and none of it good.

"Immediately following the king's murder," he said, "placards were set up accusing Bothwell."

"Set up where?" I asked.

"Nailed to the doors of the Tolbooth and the Tron kirk," he said. "And on Abbey Gate as well. With a portrait of Bothwell and the legend beneath: *Here is the murderer of the King.*"

"Who would have put them up?" I asked. I had not seen them in the market square.

He shook his head. "I do not know."

We acted very proper towards one another, and either Master or Mistress Carwood always sat in the room while we conversed, but we always spoke in whispers. I believe they thought us courting.

Joseph did not tell me of any other placards, but Master Carwood did so. He said that some of them named the queen herself, discredited because she had been seen a few days after her husband's death playing golf and pall-mall in the fields. And some named the queen's servants Francisco Busso and Bastian de Pages. "And one named your young man, Joseph, as well."

Joseph! I could not speak more, I was so frozen with fear.

"But the accusations made by Darnley's father, the Earl of Lennox," Master Carwood concluded, "carry the most weight of all. They must be answered publicly before the law."

I waited, looking down at my plate, the white soup only half eaten.

Mistress Carwood asked what I dared not. "Who does Lennox accuse, my dear?"

"Bothwell."

"When?" I asked in a hushed voice. Then louder. "When, sir, must he answer them?"

"April twelfth, Nicola, at the Tolbooth, the great hall where the Parliament meets."

"Oh," I said, allowing myself a moment of joy and hope. "Then all will be well. I'll tell the truth and then everyone will know . . ."

It was the first time I had said anything. I glanced up at the Carwoods and they both looked serious but not surprised. I supposed they had long since found out why I was in hiding. Such things are not so easily kept secret.

But Master Carwood shook his head. "Do not sew the shroud before the corpse is measured, lass. Bothwell is a powerful lord and he is Sheriff of Edinburgh. There may be nothing more than a lot of angry talk and then a summary decision in his favor. You may not get to speak at all."

"We must still hope, Master Carwood," I whispered, for the first time letting him know my mind.

"We must indeed," Mistress Carwood answered for him.

39 ⚬ TRIAL AT THE TOLBOOTH

On the day of Bothwell's trial, Joseph came to collect me.

"Are you ready, Nicola?" he asked.

I looked around the Carwoods' home. So small a place for such a big haven. "Ready indeed," I said. I kissed Mistress Carwood farewell on both cheeks and she patted me on the head.

"You look a treat in that," she told me, for I was wearing a wine-colored dress of her daughter's, with a soft green hooded cape.

Master Carwood took my hands in his. "If you speak, Nicola, tell all the truth and God will make them listen."

"I will, sir, I promise." But fear was like a large stone in my chest that would not go away.

We made our way carefully to the Tolbooth. All the way, I kept thinking: *If I can tell my story, all will be well. If the boar is slaughtered, we will all feast.*

"Look!" I whispered, pointing to a corner of the square where men with swords and muskets were positioned. Then I turned and turned again. There were armed men everywhere.

"Stand back, Nicola," Joseph warned, making sure the hood of my cape shadowed my face.

We hid in plain sight in the midst of an excited crowd and watched as Bothwell rode up the High Street from the palace with a large escort of soldiers. The sound of the horses' hooves clattering on the road was deafening. I put my fingers in my ears.

"Murderer!" a man with a red tam called out.

"Assassin, you slew our lovely laddie!" came a woman's voice, considerably louder.

Bothwell never turned his head to them, but guards marched two at a time into the crowd seeking out the speakers. No one else dared say another word against him.

"Why so many soldiers?" I asked Joseph.

"As sheriff, Bothwell is entitled to muster as many men as he thinks necessary," Joseph answered glumly. "To preserve public order. But Lennox will be allowed only an escort of no more than half a dozen men."

I clutched Joseph's arm and hissed in his ear. "Will Lennox come then?"

"Would you?"

I thought about the ill-tempered, violent Bothwell and shivered. Then I put my hands on my hips, saying smartly, "But I *am* here."

"In disguise," Joseph said, giving yet another tug to my hood.

We waited for hours in the sun for Lennox to come. I was wilting under the green hood but knew better than to remove it. I did not dare be seen by Bothwell before time. In fact every time one of the soldiers came near me, my hands trembled so much I looked like an old woman.

At first the crowd was restless, then angry in a low buzzing kind of way, and at the last turned boisterous. Men began telling stories loudly, women singing songs.

At noon hawkers selling meat pies began to make their way through the mob, and Joseph purchased a pie for me. I ate as if I were starving, but still my hands shook.

"When will Lennox get here?" I whispered to Joseph.

"In time, Nicola. In time," he said.

"In time I will have shaken myself out of my clothes," I said.

He put an arm around me.

"Perhaps I should go in and give testimony by myself," I said, snuggling against him. "Without Lennox."

Joseph held me closer. "Without Lennox there is no case, Nicola. Bothwell will win the day. You would not be allowed to open your mouth. You would simply be taken off into custody and that would be the last I would ever see of you."

I knew he was right. But so had Master Carwood been when he said God would listen.

Where is God now that we need Him? I thought. And trembled some more.

But Lennox did not come.

As Joseph had predicted, the case in court against Bothwell melted away. At the end of the day, he left the Tolbooth in triumph, heading to Holyrood, his name cleared of any involvement with the murder.

Shaking his fist at the crowd, Bothwell shouted, "I will track down the king's killers and bring them to justice."

And they cheered him! The crowd actually cheered him!

I was too angry to weep, too stunned to keep silent. I started to shout back at Bothwell. But Joseph—as if expecting it—put a hand swiftly over my mouth and dragged me away.

As we walked down the now empty streets back towards the Carwoods' house, I wept at last. "What a world, Joseph, when wild boars can roam at will and none dare raise a spear to bring them down."

• • •

Joseph visited the Carwoods the very next day, and with him came Pious Mary, who was dressed for traveling. The news they brought was even worse than we expected.

"Bothwell is more powerful than ever. Now there is no one who dares oppose him," Joseph said, as we gathered in the kitchen. Gone was any pretense as to who I was.

"I doubt Nicola is safe here anymore," said Master Carwood.

"No, she is not, Andrew," agreed Pious Mary. "That is why I have come to take her away from here."

"Does the queen know where we are going?" I asked.

Mary looked down. "We thought it best not to tell her."

Joseph held my hands. "The queen is a virtual prisoner, Nicola. Even if she knew the truth, she could not protect you."

We went by back alleys to the city's edge, where a groom waited with a trio of horses, a lovely bay mare for me, a black mare for him, and a grey gelding for Pious Mary.

"Where do we go?" I asked.

"Eight miles east," she said. "To my father's castle."

The day was soft, the color of pearl. If only we had not been escaping, I might have enjoyed the ride. But my mind was awhirl with what we were leaving behind us. I could see no way out of the maze. All I could think was: poor queen, poor Joseph, and the poor realm of Scotland under the heel of that wild boar, Bothwell.

We rode for hours. So imprisoned was I in my thoughts of the past, I did not give thought to the future. And I did not notice a thing along the way.

Lord Seton himself came out of the castle to greet us. An elderly but still vigorous man, he was dressed in somber colors, the gold crucifix around his neck marking him as a Catholic.

"Father, there was no time to notify you. This is Nicola, the queen's own fool," Mary explained. "Since Kirk o'Field, there is much danger to those who came with the queen from France. Nicola has been particularly singled out and we must make sure that no harm comes to her. The queen wishes it."

"We will do that," Lord Seton stated resolutely, "for as long as need be. The queen, poor lass, came here but two months ago to recover her wits after Darnley's death. Why should her fool not bide here with me?"

We had a cold collation of meats and cheese, sitting in perfect silence in the dining room, and then Mary got on her horse again, not even taking time to change her clothes. As she mounted, she leaned down and touched my hair with her gloved hand.

"Love God, trust the queen, and listen to my father as you would your own," she said. Then she was away, her skirts rising and falling like sea waves and the groom riding hard to keep up with her.

As I watched her ride out of sight, I felt the weight of all I had lost. My life with the queen was over as surely as my life with Troupe Brufort. France gone from me, and now—perhaps—Scotland as well?

How many lives can a person lose, I wondered miserably, *before losing the last.*

So I began a new life at Castle Seton, which was smaller than Holyrood but larger than a French château. A grey stone house surrounded by a grey stone wall in the middle of a sea of grass.

I was assigned work as a maid, as much to make use of me as to conceal my identity from any callers. Lord Seton did not believe folk in his household should be left idle, and I agreed. Idleness would have led to too much thinking—about the queen and her baby, about Bothwell, about Joseph—and thus lead me into despair. As long as I worked hard throughout the day, I had little time to think, falling exhausted into my bed.

I was grateful for the work.

Weeks went by, in the course of which I carried out my duties as a maid with gratitude to my host and protector.

I was also given leave to work in the castle gardens, assisting the gardeners. If they were surprised at my knowledge of flowers, especially the early spring bulbs, they did not ask. Nor did I volunteer where my skills had come from.

We simply did not talk about politics or insurrections or of any of the murderers being exposed. Our conversations were about the weather or what we could hold in our hands—a dusting mop, a clump of earth, a boot scraper.

I appreciated the hominess of it all.

• • •

Then one day Joseph arrived, all unexpectedly, at Lord Seton's castle, and I was called to the back garden, where the vegetables for the table were grown and espaliered plum and apple trees backed up against the walls.

Lord Seton dismissed the gardeners to work in the front so that Joseph and I might have some time together.

I cleaned my hands on my apron. "My dear Joseph," I said, tears starting in my eyes. "How I have missed . . ." But I stopped, for his face was too grim for pleasantries.

He took me by the hands and led me to a garden seat. There he drew back from me and told me his news with the bluntness of a hammer.

"The worst of all has happened. The queen and Bothwell have married."

"*Married!*" My hands went to my mouth, my cheeks, my ears. It was as if I could not keep my hands still. "But . . . how could she? Does she not know what this means? If people believe Bothwell is the king's murderer, what will they think of her?"

"They will think she planned the murder with him. That they were lovers long before the fateful fuses were lit."

"But that did not happen." I leaped to my feet. "I slept in her room after the child was born. Bothwell never came near her."

Joseph stood as well. "What is truth but what others believe? Knox has accused her from the pulpit of adultery and murder. When power is at stake, truth is at best an inconvenience."

I recalled my last sight of Bothwell, the knife in his hand as he came towards me. I shuddered. "Why did she marry him? She cannot love him."

Joseph sat down and took my hands in his. "What has love to do with royal marriages, Nicola? Some say he abducted the queen and forced her. Some say he studied the magic arts in Paris and has bewitched her. He has a kind of power that draws people to him, Nicola."

"Oh, my poor queen. Why am I here, away from her side?" I leaped to my feet. "I could have helped her. I could have . . ." I was frantic, as if blown about by a storm. Finally I turned to Joseph. "What do *you* think happened, Joseph?"

He looked down at his hands for a moment, as if the answer were written between his fingers. "I believe that she has been assailed from all sides by deceit. If there is magic, it is the world that has wrought its devilish art upon her. Is it any wonder she surrenders herself to whoever offers to silence her enemies, Nicola?"

"No! No," I said, sitting down again. "I cannot believe that of her. She is the sweetest, kindest, gentlest lady. Bothwell must have threatened her. He must have threatened her child."

"They have been married according to Protestant rites."

I put my hands up. "Then she will consider it no marriage at all. She *must* have been forced to it. She would never marry outside the one true church. Never!"

"You see those you love with a fool's eyes, Nicola," Joseph told me. "We are none of us as good as you paint us."

"Or as bad, Joseph?" I stood again, walked a few steps away, then turned. "What of the Catholic lairds? What do they say of this match?"

Joseph's mouth twisted. "I only bring you the news, Nicola. I do not make it. Do not be angry with me."

I melted at once, like a candle before a greater flame. "I am so stupid, Joseph. Trying to kill the messenger. Forgive me."

"Many of the lairds—both Catholic and Protestant—were happy enough to see Darnley killed," Joseph said. "But to have

Bothwell set over them fills them all with bitterness. Already Morton, Argyll, and Atholl are raising an army to oppose the queen and her new king."

"Aha! Then they know that he is the murderer!" I smiled.

"They guess it."

"Then why did they support him when he came to trial?"

Before Joseph could answer, a little gust of wind blew across the garden, shaking the leaves. I felt shaken, too. Shaken into awareness.

"No," I said, "do not tell me. I know why." As I spoke, I pounded my right fist into my left hand. "They thought they were using Bothwell, only to find that he had been using them all along." I turned back to Joseph. "Even a fool should have seen that. *Especially* a fool."

"Nicola, you still do not know the worst of it," he said and stood. "Bothwell counted on the fact of the nobles' complicity to keep them from opposing him. But in marrying the queen, he has seriously overstepped himself. This matter will be decided by battle. And soon." He took my hands again.

"A battle? What of the queen, Joseph? Which side will she be on?"

"I am no seer, Nicola. I only hope she chooses well."

But she did not choose well. My brave queen chose Bothwell, as a sailor clings to a bit of wreckage when a ship goes down.

Lord Seton was one of the first to summon his troops and march to the queen's defense. He had no regard for Bothwell, in fact he despised the man. But yet he was willing to die for his queen.

He took his leave of his daughter and me in the castle courtyard. From atop his splendid bay gelding, he said, "Bothwell is a bully and . . ."

"And a boar, sir?" I said.

Seton had looked startled for a moment.

"It is the little piggy eyes," I added. "Sir."

Lord Seton, that good, gentle man, threw his head back and roared. "I shall not be able to look him in the face from now on, Nicola, without seeing a boar's head and wondering where his tusks are kept," he told me. "Poor dear queen."

And away he rode at the head of his troops.

I could do nothing, of course, but wait anxiously in Seton Castle for news of any battles that were to come. It was mid-June, and the gardens were all aflower. Roses in the arbor had already opened their velvet faces to the summer sun.

But not I.

I had full autumn in my heart.

For if the queen's forces won decisively, Bothwell would remain at her side. I could never see her again. Not safely.

Yet if her forces should lose . . .

I could not believe that God would let her lose.

But He had let her lose so much already.

We had no word for days, though the castle was abuzz with rumors.

The queen is in Edinburgh, we heard.

She's riding with the troops to Borthwick, that stark twin-towered fortress near the Esk.

She's north and south, we were told. *East and west.*

No one knew a thing but everyone knew the rumors.

I longed to be with her, but I was stuck at Seton with no way to get to her except by waiting.

So I waited.

At last Lord Seton returned, looking years older than when he had left. He was grim and filthy. Dismounting, he was greeted by his daughter, who had come the evening before, sped on by news that her father might be riding home.

I watched through one of the mullioned windows as she put her arm around his shoulders for comfort. It was not my place to greet him. Besides, I was too afraid to hear what he had to say.

A servant found me in the front hall, pacing back and forth. "The master would have you take a drink with him and Lady Mary in his apartments."

I went at once, already guessing the news. Who could not, having seen Lord Seton's face?

Mary saw me before I could knock. "Ah, Nicola," she said, gesturing me in.

Lord Seton's breastplate and helmet lay on the floor, where he had dropped them. "Forgive me for not rising," he said, before taking a deep draft from his glass.

Mary handed me a drink as well, but though I raised it to my lips, I did not take so much as a sip.

Without preamble, Lord Seton began. "Face-to-face at Carberry Hill we were, about eight miles east of Edinburgh. Morton and his allies had moved more quickly than we. What's more they outnumbered us as well. We had but six hundred horses and they thousands. Even Maitland has joined their cause."

"That is no surprise," his daughter interjected. "He has no love for Bothwell."

Lord Seton waved his hand, as if to dismiss her interruption. "We held the high ground, so that they couldna easily attack us, and we stood fast under the queen's banner, the red lion of Scotland. Och, ye should have seen it whip about bravely in the wind. But

Norton's men blocked off any possible retreat, and so there we waited to see who would first spill the blood of his ain countrymen."

He took another sip of his wine. "It was hot. By God it was hot on that hill in full armor. Though the queen, bless her, never looked less than magnificent."

"Father, should you not rest now?" Mary asked.

He shook his head. "I must say it once and be done wi' it, lass. Besides, how can any of us rest, with the tale not told?"

I leaned forward. "Please, sir." My voice was small and broke in the middle. "I must know the worst."

Lord Seton smiled gently at me. "Do ye see? Nicola wants to know."

Mary sighed. "As do I, Father," she said. "Tell on." She filled his glass.

He did not pick the wine up again, but started anew. "The false lords sent a deputy, a Frenchman named du Croc. He carried their demands—that the queen should abandon Bothwell, and in turn they would restore her to her former position."

"Then why did she not give them his head?" I cried, even though I thought I knew the answer. *She loved him now out of pity.*

"Would that she had," Mary put in. "She has had not an hour of happiness from this marriage. He is cruel to her and she lacks the strength to fight him. You would not know her, Nicola, she is so altered."

Lord Seton now took another long swallow of his wine. "Poor lady, there she was wrapped in the royal colors of Scotland, a red and yellow skirt, and a jaunty black riding hat. But she was furious at the suggestion. She said it was those very lords who had sent a paper to her first urging the marriage. 'It is by ye that Bothwell has been promoted.' Those were her very words."

A steward came in with a bowl of fruit from Lord Seton's own gardens, but he was waved away. "Not now, man. Later. After I have cleaned myself up." Then Lord Seton looked at me. "Ah, Nicola, the queen tried her best to negotiate an agreement to save them both, while Bothwell swaggered around the field, offering single combat to any who would dare to face him."

"Single combat?" I said, putting down my untouched drink. "*I* would have fought him."

That brought a smile to Lord Seton's tired face. "I am certain ye would, my brave lass. And so would others. At which point he rapidly retracted his offer. A boar without any tusks at all," he said.

"Father—are you havering? Really, you must rest." Mary put her hand out towards him.

"Just a jest, my dear, between two fools, one young and one old. Do not worry, I havna lost my mind." He smiled sadly. "Though it is the only thing I havna lost this day."

"Then what was the outcome? Did the armies fight? Is Bothwell still alive? Is the queen safe?" The questions tumbled out of me.

Lord Seton raised a hand to calm me, but his hand shook so, Mary put her own over his to steady him. At last he said, "The lairds agreed that if the queen returned with them to Edinburgh, Bothwell could leave unharmed. They promised she would be permitted to address Parliament, putting her case to the people."

"Was that safe?" I asked. "I mean to return to Edinburgh with them."

Lord Seton shook his head. "Safe? The very worry I had, lass. And so I counseled her not to be overtrustful. But evening was drawing in. Many of our troops had already drifted away because of Bothwell's loathsome bragging and his cowardice when put to the point."

"I should never have left her side," I cried.

Lord Seton leaned forward. "Do not fash yerself, lassie," he said, using the old Scots phrase. "What good would ye have done her dead and one more murder on her poor conscience?"

I reached for my own wineglass then and took a sip. The sweet taste burned down my throat and was a small comfort.

"So they parted?" Mary asked.

"Aye," said Lord Seton. "Husband and wife sundered, he to the north, she to the camp of her rebellious nobles."

"And how was she treated there?" I asked, my voice hoarse with fear and the aftermath of the wine.

"She had to ride through two lines of soldiers who greeted her with jeers and insults which their leaders did nothing to suppress." His answer twisted his mouth. "They called her witch, and whore. 'Burn the murderess!' they shouted. 'Kill her! Drown her!' I do not believe she understood until then how many of her beloved Scots had turned against her."

Mary began to weep quietly but I had no tears left, having shed them all long ago. Anger consumed me, not sorrow. I was ice cold with it.

"Where is she now?" I asked.

"They have locked her up in Preston's grim mansion, without attendants or comforts or privacy. It is a small, bare house in Edinburgh." His fingers, so weak and trembling before, now clenched the goblet with such passion I feared the stem would break. "She is being treated as a common criminal while they debate whether they dare put her on trial."

"On trial." The words burst from my mouth. "They would not dare. She is the queen!"

Then I looked at Lord Seton's familiar face, now sunken and grey, and I understood for the first time how desperate things really were. The Scots lairds would dare anything.

"Father, what are we to do?" Mary asked.

"Do?" Lord Seton slumped back against his chair. "What *can* we do? There is no army left to support her, and every day Bothwell raises her a fresh crop of enemies. This is her darkest hour."

I added what we already knew. "And ours as well."

41 ❦ PLANS

Things were darker than even we had guessed, for the queen was soon spirited away from Edinburgh and locked in a fouler prison, on an island.

We were still at Castle Seton when Pious Mary told us of it. Anger and fear warred on her homely face as she spoke.

"Mary Livingstone and I had hardly an hour with the queen under the eyes of a guard. A guard!" She struck the table with the flat of her hand as her voice rose.

"How did she look?" I asked. "Was she well, my queen?"

"She was thin, worn. She had not eaten in three days."

"But why . . . ?" I leaned towards her. "Is she ill again?"

Mary shook her head. "She feared poison and dared not eat till we were there with her. Mary Livingstone and I fixed her a meal with our own hands, and only then would she try a bite."

"Poor, poor lady," Lord Seton whispered.

"Father, there is worse to come," Mary said. "We had just gotten her to accept a few spoonfuls of Lorraine soup, with Morton—that pustule—standing behind her chair and watching every bite. Suddenly the door burst open and a group of men stomped in to take her off again."

I put a hand over my mouth, shocked. I had never heard Pious Mary swear before. In fact I had never even heard her raise her voice. But war makes heroes of the least of us, and devils of the rest.

"Morton just stood there, arms crossed, calm as a post, though we women set up an awful wail," Mary said, her eyes hard, like cobbles. "The soldiers ordered her out, carrying not even a nightdress and only two chambermaids with her."

"Where did they take her?" Lord Seton asked.

"Lochleven."

Lochleven! I shivered remembering the stories I had heard of the place, that cold grey tower and keep belonging to the Douglases. It sat on a small island in the middle of a misty loch. Sentinels kept perfect watch from an elevated walkway round the inside of the parapet. No one could sail to the island or away from it without their knowing.

We discussed what we knew of the place, Mary in a fury, Lord Seton sad, and me—I hovered somewhere between the two.

"The keep there is old and the wind comes through the chinks," said Mary. "It is no place for a queen to stay. Not one who has already suffered so much and been so ill." She hesitated, her natural sense of fairness warring with her anger. "There is a bedroom that is comfortable enough, with good tapestries on the walls and a bed of green velvet. And a goodly presence chamber to meet with people." She looked a bit sheepish. "I was hawking there once with the queen."

Lord Seton's long face got longer. "The Douglases will probably take those rooms for themselves. She may be lodged instead in the Glassin Tower."

"True . . ." Mary said.

"Or in the dungeon," he added, and sighed heavily. Since the queen's removal to prison, he had fallen prey to a miasma of the heart.

"Where the queen lies, so lies majesty," I said, refusing to be drawn into his mood. "She will make even the bleakest dungeon a home." I patted his hand, but it lay beneath my touch like a dead thing. "Besides, is not Lord James a Douglas? Surely being kin to the queen they will treat her well."

"Oh fool, fool, fool." Lord Seton wept, his head in his hands.

"What have I said?" I whispered to Mary.

"The dowager Lady Margaret Douglas believes Lord James should have had the throne himself," she told me. "Lady Margaret has never forgiven the queen for coming back to take it. Her welcome will be a cold one indeed."

"Fool I am," I said to Lord Seton. "But fool I will not remain. I will find a way to get the queen out of that foul place, by myself if I have to."

"Not by yourself, dear Nicola," said Mary.

"No indeed," agreed Lord Seton. "For to get in there and get out again, you will need our help."

However we did it, it needed to be done quickly. Word came to Lord Seton that the queen was once again in ill health. Heartsick and full of despair, she had been forced to sign away the throne in favor of her year-old son. Jamie was crowned king a few days later and Lord James declared regent, which made him as good as a king.

"That old carlin, that witch Margaret Douglas, is surely crowing at this very moment," Pious Mary said as we rode to Castle Niddry, one of the ancestral homes of the Setons, to meet with the other Maries, for they were part of our plan.

The day was overcast, but the winds were hardly riding the trees at all. The road to Niddry was well traveled and we passed a small group of wagoners as we rode along.

When we arrived at the castle—a small grey stone haven within a pretty dale—Joseph was standing outside with one of the grooms. I gasped aloud and Mary was grinning ear to ear. I guessed then that she had arranged this reunion and was delighted to have kept it a surprise.

While the groom helped Mary dismount, Joseph came to my aid, lifting me down from the horse as though I weighed nothing.

"You are thinner," he said, quickly adding, "It becomes you."

"It is from worry," I told him. "For the queen's safety. And for yours."

The wind puzzled his black curls, giving him the look of an addled angel. His hands lingered on my waist and Mary called out, "I will see to our chambers." And then she left for the house, the groom—trailing the two horses—for the stables.

Joseph and I were alone under the darkening sky.

"I am surprised to see you," I said, stepping away from him, suddenly shy. "I thought you were at Holyrood."

His face was unsmiling. "I have become the latest in a long line of fugitives."

I was shocked. "You?"

"Francisco Busso and Bastian de Pages have already been arrested for aiding in Darnley's murder. I was named, too, but I escaped through the window before Morton's men could arrest me."

"But this is ridiculous!" I exclaimed. "What do the postulant lords of Scotland hope to achieve?" My voice rose alarmingly and he stepped close to me and put a hand over my mouth.

"Hush, Nicola. Even here in Seton's own house we must use caution. Morton's ears are everywhere. If you were reported and I could not save you . . ." His eyes teared up.

I nodded and he removed his hand. "I will be careful, Joseph. I promise. But tell me why they are persecuting the innocent with so many wicked around?"

"They do not care about innocence, darling fool, only scapegoats," he told me. "That way no one will stop to question the guilt of those who have seized power. These 'pustulent lords' as you call them will arrest a thousand men and execute them all if it will distract attention from themselves."

I said fiercely, "One need not be a physician to know how to deal with pustules. One quick pop between the fingers and . . ."

"Nicola!" he whispered as if shocked, but there was laughter in his eyes.

The sky began to spit down at us and we walked quickly towards the house.

"At least *you* need not stay hiding longer," he said. "Bothwell can no longer do you any harm."

"Where is he now?"

Joseph opened the door for me, saying, "He races from one end of the country to the other trying to raise an army, but it is clear that it is not the queen's cause he serves but his own. He has been publicly named as Darnley's murderer and declared outlaw. His only options now are to flee into exile or remain in Scotland until he is captured and executed."

"Good!" I said, and meant it. "Even if he is harried like a wild boar in a hunt, I will not weep for him."

Behind us the rain began in earnest. I turned to Joseph and whispered, "But what danger are you in if you remain here?"

He put his hands on my shoulders, speaking urgently. "There is a ship for France in two days time, Nicola. What belongings I have are here with me. I came for you, Nicola. Marry me and sail away from this madness."

I looked down, confused by my swirling emotions. "To be with you in France . . ." I could scarcely speak. "Married . . . It is my greatest desire." I looked up. "But, Joseph, I have to help free the queen. What is mere desire next to that?"

He shook his head and his hands tightened on my shoulders. "Nicola, even those lairds loyal to her do not know what to do. How can you and I act, who have no armies to hand?"

Tears sprang into my eyes. "What matters is to find some way to free her. Only that. I have nothing to lose but the queen. Perhaps that makes me freer to fight for her." I pulled away from him and sat down on a small wooden bench.

But Joseph was not finished. "Nicola, think—think! How many of the Scots nobles will actually want to help even should she become free? An infant king upon the throne suits them very well. There will be a series of regents and a council of lords ruling the country. By the time King Jamie comes of age, the lairds will have lined their pockets with gold many times over."

"You make things sound beyond our control," I whispered.

"Things *are* beyond our control, Nicola." He gazed at me beseechingly. "It is folly to think otherwise. The queen is locked away in an impenetrable fortress on an unreachable island. What do you think *we* can do?"

"I do not know," I confessed with a weary shake of my head. "Call it folly, if you will, but we must still try."

Joseph raised his eyes to the ceiling, spread out his hands, and gave vent to a loud string of Italian curses.

"Do not be angry with me," I begged him tearfully. "You know I cannot abandon the queen."

"I am not angry with you," he said. "I am angry at myself for being such a fool that I cannot leave you." And so saying, he took two great steps over to the bench and gathered me up in his arms.

Before we could speak further, a hidden door in the panelled wall opened and the four Maries walked into the room.

Joseph and I sprang apart, like deer startled in a copse. But we continued to hold hands.

It had been a long while since I had seen the Maries together.

Regal Mary led the way. She still had that high tilt of head, but was less animated than usual. In fact, all the Maries were curiously subdued. The flickering candlelight cast deep shadows over their faces, which seemed to make the mood even more somber.

How sad that a reunion of such old friends should take place under these troubling circumstances, I thought.

I turned from Joseph to greet them and they each kissed me, one cheek, then the other, and nodded at Joseph. Then we went into the great dining hall and sat uncomfortably around a great oak banqueting table as though for a meal, but without a thing to eat before us. Pious Mary had drawn the heavy velvet curtains so that no one might spy on us.

Just so, I thought, *ministers sit to plan a war.*

Pious Mary was the first to speak. "Thanks to the intervention of Mistress Maitland's husband," she said, "I have been given permission to join the queen at Lochleven."

I cast a glance at Regal Mary, so recently married to that chameleon, Maitland. Had she been uneasy being the intermediary between her new husband and Pious Mary? After all, Maitland had never seemed the queen's most loyal councilor. Regal Mary's cheeks had spots of red, a glow not of health but—I thought—of embarrassment.

Regal Mary said in a casual voice, "William is doing all that he can to ensure the queen's safety and comfort. He must be careful, however, for if he falls out of favor with the other lords, she will have no friends at court at all." All the while she spoke, her hands wrangled with one another.

"What about Lord James?" I asked. "How can he allow his queen and kinswoman to be treated like this?" And then I remembered how he had been put to the horn by the queen and his lands almost forfeit. Was he paying her back now?

"Lord James has made common cause with that vulture Knox," Jolly Mary reported. I had never before heard her merry voice so soured. "While Lord James bolsters the Protestant cause, Knox lauds him from the pulpit. One dirty hand washing the other."

"Can you not raise enough men to free the queen?" I asked.

Joseph put a hand on mine. "Remember Lochleven is on an island. Such a movement of men across the loch would be seen."

"And," added Regal Mary, "my husband says that would only guarantee the queen's immediate execution."

A gasp ran around the table. I was not the only one to make a noise.

"Execute a queen?" I said, rising. "They would not dare."

"You forget," Joseph said quietly, pulling me down, "she is queen no longer."

"She was *forced* to sign the abdication," I retorted.

"Nevertheless," Regal Mary said, "by law she is no longer queen. It is much simpler to execute someone who was once queen than . . ."

The rest of her sentence was shortened by the loud sounds of Pretty Mary bursting into tears.

I handed her a square of linen and she covered her mouth with it, stifling the sobs.

"If the queen is to escape," said Pious Mary, with an unaccustomed air of authority, "the plan must be executed from *inside* Lochleven. But she has not had any of her own retainers with her before. Now, however . . ."

"Hurrah!" cried Jolly Mary.

I turned and looked at Regal Mary—Mistress Maitland. She smiled tentatively as if unsure of herself.

"God will bless you," I whispered to her.

She looked down at her hands and the tears started at the edges of her eyes.

Pious Mary cleared her throat and we all looked at her again. "I am allowed a maid to accompany me."

We were silent for a long moment, then all at once her meaning was clear.

"Me," I said standing. "You must take *me* with you."

She smiled, and it was the perfectly composed smile of a nun who is certain in her mind of salvation. "I had it in mind all along."

"Even if you cannot *free* her, you can at least lighten her spirits," said Pretty Mary, her face scrubbed free of the tears. "Take her some lovely things to comfort her. I have a doublet and skirt of white satin and some cambric and linen cloth. She will want shoes. We have the same size foot. And good sheets. Maybe dry plums, and netting needles and . . ."

"Enough," Regal Mary said sharply. "You make this sound like a day at a holy day fair, while we are speaking of rescue."

"Nicola," said Joseph, taking a gentle hold of my arm and pulling me back into my seat, "*think* about what you are doing. This is not our land. From the start, we have been regarded with contempt and suspicion for our foreign speech and for our faith. We can leave now and make a new life where we will not be in danger from these quarrelsome Scots."

I turned to him. "You are the hunted man, Joseph, and you must go while you can. But my name is on no one's list."

It was not what he wanted to hear. His face closed in on itself, becoming pinched and sad.

"I will stay," he said. With an effort at lightness, he added, "There must be someone to make a worthy ballad out of your adventures, Nicola. I cannot leave so important a task to some rough-tongued Scotsman."

"Oh, Joseph!" I cried.

"If you will not run away with me," he said with a shrug, "then we will both have to remain in the lions' den a little longer."

I turned to the Maries and asked, "When do we leave?"

"In the morning," Regal Mary said, standing.

"You knew all along...."

"That you would go? Of course. It is in your nature. But I ask one favor of you, Jardinière."

I nodded and she came over to hand me a gold ring decorated with a finely-wrought picture of a lion and a mouse.

"I know that story," I said. "The mouse saves the lion."

"You told it to us many times," Regal Mary said smoothly. "Tell it again to the queen, and give her this token. Say that she has many small friends ready to chew through her bonds."

"We will need sharp teeth, my ladies," Joseph said. "Very sharp teeth indeed."

43 ~ ISLAND PRISON

ochleven was not that far from Edinburgh in miles, not far from Stirling Castle, either, but it might have been the end of the world for all of that.

At the first sight of the loch, my heart sank. The flat grey water looked forbiddingly cold. It mirrored a flat grey sky.

Out on the rugged little island in the center of the loch, the squat five-story keep rose up like a fist.

I shuddered. From where we stood, I could see there was scarcely a ribbon of land between the surrounding castle walls and the rocky island shore.

Climbing from the carriage, I whispered to Pious Mary, "An army could not make a successful assault here."

She nodded. "May God help us."

I understood at that moment that if there were to be any kind of rescue, it was up to Mary and me.

I squared my shoulders and lifted my head. I had gotten the queen out of Holyrood. I had survived Kirk o'Field. I would not let a little thing like an island prison defeat me.

"*We* can do it, Lady Mary," I told her. "We mice have very sharp teeth."

She did not answer. But she smiled.

Our escort was under strict orders to turn back once we were at the shore. The bowmen along the castle battlements watched as we made our farewells. We knew they could not hear us, but still we spoke in low voices.

Pious Mary told the captain of our guard, "Give my father my love. And tell Mistress Maitland the mice have arrived."

He gave a curt nod and then the carriage and its escort turned and started back towards Castle Seton, leaving us to the grey loch and the island prison.

At a jetty, a boatman helped us into his small vessel and began rowing us towards the island. The creaking and splashing of the oars was loud enough to alert any castle defenders of our approach. *No sneaking in,* I thought.

Suddenly a solitary heron sailed over us, its long extended neck like a lance. Then it was gone, to the farthest shore.

The mirrored water reflected only a few bare trees and the dreary Lomond hills massing on the horizon. I could feel my insides constrict, as if I had fallen into the water.

The boatman spoke not a word; I fancied his lips were frozen shut by the rising mist and cold. I began to shiver and Mary pulled her cloak more tightly about her as we neared the island, as though the castle itself were the source of the chill.

As soon as the boat reached the shore, three soldiers with drawn swords marched out from the castle gate. Bounding ahead of them like a hare before hounds came a youngish man who gallantly offered a hand to Mary. She hesitated a moment, then accepted his assistance. I clambered out without any help, and stood well away from the soldiers, pulling my cape tighter still.

Behind us the water lapped sullenly at the shore, a bleak reminder that we were now cut off from all help.

The young man turned to the soldiers. "Put yer swords away, lads. This is hardly an invasion," he commanded. Then he turned back to us. "My apologies, ladies. My brother keeps the guard on constant alert. It makes them edgy." He pushed unruly curls away from his face and grinned.

Mary acknowledged him with only the slightest of nods.

"Well . . ." he said, "welcome to Lochleven, then." He made an absurdly formal bow. "I am George Douglas, brother to Lord William Douglas, lord of this castle. I hope we can make ye comfortable."

"I am Mary, daughter of Lord Seton," Mary responded with imposing dignity. From the way she fingered her rosary, I guessed that she was nervous. "And this is Nicola, my maid."

George Douglas acknowledged me with a nod and I gave him a quick curtsy, as if I really were but a lady's maid. Then he ordered his men to carry our baggage—what little there was of it. We followed him through the gate under the eyes of dozens more armed soldiers and under an increasingly dismal sky. I saw now, even more than before, that any attempt to free the queen by force would be futile indeed.

The great square block of the stone keep towered over us.

"My family is staying in the keep. The queen's quarters are there as well," he said. "Though first she was lodged in the Glassin Tower."

"As far as possible from the landward shore," Mary noted.

George Douglas shrugged. "My brother moved her soon after she came. He says the Tower House is more easily guarded at night. Though where he thinks the queen might go . . ." He said nothing further.

By the time we got to the keep, rain was spitting down. I glanced over at the loch, where the once glassy water was now pitted.

We opened the heavy door and, one after another, walked up the narrow stairway, George Douglas in the lead.

The Tower House, which they called the keep, was certainly the most substantial building on the island, with five floors. We entered on the second floor through a cross-barred iron gate.

"Unusual," Mary commented dryly.

A wooden screen reduced the draftiness of the hall, and when we came into the presence chamber itself, there was the queen sitting against an oriel window and gazing out at the far shore.

George Douglas cleared his throat and she turned, leaped up, and almost danced across the room to greet us.

"Ah, the purest jewel of my Maries and the prettiest flower in my garden!" she declared. "What a welcome sight you are!"

At the sight of her, my breath stopped and I felt as frightened and as happy as I had that first evening we had met in the garden at Rheims. She was not radiant as she had been then, where only one death had stood between her and all the world's goodness. But she was alive.

Alive!

And I was with her.

I gave a great curtsy, sweeping down before her. "My queen!" I said.

She pulled me up and looked at me for a long time, as if drinking me in. "I knew Mary was coming, but you, Nicola—you are a wonderful surprise."

How dim a portrait she presents, I thought, *who once shone like the sun.* She had a terrible pallor. The simple wool dress she was wearing, with but a touch of lace at collar and cuffs, emphasized the awful thinning-down of all her features. She was bone on bone, her sufferings lending her an ethereal air which had a beauty all its own. But she was still the queen.

George Douglas fell on one knee before her. "I will have quarters prepared for your ladies, Madam," he said, "and as ever I stand ready to fetch anything you need."

She smiled wordlessly at him; he rose and left the room.

As the door closed after him, Mary raised an eyebrow. "I had not expected to find such a queen's knight in this cold place."

The queen smiled. "He is quite the gallant, and my one friend here. Until this moment, that is." She reached out, took our hands and, for a moment, said nothing. Then she smiled and an old beauty returned to her face. "Come, ladies, tell me all your news. I hunger for it more than food."

We sat together near the window, knee to knee to knee. I noticed the queen did not like to stray far from the view of the loch and the shore beyond. It came to me suddenly that it was all the kingdom that was left her.

Outside the rain sputtered and coughed, like a man with a catarrh. The single heron flew silently back over the loch towards the nearer shore.

"There is much to tell," Mary said. "And little."

So we told her what we could, and then she asked me about Joseph.

"He stays in Scotland for your sake, Madam," I said. "Hidden but near."

"I suspect, rather, he stays for you, my dear," she said. "You see—even through the worst of my ills . . ." She sighed and held a hand to her breast. "Even then I could not help but notice his devotion. But he must leave while he has the chance." She turned her head for a moment to look out at the loch.

"I *told* him to go," I said, my voice suddenly miserable. "But he would not."

The queen looked back at me. "I commend his constancy," she said. "But I would not have his death on my conscience."

"Nor mine, Majesty," I whispered. "But it is *your* welfare we should be concerning ourselves with, Madam."

Mary nodded, adding briskly, "You have been unwell, Highness. It is easy to see, for it is written across your face."

"Ah, Mary Seton, ever the flatterer," the queen said, smiling. Then her face went serious again. "It is true that I was ill for many weeks after coming here. I miscarried twins in the Glassin Tower, a last bitter legacy from Lord Darnley. Armed guards stood over me day and night as I struggled with the pain." She laughed but there was no merriment in it.

Oh dear queen, I thought, *who was once so happy.*

"What they thought might happen," the queen continued, "I do not know. I had scarce the strength to crawl from my bed, much less attempt escape. By the time the lairds came by with their papers of abdication, I had not the will to resist them."

"I *knew* it!" I cried, grabbing up her hands in mine. "I *knew* it!" Then, realizing what I had done—touching her without permission—I set her hands back in her lap again with infinite care.

"We all knew it," Mary said. "Madam, there are many in your kingdom who still consider you the queen."

Queen Mary sighed and looked out the window again, where the rain had begun in earnest. I could not help but feel that the very heavens were weeping the tears *I* was trying to keep in check.

The queen said very quietly, so quietly we had to lean forward to hear, "I think they hoped I would have the decency to die." She smiled sadly out at the loch, which was now almost obscured by a heavy curtain of rain. "I did not oblige them."

"An obligation," I said, in the bright voice I used as fool, "that they dare not compel."

She turned back and looked at me. "I have missed *you* especially, my dear little fool. And have thought of you often. *What would Nicola say*, I ask myself. *What story would she tell me?"*

"If any thought of me gave you peace, Madam," I said, clasping my hands as if in prayer, "then I have proved my worth."

"You have done that already a hundredfold," she said.

"Your Majesty," Mary interrupted, "is this young Douglas truly to be trusted?" There was sudden steel in her voice.

The queen gave her full attention to the question, turning from me and looking straight at Mary.

"Trusted?" The queen nodded slowly. "I believe he is mine to the core, for all that Douglas is his name." She leaned forward and whispered hoarsely. "Morton's men wanted to drag me off from here to an even more desolate spot where surely I would have met my end. It was young George who barred the way. He met them at the shore with a dozen bowmen and told them that I was under his custody and they had no authority to remove me."

"Good for George!" I said, clapping.

"He has also smuggled letters for me out to France," the queen said. "And a letter to my chamberlain at Holyrood, who is sending me—through George's good graces—several dresses, a pair of furred boots, a holland cloak, several perukes, and a box of preserves. They will see me through the hard winter . . . if indeed I must remain here all that time."

"Then he is truly a friend, Madam," I said. "Though can a Douglas be trusted?"

She smiled. "I believe it is his kindness that has given me the strength to recover my health." She patted my hands. "And now to have you two here . . ."

"All your friends are praying for your safe release," I said. "And Mary Maitland—she that was Fleming—asked me to give you this." I passed her the ring, and told the story, adding: "Remember—even the humblest of your servants might yet be of use."

"Oh, I know that very well already," the queen said. "It was a lesson I learned in Amboise. And again after dear Davie's death."

"Your Majesty," Mary began uneasily, "have the Scots lords not offered to free you if you will divorce Bothwell?"

The queen shivered, and though the room was quite chilly, I do not think she shivered with the cold. "The Scots lords! *Dogs*, rather! I trusted them at Carberry Hill and they threw me into prison," she said bitterly. "They took my crown and they took away my son." Her eyes filled up. "Poor little thing. I have not held him for these many months. He will not remember me at all."

"Madam," I said, "he will *never* forget you." But even as I spoke, I wondered if she was right. Jamie was but a baby, and hadn't I forgotten my own mother's face? And I was not a toddler when I lost her but already partly grown.

The queen waved away my words, saying angrily, "This awful marriage is the only thing left I can withhold from the Scots lords. If it causes them any pain at all, then I will cling to it with my dying breath."

An uncomfortable silence fell over the room and I began to shiver with the cold.

"Oh, Nicola, I have not been thinking. . . ." the queen said. "Let us go closer to the fire so you may get warm. I have become so used to the cold, I almost welcome it. To be as cold outside as I have become within gives me some kind of balance. I sit here in the window, away from the fire, and stare for hours out at the far shore, thinking on freedom. But look—there is nothing to see beyond my window anymore."

And indeed, the freezing downpour now totally obscured the shore. The grey loch and the grey rain were all one.

We went over to the hearth and I crouched right by it. If I had been any closer, I would have been in it, cooking like a piece of meat. Slowly the warmth began to seep into my bones.

The queen and Mary did not come so close, but rather sat together on a small pillowed bench and stared silently into the fire.

Suddenly the door opened and an angular woman bustled in. She took off a sodden cloak and came over to the hearth, chirping, "Oh, my lady, I see your maids have arrived!"

She perched herself on the edge of a high-backed chair and said, "You must be Lord Seton's daughter, and you must be her French maid." As she spoke, her head bobbed up and down. "We are going to be the *closest* of companions."

Queen Mary did her best to smooth away her annoyance at this interruption. "This is Lady Douglas," she said, "who is wife to my keeper, Lord William, elder brother to young George. She is my *constant* companion." The way she said it was no compliment.

"And very happy to be so," Lady Douglas said, clearly deaf to the queen's nuance. She bobbed her head so much, I was afraid she might peck us with her sharp little nose. "We have so few visitors, it will be a pleasure to spend time with someone of good breeding," she said to Mary.

I glanced over at the queen, who had a tight smile fixed on her face.

"Madam," I said, curtsying to the queen, "you said you had an errand for me?"

"Ah, yes, that errand," the queen said. "Fetch us something to eat and drink, please Nicola. You will have to find it on the ground floor, in the kitchens. That is, dear Lady Douglas, if it is all right with you?"

"Oh yes, oh yes," Lady Douglas said, her head bobbing again.

I left at once, glad to be away from chirrupy Lady Douglas, who—for all her fine speeches about being the queen's companion—I knew was no more than a gossipy jailer.

And while I was at my errand, I could begin to learn about the keep, the doors, and gates—and what I could of the soldiers. All those things we needed to know if we were to help the queen escape.

She cannot quit this dismal place soon enough, I whispered out to the grey and uncompromising rain.

*S*oon enough became one day and the next and the next, for the more I learned of the place, the more I despaired of escaping from it.

"We are not birds to fly away from here," I told Pious Mary. We were at the top of the tower in the queen's bedchamber, making up the queen's bed. This was the first nice day that week, and the only time the linens had been thoroughly aired. It would be another few days before the washerwomen came with fresh linen and took these back to the mainland for washing.

"Nor are we fish to swim," she added.

"Are you resigned to staying then?" I asked, fearful she might say yes.

The queen surely seemed to be, as if finding herself *safe,* she swallowed the shame of being in prison. She rarely spoke now of escape, or her son, or even of the future. Rather she dwelt on everyday pinpricks—the porridge not hot enough, her linens not clean enough, the constant chatter of Lady Douglas. The queen had even begun embroidering again, a set of chair covers for the chairs in her room, something one does if planning a long stay.

"I am *not* resigned," Mary said, matching the folds of linen to the ones in my hand.

Over the next months, at least I learned how to tolerate Lady Douglas. The most important thing was to stop one's ears to her constant chatter. She made much of little, and little of much: new embroidery techniques, gossip about noble families, the many deeds of her brave and wise and witty and wonderful husband.

"As my dear husband, Lord William, has told me . . ." was how she usually started these boring recitations. Or "Have you heard that Ogilvie's second wife has . . ." or "This pink fabric from the Continent can be made into the prettiest . . ." Every day, from early morning till after dinner, she was in the queen's small apartment. Not only did she crave the queen's company to brighten her own dull existence, she was also terrified lest the royal prisoner escape.

"If that happened," she would say, her head once again bobbing like a dipper in a stream, "Lord James will unlikely be forgiving. Oh no! Oh no!" Then a few hand waves to underline what she was saying. "It would prove the end—the very end—of dear William's advancement." For that was all the queen's misery, her shame, her loss of throne and child meant to Lady Douglas.

Often in self-defense the queen pretended to fall asleep in her chair, but I could not take such a way out. Instead I simply stopped listening, though I kept nodding and smiling while all the while I was thinking on ways to leave.

Lady Douglas's husband was her opposite in every way. Where she was sharp-nosed and chittery, Lord William was burly and thick-set, like an old ram. His voice was deep and slow, and whenever he was forced to converse with the queen, he had few sentences and fewer verbs. "I will. You won't," ran the burden of his song.

It was astonishing that he and Lord James and young George were related at all.

Lord William kept very much to himself in his countinghouse, and the few times we saw him, he was usually out riding on the far shore, on a plodding gelding that seemed to have as little personality as its master. I half suspected that Lord William had taken on a royal prisoner in order to free himself of Lady Douglas's company.

The winter months dragged by. I had hoped the loch would freeze solid, for then we might have had a chance of escaping over it with the queen.

Neither bird nor fish then, I told myself.

But though it was cold—and the tower the coldest spot on the island, which no hearthfire ever seemed able to warm to a comfortable temperature—it never got cold enough to put more than a skim of ice around the edges of the island.

We got through the winter as best we could by playing cards, chess, writing poetry. I finally developed a reasonable hand at embroidery simply because by concentrating on it I could block out Lady Douglas's chatter. My leaves looked like greenery now, and not some jagged creatures clinging hopelessly to lumpy boughs. Mary smiled her approval at a pillow cover I worked, and the queen actually used it on her bed.

Because I dared not write to Joseph for fear of revealing his hiding place, I sent letter after letter to my old friend Pierre Brufort somewhere in France, letters which George smuggled out for me. I had no hope for a return letter, and got none.

With the coming of spring the atmosphere lightened, the days grew long again, and a soft yellow haze crowned the trees on the mainland shore. Our spirits lightened as well.

We were allowed to take the queen boating on the loch, though always in the company of armed guards. Still, it was there the queen seemed happiest, crying out in delight when a trout leaped high after a darting fly or an osprey seized a fish from the black waters.

I had hoped that with winter's end there would come good news—an uprising of loyal nobles, or an intervention by Queen Elizabeth, or even some prospect of escape.

Instead it brought the worst news possible.

I was walking by the lochside while the queen napped and I was reveling in the small gales that were blowing. I had put my arms out and let the winds flap my cloak.

Oh, I thought, *if only these were wings. . . .*

It was then I saw a boat come ashore and realized it was George Douglas just returned from a trip to Edinburgh. He signalled me over.

I checked to see that no guards were by, then went quickly to him.

"Have you new gossip?" I asked, keeping my tone light in case we should be heard. "For the queen?"

"We must be more wary than ever of your mistress's safety," he told me in a low, worried voice.

I felt sick to my stomach. "What has happened?"

George rubbed his jaw anxiously. "Knox has been preaching against her from his pulpit again, saying that never was there a greater abomination in the nature of women than in her."

I recoiled. "That wicked old man," I said, forgetting that he had saved my life when he could have let me die.

"There is more." George's whisper took on an ominous tone.

"More? Has he any bile left to spew up?"

"Not Knox, no. But his sermons only underline what the lords have already done. The lords . . . ah! I have not the heart to break the news to her, Nicola."

"Tell me then and I shall tell it to her myself. Better she hear bad news from me than from you."

"It is not just bad news, Nicola. It is *terrible* news." His voice cracked.

"For Jesus's sake, tell me!" My hand balled into a fist.

He hesitated still and I thought that I would cheerfully throttle him if he did not get on with it.

"Bad news can be borne if we only know it," I said.

He blurted out, "The queen has been accused before Parliament of Darnley's murder. She may soon be tried for it."

I trembled with anger. "They cannot. *I* will not let them."

He seemed deeply shocked at my vehemence. "Nicola—they can and will. And if she is found guilty, there is only one possible penalty."

I strained towards him.

He took a deep breath and spoke it. "Death."

45 ⁊ A MINUTE FROM FREEDOM

I told the queen while she was busy with a new piece of embroidery. If I had been worried about how she would take the news, I needn't have troubled myself. She did not even raise her eyes from the stitches.

There was a long silence after I finished. The only sound was the wind buffeting the castle walls.

At last she raised her eyes from the cloth and said, "As to Knox, he is nothing. I do not think *less* of the man. I *could* not think less of him. But the others—Huntly, Argyll . . ." Her eyes were that wonderful green-gold, like jewels. "It was already clear to me that their infamy knew no bounds. They have only steeled my contempt for them."

She seemed so calm. So resolute. So accepting.

"Madam, are you not afraid?" I cried.

"They might come for you any day," added Mary, nervously twisting the chain of her crucifix.

The queen laid her work aside and stood. She walked over to the hearth and held her hands out to the fire. "Calm? Not I. I am terrified," she admitted. "But not for myself. They have already done everything to me they can, save kill me." She turned towards us. "I have been called a whore and murderess. I have had hands laid upon my person. My throne has been stolen from me, my crown and jewels. My son has been taken away. I have miscarried twins. I have lain in a foul prison." She drew in a breath, and outside the wind once more made an assault on the wall of the keep. For a second it drew her attention to the window, but only a second. "No, I am not afraid of what they will do to me, but what they will do to Scotland." Her head was high and there was a spirit I had not seen in her eyes for many months.

This—this was the queen I loved.

"Majesty," I said, and knelt before her.

"I will write again to my cousin Elizabeth and the dowager Queen of France," said the queen. "George will get the letters out to them. They will not allow me to be used in this manner. Bring me my pen, Mary, and a sheet of paper."

I stood. "I will get them, Madam," I said, and went quickly to her bedchamber. But all the while, I was thinking darkly: *If either Elizabeth of England or Catherine de Medici had wanted to go to war to free her, they would have done so already.*

There was a great tension in the air now. Not just between the queen and Lord William. There was even a roughening between Lord William and young George.

One day as I was fetching the fresh laundry from the keep where the laundresses had delivered it, I passed a chamber where Lord William was locked in a heated argument with his brother.

Eavesdropping in the queen's cause, I told myself, *is never a sin.* Besides, they were so involved in mutual accusations, they did not know I was there. So I stopped by the door and listened.

"Yer smitten," Lord William said loudly. "Ye never could hang on to yer wits in the presence of a pretty face."

"If I take pity on an innocent woman, am I to be blamed for

that?" George cast back. "I do not relish the role of jailer as much as you do, brother, especially when the prisoner is the queen."

"Queen no longer, Geordie," Lord William reminded him sharply. "She signed her abdication."

"Aye, under threat of death, which even a man might have done. And ye standing by while it happened. Like a whipped dog eager to lick the master's boots."

I leaned closer to the door.

There was the sound of rustling papers, then Sir William said, "Ambitious little toad. Ye wish to marry her. To make yerself king."

George's voice was as full of bristles as a hedgehog. "I harbor no such ambition, and well ye know it, brother! But if I serve her faithfully and ye do not, which of us then is the *traitor?*" His voice rose shrilly on the last word.

My heart had begun to pound. I thought about leaving, but I did not.

There was an ominous pause before Lord William said coldly, "Yer dangerously close, lad. Don't say more, else I will never forgive."

"Forgive? What have ye to forgive?" George retorted. He was in full roar now. "There should be truth between us, brother. Blood—if not humors—ties us to one another. But I say 'traitor' and mean each syllable. *I* will not be a party to the regent's plans. Nothing would suit him better than for the queen to die here." He paused. "Some small accident, is it? A convenient drowning, perhaps?"

I held my breath. *Where is the queen's safe haven now?* I thought. *I must tell Mary. We have to get the queen away.*

"*I* am the laird," came Lord William's cold voice. "Ye'll do as I demand. Brother or no."

"And if I do not?" George's voice matched him, ice for ice.

"Then ye'll be gone."

For a moment George was silent, as if gathering his courage. Then he said, "Yer *allies*, my dear brother, are men without honor, loyal to nothing but their own ambition."

"Go! And the while, keep yerself far from the queen. The guards have already been ordered to bar ye from her chambers."

"Go I will! Better that than become a prisoner here myself."

"Och," Lord William sighed. "Arguing with a fool is dry work. Where is my wine? Gordon? Gordon? Where are ye, stupid boy?"

As he stormed out of the room, I jumped nimbly aside, busying myself in the linen cupboard. George emerged a few moments later. His grim countenance brightened when he saw me.

"Were you listening at the door, Nicola?"

A flush spread across my cheeks.

"Good. Then you know I must go. But tell your mistress I will not be far off. Tell her . . . tell her she can count upon me when her hour comes."

I sketched a brief curtsy. "I will tell her gladly," I said carefully. "But I will miss your visits, sir. As will the queen. You are not a Douglas in heart."

"Do not say that, Nicola. I am twice the Douglas my brother is. And will prove it, to the queen and to God."

The days went by, then weeks, and we finally decided that we could not just wait for George, we would have to make a plan ourselves.

One consolation was that we were finally rid of Lady Douglas. Heavily pregnant, she had taken to her bed in the hall, clucked over by female relatives and two midwives. An April baby was expected.

"A cackle of nestlings, more like," I said to Mary and the queen, which brought a bit of laughter into our lives.

The other consolation was that the queen was no longer close-guarded. The soldiers had grown steadily lax during the winter.

The queen, Mary, and I sat huddled by the fire one morning, waiting for the sun to break through the grey long enough to let us walk outside.

"We have to have a boat," I said.

Mary clucked her tongue, as if to say, "Of course."

"And there are three ways to get one." I held up my three fingers, pointing to each in turn. "Buy one, borrow one, or steal one."

They both nodded, their fingers busy at their embroideries.

"Which do you suggest?" Mary asked.

"Borrow. That way no one else gets in trouble for helping us."

The queen smiled down at her stitchery.

"There will never be a better chance to break free," I pointed out.

At that moment, the fire in the hearth crackled loudly as if signalling its agreement.

"Do you imagine I have not considered escape?" the queen asked softly, looking up. "I consider it every day. But what is the sense in raising our hopes only to have them dashed."

Mary nodded. "George hinted at plans afoot. Should we not wait for him?"

I said hurriedly, "Whatever George meant by the queen's hour, that time had not yet come. And time, as we all know, is not on our side." What I didn't say aloud—and didn't need to—was that with a murder charge hanging over the queen's head, the executioners might come any day.

The queen stood and put her back to the fire. Such was our close companionship in this prison, neither Mary nor I felt compelled to rise with her.

"My dears," the queen said, "I could not now make a drop from the tower without breaking a leg—or worse."

"We will not have to drop from the tower or vault the gate. We will simply go *through* it," I promised. "I have been up all night thinking and have finally got it!"

Mary stared at me as if I had lost my mind. "Got what?"

"The plan!"

Toying with the ring Regal Mary had sent her, the queen said, "Perhaps if this were a magic ring, Nicola, as in one of your stories, I could become invisible, and simply walk past the guards unseen."

"You *shall* pass them by unseen," I said. "And in broad daylight, too. It will not take magic to do it."

I rushed out of the room and returned with a bundle of rough garments of linsey-woolsey which I laid out before her.

Surprised, she said, "What is this?"

"A disguise, Majesty," I said.

Her eyes widened. She had often dressed up for masques. On one occasion she had even passed as a soldier.

"As you know, I was ashore recently running some errands with the castle servants," I explained. "While they were taking refreshment at a tavern, I obtained these clothes. I said they were for rags to soften your mattress."

"Why didn't you say anything of this before?" Mary asked. Her hands were now folded atop her embroidery.

"Because I needed to think more about it. As the queen said— not wanting to raise hopes only to dash them."

The queen picked up one of the two sacklike dresses and held it under her chin. She looked thoughtful. "Do you think I can pass for a village washerwoman?"

"We will have to ruin your hair and wash off your makeup," Mary told her.

"It might work. . . ." The queen hesitated. "As long as no one notices I am gone. But Lord William insists on knowing my whereabouts at all times. His servants check on me regularly."

"*I* have an idea," Mary said. She went over to the queen's dressing table and lifted up one of the hairpieces the queen used to fill out her natural hair. "These will do."

"What do you mean?" the queen asked.

Mary held the peruke on top of her own head. "If I put on one of your dresses, Majesty, and fashion my hair into the same style as yours, I might be taken for you from a reasonable distance."

"Yes," the queen agreed somberly. "If you sit at the window as I so often do, and with your face averted, Lord William's men might well be deceived."

"And thinking you safe in the tower, like a princess in a fairy tale, they will not be looking for you elsewhere," I concluded. I had already thought of that part of the plan, but did not want to spoil Mary's obvious pleasure in proposing it.

"I wish it were not such a serious business," said the queen, "for it would make a splendid joke." There were sudden tears in her eyes. "But dearest Mary, how can we leave you behind to take the blame?"

"Once we are away," I said quickly, "Mary can get back into her own clothes and lie down in her room, to be fast asleep when it is discovered we are gone. How can they then blame her? Surely she would have come with us, had she known of our plans."

"You have thought of everything, Nicola!" the queen said, and clapped her hands. "And you, too, dear Mary. Brava!" She spun around in place and her skirts belled out around her. Then she stopped suddenly. "We must go tomorrow. Before we have time for fear."

Brava, Majesty! I thought.

The very next day the washerwomen came from the village to deliver what clean linens they had and round up the used. Normally they saved the queen's linens and her small clothes for the last.

I watched them from the window while the queen changed into her disguise. I was already in mine. At the same time, Mary stood before the mirror adjusting her false hair and tugging at her gown.

There were enough servants coming and going that the guards would pay no attention to yet another pair of common slatterns. That was important to my plan.

The queen and I got down the stairs and out of the tower without a mishap, bundles of dirty laundry in our arms.

I led the queen across the courtyard. She wore a rough plaid pulled up over her face, for her features were too striking and familiar not to be concealed. As to her walk—I had spent the morning training her and she managed to cast aside her elegant glide in favor of a longer stride and a clumsier gait.

"Never—never—look up into anyone's face," I warned her. "Your eyes, Majesty, will give you away."

We passed almost too easily up to the gate carrying the fardel of laundry without drawing so much as a glance. The soldiers were busily chatting with one another, and paid us no mind.

But the gate—that would be the big test.

For the first time in days the sun was shining brilliantly, so we had nowhere to hide.

I signalled the queen to adjust her plaid once more, and—as she did so—the great ring on her hand with the mouse and lion carving winked at me.

"Hssst," I said to get her attention, showing her my hand.

She understood and slipped the ring off, hiding it in her clothing.

We got to the castle gate, walking close, all but clinging together. The guards glanced briefly at us, then away. It was then I realized that I was holding my breath and let it out in a single *whoosh*.

One of the guards called out, "A problem, lassies?"

"Just a stink," I called back in my broadest Scots accent, "the wind off these rags."

They laughed and turned back to their own gossip.

As we made our way down to the shore, the queen winked at me. I was so astonished, I nearly dropped the laundry.

"Head down, Madam," I whispered, and she did just that, adjusting the plaid to further hide her face.

My heart was pounding, not so much with excitement but fear. It was all I could do to put one foot before another. Even when I had run from Bothwell's men in the night, I had not been so overmastered by fright. But then I had had only myself to worry about.

At last we reached one of the boats, where a man dozed in the sun.

"We are done with work, fellow," I said. "Take us back to town."

He awoke at my words, helped us into the boat, then cast off smoothly from the island, pulling leisurely on the oars. I did not dare arouse his suspicions by trying to hurry him.

The water slapped lightly, *pit-pat*, on the side of the boat as we glided along over the waves. The sun cast brilliant jewels of light on the water. Across the loch, the far shore was like a glimpse of paradise.

I glanced over to reassure the queen, who was sitting with her head downcast, as if studying her shoes, the plaid covering her head like a cowl.

Her shoes! I suddenly realized she was wearing her elegant black velvet boots. A rush of bile rose in my throat, flooding my mouth. I prayed that the boatman—who was facing us—would not notice the queen's feet.

"I have seen ye on this crossing before," he said to me.

"Yes, I am often sent on errands by Lady Douglas," I said, hoping my voice would not shake.

"And yer friend?" he asked, leaning forward. "I dinna recognize her at all."

The queen looked away and I leaned forward to take his eye on me instead.

"She is but newly come from Killin," I said. "She is still a wee bit shy." I could hear her shift behind me. "And a wee bit unwell. She is trying not to catch a chill."

"Chill?" the boatman laughed. "The sun is out full, lassie! Enjoy it while ye can. We will pay for it tomorrow." He laid down his oars. There was a curious glint in his eye. "Be it just a pretty face she hides for the sake of a jealous husband?"

Before I realized his intention, he lunged forward to snatch the queen's plaid aside. Instinctively, she reached up and grabbed his hand to stop him. He stared wide-eyed at her long delicate fingers.

"Those nae be a washerwoman's hands," he said.

She pulled herself free, and as she did so, the plaid fell away exposing her pale, beautiful face.

The boatman leaned back, his face torn between accusation and apology. "The queen . . ." He darted quick, nervous glances at the island to see if anyone was watching us.

Sitting up straight and casting aside her washerwoman bearing as though it were an old garment, the queen leaned forward. "Yes, I am your queen, boatman. But I do not command you now. Instead I *beg* your help to escape this unjust imprisonment."

The boatman's knuckles went white, so hard did he grip the oars. "I canna be a party to this escape, Your Majesty."

I could stand it no longer. "Canna? Or willna? It is only a short way. We are hardly more than a minute from freedom."

"A minute from my arrest, ye mean. They willna wait for a trial to hang *me*. Ye be royal, Ma'am," he said to the queen, "and they dare not harm ye. I have to think on mysel'—and my wee bairns."

The queen said nothing, but gazed at the mainland, now so tantalizingly close.

"If you betray us, you might still be taken as an accomplice," I said quickly. "Who will believe you could have rowed this far without recognizing the queen unless you were part of the plot? Would anyone think you such a fool?"

He shook his head but still made no move to shift the boat one way or another. It floated midway between the island and the shore, rocking slowly in the waves.

I tried to judge the distance. Heavily clad as we were, we could not possibly swim the rest of the way, even if the boatman did not cry out.

"Please," I begged, "we are so close."

The boatman shook his head. "I will take ye back to the castle, lassie, but I willna raise the alarm. Get yerselves ashore and hide all trace of yer disguise. I dare no more."

I was about to appeal again but the queen motioned me to silence.

"It is the best we can hope for under the circumstances," she said quietly, as the boatman took up the oars again. "If we remain floating here much longer, suspicions will surely be aroused."

So wordlessly we were returned to our island prison, where we made our way back to the gloomy tower, just two more unhappy slatterns from the mainland come to work.

Mary met us at the door, having watched the whole thing from the window.

"Your brief reign as queen is over, my dear," the queen said.

Those few words sent us all into doubled-over paroxysms of laughter that very soon tumbled into tears.

46 ❧ ANOTHER PLAN

Over the next few days more members of the Douglas clan arrived at the island, as though Lord William were calling in reinforcements while his wife was confined to her chamber.

A young orphaned redhead named Willie Douglas was among the first. Friendly and good-natured, he reminded me of his cousin George. For a while, I dared hope that he might act as our protector in the event Lord James's men came to take the queen. But after he had paid his respects, bringing the queen a gift of sweet comfits set in a basket as if they were eggs in a nest, we saw nothing more of him.

Two young Douglas nieces arrived soon after and attached themselves to us like limpets on a rock. Scarcely fifteen years old, they had come to the island to help with the new little laird. But they were also there to bask in the presence of the beautiful queen about whom they had heard so many tales.

The girls soon became companions as constant and unwanted as their aunt, begging Mary and me to teach them card games and show them what clothes the queen had at last been sent in her confinement. They oohed and aahed over her red satin petticoat furred with marten and the black silk tights. They cooed at the little red velvet box with the crossed *F*'s made of silver. They overpraised her embroideries. They made our quiet confinement a noisy prison.

And as we had no guarantee they would not betray our confidences, we were careful to give them none.

One day, while we were in the middle of a card game, the dowager Lady Margaret paid the tower a surprise visit. She had been spending most of her time in the hall with her new grandson, so we were not expecting to see her.

Even more surprising was the deferential manner in which she approached the queen.

"Your Majesty," she said, giving a bow whose stiffness owed more to her great age than coldness of manner.

Mary and I looked down at the cards in our hands, but the queen smiled graciously.

"Come, Lady Margaret, and sit by me. I do not know about you, but my legs get stiff with standing on these cold floors."

Lady Margaret sank gratefully into the chair.

For a moment the queen turned her attention back to her cards, but she was never unaware that the Old Lady—as everyone called the dowager—was there for a reason.

At last the Old Lady got to the purpose of her visit. "My son George has written for permission to return to the island," she said, her fingers tightly knotted around a lace kerchief. "He plans to leave for France to seek his fortune and wishes to make his farewells to his brother, despite the harsh words that passed between them. . . ."

"And a cannonball," I whispered to Mary, for a guard had told us that Lord William had fired at George across the water. But despite my sharpness, I was pleased that George was returning. Perhaps he had a plan that was better than mine had been.

The Old Lady ignored me. "His brother has relented of his ban for this purpose only—and George is not to stay the night."

So much for a plan, I thought.

"There will be many opportunities in France for a young man of George's abilities," said the queen. "I will give him any letters he might require. In France, at least, my name can still open doors."

The Old Lady's face grew as frosted as a January windowpane. "That would not be to the purpose," she stated icily. "He must remain in Scotland. He is a Douglas! A post can be arranged for him at the regent's court. After all, the regent, Lord James, is also my son."

The queen became just as frosty. "Has it *escaped* your notice, Lady Margaret, that I no longer wield influence at court? Else I would not still be here."

Both Mary and I went still as statues.

The Old Lady blinked uncomfortably, but continued on doggedly. "It is not your influence with the regent, Majesty, but your influence with young Geordie I am asking you to employ. If anyone can dissuade him from this foreign adventure, it would be you."

I dared a look from the corner of my eye at Mary. She had pursed her lips but otherwise not moved.

"Would you have me command him as a sovereign?"

The barb was not lost on the Old Lady. She bowed her head, and without raising her eyes, answered, "I would have you speak to him as a favor to a mother whose heart would break should he leave these shores. Surely you of all women can understand that."

For a moment the queen was quiet. Then in a softer tone she said, "I do indeed know what it is like to be separated from a beloved son, Lady Margaret. I will speak to George. But only in private."

"You have my word," the Old Lady agreed.

• • •

George returned to Lochleven the next morning. Even the sun seemed to shine on him with a particular brightness. The water around his boat was dotted with motes as round as gold pieces. I watched from the window as he was greeted by Lord William.

"They are acting as if the quarrel is well behind them," I said. "The laird's arm is over his shoulder."

"The Old Lady has a long reach," Mary commented dryly. She and the queen continued their embroideries as if George's arrival was of no consequence, but I could feel the excitement in the room.

It was yet another hour before George crossed the courtyard to the tower. As soon as he came up into the queen's chamber, he fell on one knee before her.

"Forgive my long absence, Majesty," he said, his voice heavy with emotion. *And your long silence,* I thought. "I have done my best to serve you well while away."

"Get up, Geordie," the queen insisted, setting down her embroidery hoop. "True friendship never asks forgiveness. If you have been driven out of your home because of your devotion to me, I hardly have cause to complain."

I shut the door carefully and put my back to it. The Douglas girls rarely came in without knocking first, but still I stood guard.

Rising, George said, "I have been visiting Lord Seton and others loyal to your cause. I have told them to expect you back soon."

"I wish I shared your optimism," the queen said, patting the chair next to her.

George went to it as eager as a lover.

"We have already attempted one escape in your absence," I said. "And yet here we are still. Freedom is not so easily won."

George leaned forward, elbows on knees, frowning in concern as we explained all that had happened.

"Laundresses—eh?" He turned and looked at the queen. "But how could you hope to disguise such majesty?"

I rolled my eyes as Mary got up to tidy the queen's table, setting a tray with her dirty dishes beside me at the door.

Sitting back, George continued. "Still—if my brother did not get wind of the attempt, it will do us no harm."

"I do not believe he knows a thing," the queen said. "Only three of us knew of the plan—and the boatman found out after. All four would have been done some injury if the escape had been uncovered. Your brother is not loath to tell us when we have done wrong."

George nodded. "Well I know. But he has no wind of what I am about, either. I have not only been meeting with nobles, but with others even more crucial to our plans. You have met my young cousin, Willie Douglas?"

"The sprightly redhead?" asked the queen. "We have. He seemed friendly enough when he arrived. Even brought me sweets. Though he has not been back since." She picked up her embroidery ring and started to work again at a picture of a phoenix rising from a flame.

"He is more than merely friendly." George gave a wide grin. Then caution overtook him. "Nicola, please check the door."

"I would have heard . . ." I protested.

"Your mother *promised* we would be alone," the queen said.

"But my brother did not."

I flung the door open, and put the tray outside. There was no one on the floor or even down on the first landing. The Old Lady had kept her word.

George looked relieved and I shut the door again, but did not leave my place.

"Young Willie has always loved the old hero tales," George said.

"When I offered him the chance to rescue a damosel from a tower, he immediately bound himself to our cause."

"A damosel!" the queen laughed merrily. It was a lovely sound, and so rare these days. I silently blessed George for that. "I am a thrice married woman with a child!"

"How bounden can wee Willie be?" Mary said sourly. "He has not been up to see Her Majesty but the once."

"I counseled him to conceal his loyalty so that he can act as our agent without suspicion," George replied.

"Boys playing at Knights of the Round Table . . ." said Mary, her own embroidery ring set down firmly in her lap, "does not get the queen out of this gloomy place. We have only a few days at best before your sister-in-law is out of childbed and rejoins us."

"Reporting every snort and sniffle to Lord William," I added. "And then there are those chattering girls. . . ."

"The Magpies!" George smiled.

I laughed, it was such a perfect name for them.

"Yes," George said, turning back to the queen, "our best chance to get you away is while my brother's wife is still confined, and the girls helping with the new baby."

At the mention of the baby, the queen's face got a misty look, as if remembering her own child.

"Perhaps we could carry you off in a great box," George said. "I could say I was transporting my papers off the isle."

"Never!" the queen cried. "I have a horror of enclosed spaces."

"Then we will need a new disguise," I put in.

"Oh, Nicola," Mary said, "not again."

"There is no other way."

"I agree." George grinned at me. "But, Nicola, it will have to be better than those washerwomen."

"Those washerwomen got us out of the tower and into the boat," I reminded them.

"But did not set us free, dear Nicola," the queen said softly.

George looked at us each in turn. "I can certainly have a boat-man in my employ standing by this time. But you will still have to get out of the castle on your own."

"Yes," I agreed. "What we need is a great distraction to be certain no one notices us in our disguises. Once was luck, but we cannot count on luck a second time."

"Did you have something in mind, Nicola?" the queen asked.

I took a deep breath. "Yes, I think I do. It is almost the end of April. Do you know, George, if there are any May Day celebrations planned?"

"My brother is not much given to celebration," George said, slowly. Then, as if he suddenly understood where I was going, added with gusto, "But I am inclined to festivity myself. I think the family *might* mount a May Day feast . . . if they believe I am going off to Paris."

"Ah—but I am to persuade you otherwise," the queen said. "I have promised your mother to try."

George made a face. "Then I will appear to be wavering. That way you will have to see me often, Majesty. But I will not make up my mind until the feast."

"Fill the castle with minstrels, tumblers, clowns!" I practically shouted. Then added softly, "By the time the revels are done, it will be too late for anyone to notice that the Queen of May is missing!"

"And I to Paris!" George crowed.

The queen laughed. "I have not enjoyed a feast in so long, I am half-minded to stay for the whole of it."

"Oh, we will have our fill of feasting before we go," George promised her. "And I will claim a galliard of my lady." There was little doubt that George Douglas was quite in love with his queen.

And I, for the first time since coming to this little island, was filled with real hope.

47 ❧ MAY DAY FEAST

George went immediately to the Old Lady and proposed a May Day celebration, telling her that he would postpone his departure for France until the end of the festivities. Given this incentive, the Old Lady agreed at once, but she did not want to spend much on it. In fact she was known throughout Scotland for her miserly hand.

"No wonder George wants to hie to France," I said, "to dance without his mother's sour face and his brother's disapproval."

"I would go, too, given such a family," agreed Mary.

The queen shook her head. "None of us is to blame for our kin. Surely, Nicola, you and I know that all too well!"

She meant Lord James and Uncle Armand, of course. I smiled ruefully at her.

"Perhaps George can get the Old Lady to turn over the planning of the festivities to wee Willie," I said.

"Suggest it to him," the queen ordered.

George was back within an hour with news.

"What a brilliant mind I seem to have," he said. "Though I feel I have thrown poor Willie to my mother, like a lamb to a lion."

"Which is which?" I asked innocently, which gave the queen another good laugh.

• • •

Word of the festival was sent out to all the performers in the area of Lochleven and Kinross. Within days their wagons and tents could be seen all around the village on the mainland.

Inside the castle everyone was hard at work making costumes and preparing special delicacies. I overheard more than one soldier praising the queen. A potboy said, "Knox's old honeypot has a sweet taste for our pleasure." Even the laundresses spoke of how different the mood in Lochleven seemed.

"And all for a feast," said one.

"The first May Day this poor island has seen," added another.

I did a little jig when I heard them, and ran off to tell the queen.

The queen, too, was thrilled with the preparations. She grabbed up my hands and whirled me around.

"I shall dance again, Nicola! Dance!" she cried, for a moment forgetting the real reason for the feast.

In the corner, a book of prayers in her lap, Mary made a tsk sound with her tongue. "It is not just a party, Madam."

We stopped spinning and the queen put her hands on her hips. "La, Mary—do not be so sour. Let us enjoy ourselves while we can. It may be the last time."

I turned away so that the queen could not see the tears that had suddenly started in my eyes.

When May Day actually came, boats overfilled with merry-makers from the mainland kept ferrying across to the island. The boatmen were earning a pretty penny for all the trips, and were paid as well with drinks from the wineskins of the revelers, so that soon many of the boats went in circles instead of straight across.

So narrow was the space between castle wall and shore, more

than one person had to be fished from the loch before day's end.

The sun shone down on us without a cloud to cover it. *God's lidless eye,* I thought, *keeping watch on us all.*

Willie Douglas was the leader of the revels, playing the Abbot of Unreason. He wore a bishop's mitre festooned with ribbons of blue and green, while his gaily-colored cassock was decorated with shells and tiny bells. He tinkled so as he walked, he was like a choir of angels. Any reveler who did not obey him or refused to laugh at his jests received a knock on the head from his shepherd's crook.

He beamed so broadly, I said to him in passing, "If your grin were any broader, you would put the sun to shame."

The musicians played merrily, old tunes and new, eagerly sweeping up any coins tossed their way. However the acrobats were not as daring as those I had known in France, and the jugglers could not keep more than five balls in the air at once.

Dear Pierre, I thought, shaking my head. *How far apart we are.* I doubted he would know me now, nor I him.

All of a sudden, Queen Mary emerged from the gloom of the tower in a green satin gown trimmed in silver and gold. A crown of spring flowers sat upon her shining hair. She was so striking a pearl in this setting of grey stone that the performers—and even a few of the soldiers—fell to their knees at the sight of her.

Willie Douglas scampered over and bowed. "As Abbot of Unreason I name ye Queen of May and my partner for the day."

Covering her face with her hands, the queen pretended to be abashed, but it was all according to our plan. Then she let the abbot lead her into a dance.

All day the queen and abbot reeled tirelessly around the courtyard and the keep's gardens, encouraging everyone else to join in the dance. The fiddlers and pipers got little rest—but much ale—which made them play faster and faster, though it added nothing to their precision.

By the time George arrived in the guise of Robin Hood, more than one soldier and most of the musicians were already heartily drunk. George passed out fresh wine and ale, mocking anyone who tried to abstain.

"Black Knox does not rule here today," he cried. "The Abbot of Unreason is our preacher. Revel is our king!"

Whenever the minstrels and musicians fell silent, George would stir them afresh by suggesting a number of saucy ballads and merry jigs and off they would go again. He was in his element for certain!

Sometimes standing on a garden bench, hands on hips, I sang with the revelers, winking at the soldiers. Sometimes I sang alone to great drunken applause. I felt at those times like the queen's own fool again, charming and entertaining.

But often as I wandered through the revelers, I recalled the queen's words—that we might be enjoying ourselves for the very last time. And each time I thought of them, a wave of sadness crashed over me.

It made me sing all the louder.

By midafternoon a lull had finally come upon the party.

George—in his guise of Robin Hood—confronted the Abbot of Unreason in front of the Glassin Tower. He brandished a quarterstaff at his cousin.

"I am the King of Thieves," George declared in a booming voice, "and I demand that you surrender the Queen of May to me."

"*Demand*, villain?" Willie retorted, sticking his chin out. "I make the rules on this day and I say thee nay."

"Surrender her," George demanded again, "or I'll knock the nonsense out of your head!" He raised his staff threateningly.

"I'll knock some nonsense into yours!" cried the abbot, waving his shepherd's crook.

The pair of them had at each other and a mighty roar went up from the crowd.

"On, Robin!" some cheered loudly.

"The abbot! The abbot!" cried others.

George and Willie carried on their mock combat with comic leaps and falls while we all whooped and laughed. Only Lord William was not amused, his fingers clenched tightly around his goblet as if half-afraid Robin would seize his royal prisoner and run off with her.

At last Robin was tripped by his opponent and he fell flat on his back. Many of the onlookers cheered loudly, throwing their tams up in the air. Then a piper blew a tremendous blast on his pipes, which the abbot acknowledged with a bow.

But others began to boo. "On, Robin! Up and at the old Roman!" Whereupon Willie charged them and they fled before his flailing crook.

At that, George clambered to his feet and approached the abbot humbly. "I admit defeat," he conceded, his head held low, "but may I claim one dance wi' the Queen o' May?"

As if accepting the surrender of an army, the abbot nodded, stroked his false whiskers, and said, "Very well. But only one."

George walked over to the queen and offered her his arm. She placed her hand lightly on it.

"A galliard!" George cried out. "A galliard for the queen."

The band tried to play one properly, but was too drunk to manage. They hooted and tooted along and it was—just barely—a recognizable tune lively enough to dance to.

George did not mind. In fact, he looked so happy, I could well believe he had engineered the escape solely for the sake of this one dance with the queen.

For a few moments they danced alone, capering and jumping. Then other revelers joined in. Soon the two were lost among the whirling, leaping couples. I, too, joined the dance, led in by a hand-some soldier with a pair of eyes the blue-green of the North Sea.

All the while, Lord William circled nervously around the court-yard, desperately trying to keep his brother and the queen in sight.

But I had *my* eye on the Old Lady, who was sitting next to the keep under a canopy to shade her from the sun. From the sour look on her face I guessed she was not pleased to see her son making merry with the queen. But she held back from chiding because she hoped his devotion might yet persuade him to remain in Scotland.

At the end of the dance, George gave a low bow. He was breath-ing in great gasps, and the underarms of his green suit had become stained a deeper green.

The queen was breathing hard as well, and she put a hand to her forehead. "I have led so quiet a life of late, I am quite worn out." She turned to Willie. "My Lord Abbot, have I your leave to retire?"

Willie made a grave show of considering this request. "I grant my permission on this one condition," he answered at last, "that you dream only the happiest and most foolish of dreams."

"That I shall certainly do," the queen smilingly assured him.

She walked back to the tower, and George Douglas's eyes fol-lowed her every step of the way.

Lord William seemed vastly relieved to see his brother sepa-rated at last from his royal prisoner. For the first time that day he ac-tually smiled. I thought it did not improve his looks.

George turned back to his mother, and I happened to be close enough to hear his farewells.

"Mother, I must go now."

"Back to the mainland, Geordie?" the Old Lady asked. "Or to . . ." She could not bring herself to mention France.

I was careful to keep the smile from my face, for I knew what she did not, that we were all going to France—the queen and George and me.

"I am not certain yet that I would find a better reception in Edinburgh than in Paris," George said. He bowed and left.

"Oh, Geordie, stay at home," the Old Lady whispered.

Then Willie was suddenly beside me, his whiskers beginning to peel off on one side, which lent him a certain lopsided charm.

"The queen has departed for her bed," he said, "so I need a new consort."

"And why should I wish to dance with a doddering old cleric like you who can hardly keep his staff upright or his whiskers straight?" I teased.

"I am the Abbot of Unreason," he proclaimed. "As a fool, ye of all people should be the first to obey me."

"On the contrary," I said, "as I am the only *genuine* fool here, I outrank you. You are merely a pretend fool for this one day."

"Rebellion!" Willie cried. "I willna stand for it!"

He took a mock swing at me with his crook which I easily dodged. Then he chased me across the courtyard and made more swipes which I ducked under, to the amusement of the onlookers.

"Answer me this," Willie demanded as we came to a halt by the well, "who is the greater fool, the fool who is always a fool and has nothing to lose by being foolish, or the fool who is foolish for only a day but risks all that he has by his foolishness."

He made his question sound like a silly riddle, in case anyone else should hear, but I knew how serious his question really was. By what he was doing today he would throw away all claim to honor and position within his family.

"The one who risks much is surely the greater fool," I said. "And the braver."

"A good answer," he said. "Now do as I command, fool, and partner me in the dance."

Happily I admitted defeat and danced several reels with him before he skipped off to find a fresh partner. Taking a sip of wine, I looked around the courtyard. The fair was winding down; people were climbing into their boats and heading back to their homes.

I saw George making his way to the postern gate, and when he turned round to spy me out, he gave me a subtle signal to join him. We walked together outside the castle walls. The far shore seemed as distant as the New World.

Since there were soldiers close by, George and I dared not speak what was really on our minds. Instead we chatted about how well the day had gone, and George joked about the bruises he had received at the hands of his cousin.

"I am black-and-blue all over," he said. "And the little pig enjoyed every minute of it."

"As you did, sir," I said.

He nodded. "As I did, Nicola." He gazed over at a boat that was pulling in to the shore and waved.

The boatman answered George's wave.

"All is well," George said with a sigh. He turned to me and handed me an earring. "Take this to the queen. Tell her you found it lying in the courtyard. She will know what it signifies."

Not daring to arouse the suspicions of his brother, George strolled down to the waiting boat alone. I curtsied to him as he got in, so nothing would seem amiss, then I watched until he was halfway over the grey waters.

When I returned to the tower, Lord William was serving the queen her dinner, an unheard-of breach in the prison protocol. His two nieces fluttered about.

The Magpies, I thought, *though it is we who will have flown off by tonight.*

Mary sat near the door, her head bent over a breviary, praying fiercely.

"My brother has departed?" Lord William asked.

"Yes, my lord, I saw him cross the loch," I said, certain Lord William already knew this, having watched us out the window. "I tendered him the queen's farewell and the hope that he would not be going to France against his mother's wishes." It was a small lie, and I hoped that God would forgive me for it.

Lord William seemed more relaxed than I had ever seen him, for he began talking about the day's revels in full sentences instead of his usual clipped speech.

"The feast went well, I thought," he said. "Much merrymaking, though perhaps a few too many drunks in the loch. But no one badly hurt, though there will be sore heads tomorrow, I suppose."

"Including my own," the queen said.

Lord William smiled. Clearly he had expected that if there were to be any trouble, it would have happened while his brother was on the island. Now that George was gone, Lord William was off his guard.

Just as we had hoped.

"Madam," I said brightly, "I found one of your earrings in the courtyard." I passed it to her. "It must have fallen off while you were dancing."

"Yes, it must have," the queen murmured. I saw her raise her eyebrows as she examined this message from George.

"Uncle—look at that!" cried one of the Douglas girls, who had been standing at the window.

Lord William strolled over to the window and, looking down, suddenly stiffened. "What is that rapscallion Willie doing down there by the boats?" he asked.

I bit my lip. It was part of our plan to chain the laird's boats together so that they could not be used to pursue us. What bad luck
that the girl had chosen this particular moment to look out.

"I expect it is just more May Day foolishness," I said quickly.
"Willie drank overmuch at the feast." Even to my ears, that expla-
nation limped along like a Glasgow beggar.

Not satisfied, Lord William leaned further out the window,
shouting and waving his fist. "Get away from there, stupid boy!"

I glanced urgently at the queen and she saw in my face what
danger our plans were suddenly in. She let out an awful moan and—
when Lord William turned at the sound—she fell back against her
chair, clutching her head. Then she slowly fell sideways. Mary and
I dashed to her side, managing to catch her before she actually hit
the floor.

"Please, sir. . . ." I cried. "We need help."

Hurrying over, Lord William gathered the queen up in his arms
and set her back into her chair while his nieces fluttered around
helplessly.

"I am so unwell," the queen murmured weakly, leaning against
Sir William. "All that dancing. Please. *Please.* A glass . . ."

Lord William was so concerned, he ran down to the kitchen
himself and brought back a pitcher of wine which he poured for the
queen.

She took a sip and sighed. "I am much better now, Lord
William. How foolish of me. I must have danced too much at the
revels. But you are so kind. Every one of you, but especially you,
Lord William."

He preened a bit, throwing out his chest like an old cock. Then,
as if suddenly aware he was dancing attendance upon his prisoner,
Lord William drew himself up.

"I will leave you now," he said, all thoughts of Willie and the boats thankfully banished. "My wife and my mother are waiting dinner."

No sooner was he gone than the Magpies began to fill the air with their twittering concern.

"Oh, Madam, ye look so flushed," said one. "What will ye have us do?"

"We could bring ye a cold compress . . ." said the other.

"A warm compress . . ."

"A bowl . . ."

"A towel . . ."

I was trying to think of a way to send them off, when the queen stood and said peremptorily, "I must go upstairs."

"Oh, let us come with ye, Madam," one of the girls pleaded.

"Lest ye faint again," said the other.

"We will be yer good right hands," said the first.

"I have," the queen said, "all the hands I need. And they will be folded first in prayer and then in sleep."

I followed the queen to the door and when I looked back, it was clear that the Douglas girls had half a mind to come after us. I caught Mary's eye.

Mary put her breviary down onto the table with a *whap*, then produced a deck of cards from her pocket, waving it in the air. "There will be time enough for piety later, girls. I have a delightful new game to show you. George taught it to me."

"Oh, George!" cried one of the girls.

"George knows the best games!" cried the other.

And intrigued, the girls were able to drag their eyes away from the retreating queen.

"It is a fortune-telling game to tell you the name of your true love," Mary said, dropping her voice to a conspiratorial whisper. She went over to the table and laid out the cards.

Both the girls giggled and sat down with her.

"Now let me see," Mary pondered, "I believe it was diamonds for fortune and hearts for fidelity."

I slipped away and hurried up the stairs to the queen's bedchamber. Mary would keep the game going for as long as possible, holding the attention of the Douglas girls by playing upon their romantic fantasies.

The queen and I had other plans.

When I reached the queen's chamber, she was already changing into her red countrywoman's gown. I changed as well, the linsey-woolsey slipping over my trembling body.

"Now it is all or nothing," said the queen. "May the good Lord be with us." She drew a plaid over her head, then handed me a similar shawl.

I crossed myself reflexively, somehow more frightened this time than the last. Then we went out of the chamber, tiptoeing past the room where we could hear Mary producing a ripple of embarrassed laughter from the Douglas girls.

"One for love," she was saying, "and one for marriage." And the gales of laughter came again.

"And one for freedom," I whispered, pulling the plaid across my mouth and chin.

When we reached the ground floor we stepped out into the courtyard, abandoning all attempts at stealth. There were servants still going to an fro. Our best chance lay in walking boldly.

We started across the courtyard, our shoes sounding unnaturally loud on the stones. I glanced over at the queen, but she seemed not to hear the noise.

Just nerves then, I told myself. And kept walking.

The guards would be mostly fuddled with drink or busy with the village girls from across the loch. Or at least we hoped so. If all went well, they would simply count us as two more villagers going home.

But as we walked, I realized our nervous silence was unnatural and suspicious. Clearing my throat, I said in my best Scots, "Do you see yon capering clown, Lizzie? He's a bra pair o' legs on him." My voice shook as I spoke, further disguising it.

The queen could barely keep from laughing nervously at my accent, but she answered me in kind. "You always had an eye for a well-turned leg, Margaret," she chided like an older sister.

We kept up our aimless chatter in low voices until we reached the postern gate, well away from the keep, where Willie was waiting. The wind off the loch feathered his hair, whirling it up in a cockscomb.

"I sent the gatekeeper for a wee dram and told him the laird had ordered me to lock up." He held up a set of keys and jangled them. "I took this from beside Uncle's plate while I was serving dinner. He does not know it is gone yet."

I hope.

All of a sudden our plan seemed terribly flawed to me. Too many things might yet go wrong. And this time young Willie and George would be condemned for it.

But Willie seemed totally undisturbed by such worries. Beckoning us through the gate, he quickly locked it behind us. Then he tossed the keys into a nearby cannon's gaping mouth.

"Stay in the shadow of the wall a moment longer," he warned, as he searched for any sign of danger.

The seconds seemed to drag on. My heart pounded and my bowels felt watery. It was still light, for we were hurtling towards midsummer when the sun scarcely sets at all. We could easily be seen. The queen reached out and grabbed hold of my hand. Her palm was as icy and as wet as mine.

"Come," Willie said at last.

He led us down to the shore where a boat was secured. The boat's owner looked up expectantly at our approach and stared about him anxiously. With a nod to Willie he walked away, leaving us to take the little vessel for ourselves.

There were several washerwomen gossiping nearby, and they seemed to be paying us no mind. But one suddenly glanced our way and cried out, "Willie, wee Willie, will ye nae stay for a dance wi' me?"

Willie tried to look carefree. "It will have to wait till the morrow," he called back airily.

Then the woman spotted the queen, and I could tell at once that she recognized her despite the disguise.

"Willie, be that . . ." she began.

Immediately alert to the danger, Willie called back, "Mind your tongue, Jennie, or there will be nae dance for you at all!"

She gave him a coy smile, then turned away, resuming her conversation with her friends, who had not noticed a thing.

"Oh, Madam," I whispered to the queen, "see—there are many who still love you and wish you well."

"My dear Scots," she whispered back. Then she lay down in the bottom of the boat, hiding beneath the seat, for we felt there was a danger that her distinctive figure might yet be recognized from the castle even as we went across the loch in the May evening's light.

Willie set to work with the oars, rowing so fast, beads of sweat popped out on his brow though there was a cooling wind now over the loch. Yet the far shore, with its small line of cottages, approached with agonizing slowness. I fought the impulse to look back at the castle to see if anyone was watching.

Inch by slow inch we crossed the grey loch. The oars occasionally slipped, slapping the water with a sound like a gunshot.

I jumped each time.

"It is nothing, Nicola," Willie said.

But it did not feel like nothing. It felt like capture, like the end of all our plans. I did not relax until the boat bumped against sand.

"We are here, Madam," I whispered to the queen. "On the mainland shore. Too far now even should you be seen from the island."

She looked up at me and smiled, but there were tears in her eyes.

Willie got out first, then turned to help me. Once I was on shore, he reached down and took the queen's hand.

She sat up, the plaid falling to her shoulders, and drew in several deep breaths. "How sweet the air is here."

"That is the scent of freedom, Madam," I said.

Just then I heard a rustling in the gorse bushes behind me, and turned to see a tall, rough-looking man emerge.

"Get behind me . . . Mother," I cried. Without thinking of the danger, I rushed him, kicking out and connecting with his shin. He grabbed me by the shoulders and held me away.

Laughing, George Douglas stepped out from behind a tree. "Is that any way to treat one of my faithful servants?"

"*Mother?*" the queen said.

"It was better than *Madam* or *Majesty,* which would have given away the game," I said.

"*Mother!*" she said again, and this time followed it with a peal of delicious laughter.

"Come, we had best get out of sight," George cautioned. "And sound," he added.

The queen took his meaning, and stopped laughing, but the smile remained on her face for a long while.

We wove our way through the thicket to where a tired groom held the reins of a pair of black horses.

The queen patted the head of one of them. "These are handsomer than any I rode that first day into Edinburgh."

"These are the finest horses in Scotland," George answered, grinning. "I stole them myself from my brother's stables." He helped the queen into her saddle, then me into mine.

"Only two horses, Geordie?" the queen asked. "What about you and Willie?"

"Willie and I will remain here to delay any pursuit, Majesty. It is only a matter of time before someone notices yer gone."

"Aye, we are not in enough trouble yet," Willie said brightly, "so we will hang about and stir up some more."

"My dear friends," the queen began, but George cut her off.

"Ye must go now, Madam," he insisted. "This is no masque. The danger is all too real. Lord Seton is waiting for you two miles down the road. Go. And God willing, I will join you later."

"God willing," the queen repeated under her breath and spurred her horse forward.

We rode so fast I half feared the horses would not be able to maintain the pace, but they were as good as George had claimed.

One mile passed swiftly, then the second.

Suddenly a group of horsemen pulled out into the road ahead of us, their horses snorting and rearing.

The queen showed no sign of slowing, but rather urged her mount on.

"Madam," I shouted as she charged ahead. But I saw then what she had already guessed, that they were friends: Lord Seton with a party of armed men. In the midst was my own dear Joseph on a high-headed bay.

He rode over to me and drew me away from the others.

"Oh, sweet Nicola, my heart rejoices to see you safe," he said. "I have hardly slept these past few nights worrying about the escape."

"You knew about it?"

"I could not be kept out. Lord Seton insisted."

"Which are you gladder to see, Joseph? The queen or me. The lion or the mouse?"

"Right now you could be either," he answered. "No lion ever had a nobler or braver spirit. No queen was ever more beautiful."

49 ❧ PARTINGS

s we crossed the sea at Queensferry, the waters were so calm for once, I believed God must have willed it.

Then we rode until midnight under a moonless sky. Such was our mood, we could have ridden straight on until morning.

We stopped at Lord Seton's palace at Niddry for the night, and the next morning the queen heard a commotion outside.

"Look out, Nicola, and tell me what you see," she said.

I threw open the shudders nervously and gazed down. "There is a mass of folk calling out for you, Majesty," I said. "It seems there is no keeping secret the good news of your escape."

She climbed out of bed and flung a dressing gown around her, then leaned out, her auburn hair all disordered about her shoulders.

A louder cry greeted her appearance. "Mary! Mary! Mary!"

"Your Majesty, you are not dressed. . . ." I said.

Ignoring me, she leaned even further out of the windows, putting her arms wide as if to embrace them all. "My own dear Scots," she cried.

The cheers went on and on and on.

Brava, Majesty, I said under my breath.

While we breakfasted at Niddry, we heard the news from Lochleven. How some countryman, recognizing her as she passed, had rowed over to report the escape. How the Douglas nieces had already found her mantle and discovered her missing. How Lord William in a passion of distress had tried to stab himself with his own dagger.

How we laughed at that.

"Though I worry what will become of my faithful Mary," the queen said, laying aside her spoon.

"God will be on her side, Madam," I replied.

By the time we had gotten to nearby Hamilton, a better place for defense than Niddry, with its high, thick walls, many of the western lords were already gathering to the queen's banner.

By the eighth of May, a week's time, Herries and Maxwell and Argyll from the far north had declared for the queen. Soon after nine earls, nine bishops, and eighteen lairds had signed a joint proclamation supporting her.

But Lord James and his allies acted just as swiftly. He summoned an army to crush those who rose up in support of the queen. "The lion unloosed," was what Lord James called the queen.

And with her amber hair on her shoulders, she indeed looked like a great lion ready to pounce.

"They say the queen now has six thousand men, Joseph," I said at breakfast in the kitchen at Hamilton. "Is that a lot?"

"It is a start," he said.

"Is it *enough*?" I pursued.

He did not answer me right away but glowered at his porridge.

"Is it enough?" I asked again, putting my hand on his arm.

He looked at me. "Enough men," he said, "but too many commanders."

• • •

Later that same day at dinner in her chambers, Lord Seton cautioned the queen of the same thing. "An army is but as good as its commanders, Majesty."

The queen listened intently, chin on hand.

By her side, as fool once more, I said what was on all our minds. "I hear they quarrel ceaselessly, like children in a game of war."

She made a face. "Dear Lord Seton, are the commanders not just trying to find the best way to return me to the throne?"

He shook his head. "I fear the worst, Majesty. We must pick our fights with care."

The first test of our strength came on the banks of the Clyde, that great slow river that halves the city of Glasgow.

As our army came to the little village of Langside, the problem of too many commanders, which both Joseph and Lord Seton had feared, proved lethal.

The first of the queen's troops, under Lord Claud Hamilton, raced forward eagerly. They headed through the village towards the other side, where it was known that Lord James and his troops were well established.

We had more men, Joseph told me, but Lord James had two very experienced generals with him—Kirkaldy and Morton. They used the little town's narrow main street to advantage, setting hagbutters at windows and doors to harry the queen's men without mercy.

Still our troops went forward, fighting bravely for each step, and we could have held the town. Of that I am certain.

But at the wrong moment, one of our commanders—Argyll—had an epileptic fit when he should have been urging his troops forward to help Hamilton. So the order was never given. And Argyll's men—who were the greatest part of the queen's army—never advanced.

Caught in a crossfire of hagbutters, harried on by unremitting pikemen, the brave men of Hamilton could do nothing but turn and flee, heading back to the Highlands.

It was an awful defeat.

The queen and I had been watching from a nearby hill when our army broke. There was nothing for us to do but go after them.

North.

North towards safety.

We rode like men, our legs clamped about the horse's broad backs, for there was no time to sit sideways like a lady. In consequence I had sores on my inner thighs, and my legs and bottom ached from the long hours in the saddle.

The queen did not complain, not once, but she must have been as sore as I, for her face was haggard and she had deep circles beneath her eyes.

Just above the village of Tongland, a sleepy little town in the mountains, our company crossed the river Dee. As we raced over an ancient wooden bridge, our horses' hooves clattered loudly enough to rouse the countryside.

As soon as all had reached the other side, Lord Herries dismounted and called his men to him.

"Destroy this bridge," he cried. "It will buy us more time."

Time, I thought bitterly, as if that was all we needed.

The men at once began dismantling the plankings. Then they levered up the crossbraces and threw them into the water. I would have offered help but it was clear they needed none from me.

• • •

That evening we camped in dense woodland, hiding like out-laws. And indeed, that is what we had become. As I crouched in front of the fire, my cape pulled around me for warmth, I suddenly realized that I could not remember any stories or songs to cheer us. The future looked as dark as the night closing in.

All we had had to eat that day was sour milk and oatmeal with-out bread. My stomach was full of needles and pins that pricked relentlessly. I put my hand on my belly and thought about moaning. But I did not. There was enough misery in the air already. There were wounded and dying men in our company. The dead we had left far behind. I knew I could at least bear a little hunger without com-plaint.

Queen Mary sat under a makeshift tent, with Lord Herries at her right hand. I had left her there to dine on more oatmeal—*wretched stuff!*—with Joseph at a smaller fire.

"I feel like a wounded deer with a pack of snarling hounds hard by," I told Joseph.

"We *are* wounded," he said, "but that is no reason to give in to despair. Look at the queen." He pointed.

She had left the sanctuary of the tent and was now strolling around the camp, offering a smile or a word of encouragement to every man there. The firelight softened her features and made her look almost young again.

So I left Joseph's side to follow the queen's lead, and suddenly all the stories and songs I knew came flooding back to me, like a river in spate. I began joking with the tired soldiers, telling them the story of the lion and the mouse, and the one about the girl who tripped while counting the money expected from the sale of her eggs, thus breaking every one.

"Lord James needs to watch his footing," I finished with a laugh.

They laughed with me, and one called out, "We will break his eggs for ye, Miss!"

"Brava, Nicola!" someone cried. I turned. It was the queen. Her face, lit by the firelight, was hollowed, like a saint's.

She beckoned me to follow her and led me to a clearing over-shadowed by the darkening sky. A half-moon shone above it like a wish only half come true.

"This is not unlike the night when we first met," she mused.

"The surroundings are wilder, but the sky very like," I agreed. There was something in her voice that warned me she was doing more than simply reminiscing.

"Do you regret that first meeting, Nicola?" she asked. "Might you have been happier if you had remained in France?"

It was an unexpected question. "I was . . . not so happy then as I have been since, Majesty. You have shown me more kindness and more beauty in the world than I could ever have imagined."

"You have also seen much that was *not* kind or beautiful," the queen reminded me. "From Amboise, to Holyrood, to Kirk o'Field, to our last battle, violence and bloodshed have dogged me. Might it not have been better if you had never been party to such things, dear Jardinière?"

I bit my lip. "Nothing was forced upon me that I did not agree to, Majesty," I assured her. "If we take pleasure in the beauty of a rose, we cannot complain if we are pricked by the thorns."

"Spoken like my own fool," the queen said, and half smiled. "So if you have no regrets, then I shall have none for you. Just memories of our happy times together."

"Memories, Majesty?" I asked.

The moon went suddenly behind a cloud and everything seemed colder. The queen pulled her cloak tighter about her shoulders. "I am haunted by the ghosts of all that might have been."

I shivered, and not just from the cold. *Memories. Ghosts.* She was talking about the past. I was suddenly afraid for the future. "What do you mean, Madam?"

She looked up again at the darkened sky. "I have made a decision, Nicola, the most difficult since I first resolved to leave France. I am going south to England to throw myself upon the mercy of my cousin Elizabeth."

"England?" I was appalled. "It was to England Lords James and Ruthven fled from your justice. Even Knox has courted the favor of the English queen. The English have no cause to love you. Oh, Majesty—do not go. For Jesu's sake, do not go."

She looked at me. "Why should I not appeal to my cousin when justice and kinship are my advocates? If I can only meet her face-to-face, she will see in me the sweet sister she has always called me."

"You *cannot* trust her," I warned with a brisk shake of my head. "She will turn you from a queen into a pawn and move you about in some wicked game of her own devising."

"I cannot deny the danger," she answered. "But I will never be a pawn. I am a queen, whether on a throne or in chains." The moon emerged from the clouds as she finished speaking, casting her face in silver.

"But what of those who love you here in Scotland?" I cried. "They need you to lead them."

She turned from me and looked back at the woods. "My supporters are scattered. Or dead. If I go now, I spare those loyal to me any further suffering. For the sake of my sweet son James, who will one day be old enough to rule on his own, I cannot let our country be wounded further."

I could tell that her mind was made up. But still I had to say what she required of me. "You are but a mortal, Majesty."

"As a mortal, I am deeply afraid, Nicola." She gave the cloak another pull around her. "But still I must go."

I thought of my beloved Joseph leaving for France. I thought of the dangers that lay across the border in England. Yet I did not hesitate. "Where my queen goes, I go, too."

She shook her head and grabbed up my hands. "Not this time, my dearest fool. You at least have life ahead of you." There was a catch in her voice. She pointed to the trees where Joseph had just emerged, leading two horses, saddled and ready to ride. "I have already spoken to Joseph this evening and he has everything you will need for your journey."

"Madam," I cried, "no!" Then I fell to my knees before her, hoping that would prove my faithfulness. "How can you send me away?"

The queen bent down and raised me to my feet. "My dearest Nicola, Joseph is a brave young man, more than worthy of your love. In this one thing I beg you to be wiser than I. In matters of the heart I am the one who has always been the fool. Do not repeat my mistakes."

A wind had started moaning through the oak trees, and I raised my voice so that she could hear me. "You will need me, Madam."

"You have done more than enough already," said the queen. "Go, like your favorite, Marie-in-the-Ashes, with her prince. Leave behind these palaces packed with danger and lies. Make instead a home filled with the laughter of children."

I felt a fire burn in my breast and the taste of bile in my mouth, burning the edges of my tongue. To choose now between Joseph and my queen—how could I make such a choice?

"If you force me to, Nicola, I will command you to go, for I am still your queen, am I not?"

"Now and forever, Majesty."

"Then do not compel me to give such an order. Go because of the love you bear me and not because I wear a crown, however tarnished that crown may be."

"As you wish," I whispered, silent tears now raining down my cheeks.

The queen took hold of my chin and tilted my head up so that I met her eyes. In the moon's small light I saw her own tears matched mine. "I am putting myself in God's hands as much as in Queen Elizabeth's," she said. "Whatever befalls, I shall take comfort in knowing you are safe, that this one flower out of all my gardens blooms still." Then she motioned me to go to Joseph, who had patiently kept his distance.

I took one step, then turned back.

"Why do you not come with us?" I asked. "There are many in France who love you still. You have lands and family there."

The queen's head drooped for a moment with the temptation. But then she shook it away, recovering her resolve.

"No, Nicola, *here* in Scotland is where I am still queen."

I tried to summon a word of farewell, but before I could speak, there was a violent stamping and crashing among the trees. I looked around in alarm, wondering if Lord James's scouts had tracked us already. Then, leaping forward, I grabbed the queen by the arm, thinking to throw her up into the saddle. But too soon battering hooves bore upon us and I had only time to pull her aside, falling to the ground on top of her, my body a fragile shield.

However, it was not a pack of hunters but a magnificent stag that burst out of a bush. The thorns had drawn thin trails of blood down his heaving flanks. In a thunder of hooves he swept past our trembling bodies, and bounded to the crest of a hillock where he paused for a moment, lifting his crowned head to the moon.

I sat up and the queen did as well, clutching my arm, staring at the stag. Part of the thornbush had been ripped off by his headlong charge and, for a brief instant, as he turned his great head in the moonlight, the broken branches formed the shape of a cross between his spreading antlers.

I got to my knees, as Saint Hubert and King David had done when the power of God had blazed before them. In that single moment, I understood all the mysterious forces that had seized hold of my life. And in that same instant I felt gratitude—for the queen's love and for Joseph, who had waited so faithfully.

Then a cloud covered the moon and the hilltop grew silent.

When the cloud moved on and it was light again, the stag had disappeared to the east, behind the hill.

The queen stood and lifted me gently to my feet. "You see, Nicola," she said hoarsely, "God is watching over us."

Just then the queen's soldiers came running towards us, swords drawn. Joseph called out for them to stop. But they did not even slow down till they saw that the queen was all right.

"Go back to the camp," she told them, brushing off her bodice and skirt. "It was a miracle sent by God. It was Saint Hubert's stag."

"Venison tonight, lads!" cried one of the soldiers.

"If you love me, that stag goes free," cried the queen, with such passion, the soldiers turned at once back to their oatmeal and soured milk.

"You must go free, too, Madam. East like the stag, to France," I told her.

She shook her head. "Though my heart goes with him, Nicola, my head tells me my fate lies south, in England."

Fato! I shuddered. "Sometimes the head is a poor councilor, Madam," I said. "Please take the advice of your fool."

"I would rather your advice than a thousand councilors, dear friend," she said. "But good advice may be given and yet not taken."

Friend. She called me *friend.* Not fool or girl or child or Jardinière, but *friend.*

She drew her hand away, squared her shoulders, and gazed at me with such sadness, I all but wept again.

"I am the queen," she said. "There is no safety in that." Then she turned away and there was in her bearing such beauty and such loneliness as I had never seen in another human being.

Joseph touched my shoulder. "She is beyond our help, Nicola," he said. "Now we must help ourselves." He boosted me onto my horse and I flinched as my sore legs touched the saddle. Then he mounted his own horse, and we turned towards the east.

When I looked around, the queen was already walking into the woods, where her little band of soldiers waited.

I knew for certain that I would never see her again.

EPILOGUE

The queen had given Joseph two leather bags, one full of gold and one with jewels, and the small casket covered in crimson with the letter *F* in silver gilt she had smuggled out of Lochleven.

"For Freedom," she had told him.

There was also an embroidery she had done in Lochleven, of a caged bird with a Latin motto arching over its head. Joseph translated it for me: "Virtue flourishes as a result of a wound."

We made it to the east coast of Scotland, just a pair of servants looking for work, and then across the sea to France. We had no problems getting there at all. Scotland was searching for a missing monarch, we posed but little interest.

Joseph sold two of the jewels for a great deal of money, and with that we bought a country house not far from Blois and made—as the queen had requested—"a home filled with the laughter of children."

There, too, we started a school for jesters. Joseph teaches our students to play the lute and sing, I how to tell stories and dance.

Twice a year Troupe Brufort comes through and they give lessons in juggling and acrobatics. Uncle Armand is long dead, having fallen under the wheels of a wine cart in Paris just months after I had left the troupe. All those years of worrying about him had been for naught!

The troupe now consists of Pierre with his wife, Bertrand with his, Annette, who has never married, and old Nadine. Little Jean has gone for a soldier.

None of them write between visits.

None of them know how.

However, once in a great while a letter comes from Queen Mary in England, bearing the prints of many hands. It seems that passage is more difficult for the queen's mail than for two frightened travelers.

Her letters always say that she is well and that she believes God will provide. But we know the letters come from a castle where her cousin Elizabeth has imprisoned her.

Dear Mary—once queen both of Scotland and France—has waited in her lonely gaol these past nineteen years, hoping for a miracle. But I fear the last of her miracles occurred on that hill where the great stag made its break east for freedom, between its antlers the Lord's own cross.

Authors' note: After almost twenty years as Elizabeth's prisoner, Mary Queen of Scots was accused of plotting to seize her cousin's throne. She was condemned to death and beheaded at Fotheringhay Castle in Northamptonshire in 1587. It took two blows by the executioner to kill her.

Pious Mary Seton had gone with the queen into captivity, though in 1583, because of ill health, she was allowed to retire to France to a convent in Rheims where, thirty-two years later, she died.

When Elizabeth herself died in 1603, she left no heirs and Queen Mary's son James became king of both Scotland and England.